FLESH AND BLOOD

ALSO BY PATRICIA CORNWELL

SCARPETTA SERIES

Dust
The Bone Bed
Red Mist
Port Mortuary
The Scarpetta Factor
Scarpetta
Book of the Dead
Predator
Trace
Blow Fly
The Last Precinct
Black Notice
Point of Origin
Unnatural Exposure
Cause of Death
From Potter's Field
The Body Farm
Cruel and Unusual
All That Remains
Body of Evidence
Postmortem

NONFICTION

*Portrait of a Killer: Jack the
    Ripper—Case Closed*

ANDY BRAZIL SERIES

Isle of Dogs
Southern Cross
Hornet's Nest

WIN GARANO SERIES

The Front
At Risk

BIOGRAPHY

*Ruth, A Portrait: The Story of Ruth
    Bell Graham*

OTHER WORKS

*Food to Die For: Secrets from Kay
    Scarpetta's Kitchen*
Life's Little Fable
Scarpetta's Winter Table

HARPERCOLLINS PUBLISHERS LTD

FLESH AND BLOOD

A SCARPETTA NOVEL

PATRICIA CORNWELL

Published by HarperCollins Publishers Ltd

First Canadian edition

HarperCollins Publishers Ltd
2 Bloor Street East, 20th Floor
Toronto, Ontario, Canada
M4W 1A8

www.harpercollins.ca

Designed by Jamie Lynn Kerner
Title page and chapter opener image by Soren Egeberg Photography/Shutterstock, Inc.

Library and Archives Canada Cataloguing in Publication information is available upon request.

ISBN 978-1-44343-670-0

RRD   10 9 8 7 6 5 4 3 2 1

To Staci

Wisdom entereth not into a malicious mind, and science
without conscience is but the ruin of the soul.

—FRANÇOIS RABELAIS, 1532

FLESH AND BLOOD

To Kay Scarpetta
From Copperhead
Sunday, May 11
(11:43 p.m. to be exact)

A little verse I penned just for you. Happy Mother's Day, Kay!!!!

(do turn the page please . . .)

The light is coming
And the dark
 you caused
 (& think you saw)
Is gone gone gone!
 Frag-
 ments of shat-
 tered gold
 and the Hangman leaves invisibly
Lust seeks its own level Dr. Death
 an eye for an eye
 a theft for a theft
 an erotic dream of your dying breath
Pennies for your thoughts
 Keep the change
 watch the clock!
Tick Tock
 Tick Tock Doc!

CHAPTER 1

COPPER FLASHES LIKE SHARDS of aventurine glass on top of the old brick wall behind our house. I envision ancient pastel stucco workshops with red tile roofs along the Rio dei Vetrai canal, and fiery furnaces and blowpipes as maestros shape molten glass on marvers. Careful not to spill, I carry two espressos sweetened with agave nectar.

I hold the delicate curved handles of the mouth-blown cristallo cups, simple and rock crystal clear, the memory of finding them on the Venetian island of Murano a happy one. The aromas of garlic and charred peppers follow me outside as the screen door shuts with a soft thud. I detect the aromatic bright scent of fresh basil leaves I tore with my bare hands. It's the best of mornings. It couldn't be better.

My special salad has been mixed, the juices, herbs and spices mingling and saturating chunks of *mantovana* I baked on a stone days earlier. The olive oil bread is best slightly stale when used in *panzanella,* which like pizza was once the food of the poor whose ingenuity and resourcefulness transformed scraps of focaccia and vegetables into *un'abbondanza.* Imaginative savory dishes invite and reward improvisation, and this morning I added the thinly sliced core of fennel, kosher salt and coarsely ground pepper. I used sweet onions instead of red ones and added a hint of mint from the sunporch where I grow herbs in large terra-cotta olive jars I found years ago in France.

Pausing on the patio, I check the grill. Rising heat wavers, the lighter fluid and bag of briquettes a cautious distance away. My FBI husband Benton isn't much of a cook but he knows how to light a good fire and is meticulous about safety. The neat pile of smoldering orange coals is coated in white ash. The swordfish filets can go on soon. Then my hedonistic preoccupations are abruptly interrupted as my attention snaps back to the wall.

I realize what I'm seeing is pennies. I try to recall if they were there earlier when it was barely dawn and I took out our greyhound, Sock. He was stubborn and clingy and I was unusually distracted. My mind was racing in multiple directions, powered by a euphoric anticipation of a Tuscan brunch before boarding a plane in Boston, and a sensual fog was burning off after an indulgent mindless rousing from bed where all that mattered was pleasure. I hardly remember taking out our dog. I hardly remember any details about being with him in the dimly lit dewy backyard.

So it's entirely possible I wouldn't have noticed the bright copper coins or anything else that might indicate an uninvited visitor has been on our property. I feel a chill at the edge of my thoughts, a dark shadow that's unsettling. I'm reminded of what I don't want to think about.

You've already left for vacation while you're still here. And you know better.

My thoughts return to the kitchen, to the blue steel Rohrbaugh 9 mm in its pocket holster on the counter by the stove. Lightweight with laser grips, the pistol goes where I do even when Benton is home. But I've not had a single thought about guns or security this morning. I've freed my mind from micromanaging the deliveries to my headquarters throughout the night, discreetly pouched in black and transported in my windowless white trucks, five dead patients silently awaiting their appointments with the last physicians who will ever touch them on this earth.

I've avoided the usual dangerous, tragic, morbid realities and I know better.

Dammit.

Then I argue it away. Someone is playing a game with pennies. That's all.

CHAPTER 2

OUR NINETEENTH-CENTURY CAMBRIDGE house is on the northern border of the Harvard campus, around the corner from the Divinity School and across from the Academy of Arts and Sciences. We have our share of people who take shortcuts through our property. It's not fenced in and the wall is more an ornamental ruin than a barrier. Children love to climb over it and hide behind it.

Probably one of them with too much time on his hands now that school is out.

"Did you notice what's on our wall?" I make my way across sundappled grass, reaching the stone bench encircling the magnolia tree where Benton has been reading the paper while I prepare brunch.

"Notice what?" he asks.

Sock is stretched out near his feet, watching me accusingly. He knows exactly what's in store for him. The instant I pulled out luggage late last night and began an inventory of tennis equipment and scuba gear he settled into a funk, an emotional hole he digs for himself, only this time it's deeper. No matter what I do, I can't seem to cheer him up.

"Pennies." I hand Benton an espresso ground from whole beans, a robust sweetened stimulant that makes both of us very hungry for all things of the flesh.

He tests it carefully with the tip of his tongue.

"Did you see someone put them there?" I ask. "What about when you were lighting the grill? Were the pennies there then?"

He stares in the direction of the shiny coins lined up edge to edge on the wall.

"I didn't notice and I've not seen anyone. They certainly weren't put there while I've been out here," he says. "How much longer for the coals?" It's his way of asking if he did a good job. Like anyone else, he enjoys praise.

"They're perfect. Thank you. Let's give them maybe fifteen more minutes," I reply as he returns to a story he's reading about the dramatic rise in credit card fraud.

MIDMORNING SLANTED SUNLIGHT POLISHES his hair bright silver, a little longer than usual, falling low on his brow and curling up in back.

I can see the fine lines on his sharply handsome face, pleasant creases from smiling, and the cleft in his strong chin. His tapered hands are elegant and beautiful, the hands of a musician I always think whether he's holding a newspaper, a book, a pen or a gun. I smell the subtle scent of his earthy aftershave as I lean over him to scan the story.

"I don't know what these companies are going to do if it gets any worse." I sip my espresso, unpleasantly reminded of my own recent brushes with cyber thieves. "The world is going to be bankrupted by criminals we can't catch or see."

"No surprise that using a keylogger has become rampant and harder to detect." A page rustles as he turns it. "Someone gets your card number and makes purchases through PayPal-type accounts, often overseas and it's untraceable. Not to mention malware."

"I haven't ordered anything on eBay in recent memory. I don't do Craigslist or anything similar." We've had this discussion repeatedly of late.

"I know how irritating it is. But it happens to other careful people."

"It hasn't happened to you." I run my fingers through his thick soft hair, which turned platinum before I knew him, when he was very young.

"You shop more than I do," he says.

"Not hardly. You and your fine suits, silk ties and expensive shoes. You see what I wear every day. Cargo pants. Scrubs. Rubber surgical clogs. Boots. Except when I go to court."

"I'm envisioning you dressed for court. Are you wearing a skirt, that fitted pin-striped one with the slit in back?"

"And sensible pumps."

"The word *sensible* is incompatible with what I'm fantasizing about." He looks up at me, and I love the slender muscularity of his neck.

I trace the second cervical vertebra down to C7, gently, slowly digging my fingertips into the Longus colli muscle, feeling him relax, sensing his mood turning languid as he floats in a sensation of physical pleasure. He says I'm his Kryptonite and it's true. I can hear it in his voice.

"My point?" he says. "It's impossible to keep up with all of the malicious programs out there that record keystrokes and transmit the information to hackers. It can be as simple as opening an infected file attached to an email. You make it hard for me to think."

"With the antispyware programs, one-time passwords, and firewalls Lucy implements to protect our server and email accounts? How could a keylogger get downloaded? And I intend to make it hard for you to think. As hard as possible."

Caffeine and agave nectar are having their effect. I remember the feel of his skin, his sinewy leanness as he shampooed my hair in the shower, massaging my scalp and neck, touching me until it was unbearable. I've never tired of him. It's not possible I could.

"Software can't scan malware it doesn't recognize," he says.

"I don't believe that's the explanation."

My techno-genius niece Lucy would never allow such a violation of the computer system she programs and maintains at my headquarters, the Cambridge Forensics Center, the CFC. It's an uncomfortable fact that she is far more likely to be the perpetrator of malware and hacking than the victim of it.

"As I've said what probably happened is someone got hold of your card at a restaurant or in a store." Benton turns another page and I trace the straight bridge of his nose, the curve of his ear. "That's what Lucy thinks."

"Four times since March?" But I'm thinking of our shower, the shiny white subway tile and the sounds of water falling, splashing loudly in different intensities and rhythms as we moved.

"And you also let Bryce use it when he places orders for you over the phone. Not that he would do anything reckless, at least not intentionally. But I wish you wouldn't. He doesn't understand reality the way we do."

"He sees the worst things imaginable every day," I reply.

"That doesn't mean he understands. Bryce is naïve and trusting in a way we aren't."

The last time I asked my chief of staff to make a purchase with my credit card was a month ago when he sent gardenias to my mother for Mother's Day. The most recent report of fraud was yesterday. I seriously doubt it's related to Bryce or my mother, although it would fit neatly with the history of my dysfunctional familial world if my good deed were punished beyond my mother's usual complaints and comparisons to my sister Dorothy, who would be in prison if being a self-consumed narcissist were a crime.

The gardenia topiary was an insensitive slight, since my mother has gardenias in her yard. *It's like sending ice to Eskimos. Dorothy sent the prettiest red roses with baby's breath,* my mother's words exactly. Never mind that I went to the trouble to send her favorite flowering plant and unlike cut roses the topiary is alive.

"Well it's frustrating and of course my replacement card will get here while we're in Florida," I remark to Benton. "So I leave home without it and that's not a good way to start your vacation."

"You don't need it. I'll treat."

He usually does anyway. I make a good living but Benton is an only child and has old family money, a lot of it. His father, Parker Wesley, shrewdly invested an inherited fortune in commodities that included buying and selling fine art. Masterpieces by Miró, Whistler, Pissarro, Modigliani, Renoir and others for a while would hang in the Wesley home, and he also acquired and sold vintage cars and rare manuscripts, none of which he ultimately kept. It was all about knowing when to let go. Benton has a similar perspective and temperament. What he also absorbed from his New England roots are shrewd logic and a Yankee steely resolve that can endure hard work and discomfort without flinching.

That doesn't mean he doesn't know how to live well or gives a damn what people think. Benton isn't ostentatious or wasteful but he does what he wants, and I scan our beautifully landscaped property and the back of our antique frame house, recently repainted, the timber siding smoky blue with granite gray shutters. The roof is dark slate tile with two dusky redbrick chimneys, and some of the windows have the original wavy glass. We would live a perfectly charmed and privileged existence were it not for our professions, and my attention returns to the small copper coins not far from us, flaring in the sun.

Sock is perfectly still in the grass, eyes open and watching my every move as I step closer to the wall and smell the perfume of English roses, apricot and pink with warm shades of yellow. The thick thriving bushes are halfway up the vintage bricks, and it pleases me that the tea roses are also doing especially well this spring.

The seven Lincoln pennies are heads up, all of them 1981, and that's peculiar. They're more than thirty years old and look newly minted. Maybe they're fake. I think of the date. Lucy's date. Her birth year. And today is my birthday.

I scan the old brick wall, some fifty feet in length and five feet high, what I poetically think of as a wrinkle in time, a wormhole connecting us to dimensions beyond, a portal between *us* and *them,* our lives now and the past. What's left of our wall has become a metaphor for our attempts at barricading ourselves from anyone who might want to harm us. It's really not possible if someone is determined enough, and a sensation flutters inside my mind, deep and unreachable. A memory. A buried or scarcely formed one.

"Why would someone leave seven pennies, heads up, all the same date?" I ask.

THE RANGE OF OUR security cameras doesn't include the far corners of the wall, which leans slightly and terminates in limestone pillars completely overtaken by ivy.

In the early 1800s when our house was built by a wealthy transcendentalist, the estate was an entire block surrounded by a serpentine wall. What's left is a crumbling brick segment, and half an acre with a narrow driveway of pavers and a detached garage that originally was a carriage house. Whoever left the pennies probably won't have been caught on video and I feel the same uneasiness again, a remnant of what I can't recall.

"They look polished," I add. "Obviously they are unless they're not real."

"Neighborhood kids," Benton says.

His amber eyes watch me over the top of the *Boston Globe,* a smile playing on his lips. He's in jeans and loafers, a Red Sox windbreaker on, and he sets down his espresso and the paper, gets up from the bench and walks over to me. Wrapping his arms around my waist from behind, he kisses my ear, resting his chin on top of my head.

"If life were always this good," he says, "maybe I'd retire, say the hell with playing cops and robbers anymore."

"You wouldn't. And if only that was what you really played. We should eat fairly soon and get ready to head to the airport."

He glances at his phone and rapidly types what looks like a one- or two-word response to something.

"Is everything all right?" I hug his arms around me. "Who are you texting?"

"Everything's fine. I'm starved. Tease me."

"Grilled swordfish steaks Salmoriglio, seared, brushed with olive oil, lemon juice, oregano." I lean into him and feel his warmth, and the coolness of the air and the heat of the sun. "Your favorite *panzanella*. Heirloom tomatoes, basil, sweet onions, cucumbers . . ." I hear leaves stirring and smell the delicate lemony fragrance of magnolia blossoms. " . . . And that aged red wine vinegar you like so much."

"Full-bodied and delicious just like you. My mouth is watering."

"Bloody Marys. Horseradish, fresh-squeezed key limes and habanero to get us in the mood for Miami."

"Then we shower." He kisses me on the lips this time, doesn't care who sees it.

"We already did."

"And we need to again. I feel extra dirty. Maybe I do have another present for you. If you're up for it."

"The question is are you?"

"We have a whole two hours before we need to leave for the airport." He kisses me again, longer and deeper as I detect the distant rapid stuttering of a helicopter, a powerful one. "I love you, Kay Scarpetta. More every minute, every day, every year. What is this spell you have over me?"

"Food. I'm good in the kitchen."

"What a happy day when you were born."

"Not if you ask my mother."

He suddenly pulls back from me almost imperceptibly as if he just saw something. Squinting in the sun, he stares in the direction of the Academy of Arts and Sciences a block north of us, separated from our property by a row of homes and a street.

"What?" I look where he's looking as the helicopter gets louder.

From our backyard we can see the corrugated metal roof the green color of copper patina peeking above densely wooded grounds. The world's top leaders in business, government, academia and science routinely speak and meet at the Academy's headquarters, the House of the Mind as it's called.

"What is it?" I follow Benton's intense stare, and the roar of a helicopter flying low is coming closer.

"I don't know," he says. "I thought I saw something flash over there, like a camera flash but not as bright."

I scan the canopies of old trees and the multiangled green metal roof. I don't notice anything unusual. I don't see anyone.

"Maybe sunlight reflecting off a car window," I offer and Benton is typing on his phone again, something brief to someone.

"It came from the trees. I might have noticed the same thing earlier, caught it out of the corner of my eye. Something glinted. A flick of light maybe. I wasn't sure . . ." He stares again and the helicopter is very loud now. "I hope it's not some damn reporter with a telescopic lens."

We both look up at the same time as the deep blue Agusta comes into view, sleek with a bright yellow stripe and a flat silver belly, its landing gear retracted. I can feel the vibration in my bones, and then Sock is cowering on the grass next to me, pressing against my legs.

"Lucy," I say loudly and I watch transfixed. She's done this before but never at such a low altitude. "Good God. What is she doing?"

The composite blades whump-whump loudly, their rotor wash agitating the tops of trees as my niece overflies our house at less than five hundred feet. She circles in a thunderous roar then pauses in a hover, nodding the nose. I can just make out her helmet and tinted visor before she flies away, dropping lower over the Academy of Arts and Sciences, circling the grounds slowly, then gone.

"I believe Lucy just wished you a happy birthday," Benton says.

"She'd better hope the neighbors don't report her to the FAA for violating noise abatement regulations." All the same I can't help but be thrilled and touched.

"There won't be a problem." He's looking at his phone again. "She can blame it on the FBI. While she was in the area I had her do a recon. That's why she was so low."

"You knew she was going to buzz the house?" I ask and of course he did and at exactly what time, which is why he's been stalling in the backyard, making sure we weren't in the house when she showed up.

"No photographer or anybody else with a camera or a scope." Benton stares in the direction of the wooded grounds, of the cantilevered green roof.

"You just this minute told her to look."

"I did and in her words, *no joy*." He shows me the two-word text on his iPhone that Lucy's partner Janet sent, aviation lingo meaning they didn't see anything.

The two of them are flying together, and I wonder if the only reason they're up is to wish me a very loud and dramatic happy birthday. Then I think of something else. Lucy's twin-engine Italian helicopter looks law enforcement, and the neighbors probably think it has to do with President Obama arriving in Cambridge late today. He'll be staying in a hotel near the Kennedy School of Government, barely a mile from here.

"Nothing unusual," Benton is saying. "So if someone was there up in a tree or wherever, he's gone. Did I mention how hungry I am?"

"As soon as I can get our poor rattled dog to potty," I reply as my attention wanders back to the pennies on the wall. "You may as well relax for a few more minutes. He was already stubborn this morning and now he'll only be worse."

I crouch down in the grass and stroke Sock, doing my best to soothe him.

"That noisy flying machine is gone and I'm right here," I say sweetly to him. "It was just Lucy flying around and nothing to be scared about."

CHAPTER 3

I T'S THURSDAY, JUNE 12, my birthday, and I refuse to preoccupy myself with my age or how time flees faster with each passing year. There is much to be in a good mood about and grateful for. Life is the best it's ever been.

We're off to Miami for a week of reading, eating and drinking whatever we want, maybe tennis and a few scuba dives, and long walks on the beach. I'd like to go to the movies and share a bucket of popcorn, and not get up in the morning until we feel like it. I intend for us to rest, play, to say the hell with everything. Benton's present to me is a condo he rented on the ocean.

We've reached a point in life where we should enjoy a little time off. But he's been saying that for as long as I can remember. We both have. As of this morning we're officially on leave, at least in theory. In fact there really isn't such a thing. Benton is an intelligence analyst, what people still call a profiler. He's never off his FBI leash, and the cliché that death never takes a holiday is true. I'm never off my leash, either.

The pennies are lit up in the morning glare, fiery and too perfect and I don't touch them. I don't recall seeing them earlier lined up precisely straight on the wall, all oriented exactly the same way. But the backyard was mostly in shadows the first time I ventured out, and I was distracted by my pouty dog's unwillingness to potty and by my landscaping check-list. The roses need fertilizing and spraying. The lawn needs weeding and should be mown before a storm ushers in a heat wave as predicted for tonight.

I have instructions written out for Bryce. He's to make sure that all is taken care of not only at the CFC but also on the home front. Lucy and Janet are dog nannies while we're gone, and we have our usual trick that isn't flawless but better than the alternative of leaving Sock alone in an empty house for even ten minutes.

My niece will arrive and I'll walk him out the door as if I'm taking him with me. Then I'll coax him into whatever she's driving, hopefully not one of her monster machines with no backseat. I asked her pointedly to use her SUV, not that it's a normal vehicle, either. Nothing my former law enforcement computer genius power-addicted niece owns is for the hoi polloi—not her matte black stealth bomber of an armored SUV, not her aggressive 599 GTO that sounds like the space shuttle. Sock hates supercars and doesn't like Lucy's helicopter. He startles easily. He gets scared.

"Come on," I encourage my silent four-legged friend from his snooze in the grass with eyes wide, what I call playing possum. "You need to potty." He doesn't budge, his brown stare fixed on me. "Come on. I'm asking nicely. Please, Sock. Up!"

He's been out of sorts all morning, sniffing around, acting skittish, then lying down, his tail curled under, tucking his long narrow nose beneath his front paws, looking completely dejected and anxious. Sock knows when we're leaving him and gets depressed, and I always feel rotten about it as if I'm a terrible mother. I lean over and stroke his short brindle fur, feeling his ribs, then gentle with his ears, misshapen and scarred from former abuses at the racetrack. He gets up, pressing against my legs like a listing ship.

"Everything's fine," I reassure him. "You're going to run around on acres of land and play with Jet Ranger. You know how much you love that."

"He doesn't." Benton reseats himself on the bench and picks up the paper beneath spreading branches of dark green leaves loaded with waxy white blossoms the size of pie pans. "It's fitting you have a pet that doesn't listen and completely manipulates you."

"Come on." I lead him over to his favorite privacy area of shaded boxwoods and evergreens in thick beds of pine-scented mulch. He's not interested. "Seriously? He's acting odd."

I look around, searching for anything else that might indicate something is off and my attention wanders back to the pennies. A chill touches the back of my neck. I don't see anyone. I hear nothing but the breeze whispering through the trees and the distant sound of a gas-powered leaf blower. It slowly comes to me, what I didn't recognize at first. I see it. The tweet with the link that I got some weeks ago. The attachment was an odd note to me and a poem, I recall.

The Twitter name was *Copperhead* and I remember only snippets of what the poem said. Something about the light coming and a hangman that struck me as the ramblings of a deranged individual. Delusional messages and voice mails aren't uncommon. My Cambridge Forensic Center email address and phone number are public information. Lucy always traces unsolicited electronic communications and lets me know if there is anything I should worry about. I vaguely recall her telling me the tweet was sent from a hotel business center in Morristown, New Jersey.

I need to ask her about it. In fact I'll do it now. Her cockpit is wireless, her flight helmet Bluetooth enabled. For that matter she's probably already landed, and I slide my phone out of a pocket of my jacket. But before I get the chance someone is calling me first. The ringtone sounds like an old telephone. Detective Pete Marino, and I recognize his mobile number in the display, not his personal phone but the one he uses on the job.

If he were calling to say happy birthday or have a nice trip he wouldn't be on his Cambridge police BlackBerry. He's careful about using his departmental equipment, vehicles, email or any form of communication for anything remotely personal. It's one of life's many ironies and contradictions when it comes to him. He certainly wasn't like that all the years he worked for me.

"Oh God," I mutter. "This had better not be what I think it is."

"Sorry to do this to you, Doc," Marino's big voice sounds in my earpiece. "I know you got a plane to catch. But you need to be aware of what's going on. You're my first call."

"What is it?" I begin slowly pacing the yard.

"We got one on Farrar Street," he says. "In broad daylight, plenty of people around and nobody heard or saw a thing. Just like the other ones. And the victim selection bothers the shit out of me, especially the timing with Obama coming here today."

"What other ones?"

"Where are you right now?" he asks.

"Benton and I are in the backyard."

I feel my husband's eyes on me.

"Maybe you should go inside and not be out in the open. That's the way it happens," Marino says. "People out in the open going about their business . . ."

"What other ones? What people?" I look around as I pace.

Sock is sitting, his ears folded back. Benton gets up from the bench, watching me. It continues to be a beautiful peaceful morning but it's a mirage. Everything has just turned ugly.

"New Jersey right after Christmas and then again in April. The same M.O.," Marino says and I interrupt him again.

"Hold on. Back up. What's happened, exactly? And let's not compare the M.O. to other cases before we know the facts."

"A homicide not even five minutes from you. We got the call about an hour ago . . ."

"And you're just notifying my office now? Or more specifically, notifying me?"

He knows damn well that the more quickly the body can be examined in situ and transported to my office, the better. We should have been called instantly.

"Machado wanted to secure the scene."

Sil Machado is a Cambridge PD investigator. He and Marino are also good friends.

"He wanted to make sure there's not an active shooter still there waiting to pick off someone else. That's what he said." Marino's tone is odd.

I detect hostility.

"The information we've got so far is the victim felt someone was after him. He'd been jumpy of late, and that's true in the two Jersey cases," Marino says. "The victims felt they were being watched and screwed with and then out of the blue they're dead. It's a lot to explain and right now we don't have time. The shooter may still be in the area even as we speak. You should stay inside until I get there. I'm maybe ten minutes out."

"Give me the exact address and I'll get myself there."

"No way. Not happening. And wear a vest."

I watch Benton fold the paper and pick up his coffee, his happy demeanor eclipsed by what he senses. Life is about to change on us. I already know it. I look at him, my expression somber as I stop pacing and pour my espresso into the mulch. I did it without even thinking. A reflex. A relaxing cheerful day has ended as abruptly as a plane slamming into a mountain socked in by fog.

"You don't think this is a case that Luke or one of the other docs can handle?" I ask Marino but I already know the answer.

He's not interested in dealing with my deputy chief, Luke Zenner. Marino isn't going to settle for any of my other medical examiners.

"Or we can send in one of our investigators if that would suffice. Jen Garate certainly could handle it and Luke can do the post immediately." I try anyway. "He's probably in the autopsy room. We have five cases this morning."

"Well now you got six. Jamal Nari," Marino says as if I should know who he's talking about.

"SHOT IN HIS DRIVEWAY as he was getting groceries out of his car between nine-forty-five and ten," Marino says. "A neighbor noticed him down on the pavement and called nine-one-one exactly one hour and eight minutes ago."

"How do you know he was shot if you haven't been to the scene yet?" I check my watch. It's eight minutes past eleven.

"He's got a nice hole in his neck and another one where his left eye used to be. Machado's there and has already gotten the wife on the phone. She told him some weird shit's been happening in the past month and Nari was concerned enough to start changing his patterns, even his car. At least that's what Machado's passed on to me." That tone again.

Hostility, and it makes no sense. The two of them go to baseball and hockey games together. They ride Harleys, and Machado is largely responsible for convincing Marino to resign as my chief forensic investigator and go back to policing. This was last year. I'm still adjusting to his empty office at the CFC and his new habit of telling me what to do. Or thinking he can. Like right now. He's demanding my presence at a death scene as if I have no say about it.

"I've already got a few emailed pictures," Marino explains. "Like I said it reminds me of the lady killed in New Jersey two months ago, the one whose mother I went to high school with. Shot while she was waiting for the Edgewater Ferry, people everywhere and no one heard or saw a damn thing. Once in the back of the neck, once in the mouth."

I remember hearing about the case and the original suspicion that it was a murder for hire, possibly domestic related.

"In December it was the guy getting out of his car at his restaurant in Morristown," Marino continues as my mind jumps to the peculiar poem again.

It was tweeted from a hotel in Morristown. *Copperhead.* My attention wanders back to the seven pennies on the wall.

"And I was there for that one, during the holidays, hanging out with some of my cop buddies, so I went to the scene. Shot once in the back of the neck, once in the gut. Solid copper bullets, high-speed velocities with so little frag we can't do positive ballistics matching. But there's a definite consistency in the two cases. We're pretty sure the same rifle was used, an unusual one."

We. At some point Marino inserted himself into an investigation that is outside of his jurisdiction. Serial murders, possibly sniper kills or at least that seems to be what he's implying, and there's nothing worse than an investigation launched by assumptions. If you already know the answer you torque everything to fit the theory.

"Let's go slowly until we know exactly what we're dealing with," I say to him as I watch Benton watching me and checking his phone.

I suspect he's skimming through news feeds and emails, trying to find out for himself what is going on. He continues to glance in the direction of the Academy of Arts and Sciences where he saw something flash like a camera flash, only duller. A glint, a flick of light, he said. The lens of a riflescope enters my mind. I think of the low dispersion glass or kill-flash devices used by snipers and competition shooters.

I meet Benton's eyes and indicate we need to go inside the house slowly, calmly, as if nothing is the matter. I pause on the patio, checking the grill. I cover it with the lid, acting unflustered and unconcerned. If someone is watching us or has a riflescope trained on us there is nothing we can do about it.

Sudden movements or an impression of panic will make matters worse. Lucy and Janet didn't notice anyone when they did an aerial recon but I don't put much stock in that. The person could be camouflaged. Maybe he ducked out of sight when he heard the helicopter's approach. Maybe he's back.

"You know who Jack Kuster is?" Marino asks.

I tell him I don't as Benton and I climb the back steps with Sock on our heels.

"Morristown," Marino says. "Their lead investigator and a master forensic firearms instructor. He's suspicious we're talking about a 5R like you see with sharpshooters and snipers who build their own rifles. My buddies there have been keeping me up to speed. And I got a personal interest."

Marino grew up in Bayonne, New Jersey, and loves to attend concerts and sports events at the MetLife. This past February it was the Super

Bowl. He claimed his cop friends with the Morris County Sheriff's Department managed to get tickets.

"There's copper frag at the scene, more of the same glitter where the bullet exited his body and slammed into the pavement," Marino says.

"The body's been moved?" That had better not be what he's implying.

"Apparently some of the frag's in blood that flowed out from under his head. Don't worry. Nobody's touched anything they shouldn't."

Benton shuts the screen door behind us, then the heavy wooden inner door, deadbolting it. I stand in the hallway on the phone while he disappears toward the kitchen. I end the call because someone else is trying me and I look to see who it is.

Bryce Clark.

Then I have him in my earpiece.

"Remember the high school music teacher who made the big stink about being persecuted by the government and ended up having a beer and barbecue with Obama?" Bryce says right off and now I understand. "A real jerk to you, remember? Dissed you right in front of the president? Basically called you a body snatcher and a Nazi who sells skin, bones, eyes, livers, lungs to the highest bidder?"

Jamal Nari. My mood gets worse.

"Did I mention a shit storm?" Bryce says. "It's already all over the news. Don't ask me why they released his identity instantly. Waited what? An hour? Maybe ask Marino that?"

"What are you talking about?"

"I mean it's no secret where Nari lives—or lived—obviously since there were news crews including CNN and Reuters and my fave GMA camped out there when that disastrous PR faux pas happened that landed him at the White House during happy hour. But they're saying it's him for sure. How did it happen that they released this all over the planet?"

I don't have an answer.

"Are you going to the scene or should I tell Luke to head there? Before you answer? My opinion? It should be you," adds my talkaholic chief of staff. "They're already tweeting conspiracy theories. And get this? A tweet about a Cambridge man *possibly murdered on Farrar Street?* It's been retweeted a million times since nine A.M."

I don't see how that's possible. I recall Marino saying Nari was killed between nine-forty-five and ten. I tell Bryce to get transport to the scene ASAP and make sure they bring a barrier shelter and set it up. I don't want people gawking and taking pictures with their phones.

"We release absolutely nothing to anyone," I instruct. "Not one word. Alert the cleanup service, and as soon as we've documented the scene I want blood and any other biological material removed as if it was never there."

"I'll get right on it," he says. "Oh yeah! And happy birthday, Doctor Scarpetta! I was going to sing it to you. But maybe later's better . . . ?"

CHAPTER 4

IT WAS A COMPUTER error, a terrible blunder. Jamal Nari was mistaken for someone with terrorist ties and suddenly found himself on a No Fly List and under surveillance.

His assets were frozen. The FBI appeared at his home with a search warrant. He resisted, ended up in handcuffs and next was suspended from teaching. This was maybe a year ago. It was all over the news and went viral on the Internet. The public was incensed and he was invited to the White House, which only offended people further. I'd completely forgotten his name. It's possible I'd blocked it. He was rude to me, a pompous ass.

It happened in the White House basement where there are small rooms collectively called the Mess, elegant with fine linen and china, fresh flowers and rich wooden paneling hung with maritime paintings. I was meeting with the director of the National Institute of Standards and Technology, the NIST, discussing the lack of consistency in forensic disciplines, the inadequate resources and the need for national support. Happy hour and the president appeared to buy a beer for Jamal Nari, who made a point of insulting me.

Another call and Marino lets me know he's in my driveway.

"Give me fifteen minutes to get my things," I tell him.

Sock nudges the back of my legs as I follow the paneled hallway hung with Victorian etchings of London and Dublin scenes, then into my kitchen of commercial grade stainless steel appliances and antique alabaster chandeliers. Benton is standing by a counter using one of many Mac-Books stationed about, skimming through security camera video footage.

"Any word from your people?" I'm wondering if the FBI's Boston Field Division has contacted him yet about Jamal Nari.

"It wouldn't be ours at this stage unless Cambridge invites us. And Marino won't, and at the moment there's no need."

"You're saying the FBI has no reason to think the shooting is related to Obama coming here today."

"At this time we don't but security will be intensified. It could be someone making an anti-Islamist statement because of the timing. The president's press conference tomorrow in Boston," Benton reminds me. "He plans to address the hatred, the threats ramping up as we get closer to the Boston Marathon bombing case going to trial."

"Jamal Nari wasn't a terrorist. I don't recall that he was Muslim, either."

"Perception," Benton says.

"And Marino's perception has nothing to do with anything political or religious. He believes this case is connected to ones in New Jersey. If that's true," I reiterate, "the FBI certainly has more than a passing interest."

"We don't know what we're dealing with, Kay. The shooting could be self-inflicted. It could be accidental. It could be anything. It might not even be a shooting. I don't trust what anyone says until you actually see the body yourself."

"You don't want to come?" I cover the *panzanella* with plastic wrap.

"It's not appropriate for me to show up."

The way he says it makes me suspicious. I know when Benton is telling me what I should hear and not necessarily what is true.

"Anything?" I ask him about the video recording.

"Not so far, which isn't making me happy. For sure someone was at our wall. If it was completely missed by our cameras then the person knew exactly how to come and go without being seen or recorded."

"Unless this really is nothing and whoever did it just happened to miss cameras he didn't even know about," I remark.

"A coincidence?" He doesn't believe it and I don't either.

The Tuscan salad goes into the refrigerator where the swordfish and pitcher of my spicy Bloody Mary mix will stay. Maybe tonight we can have a nice dinner that was supposed to be brunch. But I doubt it. I know how days like this go. Sleepless, relentless, take-out pizza if we're lucky.

"Our agents gave Nari a rough time. Doesn't matter who started it." Benton gets back to that.

"I'm not surprised. He certainly didn't strike me as easy or nice."

"If we rush in uninvited it won't look good. The media will make something of it. There are protests in Boston and Cambridge tomorrow and a march scheduled on Boylston Street. Not to mention anti-FBI and antigovernment protestors, and even local cops who are bitter about how we handled the bombing."

"Because you didn't share information that might have prevented MIT Officer Collier from being murdered." It's not a question. It's a re-minder. I'm judgmental about it.

"I can try to get us on the seven P.M. flight into Fort Lauderdale."

"I need you to do something for me." I open a cabinet near the sink where I keep Sock's food, medications, and a box of examination gloves because I hand-feed him. I pull out a pair and give them to Benton. Then I give him a freezer bag. From a drawer I retrieve a Sharpie and a measuring tape.

"The pennies," I explain. "I'd like them photographed to scale and collected. Maybe they really are nothing but I want them preserved prop-erly just to be on the safe side."

He opens a drawer and retrieves his Glock .40 cal.

"If Jamal Nari was murdered then his killer wasn't far from here this morning, not even half a mile away," I explain. "I also don't like the fact that you noticed something glinting from the trees, and added to that I got a strange communication last month from someone who mentioned pennies. There was something in it about keeping the change."

"Directed at you?"

"Yes."

"You're just telling me this now?"

"I get whacky communications. It's nothing new, and this one didn't seem all that different from other ones—not at the time. But we should be careful. Before you go back into the yard I think it would be a very good idea to get the state police chopper to do a flyover, check the woods, the Academy, make sure there's no one on the roof or in a tree or lurking around."

"Lucy already checked."

"Let's do it again. I can ask Marino to send some uniforms over there too."

"I'll take care of it."

"You might want to book our flight for tomorrow," I decide. "I don't think we're going anywhere today."

I head upstairs. Sunlight streams through the French stained glass over the landings, illuminating wildlife scenes like jewels. The vivid reds and blues don't inspire happiness at the moment. They remind me of emergency lights.

INSIDE OUR MASTER SUITE on the second floor I take off my jacket and drop it on the bed, which I've not gotten around to making. I was hopeful we hadn't finished with it yet.

Through windows facing the front of the house I can see Marino leaning against his unmarked dark blue Ford Explorer. His shaved head is shiny in the bright sunlight as if he polishes his big round dome, and he has on wire-rimmed Ray-Bans that are as old-fashioned as his worldview. He doesn't seem particularly worried about an active shooter at large as he lingers in the middle of our driveway.

I can tell he was off duty when he got the call. His voluminous gray sweatpants and black leather high-tops are what he usually wears for heavy bag training at his boxing club, and I suspect there's a vest under his zipped-up Harley-Davidson windbreaker. I don't see Quincy, his rescued German shepherd that Marino has deluded himself into believing is a service dog. He shows up at most crime scenes these days, snuffles around and typically pees on something disgusting or rolls in it.

Inside the bathroom I wash my face and brush my teeth. Stripping off my drawstring pants and pullover I'm confronted by myself in the full-length mirror on the back of the door. Handsome, attractive in a strong way according to journalists, and it's my belief they're actually thinking about my personality when they make such comments. I'm small, formidable, generously built, petite, medium height, too thin, sturdy, depending on who you ask. But the fact is that most journalists have no idea what I really look like and rarely get my age right or understand anything about me at all.

I examine the faintly etched laugh and smile lines, the hint of a furrow from frowning, which I try not to do because it makes nothing better. Mussing my short blond hair with gel and adding a touch of lipstick are an improvement. I brush a mineral sunblock over my face and the backs of my hands.

Then I pull on a T-shirt and over that a soft armor tactical vest, level IIIA, coyote tan, mesh lined. In a drawer I find cargo pants and a long-sleeved button-up shirt, navy blue with the CFC crest, my winter uniform when I respond to deaths or related scenes. I haven't bothered swapping out for lightweight khaki yet. I was going to do it after Florida.

Back downstairs I retrieve my rugged black plastic scene case out of the closet near the front door. I sit on the rug to pull on ankle-high boots that I decontaminated with detergent after I wore them last. I think of when that was, the end of April, a Sunday. The nights were still dipping into the low forties when a Tufts Medical School professor walking a trail in Estabrook Woods got lost and wasn't found until the next day. I remember his name, Dr. Johnny Angiers. His widow is owed life insurance benefits thanks to me. I can't undo death but I can make it less unfair.

Grabbing my case, I head down the brick front steps. In and out of sunlight I pass beneath flowering dogwoods and serviceberry with white clusters on the tips of twigs. Beneath them are wild ginger and cinnamon fern, then the old dark red brick pavers of our narrow driveway which is completely blocked by Marino's SUV.

"Where's Quincy?" I look at the empty dog crate in the backseat.

"I was at the gym when I got the call," Marino says. "Raced home on my motorcycle and grabbed my car but didn't have time to change or deal with him."

"I'm sure he wasn't happy." I think of my own unhappy dog.

Marino taps a cigarette out of the pack.

"Nothing like it after a workout," I say pointedly at the spurt of the lighter, the toasty tobacco smell.

He takes a big drag, leaning against the SUV. "No nagging about smoking. Be nice to me today."

"This minute I might just light one up." I sit inside the SUV and talk to him through the open door.

"Be my guest." He sucks on the cigarette and the tip glows brighter like a fanned hot coal.

He shakes another one loose, the brown filter popping up. Greeting me like a lost friend. Like the old days. I'm tempted. I fasten my shoulder harness and suddenly Benton is on the driveway striding toward us with purpose.

CHAPTER 5

THE BRIGHT COPPER COINS shine through the freezer Baggie Benton carries. He sealed it with tape that he initialed and labeled.

"What the shit?" Marino's words blow out in a cloud of smoke. "What are you giving this to me for?"

"Either take care of it or it ends up at the FBI labs in Quantico." Benton hands him the Baggie and a Sharpie. "Which wouldn't make any sense. No pun intended. I've emailed the photographs to you."

"What? You auditioning to be a crime scene tech? Reading your crystal ball's not enough anymore? Well I can check. But I'm pretty sure Cambridge isn't hiring."

"They're not fake and they definitely were polished," Benton says to me. "If you look at them under a lens, each has the same very subtle pitting. It may be that a tumbler was used. Gun enthusiasts who hand-load their own ammo often use tumblers to polish cartridge cases. The pennies need to go to the labs now."

Marino holds up the Baggie. "I don't get it."

"They were left on top of our wall," I explain. "It could have waited until we were sure nobody is around," I say to Benton.

"Nobody is. That's not how an offender like this works."

"An offender like *what*?" Marino asks. "I feel like I missed the first half of the movie."

"I've got to go." Benton holds my gaze. He looks around and back at me before returning to the house where I have no doubt he's been making plans he's not sharing.

Marino initials the Baggie, scribbles the time and date, screwing shut one eye behind his Ray-Bans as smoke drifts into his face. Another drag on the cigarette and he bends down to wipe it against a brick, scraping it out, and he tucks the butt in a pocket. It's an old habit that comes from working crime scenes where it's poor form to add detritus that could be confused with evidence. I know the drill. I used to do it too. It was never pretty when I'd forget to empty my pockets before my pants or jacket ended up in the washing machine.

Marino climbs into the SUV and impatiently shoves the Baggie into the glove box.

"The pennies go to fingerprints first, then DNA and trace," I tell him as we shut our doors. "Be gentle with them. I don't want any additional artifact introduced such as scratches to the metal from you banging them around."

"So I'm taking them seriously, really treating them like evidence? In what crime? You mind explaining what the hell's going on?"

I tell him what I remember about the anonymous email I received last month.

"Did Lucy figure out who it is?"

"No."

"You're kidding me, right?"

"It wasn't possible."

"She couldn't hack her way into figuring it out?" Marino backs out of the driveway. "Lucy must be slipping."

"It appears the person was clever enough to use a publicly accessed computer in a hotel business center," I explain. "She can tell you which one. I recall she said it was in Morristown."

"Morristown," he repeats. "Holy shit. The same area where the two Jersey victims were shot."

We back out onto the street and I'm struck by how peaceful it is, almost mid-June, close to noon, the sort of day when it's difficult to imagine someone plotting evil. Most undergraduate students are gone for the summer, many people are at work and others are home tending to projects they put off during the regular academic year.

The economics professor across from our house is mowing his grass. He looks up at us and waves as if all is fine in the world. The wife of a banker two doors down is pruning a hedge, and one yard over from her a landscaping truck is parked on the side of the street, SONNY'S LAWN CARE. Not far from it is a skinny young man wearing dark glasses, oversized jeans, a sweatshirt and a baseball cap. He's loud with a gas engine leaf blower, clearing the sidewalk, and he doesn't look at us or do the polite thing and pause his work as we drive past. Grass clippings and grit blast the SUV in a swarm of sharp clicks.

"Asshole!" Marino flashes his emergency lights and yelps his siren.

The young man pays no attention. He doesn't even seem to notice.

Marino slams on the brakes, shoves the SUV into park and boils out. The blower is as loud as an airboat. Then abrupt silence as the young man stops what he's doing. His dark glasses stare, his mouth expressionless. I try to place him. Maybe I've just seen him in the area doing yard work.

"You like it if I did that to your car?" Marino yells at him.

"I don't have a car."

"What's your name?"

"I don't have to tell you," he says in the same indifferent tone, and I notice his hair is long and carrot red.

"Oh yeah? We'll see about that."

Marino stalks around the truck, inspecting it. He pulls out a notepad and makes a big production of writing down the truck's plate number. Next he photographs it with his BlackBerry.

"I find anything I'll write you up for damaging city property," he threatens, the veins standing out in his neck.

A shrug. He isn't scared. He doesn't give a shit. He's even smiling a little.

Marino gets back in and resumes driving. "Fucking asshole."

"Well you made your point," I reply dryly.

"What the hell's wrong with kids these days? Nobody raises them right. If he was mine, I'd kick his damn ass."

I don't remind him that his only child, Rocco, who is dead, was a career criminal. Marino used to kick his ass and a lot of good it did.

"You seem very agitated today," I comment.

"You know why? Because I think we're dealing with some type of fucking terrorist who's now in our backyard. That's my gut and I wish to hell it wasn't, and me and Machado are having a real beef about it."

"And you started thinking this when exactly?"

"After the second case in Jersey. I got a real bad feeling Jamal Nari is the third one."

"Terrorists generally claim responsibility," I remind him. "They don't remain anonymous."

"Not always."

"What about enemies?"

I get back to the reason my vacation is being delayed and possibly ruined. More to the point, I need Marino to focus on what's before us and not on connections he's making to cases in New Jersey, to terrorism or to anything else.

"I would imagine that after the storm of publicity Jamal Nari must have gained a few detractors," I add.

"Nothing to account for this that we know about so far." Marino turns on Irving Street.

A light wind stirs hardwood trees and their shadows move on the sunny pavement. The traffic is intermittent, a couple of cars, a moped, and a boxy white construction truck that Marino tailgates and blares his horn at because it's not going fast enough. The truck pulls over to let him pass and Marino guns the engine.

He's in a mood all right and I doubt it's solely related to his so-called beef with Machado. Something else is going on. Marino might be scared and going out of his way to act like he's not.

"And the highly publicized problem with the FBI was about this time last year?" I'm asking him. "Why strike now? A lot of people have forgotten about it. Including me."

"I don't know how you forget after the way he treated you at the White House. Accusing you of selling body parts, saying autopsies are for profit and all that bullshit. Kind of an irony that the very thing he went after you about is now going to happen to him."

"Did he live alone?" I ask.

"Second marriage. Joanna Cather. She was one of his students in high school and now works there as a psychologist." Marino has gone from angry to subdued. "They started dating a couple years ago when he got divorced. Needless to say she's much younger. She kept her name when they got married for obvious reasons."

"What obvious reasons?"

"The name Nari. It's Muslim."

"Not necessarily. It could be Italian. Was he Muslim?"

"I guess the Feds thought he was which is why they went after him."

"They went after him because of a computer error, Marino."

"What matters is the way it looks and assumptions they make. If people thought he was Muslim, maybe that has something to do with why he's been murdered. Especially with Obama coming here and the fact that Nari met him at the White House last year. Since the marathon bombings there's a lot of sensitivity around here about jihadists, about loser extremists. Maybe we're dealing with a vigilante who's taking out people he thinks should die."

"Jamal Nari was a Muslim and now suddenly he was a jihadist or extremist Islamist upset about the wars in Iraq and Afghanistan?"

He clams up, his jaw muscles clenching.

"What's going on with you, Marino?"

"I'm not objective about it, okay?" he erupts again. "The Nari thing is pushing my wrong buttons and I can't help it. Because of who and what he was and the fucking reward he got? A trip to the fucking White House? He gonna be on the cover of *Rolling Stone* next?"

"This isn't about him, it's about the bombings. It's about the murder of an MIT police officer who was minding his own business, sitting in his patrol car on a night when you were on duty. It could have been you."

"Asshole terrorists, and if the Bureau had bothered telling us they were in the Cambridge area . . . ? I mean a detail like that and no cop is going to be sitting in his car, a damn sitting duck. I'm not back in policing even six months and something like that goes down. People killed in cold blood and their legs blown off. That's the world we live in now. I don't see how you get past it."

"We don't. But I'm asking that you put it on hold right now. Let's talk about where Jamal Nari lived."

"A one-bedroom apartment." Marino's Ray-Bans stare rigidly ahead. "They moved in after they got married."

"This part of Cambridge is expensive," I reply.

"The rent's three-K. Not a problem for them for some reason. Maybe because after he was suspended from teaching he sued the school for discrimination. Figures, right? I don't know the settlement but we'll find out. By all appearances so far he did a little better than your average high school teacher."

"This is from Machado?"

"I get info from a lot of places."

"And where was Joanna Cather this morning when her husband died?"

"New Hampshire, heading to an outlet mall, according to her. She's on her way here." Sullen again, he refuses to look at me.

"Are you aware that by nine A.M. it was already on the Internet that a Cambridge man on Farrar Street possibly had been shot? It was retweeted before the alleged shooting had even occurred."

"People are always screwing up the time they think something happened."

"Regardless of how people screw up things," I answer, "you should know exactly what time the nine-one-one call was made."

"AT TEN-OH-TWO exactly," he says. "The lady who noticed his body on the pavement said she'd seen him pull up and start getting groceries out of his car around nine-forty-five. Fifteen minutes later she noticed him down on the pavement at the rear of his car. She figured he had a heart attack."

"How did anyone get the information before the police were even called?" I persist.

"Who told you?"

"Bryce."

"Maybe he's mixed up. It wouldn't be a first."

"Unfortunately, these days you have to worry about students," I say as we slow at a four-way intersection. "If you're a teacher or work in a school you could be targeted by a teenager, by someone even younger. The more it happens the more it will."

"This is different from that. I already know it," he says.

A jogger goes by in the crosswalk and starts to turn onto Farrar Street but apparently notices the emergency vehicles, the news trucks. He looks up at several helicopters hovering at about a thousand feet. Heading to Scott Street instead he nervously glances back and around as he picks up his pace.

"Obviously, we need to consider his students and any his wife had contact with," I add. "Have you talked to her yourself?"

"Not yet. I only know what Machado's been saying. According to him she sounded shocked and upset." Marino finally looks at me. "Lost her shit in other words and it came across as genuine. She mentioned a kid she's been helping, said she has no reason to think he'd hurt anyone but he has a thing for her. Or maybe Nari was shot during an attempted robbery. That was her other suggestion."

"She said he was shot?"

"I think she got that from Machado. I didn't get the impression that she already knew it."

"We should make sure."

"Thanks for helping me do my job. Obviously I couldn't connect the dots without you."

"Are you angry with me or just angry in general about terrorists? Why are you and Machado not getting along?"

He doesn't say anything. I let it go for now.

"So Jamal Nari went grocery shopping." I unlock my iPhone and execute a search on the Internet. "Was that a typical routine on a Thursday morning during the summer?"

"Joanna says no," Marino replies. "He was stocking up because they were going to Stowe, Vermont, for a long weekend supposedly."

Jamal Nari is on Wikipedia. There are scores of news accounts about his run-in with the FBI and trip to the White House. Fifty-three years old, born in Massachusetts, his father's family originally from Egypt, his mother from Chicago. A gifted guitarist, he attended the prestigious Berklee College of Music in Boston and performed in musical theater and bands until he decided to settle down and teach. His high school chorus is consistently one of the top three in New England.

"Well this is a mess already," I decide as we roll up on the scene.

I recognize the two helicopters directly overhead, Channel 12 and Channel 5. There must be at least a dozen cars, marked and unmarked, plus several news trucks in addition to other vehicles that might belong to reporters. The media has wasted no time, and that's the way it is these days. Information is instantaneous. It's not unusual for journalists to arrive at a scene before I do.

We park behind a CFC windowless white van rumbling on the shoulder of the road. The caduceus and scales of justice in blue on the doors are tasteful and subtle but nothing can disguise the ominous arrival of one of my scene vehicles. It's not what anyone would ever wish to see. It can mean only one thing.

"Suddenly he gets a brand-new red Honda SUV." Marino points out what's parked in front of the house. "That would have set him back a few."

"And you presume he changed cars because he thought someone was after him?" That doesn't seem logical to me. "If someone was stalking him I wouldn't think changing cars would make a difference. The person would figure it out soon enough."

"Maybe it doesn't matter what I think. Maybe the Portuguese Man of War is in charge of this investigation. At least for five minutes."

"You two need to get along. I thought you were good friends."

"Yeah well think again."

We climb out as my transport team, Rusty and Harold, open the back of the van. They begin pulling out a stretcher and stacks of disposable sheets.

"We got the barrier screens up," Harold says to me.

"I can see that," I reply. "Good job."

The four large black nylon panels are fastened by Velcro straps to PVC frames and form an ominous boxy shelter roomy enough for me to work in while shielding the body from prying eyes. But like similar screens used roadside in motor vehicle fatalities to prevent rubbernecking, the temporary shelters also signal carnage and they won't stop helicopters from filming. Despite our best efforts we won't be able to keep Jamal Nari's dead body out of the news.

"And we've got sandbags on the rails just to make sure somebody doesn't accidentally knock one over," says Harold, a former undertaker who might just sleep in a suit and tie.

"Or in case we get a chopper gets too damn close." Rusty is clad as usual in a sweatshirt and jeans, his long gray hair pulled back in a ponytail.

"Let's hold here," I say to them.

They need to stay put until I give them the signal. I don't have to explain further. They know the routine. I need time to work and think. I count six uniformed cops sitting in their cruisers and posted at the perimeter. They're making sure no one unauthorized enters the scene while they keep a lookout for the possible killer. I recognize two Cambridge crime scene techs who can't do much until I'm done, and I find Sil Machado's SUV, a dark blue Ford Explorer the same as Marino's only not as shellacked with wax and Armor All.

Machado—the good-looking dark-haired Portuguese Man of War—is talking to a heavyset young woman, brunette, in sweats. The two of them are alone in the shade of a maple tree in front of the slate tower-roofed Victorian, a splendid three-story house turned into condominiums. Marino tells me Nari's unit is on the first floor in back.

I lift out my scene case but hold my position at the rear of Marino's SUV. I stand perfectly still. I get the lay of the land.

CHAPTER 6

Tape is wrapped around big oak trees and iron lampposts, bright yellow with police line do not cross in black. It encircles the property, threaded through railings, barring the front entrance covered by a peaked roof.

I note the red Honda's temporary tags, the open tailgate, the cartons of milk and juice, the apples, grapes, bananas, and boxes and bags of cereal, crackers and potato chips scattered on the pavement. Cans of tuna have rolled to the curb, resting not far from my feet, and honeydew melons are cracked and oozing sweet juice that I can smell. A jar of salsa is shattered, and I detect its spicy tomato odor too. Flies have gotten interested, alighting on spilled food warming in the sun.

What once was the front yard is now a paved parking area with space for several cars. A motor scooter is chained to a lamppost. Two bicycles are secured by locked heavy cables hugging columns on a wraparound front porch centered by a bay window. Probably students living here, I decide, and a fifty-three-year-old high school music teacher married to a second wife named Joanna who supposedly was shopping at a New Hampshire outlet mall when the police gave her the shocking news.

I continue to ponder that fact as I move in, ducking under the tape. If Nari and his wife were heading to Vermont for a long weekend, why was she off to an outlet mall a two-hour round-trip away? Did she need to shop this morning because of their impending trip? Or was she careful not to be home or even in Massachusetts at nine-forty-five A.M.? I reach the privacy screens. Velcro makes a ripping sound as I open the panel closest to the back of the red SUV. I make sure that the slowing cars and gathering spectators on sidewalks and in their yards can't see what is none of their business.

I don't enter the black boxy barricade yet as I think about what Marino said Joanna told Machado. She has no idea why anyone would have killed her husband. But she mentioned a high school student she was trying to help. She also offered the possibility of a random robbery gone as wrong as one could, and that's not what this is.

I set down my scene case just outside the privacy screens, the sun almost directly overhead now, illuminating what's inside. I smell the iron pungency of blood breaking down. Blowflies drone, honing in on wounds and orifices to lay their eggs.

HIS BODY IS FACEUP on the pavement, his legs straight out, the left one only very slightly bent. His arms are loosely by his sides. He didn't stumble. He didn't try to catch himself when he fell or move after he did. He couldn't.

Blood is separating from its serum at the edges, in the very early stages of coagulation, consistent with his being shot within the past two hours. Postmortem changes will have begun but not escalated because the temperature is in the upper sixties, the air dry with a cool breeze and he's fully clothed. I estimate his body temperature will be around ninety-four degrees and he's begun getting stiff. Then my attention is pulled back to the blood.

It flowed from the wound in his neck. Following the gentle slope of the tarmac it soaked the upper back of his white shirt, terminating some three feet from his body. The wound to his eye doesn't appear to have bled much at all, just a trickle down the side of his face, staining his collar. A small amount flowed from the back of his head. It wasn't much bleeding for such profound injuries to vascular areas. His heart stopped beating quickly. It may have stopped instantly.

I note the car key nearby, the two brown paper bags from Whole Foods, their contents spilled. He had the key and two bags in hand when he went down like an imploded building. Eight additional bags are still inside the SUV's open tailgate, the interior light on, and already I'm perplexed by the extensive shopping he did for a three-day trip.

I catch glimpses of paper towels, toilet paper, boxes of aluminum foil and trash bags, and a Smirnoff vodka box with bottles of wine and liquor inside the dividers. If there are additional bags inside the apartment then Nari must have left home quite early to do this much shopping at more than one location. Whole Foods doesn't carry liquor.

He looks familiar but he probably would even if we hadn't briefly met. I would have seen him on the news. It's possible I've seen him in passing in the neighborhood, although I have no recollection of it. I look closely at his body before touching it, getting an overview and immediate impressions. I will myself not to think about our unpleasant encounter in Washington, D.C., and the president's raised eyebrows, his bemused smile when Nari lit into me.

He has short gray hair that's receding, and a rugged face with a strong prominent jaw hinting at an underbite. Clean-shaven, he's of average height and slender with little body fat but he has a swollen belly that I find curious. Possibly he's a heavy beer drinker. I put him at about five-foot-eight, 160 pounds, someone youthful for his age.

"Anything I can help you with, Chief?" The voice with the Spanish accent belongs to CFC Investigator Jen Garate, long dark hair, blue eyes, olive skin, mid-thirties, pretty in an exotic overblown way.

She likes tight clothes that accentuate her voluptuous build, and I watch Machado watching her. He's still talking to the young woman in sweats. She seems agitated and excited and he looks at me. He excuses himself and comes over.

"I'm all set here," I tell Jen.

"You picked a good day to head out on vacation," she says ironically. "I would have gotten here sooner but the little girl who drowned?"

I don't know who she means and I'm not going to ask, not now.

"Stupid ass kids, right?" she tells me anyway. "The water was freezing and she decides it's a good idea to jump on the pool cover. Good thing we keep dry suits in the back of the trucks. But the collar gasket leaked and I had to clean myself up."

"Thanks for your help." My tone doesn't invite her chatty conversation.

"I wonder if Lucy's still up." She stares off at a distant helicopter, twin engine but with skids, and her observation is peculiar.

Why would she know that Lucy was flying today? They aren't friends, not even cordial. I recognize the fuselage shape of a Eurocopter, possibly MedFlight.

"I'm just curious," she says. "Obama's coming here today so how does she manage permission to fly in a prohibited airspace? I guess your DOD connections don't hurt, not to mention your husband."

"Permission depends on who's been vetted by the TSA and has advance clearance." I've stopped what I'm doing and am meeting her gaze. "I have no influence with the FAA and I'm not sure what you're implying."

"I just think it's cool to be a pilot, that's all."

"I'll see you back at the office." It's my way of dismissing her.

She hesitates in her cargo pants and long-sleeved T-shirt that look painted on, then she smiles at Machado as his eyes wander over what she never fails to flaunt.

Male or female, Jen doesn't care who stares. My new chief of investigations is a shallow narcissist it's just my luck, and I hired her because I had to hire someone after Marino left. Skilled and New York trained she's smart and competent but a mistake I've found out. I can't fire her because she's inappropriate and certain people don't like her. I can't tell her how to act or dress because that for sure would get me sued, and I watch her head back toward the street, swaying her hips, her round buttocks pumping.

"Doc?" Machado greets me, his eyes masked by Oakleys, a style called Half Jacket that's popular with the cops and the military.

He is typically neat in crisp khaki slacks, a white shirt and blue striped tie, and a navy blue windbreaker with CAMBRIDGE POLICE in yellow on the back. The windbreaker is oversized, snapped up to conceal a tactical vest. He obviously was on duty when the call came in and it doesn't escape my notice that Marino crosses his arms, his face hard, his jaw muscles clenching again.

"I hear we ruined your day," Machado says to me.

"My day's not as ruined as his."

"Sorry about your vacation."

"Right now it doesn't seem very important, considering." I open the sturdy plastic clasps of my scene case and retrieve white Tyvek coveralls packaged in cellophane.

"What's been done?"

"We've got photographs and I've checked out his apartment, just a quick go-through to make sure nobody was inside who shouldn't be. The door was unlocked and ajar. It appears he'd already carried in three bags and was getting more out of the car when somebody nailed him."

Machado flips through a notepad as I work the coveralls over my clothes. At the bottom of my scene case I find boot covers and pull them on, standing on one foot at a time. Suiting up is an art. I've witnessed seasoned investigators put things on backward or lose their balance.

"That lady?" Machado glances at the one he was just talking to. "She lives in the unit on the top floor, Harvard grad student, said she was working at her desk when she saw Nari drive up. Next thing she noticed him where he is now."

"Did she hear gunshots or anything that might have been gunshots?" I pull on gloves.

"She says she didn't, and there were no reports of shots fired in the area. We're already questioning the neighbors. So far coming up zero. But the grad student?" He glances back at the woman, standing rather dazed on the side-walk now. "Angelina Brown, twenty-four, getting her doctorate in education."

Marino is jotting down the information, his mouth set as if he just ate something that didn't agree with him.

"She did make one interesting comment," Machado continues, "and for sure we'll follow up on it. Apparently her desk is in front of the window facing the street and she has a bird's-eye view of who's out front or entering or leaving the house. She says she's seen a kid in the area. He rides his bike back and forth up and down the street. Not so long ago Joanna Cather was outside talking to him and then they went around back, maybe head-ing into her apartment. Angelina says she's pretty sure Nari's car wasn't here at the time. It struck her as weird that Joanna was possibly inviting a male into the apartment when her husband wasn't home."

"We know the kid's name or have a description?" Marino continues to write down the information.

"Short, thin, always has a cap on."

"That could only be a couple of people," Marino says snidely and Machado ignores it.

"She says the kid looks maybe sixteen," Machado continues. "Could be a little older or a little younger, you know with pants half mast, the usual baggy bad-boy clothes."

"Huh. Let me guess. The kid Joanna claims she's been trying to help," Marino says. "Yeah, well maybe she's been giving him more than advice."

"If your witness is right and the person she's seen riding his bike is this same student Joanna supposedly is helping, it appears he doesn't live too far from here," I reply, and Tyvek makes a papery sound as I crouch on the back of my heels just inside the opening of the barrier. "Otherwise he wouldn't be on a bike, my guess is."

"I'm gonna talk to her," Marino says brusquely, and I glance back at his NBA-huge black high-tops behind us.

"Help yourself," Machado replies.

"Don't worry, I will." Marino walks off as I check the dead music teacher's hands.

I bend his fingers and feel rigor mortis forming in his small muscles. He's still warm. I begin to unbutton his shirt and discover tattoos. Trees with flying crows are on his left chest, and on his right shoulder is a logo of some sort, *RainSong* in stylized letters. Machado crouches next to me.

"I assume the witness, Angelina Brown, didn't mention whether she'd noticed this same kid in the area this morning?" I insert a long thermometer under the right arm and set a second thermometer in the top drawer of my scene case.

"I asked her that. She says no." Machado watches what I'm doing. "But it's not like she's looking out her window every minute, either. It's possible he could have come around through the backyard and she wouldn't have seen him."

"Any chance she really wasn't in New Hampshire when you reached her?"

"We'll be able to determine that from cell towers that picked up her phone signal when I called her."

I rock the body toward me and it rests heavily, limply against my knees as I check for livor mortis, the settling of noncirculating blood due to gravity. It's just beginning to form on his back, a blush of dark pink that blanches when I press it.

"I'm wondering," I continue, "if it might be possible she actually was inside the apartment. I wonder if she had a visitor while her husband was shopping and then she left either intentionally or unintentionally at a strategic moment right before he got home."

"Exactly. The cell towers will tell us if she's lying. But I'm wondering why you're wondering it." His attention is fixed on me.

"Because I've seen things like it before. And there are still a lot of people out there who don't realize just how much information their cell phones are giving to anyone interested. They lie because they have no clue how easily they'll be caught."

"She shouldn't be naïve though, not after what they went through with the FBI." Machado makes a good point.

"I don't guess your witness noticed if Joanna's car was here this morning," I add.

"Well here's an interesting detail. It just so happens she's driving a rental car today."

"Why?"

"I don't know but I'd say it's open season on possibilities," Machado replies. "Which is one reason we don't want anybody inside the apartment until we get a chance to go through it with a fine-tooth comb. All we're waiting on is the warrant."

He's suspicious the wife had something to do with her husband's murder, and it's no wonder that would enter his mind early on. But based on what the witness Angelina Brown said and also on what I'm already seeing, Jamal Nari wasn't taken out by some jealous high school kid packing a pistol. He wasn't picked off by a contract killer who walked up and shot him and kept on going.

Had a gun been fired on the property someone would have heard it. I strongly suspect that Nari was shot long range by someone experienced and skilled who had a point to make. I retrieve a magnifying hand lens to get a better look at the small tangential hole in the back of the neck at the hairline. I take photographs. I turn the head slightly to the right, and blood spills out of the wound, an entrance wound. I move the head some more and shine a flashlight. Fragments of copper light up like gold in a mush of coagulating blood, hair and brain tissue.

CHAPTER 7

THE WOUND TO THE eye is also an entrance, the bullet smashing through the sunglasses Nari had on. I photograph them on the pavement, the left lens gone, the tortoise frame intact.

Shards of polarized plastic are scattered over his white button-up shirt and on the pavement next to his face. He was down when he was shot through the eye, in the exact position he's in now, and I back out of the cool shade of my privacy shelter. I look up and around at windows in other homes and town houses. I look at the apartment buildings at the end of the street a block from here, rows of them like barracks, three story, flat rooftops.

Finding a six-inch ruler and a tape measure, I duck back inside my big black box and photograph him from every angle, noting that when the bullet struck his sunglasses, the force and trajectory knocked the frames off his face. They landed exactly three feet four inches to the right of his head, and I palpate his bloody gray hair.

My gloved fingers find what I'm looking for, fractured bones in his occipital skull and lacerations where at least one bullet exited. But no bogginess. He had scarcely any vital response at all. He was dead by the time he hit the ground. I remember the anonymous poem again and its reference to a hangman.

Instant death is rare. It can be caused by the dislocation of the C2 from the vertebral body. When I see this it's usually in hangings with long sudden drops such as from a bridge or a tall tree, and in motor vehicle and diving accidents when the victim suffers a hyperflexion injury after striking his head on a dashboard or the bottom of a pool. If the spinal cord is severed, the brain is no longer attached to the body. The heart and lungs instantly quit.

"I think you can rule out a drive-by shooting or foiled robbery or anything else that might have involved a handgun," I tell Machado.

"You think it's completely out of the question somebody could have come up behind him and shot him in the back of the neck? And when he dropped, shot him in the face?"

"In broad daylight with people around?"

"It's amazing what people don't hear or just assume is a car backfire."

"There's no stippling or any other evidence indicating the shot was close range." I look carefully at the wound at the hairline. "If it was a pistol, there are no ejected cartridge cases."

"The shooter could have picked them up."

"That's a lot of activity in a wide open area in the middle of the morning."

"I'm not arguing," Machado says. "I just want to cover every base. For example is it possible the bullet to the back of his neck exited through his eye? And we're talking only one shot?"

"No. The wound to his eye is an entrance, and there wouldn't be frag under and around his head if he was shot only once and while he was standing."

"So that bullet—the first bullet—could be anywhere."

"We'll know more when we get him to my office. But what I'm seeing so far indicates two different flight paths. One when he was upright and another when he was down. The second shot exited the back of his skull, which is pretty much pulverized, held together by his scalp. The frag is right here." I indicate the blood under and around the head. "The bullet disintegrated when it exited and struck the asphalt. In other words when he was shot through the eye he was in the position he's in now."

"Luck of the draw," Machado says. "A bull's-eye."

"I don't know if it was a lucky shot but it certainly wasn't lucky for him except he didn't suffer. In my opinion this was a lightning strike seemingly out of nowhere because it was made from a distance by someone who was set up for it."

"How much of a distance?"

"It's not possible to tell without doing detailed shooting reconstructions. And we will. And I suggest you pay close attention to any buildings around here where someone may have set up with a rifle. The frag appears to be solid copper, and if we're talking about a handgun round such as a nine-millimeter solid copper hollowpoint, there wouldn't have been sufficient muzzle velocity for the bullet to fragment like this. I think these were distant shots with heavy loads fired by someone with a high-power-rifle who is extremely precise and deliberate," I reiterate.

"It's exactly like I was telling you." Marino is back, and I notice his shoes behind me again. "Maybe the same damn sniper that took out two people in New Jersey."

"Jesus." Machado's dark glasses stare at the apartment buildings. He scans the nearby houses, pausing on the Federal-style brick multiunit dwelling directly across the street. "There we go with that again."

"Didn't you mention that those two victims were shot in the back of the neck?" I ask Marino.

"High up," he says. "At the base of the skull."

"And a second shot after they were on the ground?"

"You got it," he replies. "Like some terrorist sending a message, making us feel nobody is safe taking the ferry or getting groceries out of the car."

"Someone motivated by terrorism or possibly someone having fun target practicing with human beings." I rip open a packet and remove a pair of plastic tweezers. "In either case you're right. It sends a message that nobody's safe."

"Me? I'm keeping an open mind," Machado says with an edge. "I want to find the kid on the bicycle before I start thinking murders committed by some ex-military guy gone berserk."

"An open mind?" Marino says loudly. "That's a joke. Your mind's about as open as the Federal Reserve."

"Watch it," Machado says with the metallic ring of a warning in his tone. "You don't ease up I'll have you reassigned."

"Last I checked you don't supervise me. And the commissioner and me are tight. Threw back a few at Paddy's the other night with him and the district attorney."

Their squabbling and swipes are depressingly unhelpful and in poor taste. It's as if they have forgotten the dead man who was minding his own business when someone violently stole his life and upended the worlds of everyone around him. I'm going to put a stop to the bickering the only way I can. I'll separate them. I find a Sharpie in a drawer of my scene case.

I label a small cardboard evidence box and with the tweezers begin plucking each fleck and shred of bright copper from hair, from brain tissue and blood. The largest piece of frag is the size of a baby tooth, curved and as sharp as a razor. I place it on the tip of my index finger. I look at it with the magnifying lens and see one land, a partial one, and a groove imprinted into the copper by the rifling of the gun barrel. Then Marino is next to me, squatting, his hands gloved in black. I feel his heat. I smell the dried sweat from his workout in the gym.

"We'll get ballistics on this right away," I say to him. "Can you ask the investigators in New Jersey to email photographs from the two cases there?"

"Hell yes. Jack Kuster is the man."

"Who?" Machado asks rudely.

"Only the top guy in shooting reconstructions who also happens to know more about guns than anyone you'll ever meet." Marino is boisterous, and I feel the anger between them.

"Get me anything as fast as you can," I say to Marino. "The autopsy reports, lab results."

"What if it turns out the ballistics don't match?" Machado pushes back at me now.

"My concern at the moment," I reply, "is that the M.O. and pattern of injuries are quite similar. A fatal shot to the back of the neck followed by a second shot that seems gratuitous and possibly symbolic. A shot to the mouth, a shot to the gut, a shot to an eye. We also have distant shots and solid copper bullets in common. Even if the ballistics don't match, I suggest that we compare notes with Morristown. It's in the realm of possibility that a shooter might not always use the same firearm."

"Not likely," Machado counters. "If you're talking about a sniper, he's going to use what he knows and trusts."

"There you go with your assumptions," Marino retorts.

"Jesus," Machado mutters, shaking his head.

"Somebody's got to work this intelligently before the fucker does it again."

"Back off, buddy," Machado snaps at him.

"I'm calling Kuster right now." Marino pulls off his gloves and dips into a pocket of his jacket for his phone.

I place the bloody copper frag into the cardboard box. I tape the lid securely, handing the packaged evidence to Machado. I've just made it his responsibility to receipt it to the CFC and in the process I'm separating Marino and him. I remind Machado that the bullet fragments should be processed in the Integrated Ballistic Identification System, IBIS, immediately.

"There's a problem with that. She's not in . . . ," he starts to say, and I know what he's alluding to and find it strange.

My top firearms examiner, Liz Wrighton, has been out sick with the flu for the past few days. I'm not sure why Machado would know about it.

"I'm calling her at home," I reply.

I need her to use IBIS software to image the marks on the frag and run them through the National Integrated Ballistic Information Network, NIBIN. If the firearm in question has been used in other crimes we could get a hit in a matter of hours. I peel off my gloves.

"HELLO?" SHE SAYS STUFFILY.

"Liz? It's Doctor Scarpetta."

"I heard about the shooting on the news."

"Apparently everybody has." I look around as I talk.

Some of the neighbors are outside loitering on the sidewalks, in the street, and every car that passes slows to a crawl as people gawk. The sound of the news choppers is constant, and I notice a third one in the distance.

"The case is maybe two hours old. The media got here before I did," I say to Liz.

"I saw it on Twitter," she replies. "Let me see, I'm looking. *Boston-dot-com* says there was a shooting homicide in Cambridge, victim Jamal Nari. And another tweet reminds us who he is, you know, his *pulled pork powwow* with Obama. And I'm quoting. No disrespect on my part."

"Can you come in? I'm really sorry. But this is important. How are you feeling?"

"Congested as hell but not contagious. I'm actually at CVS buying more drugs." She coughs several times. "I can be there in forty-five."

I look at Machado and nod that he can head to the CFC, and he walks swiftly to his SUV. Next I get my radiologic expert Anne on the phone. I tell her she has a case coming in that I want scanned immediately.

"I'm especially interested to see if he has a hangman's fracture," I explain.

A pause, then, "Okay. I'm confused. I thought this was a shooting."

"Based on the position of the wound at the back of his neck and his lack of a vital response after being shot, I have a hunch we're going to find a fracture involving both pars interarticularis of C-two. On CT we should be able to see the extent of his cervical spine injury. I'm betting his cord was severed."

"I'll do it as soon as the body arrives."

"It should be there in half an hour. If I'm not back by the time you're done, see if Luke can get started on the autopsy."

"I guess no Florida," Anne says.

"Not today," I reply, and I end the call and crouch back inside the shelter of the privacy screens.

I tape small paper bags over the hands and a larger one over the head to preserve possible trace evidence. But I don't expect anything significant beyond copper frag. I don't think the killer came anywhere near his victim, and I stand up and look at Rusty and Harold still holding back at the CFC van. I motion to them.

They head in this direction as I pack up my scene case. Wheels rattle toward me as they roll the stretcher. Piled on top of it are white sheets and a neatly folded black body bag.

"You want to take a look inside his apartment?" Marino asks me. "Because that's where I'm headed. I mean if you want to do your usual thing with the medicine cabinet, the fridge, the cupboards, the trash."

He wants my company. He usually does.

"Sure. Let's see what kind of meds he was taking," I reply as a uniformed officer approaches him with paperwork I recognize as a warrant.

CHAPTER 8

IT'S A FEW MINUTES past one when Marino walks me around to the back of the Victorian house.

The first floor of it is clapboard, the upper stories and gables shingled. Up close I see the dark green paint is peeling and drainpipes are rusting. What's left of the yard has been sutured by an ugly wooden fence, and the trunks of old trees crowd against it like something massive and lumbering trying to escape. I can imagine what an estate this must have been in an earlier era. What's left of the subdivided property is no more than a sliver of land crowded by recently built bright brick town houses on three sides.

The windows of the corner first-floor apartment are small. The curtains are drawn, and the door they used to access their apartment has no patio or overhang. It must have been unpleasant hurrying inside when the weather was bad, especially if one was carrying groceries. It would have been awful in the ice and snow, treacherous in fact.

"So this is the exact way he came after he got out of his car," Marino says as we walk through unbroken shade, chilly and still beneath leafy canopies, the earth pungent and spongy under my booted feet. "He carried three bags, walked around to the back of the house and let himself in with keys that are on the kitchen counter. There's a knob lock and a dead bolt."

"What about an alarm system?"

"He probably disarmed it when he went in unless it hadn't been set, and I've got a call to the alarm company to find out the history for earlier today." He glances at his phone. "Hopefully I'll be getting that any minute."

"Machado certainly handed off a lot of detail considering how much the two of you don't seem to like each other at the moment." I'm going to make him talk about it. "There's no room in a homicide investigation for personal problems."

"I'm a hundred percent focused."

"If you were I wouldn't have noticed that anything is wrong. I thought you were friends."

His gloved hand turns a modern satin chrome knob that is an insult to the vintage oak front door.

"It's completely closed now but when the first responding officers got here it was ajar." He continues to ignore my questions.

I follow him in and stop just beyond the jamb, pulling the door shut. Opening my scene case I retrieve shoe covers for both of us as I glance around before stepping farther inside. The apartment is tiny, the kitchen and living area combined, the oak paneling painted chocolate brown. The wide board flooring is heavily varnished and scattered with colorful throw rugs. One bedroom, one bath, two windows across from me and two to my left, the drapes drawn, and I take my time near the door. I'm not done with him.

He and Machado are fighting and I wonder if it's over a woman, and my thoughts dart back to Liz Wrighton. I'm rather startled but probably shouldn't be. Single, in her late thirties, attractive, and I recall that when Marino worked for me, the two of them sometimes went shooting together or grabbed a few drinks after work. She's been out sick since Monday and for some reason Machado knew about it.

"Did you mention to Machado that Liz has been out sick?" I ask.

"I didn't know about it."

"Is that a yes?"

"It isn't."

I look up at two rubbed bronze hanging fixtures shaped like inverted tulip bulbs. Cheap. What's called *antique inspired*. Their bulbs are glaring, the dimmer switches near the door pushed up as bright as the lights will go. I doubt Jamal Nari did that when he came in with groceries and left the door ajar. I have a feeling Machado did plenty of looking around when he did his walk-through, and I suggest this to Marino. I ask him if the lights were on when the police got here or if Machado might have done it.

"I'm sure he turned them on so he could see anything in plain view before we got the warrant." Marino is skimming through it, his mouth set angrily. "And guess what? I don't see a sniper rifle on it. What if we find one in the closet or under the bed? It's not like I didn't damn tell him."

"I don't understand. Are you implying Joanna Cather shot her husband with a rifle they keep in the apartment?"

"I'm implying that Machado is being bullheaded and jerking me around. What he doesn't want to hear is we're probably looking for a special type of firearm. One that not so long ago wasn't readily available to the public. So he's not acknowledging anything I tell him." Marino's gloved hands pick up keys on the kitchen counter next to three upright brown paper Whole Foods bags. "A 5R. Like the rifle used in New Jersey."

He's talking about the engraving on the bullet made by the rifling of the barrel.

"Five lands and grooves with rolled leading edges," he says. "And when do you see that in shooting cases?"

"I'm not sure I have."

"I personally don't know of any homicides where the shooter used a rifle with a 5R barrel except the two Jersey cases," Marino says. "Even now there's only a few models out there unless you custom-build, and most people don't know crap about barrels or even think they're important. But this shooter does because he's damn smart. He's a gun fanatic."

"Or he somehow got hold of a gun like that . . ."

"We need to look for anything that might be related, put everything on a warrant including solid copper bullets, cartridge cases, a tumbler."

Marino talks over me. "Anything you can think of in any place we search including any vehicles like the wife's rental car. But Machado's fighting me. Basically he's giving me the finger because if I'm right it's a huge case and it's mine not his."

"Under ordinary circumstances it should be both of yours."

"Well the circumstances aren't ordinary and I should be the lead investigator. He's already run the wrong way with the ball."

"Your hope is that it's Machado who gets reassigned."

"Maybe he will and maybe he should before there's a bigger problem."

"What bigger problem?" There's more to this than Marino is saying.

"Like him pinning this murder on some kid who maybe was fooling around with the dead man's wife. A kid didn't do this," Marino says but that's not his reason. There's something else.

HE OPENS HIS SCENE case on the floor as I survey the sitting area.

A chesterfield brown leather sofa and two side chairs. A coffee table. A flat-screen TV has been dismounted from the wall and so have framed Jimi Hendrix, Santana and Led Zeppelin posters. In a corner are three black carbon fiber guitars on stands, iridescent like a butterfly wing when the light catches just right, and I get close to inspect.

RainSong.

"He must have really loved his guitars to get a tattoo," I comment, and I'm in the kitchen now.

Four wall-mounted cabinets, a three-burner stove, an oven, a refrigerator. On the counter are a microwave, the keys and bags of groceries Nari carried in before he returned to his car and was shot to death. I work my hands into a pair of fresh gloves before inspecting what he bought.

"Sliced cheeses, coffee, jars of marinara sauce, pasta, butter, several different spices, rye bread, detergent, dryer sheets," I go through the inventory. "Advil, Zantac, valerian. Prescriptions for Zomig, Clarinex, Klonopin filled at the CVS at nine this morning, possibly after he bought the groceries and right before he drove home."

I look at Marino as he slides the trash can out from under the sink.

"Who does this much shopping for a long weekend?" I open the refrigerator.

There's nothing inside but bottles of water and an open box of baking soda.

"I'm thinking the same thing you are. Something's wrong with this picture." Marino lifts the trash bag out of the can. "Nothing in it but a bunch of paper towels. They're damp. It looks like they were used to wipe something down. What do the meds tell you?"

"It would seem that one or both of them suffer from headaches, possibly migraines in addition to allergies and stomach problems," I reply. "And valerian is a homeopathic remedy for muscle spasms and stress. Some people use it to sleep. Klonopin is a benzodiazepine used for anxiety. The name on all of the prescriptions is Nari's. That doesn't necessarily mean his wife wasn't sharing."

Marino heads toward the bedroom and I follow him. Another former jewel that is sad to see, the oak flooring original to the house and painted brown. The crown molding like the paneled walls is painted an insipid yellow. On top of the double bed are two guitar cases, hard plastic and lined with plush red fabric, and on the handles are elastic bands from baggage tickets. There are nightstands and lamps, and near the open closet door are suitcases and stacks of taped-up Bankers Boxes.

On top of the dresser are two laptop computers plugged in and charging, and Marino's gloved fingers tap the mouse pads and the screen savers ask for passwords. He returns to the living area. Then he's back with evidence tape and plastic bags.

"They weren't going away for just the weekend. It's obvious they were moving." I step inside the bathroom.

It's not much bigger than a closet. The vintage claw-foot tub has been outfitted with a showerhead and a yellow plastic curtain on enclosure rings. There's a white toilet, a sink and a single frosted window.

"Didn't you mention that they just rented this apartment a few years ago?" I ask. "And now they're moving again?"

"It sure looks that way," Marino says from the bedroom.

"The guitars aren't in their cases." I direct my voice through the open doorway so he can hear me. "And I would think that's significant since they were important to him. Almost everything else is packed up but not his guitars."

"I don't see a third case anywhere. Just the two on the bed," Marino says and I hear him opening a door, I hear coat hangers scraping on a rod.

"There should be three. One for each guitar."

"Nope and nothing in the closet."

I open the medicine cabinet, the mirror old and pitted. There's nothing inside. In the cabinet under the sink are nonlubricated condoms and Imodium. Boxes and boxes of them, and it's unusual. I wonder why these were left in here when nothing else was. They're perfectly arranged, the boxes lined upright like a loaf of sliced bread, each label facing out. None of them are open. I detect a chlorine smell. Possibly a bathroom cleanser that was stored in here before it was packed or thrown out.

"I wonder where the building empties garbage?" I ask.

"There's a Dumpster."

"Someone should go through it to see what they might have tossed." I return to the bedroom.

I notice the Bankers Box on top of the stack. The tape has been cut. Someone opened it. The lid is marked BATHROOM. I take a look. It's half empty, nothing inside except a few toiletries that appear to have been rummaged through. I look at the other boxes, eleven of them and they're taped up. They look undisturbed and I get the same weird feeling I had when I noticed the condoms and Imodium in the cabinet.

"You gotta see this." Marino is opening dresser drawers now. "More of the same, friggin' unbelievable. Something was definitely going on. Like they were on the damn run."

"If so he didn't exactly make it very far," I reply as I hear voices outside the apartment.

"Maybe that's why. Someone decided to stop him." The dresser drawer he pulls open is completely empty and wiped clean.

I can see the swipe marks and lint of the wet paper towels used, perhaps the ones he found in the kitchen trash. I suggest he bag them as evidence.

"Let's make sure it was only dust and dirt being cleaned out of drawers," I add as the voices get closer and sound argumentative, a man and a woman. She's extremely upset.

"No question about it." Marino checks the drawers in the nightstands and they're empty. They also have been wiped clean. "They were getting the hell out of Dodge. And I'm guessing someone good with a rifle wasn't happy about it."

We return to the living room as the voices get louder.

"Ma'am, you need to hold here," the male voice says from the other side of the front door. "You can't go in until I check with the investigator . . ."

"This is where we live! Let me in!" a woman screams.

"You need to hold here, ma'am." And the door opens, and a uniformed officer steps halfway inside, blocking the woman behind him.

"Jamal! Jamal! No!"

Her screams pierce the quiet apartment as she tries to push past the officer, a heavyset man, gray hair, in his fifties, an impassive air I associate with cops who have been at it too long, and I try to place him. Ticketing parked cars. Picking up personal effects in the autopsy room.

"Let me in! Why won't you tell me anything! Let me in! What's happening? What's happening?"

Her anguish and terror come from where no one should have to go, a wrenching hopeless place. It's not true that we are never given more than we can bear. Only it isn't given. It simply happens.

"It's okay. No problem," Marino says to the officer. "You can let her in."

CHAPTER 9

JOANNA CATHER ISN'T WHAT I expected.

I'm not sure what I imagined but not the tiny girlish woman weeping and staring glassy-eyed in grief and terror. She's pretty in a delicate, fragile way like a porcelain doll that might break in half if you knocked her over, dressed in black leggings, boots and a pink COLDPLAY sweatshirt that hangs to her knees. She wears multiple rings and bracelets, her nails painted turquoise, and her long straw-blond hair is so straight it looks ironed.

"Did you see them in Boston?" I indicate her sweatshirt and she stares blankly as if she doesn't remember what she has on. "I'm Doctor Kay Scarpetta. I'm trying to think back to when it was. Maybe two summers ago."

My offhand reference to the British rock band and query about when it performed in the area reboots her shocked distraction, a tactic I learned early on when people are too fragmented by hysteria to give me what I need. I make a nongermane observation about the weather or what they're wearing or anything at all we might have in common. It almost always works. I have Joanna's attention.

"You're a doctor?" Her eyes fasten on me, and I'm mindful of the hard stiffness of the vest underneath my shirt, of my hands still gloved in purple nitrile, of my boots cocooned in boat-shaped blue shoe covers.

"I'm handling Jamal's case, the medical aspects of it." I'm gentle but sure of my position, and I sense the beginning of trust.

She pauses, staring with a hint of relief and says, "July two years ago. We had VIP backstage passes. We never miss them."

One of the band's tour stops was Boston where they played for several nights, and Lucy got seats two rows back, center stage. We may have been at the same concert, perhaps near Joanna and her musician husband, all of us there on a rock-and-roll high.

It happens in the blink of an eye. A lightning strike. A heart attack. A wrong place. A wrong time.

"You . . . You saw Jamal," she says to me. "What happened to him? He was shot?"

"Preliminarily that's the way it looks. I'm very sorry."

"The way it looks? You don't know?"

"He needs to be examined. Then I'll have answers I can be sure of." I'm next to her now as if she's in my care, and I tell her I regret that I don't have more information at the moment.

I repeat how sorry I am for her terrible loss. I say all the right things as she starts crying again and this is exactly how Marino wants it to go. We've danced this dance since the beginning of our time. I'm the doctor who's not here to accuse or cause further harm. The more he leans on her, the more she'll bond with me, feeling I'm on her side. I know exactly how to insert myself without violating the boundaries of what I have a right to answer or ask. I also know how to be useful without saying a word.

"We got it from here," Marino tells the officer hanging back in the doorway. "Make sure none of the reporters out there get any closer to the house."

"What about the residents?" The officer whose silver name tag says T. J. HARDY watches me pull off my shoe covers and gloves and drop them in a red biohazard bag on the kitchen counter.

I wear no personal protection clothing now, just my field clothes, which are official-looking with their many pockets and CFC crest. But I'm not threatening. I return to Joanna's side as T. J. Hardy begins to explain that residents are trying to return to their apartments.

"Two of them just pulled up in their cars, are in front of the house as we speak. They're getting upset that we won't let them back in." His Massachusetts accent is elastic and strong, his *r*'s sounding like *w*'s.

His voice triggers memories of him showing up in the autopsy room on several occasions for motor vehicle fatalities, and I'd had the distinct impression it was the last place he wanted to be. He'd collect personal effects and keep his distance from the steel tables. He'd avert his gaze, breathing out of his mouth because of the stench.

"Positively ID them and escort them into their apartments," Marino says to him. "I want their names and how to reach them. Email me the info ASAP. Nobody gets near the red SUV and the immediate area around it. We're clear on that?"

"Got it."

"You parked out there?" Marino directs this at Joanna, and she nods, not meeting his eyes.

"What kind of vehicle?"

"A Suburban. A rental. We're moving things . . . We were supposed to move things around and needed something big." She looks past him in a fixed wide-eyed stare.

"You don't own a car?" Marino asks.

"We traded in both of ours on his new Honda." Her voice quavers. "The red one out there."

"The cleanup crew wants to start picking up the spilled groceries. And . . ." T. J. Hardy glances at Joanna as he chooses his words. "And you know, start tidying things up."

Marino looks at me. "We're done, right?"

The body is at the CFC but I don't mention it. The blood, the gore certainly need to be gone and I'm not going to say that either. I tell Marino that cleanup can get started, and Joanna quietly cries in spasms. Officer Hardy steps back outside. The solid sound of the oak door shutting startles her and her knees almost buckle. She gasps and holds a tissue over her nose and mouth, her eyes bloodshot and smeared with makeup.

"Why don't you come sit and let's talk," Marino says to her, and he introduces himself, adding, "Doctor Scarpetta is the chief medical examiner of Massachusetts and also works for the Pentagon."

"The Pentagon?" Joanna isn't impressed and he just scared her.

"It just means I have federal jurisdiction in certain cases." I dismiss it as nothing.

"What? You're the fucking FBI." The look in her eyes changes just like that.

Marino had to brag and now I have to undo it. I explain I'm an Air Force special reservist affiliated with the Armed Forces Medical Examiners. She wants to know what that means. I tell her I assist the federal government with medical intelligence and help out with military matters but I also work for the state and my office is here in Cambridge. The more detail I give the more she glazes over. Wiping her eyes. Not listening. She doesn't care about my pedigree. She's not threatened by it and that's what I want.

"Point being you couldn't be in better hands," Marino adds. "She may have a few questions about medications, about any general health details she should know about your husband."

He's says it as if I'm their family doctor and it's a tried-and-true manipulation, a familiar one I wish wasn't needed. Nari's prescription drugs and health history have nothing to do with what killed him. A gun did. But Marino wants me present, and if Joanna thinks what he's saying is a ploy she makes no indication. Instead she's suddenly deflated as if there's no point in fighting what can't be changed. There's no protest or argument that will make it untrue.

"Where is he? Where's Jamal?" Her tone is dead. "Why is that big black box set up in front of the house? I don't understand. Was that where they put him? They wouldn't let me look inside it. Is he in there? Where is he?"

"He's been taken to my office for examination." I repeat what I've already told her. "The black enclosure was to ensure privacy and respect. Come sit down." I touch her elbow and lead her to the couch, and she sits stiffly on the edge of it, wiping her eyes.

"Who did this? Who would do this?" Her voice shakes and catches.

"Well that's what this is all about, Joanna. We gotta find that out." Marino sets a chair directly across from her and sits down. "I'm real sorry. I know how hard this is but I've got a lot of questions I need you to answer if you're going to help us figure out what happened to Jamal, okay?"

She nods. I sit down off to the side.

"Starting with what time you left here this morning, where you were headed and why." Marino has his notepad out.

"I already told the other one that. He said Jamal was shot while he was getting groceries out of the car. That someone shot him." She looks at me. "But you said you don't know if he was shot."

"He needs to be examined so we can be sure of exactly what happened." I avoid using the word *autopsy*.

Her eyes race around the living room and then she stares at the three guitars. "Who did that? Her voice goes up a notch and is louder as she stares accusingly at us. "Jamal packed them in their cases. He's so careful with his guitars. Who put them back on their stands?"

"That's interesting," Marino says. "There's two cases on the bed. Where's the third one?"

"You had no right! Touching his things, you had no right!"

"We didn't touch his guitars," Marino says and I think of Machado.

But he wouldn't do that. I look across the room at the guitars, different shapes, black carbon fiber, one a matte finish, two shiny and shimmering with mother-of-pearl inlays. Upright on stands, a rubber gooseneck clamped over the strings. Facing out. Perfectly, precisely arranged, and I get out of my chair. I walk over to them and detect the vague chlorine smell of bleach, what I smelled in the bathroom. Someone was inside this apartment here who shouldn't have been, and then I check the kitchen again.

The paper towels in the trash have no odor at all. Bleach destroys DNA. Something else was used to wipe out the drawers. Two different types of evidence, two different means of eradicating it. Possibly two different people. I sit back down. I give Marino a look that he understands.

Jamal Nari's killer may have been inside this apartment at some point, and I think of Machado again at the same instant Marino asks Joanna about him.

"I know you two talked." He keeps the annoyance out of his voice and there's no sign of it on his face.

But I know what he feels. Machado shouldn't have offered details to her. He shouldn't have said her husband was shot. If she'd said it first it would have been significant.

"You told Detective Machado you were in Tilton, New Hampshire. At the Tanger Outlets?" Marino asks her.

"He was shot in broad daylight by his car?" She's trembling hard and maybe this time for a different reason. "Did anyone see who did it or try to help?"

When he doesn't answer as he flips through pages in his notepad, she gets more agitated and anger glints.

"Did anyone try to get an ambulance? Didn't anyone try to help him?" She's asking me this.

"It was a fatal injury." I select my words carefully.

"You mean there was nothing that could have been done. Nothing at all?"

"Your husband died very quickly."

"I'm hoping you might know something that will help us," Marino says.

She glares at him. "I have no idea who did this."

"Detective Machado called your cell when you were on your way to New Hampshire." Marino baits the trap.

"I was already there at the luggage store."

"Was it Tanger or Merrimack?" Marino frowns, flipping pages. He looks confused. "You know the one in Tanger or the bigger outlet mall about an hour from here?"

"The bigger one. I was returning a bag with a broken zipper and he called. I asked him how he got my number and I thought maybe it was the police harassing us again."

"As I remember it the FBI was investigating your husband not the police. In light of your bad experience it's real important you make that distinction, Joanna." Marino is leaning forward, his big gloved hands on his big knees. "We're not the FBI. We're not the ones who put you through all that."

"It's never been the same." She shreds the tissue in her lap. "Is that why? Because of that someone targeted Jamal? We got a lot of hateful things from people. On the Internet. Mail. Stuff left by our cars at school and here."

"Is that what you think?" Marino is baiting her again.

He knows what she offered to Machado when she first got the news. About the student she was helping. About a robbery gone bad.

"I don't know what to think!" Tears flood her eyes and spill down her cheeks, streaking her makeup, the flesh around her eyes a mascara smear.

Marino slowly gets up from his chair. He walks to the kitchen, looks at the bags of groceries. He peers through the open bedroom doorway, looks at the luggage, the stacks of taped-up Bankers Boxes. His black gloved thumbs type on his BlackBerry.

"What did you say the name of the luggage store is?" he asks from the kitchen, turning his broad back to us.

"What?" She seems numb.

"The luggage store where you took the bag with the broke zipper."

"It was just a luggage store. I . . . I don't remember the name of it."

"*Tommy Bahama*? *Nautica*?" He's checking, seeing what stores are located in the outlet mall she claims to have visited.

"Yes," she says.

"YES?" MARINO WALKS BACK to us, his footsteps heavy, the blue plasticized paper shoe covers making a sliding sound over hardwood. His feet look as big as Frankenstein's.

"It could have been one of them," she says warily.

"Ms. Cather, you don't remember what kind of luggage you own? The suitcases in the bedroom are Rockland. A leopard pattern with pink trim, and I'm guessing those are yours. The others are American Tourister, black, and I'm guessing those are your husband's."

"How do you expect me to think of something like that right now?" She knows she's been caught.

"If you find the receipt maybe it will refresh your memory." Marino reseats himself, looking right at her as she blushes, staring down at her hands and when she talks her mouth sounds dry.

"Okay. I think I have it. I think it's in my wallet. It should be there." Her tongue sounds sticky as she continues evasions she knows are failing.

I go to the refrigerator and get her a bottle of water while she sits and Marino waits. Her pocketbook is on the couch and she starts digging inside it, inside her wallet, but it's an act and not a skillful one. There's no receipt. It's useless to pretend.

CHAPTER 10

"YOU KNOW ANYTHING ABOUT cell towers, Ms. Cather?" Marino is scrolling through text messages, and she's not Joanna anymore.

He's gotten information and is distancing himself. His tone has chilled. He's playing the role he'd already scripted and getting external validation for it, finding out things that aren't good for her.

"Cell towers?" She takes a swallow of water, talking to him but looking at me. "I know what they are. But I don't know anything about them."

"That surprises me. The FBI didn't tap your phones? They didn't check out your locations or more specifically his? They weren't in your email when they thought Jamal was a terrorist?" he says.

"How could I possibly know what they did? It's not like they tell you."

"They would have notified your lawyer."

"Jamal would know more about it than I do. He's who they were after. It was his lawyer not mine." She's crying again but there's anger and beneath it is rage. Beneath all of it is grief that hurts so much it's physical. And fear. Whatever she's afraid of is prompting her to lie.

"I need you to tell the truth whatever it is," Marino says. "But first I'm going to remind you of your rights. I always like to get that out of the way . . ."

"My rights?" She looks bewildered, her eyes on me as if I might save her. "You think I did this? Are you arresting me?"

"It's just a preventive measure," Marino replies casually. "I'm making sure you know you don't have to talk to us. Nobody's forcing you. If you'd rather have an attorney present that's what we'll do. What about the attorney your husband used? Maybe you want to call whoever that was? We'll sit here and wait until he shows up or he can meet us at the station."

He goes on bluffing and Mirandizing while she stares at him without blinking, her eyes turning hard and furious, thoughts flickering like static on an old TV. She's been through this before when the FBI raided their home and hauled away her husband in handcuffs.

"I don't want a lawyer," she says and a calm comes over her, flat and still. "I would never do anything to physically hurt Jamal."

I notice her use of the word *physically*. It seems important she make the distinction between hurting her husband physically as opposed to in some other way. I think of the boy on the bicycle she was seen chatting with.

"We don't own a gun so I don't know why you think . . . Except it's easiest, isn't it?" Her eyes are hot and resentful on Marino as he reads a message that landed on his phone. "All of you people are the same."

"You weren't in New Hampshire today," he says as a matter of fact, typing a reply to someone who is texting him. "Let's talk about where you really were."

BEFORE SHE CAN ANSWER Marino lets her know he has proof of exactly where she's been since seven-fifteen A.M. He knows every mile she drove and every call she made on her cell phone including three to a moving company.

"But I'd rather you tell me the details yourself," he adds. "I'd rather give you a chance to be truthful so maybe I start feeling better about you than I do right this minute."

"I've been falsely accused." She directs this to me and she's not talking about her husband's homicide.

I can tell she means something else.

71

"When Detective Machado reached you on your cell phone," Marino asks her, "what did he say to you exactly?"

"He identified himself. He told me what happened." She stares down at her hands tightly clasped in her lap.

"And you told him you were in New Hampshire. Even though it wasn't true."

She nods yes.

"You lied."

She nods again.

"Why?"

"I've been falsely accused." Again she says this to me. "I thought that's why he was calling, that the police were coming after me. I wanted to buy myself time so I could figure out what to do. I panicked."

"And you didn't change your story about where you were even after Detective Machado informed you of the real reason he was calling," Marino says.

"It was too late. I'd already told him . . . I was scared. So scared I was stupid." Her voice shakes badly, tears spilling. "And then all I could think about was Jamal. I wasn't thinking about the lie or why I told it. I'm sorry. I'm not a bad person. I swear to God I'm not."

She digs into her pocketbook and finds a towelette. Tearing open the packet she wipes ruined makeup off her eyes, her face and I smell the fresh scent of cucumber. She suddenly looks years younger, could pass for twenty but probably is closer to thirty. A career as a high school psychologist requires college then a master's degree. She's been married three years. I calculate she's twenty-seven or twenty-eight.

"This is a nightmare. Please let me wake up from it." She stares at me.

Then she looks at the items I took out of the bags her husband carried in, the food, the drugs. Her attention fixes on the drugs.

"Your husband had prescriptions filled at a CVS this morning," I say to her. "Including one for Klonopin."

"For stress," she says.

"His stress?"

"And recently mine. Both of us."

"Can you tell me what's been going on with him?" I'm deliberate about what tense I use. "If he's been anxious, stressed it's helpful if I know why. A drug screen will tell us exactly what he has in his system. But if you have information I'd appreciate it."

My mention of a drug screen startles her. Apparently she hadn't thought of it.

"Klonopin," she says. "I saw him take one this morning when we got up, and he said he was almost out. That he planned to stop at CVS while he was running errands."

"Might he have taken anything else?" I ask.

"I . . . I don't know. I wasn't around him . . . I left at about seven."

I think of the damp paper towels in the trash, the drawers wiped clean. Not a week goes by that I don't see a heroin-related death in my morgue.

"What about street drugs?" I ask and then Marino jumps in.

"The slightest residue and a drug dog's going to hit on it," he says. "I got a K-nine. Maybe I should go get him."

If the situation weren't so tragic I would laugh. Quincy couldn't tell the difference between heroin and baby powder. I text Anne to check Jamal Nari carefully for needle tracks, for damage to his septum, to do it right now.

"Has your husband ever been on prescription pain medications?" I ask Joanna.

"His back," she says. "A bicycle accident when he was in his twenties, and he has ruptured disks."

"OxyContin?"

She nods as my suspicions continue to gather. It's not unusual for people who abuse OxyContin to switch to an opiate that's less expensive. On the street an 80-milligram pill can cost as much as eighty dollars while a bag of heroin might go for a fraction of that price.

"He's been clean and sober for over ten years," Joanna says to me.

"But he's been under stress? Do you know why?"

"He was shutting me out. He'd disappear and not tell me where he was going or where he'd been." She continues to stare at the prescriptions on the kitchen counter.

"Was it you who cleaned the inside of all the drawers?" Marino asks and she doesn't answer. "Did Jamal do it or you?"

"I don't know. He might have. I told you he's been paranoid, worried someone's out to get him."

"Coke? Heroin? What was he using?"

"Nothing. I've told you, nothing."

"Nothing?" Marino drops his notepad, the pen on the coffee table. "Then who were you worried might find something?"

"The police," she says. "We've been worried about it for days. That's why I was so sure about the reason for the call. I thought it was about that."

I glance at my phone as a text message lands.

"About what exactly?"

Old scars on legs were covered with tattoos. That's as much as Anne can tell at this point but it's enough.

Nari used to mainline drugs and attempted to disguise the needle tracks with tattoos. At a glance there's nothing fresh that would indicate current drug abuse. But it doesn't mean he was finished with that part of his life.

Have you scanned him yet? I write back.

Getting ready to.

"I'm not following you about the police," Marino pushes Joanna.

"Because they've been after us before for no good reason! They'd like nothing better than to make it stick this time! Do you have any idea what it's like to go through that?"

"The FBI did that." Marino makes that point again. "It wasn't us."

She wipes her face and I smell cucumber again. I remember the odor of bleach and I ask her. Did she or her husband use something with chlorine in it, maybe bleach to clean out the drawers and she says no. I tell her the paper towels in the trash will be tested in my labs and she looks dejected but she doesn't change her answer about bleach. She's allergic to it. She breaks out in hives. They never have it in the house.

"Jamal thought someone was following him, stalking him," she says. "Someone wearing a cap and dark glasses was riding his bumper. He thought it was the FBI again. One night he got up to use the bathroom and there was a face looking through the window. After that we frosted the glass in there and started closing all the curtains."

"When did he start feeling this way?" Marino picks up his notepad, begins taking notes again.

"A few months ago."

"That's why you suddenly decided to move?"

"No." She tells us the boy she's been seen talking to is Leo Gantz.

He's fifteen years old, a freshman at Emerson Academy where Nari taught music and Joanna is a psychologist. A nationally ranked tennis player, Leo Gantz has a scholarship and an abusive father. In January Leo was sent to her office because of his behavior. He'd started sneaking alcohol. He keyed a car and was "mouthing off" to his teachers. In early May he was suspended from the tennis team after showing up at practice drunk and hitting the coach with a ball hard enough to bloody his nose.

"He started having too much spare time because he didn't have practice anymore and now school's out," Joanna explains. "He was bored, lonely. He started riding his bike past our house all the time. Angie . . ."

"Angelina Brown," Marino says. "Your upstairs neighbor."

"Yes," Joanna replies. "She would see him from her window. Her desk is in front of her window and she would see him riding back and forth in front of the house."

"Maybe he was the one stalking your husband? Did that ever occur to you?"

"Leo doesn't have a license yet or access to a car."

"Was he ever inside this apartment?"

I glance down at a text message from firearms examiner Liz Wrighton as Joanna goes on to say that she always talked to Leo outside. He was never in here.

"I tried to help him." Her tone turns to iron, and I don't let on that what I'm reading is stunning, both extremely good and awful.

We have a high-confidence candidate. That's Liz's cautious way of saying we got a hit in the National Integrated Ballistic Information Network, NIBIN. A comparison of digital images from New Jersey and the frag Machado dropped off at her lab shows that the measurements, the lands and grooves match. The same gun was used.

A sniper. Three victims who seem to have nothing in common.

"And there's no reason, absolutely nothing I ever did except care about him." Joanna's eyes blaze. "Except to treat him nice, to be helpful and that's what he does to thank me!"

CHAPTER 11

THE CHARLES RIVER SHINES deep blue in the midafternoon sun, barely ruffled by a light breeze. Sycamores, weeping willows and Bradford pears that have lost their flowers and I remember when they fell like snow, covering sidewalks and drifting into the street. For a while I drove to and from my office in a blossomy storm that made me happy.

I look out my side window at rowers leaning their backs into long slender oars, slicing through the water in blade-like sculls. The DeWolfe Boathouse is to our right, and on our left the stair-step-shaped Hyatt Hotel, then the Massachusetts Institute of Technology's spreading campus. In Marino's SUV again, headed to the CFC, and we're on the subject of the cell phone signals picked up when Joanna Cather claimed to be in New Hampshire this morning.

She absolutely wasn't. Not at any time. She was telling us the truth about her lie. At shortly after seven A.M. she drove out of her cell area in Cambridge, her phone's signal picked up by FCC-registered antenna towers along I-90 East and Massachusetts Avenue, then I-93 South. Her final destination was Gallivan Boulevard in the Boston neighborhood of Dorchester where she and her husband had planned to move today.

They'd rented a two-story shingle-sided Colonial with a stone cellar, a sunporch, a garage, hardwood floors and a security system. Marino has shown me photographs of the listing on the Internet, a handsome house with character built in the 1920s. The asking price is $4,000 per month, unfurnished, utilities not included, a lot of money for the high school faculty couple. The Realtor's name is Mary Sapp and Marino has left a message for her to call him as soon as possible.

"I got a hunch about it." He's switched to another topic, the timing, why the killer struck now. "I think their suddenly deciding to move triggered something so to speak. And the reason they decided to skip town is also why Nari wiped down the drawers. I think Leo Gantz's accusation opened a can of worms in more ways than one."

His story is ruinous no matter the outcome. Consensual sex and it's Joanna's word against his. As she was telling us what she called a bald-faced lie, I sensed she has feelings for him. Not just hateful ones.

"Nari was worried the police were going to show up with a search warrant any minute," Marino says, "and while they were at it bust him for drugs."

"His wife claims he's clean," I remind him. "His needle tracks are old."

"He could be snorting or smoking."

"Tox will tell."

"Plain and simple there was something he didn't want the cops to find a trace of and I'm putting my money on heroin. The cops being Cambridge, in other words yours truly," he adds. "A complaint of sex with a minor and we were going to be called."

But Cambridge PD hasn't been. Leo's unemployed father began threatening Nari and his wife but didn't call the police.

"Wait and see. This is about money," I reply. "Leo's father probably figures they got a big settlement after suing the school. The irony is they haven't gotten a dime."

I had Lucy check. Motions are still being filed in Jamal Nari's discrimination suit against Emerson Academy. Depositions have been scheduled, a trial date set, the usual game of chicken that only the lawyers win. The information can be found in legal databases but it hasn't been in the press. If Leo Gantz's father has been paying attention he could easily infer that Nari and his wife recently had come into money. The new Honda alone was enough to cause assumptions.

"If it had been me showing up to investigate whether she and Leo had sex inside the apartment I would have done everything I just did." Marino is suddenly watching his mirrors. "You know me. No stone unturned."

There was no cushion unturned either. Before we left the apartment he searched it again, looking under the mattress, the furniture and rugs, and inside pillows, whatever might be a hiding place. He scoured the Honda SUV and the rented Suburban. Marino processed everything that didn't move for prints, for trace evidence.

He swabbed for DNA and when he sprayed a chemical reagent on the guitars they luminesced faintly and for a brief duration. So did the two empty guitar cases on the bed and the Bankers Box that looked rifled through plus the condoms, the Imodium under the sink. All of it glowed the whitish blue false positive for blood, a typical reaction to bleach.

He's looking in the mirrors, an angry expression on his face. He slows down.

"What's the matter?" I ask.

"I don't believe it." He slows even more, almost to a crawl. "The same asshole," he says.

I LOOK IN MY side mirror and recognize the pickup truck we saw earlier today when Marino confronted the young man with the leaf blower. Gray with a lot of chrome, a Super Duty truck, an older one in mint condition.

It passes us in the right lane, a HANDS ON MECHANICS logo and phone number on the door, and the driver is light-skinned with short dark hair. I don't see anybody with him or evidence of lawn care equipment.

"That's not who we saw earlier, the kid with the leaf blower," I puzzle. "Is it the same plate number?"

"Pretty damn sure."

"The truck we saw on my street had Sonny's Lawn Care on it."

Marino holds up his BlackBerry, showing me the photograph he took this morning. The license tag is the same as the one on the gray truck that just passed us. The phone number is also the same. The truck is far ahead of us now, in the right lane with its right-turn signal on.

"A magnetic logo," Marino decides. "The type that's removable, has to be. What was on there this morning definitely said Sonny's Lawn Care with the phone number under it. Maybe he's got more than one business that share the same phone line."

"Then why not advertise everything on the same sign?"

"Maybe the jerk-off kid has nothing to do with it," Marino then says. "Maybe he just happened to be clearing off a sidewalk near where the truck was parked."

It would explain why he wasn't concerned about Marino storming around like a maniac, taking a picture of the license plate and threatening him, I think but don't say.

"You ever seen this same truck in your neighborhood before today?" he asks.

"Not that I recall but that doesn't mean anything. I'm rarely home during the day."

Marino watches the gray truck turn right onto the Harvard Bridge, and I can tell he's deliberating whether to follow it. Instead we swing left onto Audrey Street and into an MIT apartment building parking lot where we stop.

"It's probably nothing but I'm not taking any chances," he says. "And I don't want whoever's driving it to think we're paying attention."

"You slowed down so he could pass us," I remind him.

"He doesn't know it had anything to do with him."

I'm not convinced of that. Marino was reminded of the incident this morning and got angry all over again. Had the driver of the pickup truck been observant and able to read lips he certainly would have seen Marino glaring and cursing. But I don't mention that either as I scan our surroundings, the MIT athletic fields and football stadium just ahead. Across the river the old buildings of Back Bay are dark red brick and gray roofed.

In the distance the skyline of Boston is dominated by the Prudential Tower with its radio mast rampant like a jousting lance, and the Hancock is slightly taller, the shapes of clouds reflected in its glass. Far off the light changes the way it does over great expanses of water, the Charles flowing northeast into the harbor, then sweeping around Logan Airport and the barrier islands before emptying into bays and finally the sea. I'm reminded of what a beautiful spring day it is, the sky bright blue, the trees and grass a vibrant green.

Right now Benton and I should be on the plane to Fort Lauderdale, and I think about a condo he rented on the ocean, my birthday surprise. Knowing his taste it will be extremely nice, and then I force such thoughts from my mind because nothing good comes from imagining what isn't going to happen. I already know our week away will be postponed, and for us that's the same as being canceled. Our taking time off isn't about accumulating vacation days. It's about bad things stopping long enough for us to have nothing to worry about.

I send him a text. *You OK? Heading to my office. We need to talk.*

"I got a gut feeling something isn't right." Marino is still on the subject of the truck. "I was only a few blocks from where Nari was shot, not to mention near your house where someone left pennies on your wall that might have been polished in a tumbler like cartridge cases."

He calls the dispatcher on his portable and asks her to run the plate number.

"Let's see what happens." He rechecks the photographs on his Black-Berry. "How about dialing the number for me." He reads the number that was on the truck.

"It's not a good idea to have my phone involved."

"Caller ID's blocked on it."

"It doesn't matter. I don't want a record of my calling a number that's unrelated to what I'm responsible for. If there's an issue it's hard to explain. And attorneys are always looking for issues."

More to the point I'm not Marino's assistant. I don't answer to him and I'm not his partner either. But he can't seem to remember that. I recite the number back to him and he enters it. A few seconds later a phone rings twice and someone picks up.

"Hello?" a female voice asks over speakerphone.

"Is this Sonny's Lawn Care?"

"Excuse me? Who are you trying to reach?"

Marino repeats himself and the woman replies that he has the wrong number. He tells her who he is.

"The police? Oh my. Is something wrong?" She sounds confused and worried. "Is this about Johnny? Why is Cambridge calling me? We live in Carlisle . . . I do, I mean. I don't live in Cambridge. I live in Carlisle."

"Ma'am, I'm sorry to bother you. I'm wondering if you've gotten other calls from people thinking they're reaching Sonny's Lawn Care or maybe Hands On Mechanics. Your number's on the side of one of their trucks."

"You must be mistaken."

"I'm not. It's this number." He recites it to her.

"I don't know what to think. We've had this same number for more than twenty years. It's our home number . . . my home number. Well if you look in the phone book you'll see it listed under my late husband's name. Doctor John L. Angiers."

It takes a moment for comprehension. Then it hits me hard.

CHAPTER 12

Dr. JOHNNY ANGIERS'S WIDOW says she doesn't answer the phone anymore if she doesn't know who's calling.

"You just answered," Marino reminds her but he's kind about it. He's not aggressive with her. "And you don't know me, right?"

"I'm not sure why I did. I wasn't thinking. There have been some odd messages in voice mail and maybe what you're saying explains it. Now and then calls from people wanting trees pruned, sod put down. Earlier today it was someone who wanted his car fixed. If they get me directly I hang up on them." She sounds upset. "I'm going to have to change my phone number and I don't want to. I don't want to change a number we've had for twenty years."

"When did the calls start?" Marino asks.

"It's been very recent. In the past several weeks."

"What's your name, ma'am?"

"Sarah Angiers."

I check the calendar on my phone. April 28, a Monday, and I roll back my memory, pulling up the case in my thoughts. It's one hard to forget. I found it particularly tragic and poignant, and I gave Sarah Angiers all the time she wanted when she came to my office to discuss her husband's death. Tall and thin, she'd bothered to dress up as if she were going to church or the symphony, in a smart suit with her white hair neatly styled. I remember her as lucid and forthcoming and completely devastated.

She said she'd always been nervous about her husband going off on his own, hiking in Estabrook Woods, more than a thousand acres of undeveloped forest, hills and horse trails. She said he could be somewhat difficult when he had his mind made up and she described how much he loved to follow what she referred to as "the path" from their backyard in Carlisle all the way to Hutchins Pond in Concord.

When I examined his body in the heavily forested area where he died I was very close to Fox Castle Swamp and nowhere near Hutchins Pond. The phone signal was bad to nonexistent there, and the dozens of calls he'd made to his wife and 911 had failed. They were all right there on his outgoing log when his phone was recovered in addition to a text to his wife that wasn't delivered. He said he was cold and exhausted so he'd found a place to sit. He was lost and it was getting dark. He would always love her. The police had nothing to go on except where he usually hiked, which was some two miles south of where he'd actually wandered.

I suspect that early into his hike he wasn't feeling well and became disoriented, heading in the direction of Lowell Road instead of Monument Street. He realized he didn't know where he was, and unable to reach anyone he sat on the fallen tree, getting increasingly anxious and agitated as night came. He may have panicked, suffering shortness of breath, dizziness, nausea and chest pains. Acute anxiety would have felt like a heart attack, and a heart attack would have felt like acute anxiety.

When the pain began spreading from his chest into his shoulders, neck and jaw, Johnny Angiers, a professor of medicine at Tufts, would have recognized that he was in serious trouble. He may have realized he was dying. He'd never been diagnosed with coronary artery disease but his was significant, and as I explain all this to Marino I continue to feel incredulous. I feel as if ground is moving under my feet, as if I can't get my balance. I have no idea what is happening but it all seems too close to me like the pennies in my own backyard and the pickup truck on my street.

"One of my cases and not that long ago," I explain. "And their phone number was on the side of a truck parked on my street this morning, not even two blocks down from my house? What the hell is going on?"

"Nothing good," Marino says.

I Google Sonny's Lawn Care. There's no such company in Massachusetts. I try Hands On Mechanics and there's no listing for that either.

"This is only getting more disturbing," I say as the dispatcher gets back to Marino.

She tells him that the plate number belongs to a 1990 gray F-150 Ford pickup truck. It's registered to an eighty-three-year-old white male named Clayton Phillip Schmidt with a Springfield address, some ninety miles west of here, almost across the border into Connecticut.

"Any record of the plate or vehicle being stolen?" Marino asks.

"Negative."

He requests that all units in the area be on the alert for a 1990 gray Ford pickup truck with that plate number.

"Saw it maybe ten minutes ago on Memorial Drive, eastbound." Marino holds the radio close to his mouth. "Took a right on the Harvard Bridge. Same vehicle was spotted around twelve hundred hours in the area of the incident on Farrar Street. Had Sonny's Lawn Care on the door. Now has Hands On Mechanics. Possibly using different magnetic signs."

"Thirteen to thirty-three," another unit calls.

"Thirty-three," Marino answers.

"Saw vehicle at approximately noon, corner of Kirkland and Irving," unit thirteen, a female officer advises. "Had Sonny's Lawn Care on it at that time."

"Parked or moving?"

"Pulled off onto the shoulder."

"You see anybody?"

"Negative."

I open a text message Benton has just sent to me.

An unexpected development. Will tell you when I see you, I read.

I envision him in our backyard earlier today, and the pennies on our wall and the flick of light he saw. I think of *Copperhead,* of the odd poem tweeted to me from a hotel in Morristown. Now a mysterious truck has a phone number on it that is connected to a recent death I handled—one I really don't want further scrutinized.

I didn't misrepresent the medical facts in Johnny Angiers's case but I was liberal in my interpretation and decision to sign him out as an accidental death due to hypothermia. When his insurance company questioned me, pointing out that my autopsy report indicated a finding of ruptured plaque due to coronary artery disease, I held my ground. Johnny Angiers wasn't diabetic but his vitreous glucose was elevated and this is typical in hypothermia deaths. There were skin changes, gastric lesions and damage to his organs consistent with exposure to cold temperatures.

Hypothermia may have precipitated cardiac arrest or it could have been the other way around. It was impossible to say with certainty and if I were going to err it was on the side of compassion. The accidental life insurance policy didn't cover death by heart attack even if it was a heart attack that caused a fatal accident such as a fall or a car crash or exposure to cold. It wasn't fair. It wasn't right. The company TBP Insurers is huge. It's notorious for finding ways to avoid payment to people who have just been traumatized by the unexpected loss of a loved one.

Had I not filled out the autopsy report and death certificate the way I did, Johnny Angiers's widow would have been forced to sell their house and stop any financial assistance they were giving to grandchildren in college and graduate school. I had ample justification to make sure that didn't happen, and I have a deep-seated disdain for greedy unethical insurance companies. I constantly see the lives they rob and ruin, and unfortunately my run-ins with TBP aren't new.

"I hope what's happening doesn't in any way compromise her," I remark as Marino tries a number and gets voice mail. "We should head on to my office," I add as we continue to sit in the parking lot.

"Compromise Mrs. Angiers? Why would what's on a pickup truck compromise her? It's not her fault."

"The insurance company. Anything that draws attention to her or her husband's case may not be helpful." I'm grateful I didn't use my phone to call a number that turns out to be hers.

TBP would make something of it.

"She's eligible to collect the insurance money but obviously hasn't gotten it yet," I add.

"How do you know what she's gotten?"

"One of their investigators called Bryce the other day wanting to set up an appointment with me about the case. In person this time. They wouldn't do that if they weren't still fighting it."

"You going to sit down with them?"

"It's not been scheduled yet since I'm supposed to be out of town. Bryce gave them dates and we haven't heard back, which is their typical M.O. The longer they stall, the better for them. The only person in a hurry is the one who needs the money."

"Fuckers." Marino tries another number on his phone.

"So now it's in your backyard, buddy," a man answers right off. "Unbelievable."

"THAT'S HOW IT'S LOOKING. Your two shootings linked with the one we got here, not to mention weird shit going on," Marino says, and I realize he's talking to Morris County investigator Jack Kuster. "You ever hear any reports of a gray pickup truck spotted in your area, maybe one that had a company logo on the doors?"

"Not a gray one funny you'd ask. But a white truck, you know like a Ryder or U-Haul bobtail rental truck but with no name on it. Not a huge truck, maybe a ten-footer. I thought I told you about it that night you got so shit-faced at Sona. Oh yeah. That's why you don't remember." Jack Kuster has an easygoing baritone voice with a heavy New Jersey accent. "I think you must'ave been drinking Blithering Idiot."

"Skull Splitter Ale I'm pretty sure," Marino deadpans. "What about the white truck?"

"The day before Julie Eastman was shot while she was waiting for the Edgewater Ferry, the truck I'm talking about was spotted at a construction site that had been shut down. From there it went down the road a little ways into the ferry landing parking lot."

"I guess there's only one white truck in all of Jersey," Marino says.

"The reason this particular vehicle came to anyone's attention is it hit a car that was backing up and the truck hauled ass out of there. Two things about it caught my interest after the homicide. A recovered paint chip showed the truck had been repainted multiple times and the tag number came back to a plate belonging to someone dead. From Massachusetts as a matter of fact."

"Jesus," Marino says. "A commercial plate I assume."

"No. A regular noncommercial one. Obviously stolen from a noncommercial vehicle, a thirty-something-year-old Pontiac that had been totaled back in November, thus explaining why the owner is deceased."

"Anybody take a picture of the truck?"

"No one has come forward if they did." Kuster's voice is loud over speakerphone, and Marino pushes the SUV gearshift into reverse. "The person whose car was hit by it got the plate number, like I said, and described it as *a white moving truck* but didn't get a look at the driver, just someone wearing a hat and glasses."

"Doesn't sound like the same thing here," Marino says. "And it's probably a wild-goose chase."

"If it wasn't for chasing geese I'd have to get a job."

"You around tomorrow if the Doc and me drop by?" As usual Marino doesn't bother to clear it with me first. "We need to compare notes and see if we can figure out the distance this psycho is shooting from."

"Funny you would mention that too. I got a theory and a way to test it. Especially now since you got a relatively undamaged solid bullet in your case."

"News to me. But we haven't been to her office yet. We haven't had time to take a whiz for that matter."

"Liz Wrighton sent me a photo," Kuster says. "Right hand, one-ten twist, 5R rifling, one-ninety grain solid copper, ballistic tip. Five lands and grooves with a rolled leading edge. I'm thinking a .308 with a freaking accurate barrel like a Krieger Match. Not the sort of rifle you carry around when you're hunting. Tough to shoot unsupported. You'd set up with a bipod or bag rests filled with sand, rice, popcorn, whatever."

"Hunting meaning people." Marino stops at the intersection of Audrey Street and Memorial Drive, waiting for a break in traffic.

"A typical tactical magnum rifle, only what I'm thinking about isn't typical. I can set us up on the range, borrow what I need from SWAT. Last fall they got the latest greatest for the Super Bowl, had it all ready to go on the stadium roof just in case. Maybe you don't remember that either, were too busy throwing back beers and tequila and telling war stories about Scarpetta and your high school days plus being pissed at Machado. Where's he at during all this?"

"Getting in the way," Marino says. "The Doc's here in the car and we're on speakerphone, headed to the morgue so maybe stop talking about her."

"Nice to meet you, Doctor Scarpetta. What I'm referring to is a PGF. A Precision Guided Firearm that can turn a rookie shooter into a top gun sniper who can hit a target dead center at a thousand yards out or more. Unfortunately police and the military aren't the only ones who can buy something like this. That's what I have nightmares about. It's just a matter of time."

Marino ends the call and uneasily looks around us while we sit perfectly still, the traffic heavy on Memorial Drive. He's glancing in his mirrors, out the windows, up at rooftops and suddenly accelerates across three lanes into eastbound traffic to a cacophony of blaring horns.

"How about you don't get us killed by driving like a kamikaze pilot." I start picking up what just spilled out of my shoulder bag.

"No point in being a damn sitting duck." His eyes continue darting around, and his face is red. "We need to go see Kuster tomorrow. We can't waste time on this."

"It would be nice if you'd ask before making plans that include me."

"He can help with shooting reconstructions." Marino takes off his Ray-Bans. "No one better. You mind cleaning these for me?"

He drops his sunglasses in my lap.

I dig a tissue out of my jacket pocket. "What about brushes with law enforcement? Did the other victims have any reason to fear the police? What about drugs?"

"Not that I've heard." He pulls down the visor and a stack of napkins flutter into his lap. "But it makes sense that Nari and his wife were scared shitless. Imagine being accused of having sex with some screwed-up juvenile? When Machado called she probably did think she was about to get arrested."

"I'd say life couldn't get much worse for her right now." I continue to work on his Ray-Bans. "They need to be washed with soap and water. They're also badly scratched. You've had these how long?"

"Gotta get new ones but hate to spend the dough." He takes his glasses from me and puts them back on. "A hundred and fifty bucks a pop."

I know what to get him for his birthday next month. He crams the napkins into the glove box and I catch a glimpse of the bagged pennies inside. I imagine a sharpshooter with a PGF and very specific ammunition that is difficult to trace because so far all that's left is frag. I'm already puzzled by a detail I didn't know, what Kuster said about an intact bullet. Luke Zenner must have recovered one from Nari's body and that's very surprising. It's hard to believe.

Marino is chewing gum, his jaw muscles clenching. He's chomping away because he really wants to smoke and he continues to feel for the pack of cigarettes in his jacket pocket. Pretty soon he'll pull out a cigarette and not light it. As I'm thinking it he does it and then his cell phone rings through the speakerphone.

"Yeah," he answers gruffly.

"This is Mary Sapp," a woman says. "I'm returning your call from the house on Gallivan. There's a truck parked in front and I'm not sure I should leave."

CHAPTER 13

HE SIGNED THE LEASE this past Monday, agreeing to the asking price and three months' rent in advance. Jamal Nari paid twelve thousand dollars so he and his wife could get in instantly.

Usually a renter has an attorney review a contract—especially a renter who has experience with litigation and has no reason to be trusting. But he was in too much of a hurry according to Realtor Mary Sapp, who has completely rerouted us. Across the Harvard Bridge, on Massachusetts Avenue now, and Marino is driving fast. He's flying. Whenever a car doesn't get out of his way, he flips on his emergency lights and whelps the siren.

It doesn't matter that we've entered Boston and he's left his jurisdiction without letting a Cambridge dispatcher know. He's requested a backup from Boston PD and he hasn't bothered telling Machado or anyone else what is going on. Nor is he concerned that I'm not headed to my office when I have cases to supervise, where I have a job and my own responsibilities and my own problems to worry about. He didn't ask if my coming along for the ride is okay and I message Bryce Clark that I've been held up.

OMG! Do you mean robbed? he fires back, and I don't know if he's trying to be funny.

I'm with Marino. How is Luke doing?

Finished with post but assume you don't want him released? I mean case from Farrar Street, not Luke.

Do not release, I reply as I overhear what Marino is asking Mary Sapp. *I need to take a look at him.*

Marino is reassuring the Realtor that she is safe as long as she stays inside the house. But she doesn't sound as if she's worried about being safe. She doesn't sound afraid. In fact she sounds something else. Dramatic, overly charming and helpful. It occurs to me that she might be enjoying herself.

No funeral home picked out anyway. Another message from Bryce appears in a gray balloon.

Then don't ask me if he should be released yet, I think but I'm not going to put that in writing.

I talked to the wife. She's in a fugue state, doesn't have a clue what to do no matter what I tell her, Bryce writes and he shouldn't editorialize.

Will let you know when I'm headed in. I end our dialogue.

" . . . I probably wouldn't have thought much about it except for what's all over the news." Mary Sapp's voice fills the car, a voice that is too cheerful in light of the circumstances.

Already I don't have a good opinion of her.

"I'm glad you're thinking about it and are smart enough to stay put inside the house." Marino encourages her to do as he says. "And you're sure about the description."

"Oh yes. Yesterday around two or three in the afternoon. I was doing another walk-through of the house, taking more photographs, making notes, making sure they didn't damage anything when they dropped by," she replies.

"Dropped by for what?"

"She's been carrying in boxes of their belongings. Sometimes people scuff and bang up a place and then claim it already was like that before."

"What you're saying is it wasn't the two of them. It was just Joanna dropping by."

"That's right. I only met him once, when I first showed them the house about a week ago. The rest of the time I've dealt with her."

"And at around two or three yesterday afternoon you saw the truck."

"When I happened to look out the window, I noticed it drive by. A big gray pickup truck with a sign of some sort on the door."

"Any particular reason you noticed it?" Marino asks.

"It was going so slowly that I thought it was going to stop in front of the house. Some type of lawn care company and then there it was again this morning when I was meeting with Joanna."

"Did she drop by or were you scheduled to meet?"

A pause, then, "It was scheduled."

"Maybe she was moving more boxes in," Marino suggests, and Mary Sapp pauses again.

"She'd moved most of them already like I said, and I suggested she hold off on moving any more or unpacking anything. That's what I wanted to talk to her about."

"So you scheduled the meeting this morning. It was your idea," Marino says, and I know what he's thinking.

If the Realtor scheduled the meeting it defeats the argument that Joanna contrived a reason to be out of the house at the time her husband was murdered. But that won't stop certain parties from pushing through with their theory, and I suspect I know who will be pushing the hardest. Joanna lied to Machado and no matter her reason it was a very bad way, perhaps the worst way, to start off with him. Matters are further complicated by his relationship with Marino. They're competing with each other, and then there's the bleach.

Someone may have attempted to eradicate DNA from items that appear to be part of a staged scene. Guitars taken out of their cases and displayed on their stands, items returned to a bathroom cabinet, a box of belongings rummaged through, and I have little doubt it was the killer who did all this. Machado took his time notifying Marino or my office about the homicide. He got there first and was inside the apartment, possibly turning on the lights and looking around. He shouldn't have done this alone. He would have done it with Marino were they not at each other's throats.

"I asked her if she could stop by the house," Mary Sapp is saying, "and we agreed to meet early because she said they had a very busy day ahead, running errands. And of course the move they were still planning on."

They were planning on it. But it doesn't sound as if she was.

"We agreed on eight o'clock and she did show up at that time. To give her credit, she was punctual," she says and something has caused her to disapprove of Joanna Cather.

"Why did you suggest that she hold off moving their belongings?" Marino asks as my suspicions about the Realtor darken.

"Details. We had details to discuss that unfortunately were problematic. I thought it better to do so in person and not in writing," she says. "And before I could explain, I saw the truck again."

"What time was this?" Marino asks and we're on I-93 South now, on the waterfront.

"About eight-fifteen, eight-thirty. I noticed it and even said to her, 'I think that truck is cruising for business around here, and it won't get him anywhere.' My company has quite a few listings in this area and we have certain companies we recommend of course."

"Do you have any idea who was in the truck when you saw it yesterday and again this morning? Did the driver look familiar?"

"No one I've ever seen before. An unattractive man wearing dark glasses. I don't know who it is."

"What about Joanna? Did she say anything about it?" Marino flicks his lights again, riding the bumper of the car in front of us and it changes lanes to let him pass. "Did she mention if she'd ever noticed the truck before?"

"She didn't seem happy about it," she says. "Then she stepped away from me for a minute and made a phone call. I got the impression she was talking to the husband."

THE HUSBAND, I THINK about what she just said. She has distanced herself from Jamal Nari and depersonalized him. Mary Sapp has information she wants to keep from Marino and I don't trust her in the least.

"What was Joanna's demeanor this morning?" Marino asks as we drive past acres of solar panels and the National Grid gas storage tank with its rainbow design, a landmark in Dorchester and a waypoint on the Quarry Route that Lucy often follows when flying her helicopter in and out of Logan.

"Somewhat frantic and irritable but that's not unusual when people are moving. And eventually she sensed there was an issue, a problem and she became difficult." Another pause. "Are you thinking the gray truck out front has something to do with what happened to the husband? That maybe it's someone he was involved with?" she asks, and I think about drugs again.

Heroin-related crimes are epidemic in this area of Boston.

Marino says, "Ms. Sapp, did Joanna seem afraid of anything when you were with her this morning?"

She hesitates before she answers. "I'm not sure. Well, I don't think so."

"I'm just wondering if she or maybe her husband might have mentioned they were having some sort of trouble," Marino says.

"Privacy. I know that came up several times. They didn't want people bothering them anymore."

"Anymore?"

"Yes."

She goes on to claim that she doesn't know for a fact why the couple's need to move was urgent. She knows only what Nari mentioned last week, which was that they wanted something bigger and preferred not living in the same city where he worked.

"I know privacy was a big concern," Mary Sapp repeats, and she describes Nari as a popular musician and teacher who had been in the news last year and was "pestered by his students" because he lived too close to the school. If she'd had any inkling they were in any kind of trouble, she wouldn't have leased the house to them "to begin with and this entire ordeal would never have happened."

She makes the point that she was under the impression Joanna recently had quit her job as a school psychologist so she could "stay at home and start a family." She says the couple never let on that maybe "their circumstances" had changed and weren't at all what was represented when she first showed them the house on Gallivan Boulevard. After Joanna made the phone call, possibly to her husband, she and the Realtor got "into a discussion." It wasn't pleasant.

"I tried in the nicest way to convey to her that I no longer thought the property was well suited for them," she explains, "and she said it was a done deal. Her exact words. She began unpacking things over my objections, threatening to sue me for breach of contract."

"Were you still at the house with her when she got the call about her husband's death?" Marino asks.

"I wasn't. I finally left. That man is just sitting," she says. "I think he's waiting for me but I can't imagine why."

I recall that Joanna told us the moving truck was scheduled to pick up their furniture today at three P.M. and bring it to the house in Dorchester. If she's still planning to go ahead with the move she should be arriving at any moment but I have a strong feeling she won't. She hasn't even picked a funeral home yet and Bryce described her as being in a *fugue* state. If she can't make a decision about what to do with her husband's body then it's unlikely that she's made any other important decisions either. She's in shock. I hope she has family. I hope she has friends.

"I'm two minutes from you," Marino says to the Realtor. "Just stay where you are, okay?"

"He's sitting in the same place, right behind my car. He's just sitting inside the truck. It says 'Hands On Mechanics' on the door and I don't know why someone like a mechanic would be waiting here if that's what he's doing. It's odd though. When I saw the truck yesterday I thought it was a lawn care person, like I said. He might be eating something. I can't really tell from where I am."

"I'm going to get off the phone now." Marino is very calm. "You just stay put. You've got the doors locked and the alarm on?" He's asked her this before, and she says yes, she's made sure of it, and Marino ends the call. "There's got to be an explanation," he says to me. "If he just killed Jamal Nari he sure as hell wouldn't drive over here and sit in front of their house."

"The fact is we don't know what we're dealing with," I answer. "Including with Mary Sapp. I don't trust her."

ON GRANITE AVENUE WE drive over water. For a moment we're surrounded by it and I feel airborne. On our right is the Dorchester Bay with its sliver of tawny beach, on our left the Neponset River where small boats are moored.

Marino blasts through an intersection of bright-white-painted crosswalks, no pedestrians in sight, and he hangs a sharp left on Gallivan Boulevard and floors it. I recognize the small shingle-sided house from photographs on the Internet, a white Mercedes parked directly in front and behind it the gray Ford pickup truck.

If the truck's driver seems concerned that an unmarked police vehicle has pulled up behind him, he makes no sign of it. If the strobing blue and red grille lights are disconcerting or even a surprise there is no indication. He appears to be drinking a large coffee, his sunglasses watching us in the rearview mirror. But he makes no move to get out of the truck even as a Boston Police Department cruiser speeds around the corner and stops in the middle of the street next to us.

"You sit tight and let's see what the hell this is." Marino opens his door at the same time the uniformed officer in the cruiser opens his.

At least Marino left the engine running. I unlock the windows and roll mine down so I don't get any more surprises or feel trapped. I watch him approach the old gray truck, his Harley windbreaker moved out of the way of the .40 caliber Sig on his right hip. He raps the driver's window with his knuckle as the uniformed officer lowers his hand to his gun and steps around Marino to get a different perspective of the person inside.

"What can I help you with?" I hear a rude male voice say as the window goes down.

"License and registration and step outside," Marino says.

"Have I done something wrong?"

"Maybe I should be asking you that."

"I'll assume you just did and the answer is no. I've done nothing wrong," he says and I have the unsettling sensation that I've heard the voice before, aggressive and unpleasant.

"Sir, you need to step out of your truck," the uniformed officer says rather fiercely, young, dark skinned with a V-shaped build and biceps bulging from the short sleeves of his blue shirt.

The driver's door opens as the man says, "Don't get excited and do something stupid. I need to get my wallet and the registration out of the glove box, that's what I'm reaching for."

"Sir, do you have a gun in your vehicle?" the uniformed officer almost shouts.

"I do not. For God's sake don't shoot me."

CHAPTER 14

MARINO AND THE UNIFORMED officer have their hands by their guns, their attention riveted to the driver's every move.

I can see him leaning to the right, his right arm reaching, and the same thought replays itself in my mind, caught in a loop, I keep thinking it. If the worst happens, there's nothing I can do except call 911. Not all police vehicles have built-in radios anymore. Marino's SUV doesn't. He uses his portable instead and has it in hand, leaving me alone with an iPhone, the vest beneath my shirt and my wits.

I didn't bother with my .380 today, and I wish I had as I watch the driver step out of the truck, the same light-complexioned man who passed us on Memorial Drive. He has short curly black hair, is coarse featured, slender, medium height, dressed in jeans and a baggy denim shirt that isn't tucked in. In the lobe of his left ear is a small diamond stud, and his watch is military-looking, a black dial with a rotating bezel on a black silicone band. He hasn't shaved for days. He's not afraid. His demeanor is mocking and defiant.

"Move your glasses out of the way," Marino says loudly.

"Do what . . . ?"

"Take them off."

The man parks the sunglasses on top of his head and blinks in the brightness. There's something wrong with his eyes. They aren't symmetrical, are different sizes, one slightly lower than the other. I try Benton's cell phone and he answers.

"Arms out!" Marino steps closer to the truck and looks through the open window. "Nice scanner. Handheld. You make it your practice to monitor the police around here? What you got it set on? Let me guess. One-thirty-one-point-eight."

I tell Benton where I am and then I tell him about Machado. I mention the bleach as I watch Marino reach inside the truck and pick up the scanner. Benton recalls that Machado was at the scene about an hour before Marino was called, before I was.

"Yes," I confirm. "That's right."

"Poor judgment if nothing else," he says.

"At the very least."

"I'm glad you told me."

"Marino's not in a position to be objective about it. I'm not saying it's anything . . ."

"I understand what you're saying and it's a problem no matter what," Benton replies. "Something gets compromised and it can't always be fixed."

We end the call as I watch Marino toss the handheld scanner back on the seat.

"BAPERN," he says to the man. "So you can monitor what we say to each other and our pursuits and descriptions of assholes like you."

The Boston Area Police Emergency Radio Network is intercity. Its 131.8 frequency covers most police departments in the greater Boston area, and I wonder who he is. Maybe a journalist, maybe a cop, but neither makes sense unless he's on some oddball assignment that includes displaying magnetic signs and wrong phone numbers on a truck that's registered to an eighty-three-year-old man in Springfield.

"I'm not wanted," he says.

"Right now you are."

"And you don't have a warrant to search my truck." He points a finger at Marino.

"Arms out!"

"I don't have a weapon." He holds out his arms, waving his vehicle registration and a wallet.

"Take your license out of your wallet."

He does it.

"Arms out! Don't make me tell you again!"

"Don't shoot me! Don't tase me!" he exclaims as if either is imminent.

"Turn around and place your hands on the truck," Marino orders him.

"You don't need to be so nasty."

The voice is familiar. I try to place it and I can't. I watch Marino frisk him, and satisfied he's unarmed he takes the license and registration. He looks them over and calls them in to the dispatcher. Rand Bloom, thirty-two years old, a South Boston address. I can hear every word of it over the radio Marino holds and the scanner inside the pickup truck.

"This your truck?" Marino asks.

"My grandfather's." Rand Bloom leans against it, crossing his arms. "Clay Schmidt. He lives in a retirement community in Springfield but I'm guessing you already know that. What's your interest in me?"

"I'm the one asking the questions here."

"Ever heard of the First Amendment, freedom of speech? Maybe not since you don't seem to know about illegal searches."

"You want to tell me what you were doing in Cambridge this morning and why you had a different sign on this truck?"

"No. I don't want to tell you." He doesn't sound remotely intimidated.

In fact he seems amused as if the joke is on the police and he knows they're about to find that out.

"Thirty-three," the Cambridge dispatcher sounds.

Marino answers without taking his eyes off Bloom, who has no outstanding warrants. Arrested this past March for trespassing, he currently has a restraining order against him and lists his occupation as Specialized Investigations. I realize why his bitchy, condescending voice is familiar. I open my door and step out of the SUV.

MARINO WATCHES AS I approach. Then Rand Bloom is staring at me. He smiles as if we're friends.

"Nice to see you up close and personal, Doctor Scarpetta." His asymmetrical eyes are lasers locked on mine, a yellowish brown like a snake's or a cat's. "We've spoken on the phone, had several very pleasant conversations as a matter of fact."

"I know who you are," I reply. "And our conversations haven't been pleasant."

"You know each other?" Marino is knocked off his game, then he gets it back. "How?" he asks.

"Mister Bloom is an investigator for TBP Insurers."

"There we go," Marino says to him. "I knew you were a bottom-feeder."

"It looks like you got another unfortunate case, not that any of them are fortunate in your line of work," Bloom says to me, and I don't answer as I hold his intense stare. "A really bad day, a really tough one, and now you've got a canceled vacation. What a shame. But just so you know," he adds and I don't say a word, "I'm not here about his murder."

"Oh really?" Marino says. "Why would you assume we'd think you're here because of a murder? And what murder are you talking about? *His* murder? *Whose* murder?"

"It's on the news, all over it like I'm telling you something you don't know." Bloom stares at me, unwaveringly like a cobra I decide, swaying to his own music before he spits venom in my eyes. "Very sad but his death isn't covered by us and as depressing as it is life goes on. Well for most of us. Maybe not for you, Doctor Scarpetta."

"His death isn't covered by you?" Marino moves closer to him, almost nose to nose. "What the hell are you talking about?"

Bloom doesn't answer, and I take in the faint scars on his face, the deformity of his right eye from old lacerations and a fractured orbit. An obvious bridge, not a good one, replaces his upper front teeth. I can't tell about the lower ones. At some earlier time he suffered a violent event that injured his face and mouth. A car accident or a bad fall. Maybe he was beaten.

"Your life just stops when someone dies, am I right? And by the way Fort Lauderdale is a perfect eighty degrees and sunny. Well actually, North Miami Beach, right?" He looks me up and down, his gaze lingering where it shouldn't and I can feel the heat of Marino's anger. "Have you seen the building, Haulover Towers? I'm just wondering because it's right across the inlet from Haulover Park, thus the name. The park is public, constant barbecues, parties, music and ice cream trucks. Can be extremely loud. Same with the causeway, all those cars."

"Why don't you shut the hell up?" Marino is glancing at me and at messages landing on his phone, and his face is dangerous.

"The fact is Joanna Cather and I have unresolved business pertaining to her husband's frivolous suit against my company's client Emerson Academy." Bloom continues to ignore Marino and direct his comments to me, and I don't show my outrage.

I don't show my shock.

CHAPTER 15

He KNOWS ABOUT THE condo in Bal Harbour. How is that possible?

Benton wouldn't lease or purchase a property in either of our names. He always uses Limited Liability Companies, LLCs. He's FBI, former undercover, former protected witness, a seasoned profiler who has seen it all. He's as secretive as anybody could possibly be and ferocious about protecting our personal lives.

"Unfortunately Jamal Nari's tragic death doesn't change the fact he and his wife are greedy and unreasonable," Bloom is saying. "I was going to try to talk some sense into her and had no choice but to hang out and wait."

"Some sense into *her*?" Marino asks. "You decide to have this little chat with *just her* after you found out her husband is dead?"

"Joanna doesn't return my phone calls. If she did I wouldn't have to resort to such measures."

"The thing is you were seen in this neighborhood yesterday," Marino continues to pound away at him. "Before her husband died. You were seen driving past when Joanna was inside the house early this morning. Then I saw your truck in Cambridge later, around eleven, an hour after his death. Can you explain?"

"I'm an easygoing guy. I hate it when people push me against a wall and I can no longer be polite."

"No longer being polite means killing somebody, if necessary? So they can't collect insurance money?"

"I didn't say anything even close to that."

"You need to leave Joanna Cather the hell alone starting right now," Marino threatens as I notice the house, someone looking out a window, and then the front door opens.

The woman who emerges must be Mary Sapp, overblown in a short green dress with long brassy blond hair and bright red lipstick. She shields her eyes with her hand, squinting at us in the low sun. Then she ducks back inside to set the alarm. I can hear its warning beeps as she reappears and shuts the door behind her. She snaps a lockbox over the outside handle, and that piques my attention.

It's not the sort of thing one does when a house is no longer on the market, and the practice is a dangerous one. Lockboxes hold keys and sometimes alarm codes, allowing other Realtors to show a property without the listing agent present. Given the right tools, the shackles can be cut and the metal vaults can be forced open, which was what happened in Nantucket last Thanksgiving, a case that hasn't been solved, a horrific one.

A Realtor arrived at an oceanfront estate to check on damage after a bad storm and discovered the lockbox was missing. Thinking nothing of it she returned to her office for a key and the alarm code, and when she entered the house someone was waiting. She was savagely beaten and stabbed during a struggle that began in the foyer and ended in the flooded basement where she was drowned and hanged from a pipe. The murder was sensational enough to cause most Massachusetts Realtors to stop using lockboxes. I don't understand why Mary Sapp does unless she's careless.

Patty Marsico, I think of the victim and envision her contused bloody face, the bones shattered in it, her jaw and teeth broken, one of her eyes avulsed from its socket. It looked as if someone had spray-painted blood all over the house and I remember something else. Another ugly coincidence, and when there are enough of them, they likely aren't chance or random. I send Bryce a text: *Patty Marsico, last November. Wasn't TBP Insurers involved?*

"You can't stop me from talking to her." Bloom confronts Marino. "I'm just doing my job and you have no right to tell me what to do unless I'm guilty of a crime. And I'm certainly not." He smiles boldly, his dental bridge very white and horsey. "And you know that, of course. Because if I were guilty of anything at all I'd be in cuffs that are much too tight and thrown into the back of a filthy cruiser that has a cage."

"I'll tell you what you're guilty of," Marino says, "being an asshole. And I'm not done with you but guess what? We'll wait and follow up at the station. You got some explaining to do."

"I'll check my calendar and call my lawyer."

"Be as cocky as you want. It won't help." Marino is seething and his letting Bloom go for now tells me a number of things.

Marino doesn't want Boston PD involved any more than it already is, and whatever information he's getting through messages and emails isn't offering sufficient justification for him to bring in Bloom right now on suspicion of murder or any other charge. Something else is going on that is making Marino angry and agitated, his bad mood not simply about a smart-ass insurance investigator.

I wonder what Machado is digging up in the Nari case, and I watch Mary Sapp take her time following the sidewalk to the street, pausing every other step in her high-heeled shoes, on her phone, the busy successful Realtor who drives a hundred-thousand-dollar car. She stops and says something about rescheduling a showing as she looks at her watch, gold, a sparkle of diamonds. She tucks the phone in her shoulder bag, an expensive designer one.

I glance at a message from Bryce. *Affirmative. TBP Insurers. That same A-hole too. Rand Bloom, who's called me at least fifty times trying to get to you, and why you ever return his calls, I don't know. Victim's husband sued her real estate company for negligence or something. You were deposed, remember? Why are you asking? Oh, let me guess. Another death, another claim? Another day, another dollar?*

Too much information! Dammit, I think. My staff can't get it through their heads that anything written creates a record. It can end up in court.

It doesn't matter if it's a text message or a Post-it and Bryce is the worst offender. He's going to get me into trouble one of these days.

"Is everything all right here?" Mary Sapp asks when she reaches us. "Did you need to speak to me?" She directs this to Bloom. "Have we met?"

He introduces himself and her reaction conveys the truth. She looks slightly flustered and then has no expression on her heavily made-up face. She feigns ignorance and indifference. She seems distracted as if she has places to go and people to see, and I don't believe it. She may have no trouble misrepresenting a property or taking advantage of a client but she's not a good actress. I suspect she and Bloom haven't met and she had no idea he was the person she was seeing in the gray truck. But that doesn't mean they aren't familiar with each other.

"No, ma'am. I'm not here to speak to you. You're not who I've been looking for," he says too sweetly, too politely. "I've been trying to have a word with your lessee. But while I have a moment of your time, I have to ask if you're fully aware that there are some things you should be concerned about? Unless of course you don't care if you rent a nice property like this to, well, a tenant of questionable character."

"This property is no longer under agreement," she says and the way she says it confirms she has information.

Of course she does. She's already gotten it from him, probably over the phone. Rand Bloom is too streetwise to do his dirty work by email or any other form of communication that leaves a trail.

"Jesus," Marino exclaims. "You talked to her, didn't you?" He glares at both of them, and she glances at her car, fidgets with her keys, shifting her crocodile bag to her other shoulder. "You get her on the phone first? You pass on a lot of unsubstantiated shit so maybe Joanna's not welcome here anymore? What kind of dirtbag does something like that?"

"I'm sorry," the Realtor says coldly. "The contract clearly states that the lease is null and void if there is reason to suspect criminal activity."

"Reason to?"

"That's what it says. Close enough."

"And what criminal activity might that be?" Marino asks. "What bullshit did you feed her?" He glares at Bloom as if he might tear him apart.

"In reality there's the not so trivial problem of why Joanna really quit her job. Added to that is her late husband's extracurricular activities." He crosses his arms at his chest, and the veins in his hands are ropey. He's sinewy and strong. I imagine he's a dirty fighter.

"Cut the crap before I do it for you!" Marino bellows.

"I'm going to show you something." Bloom focuses on him, ignoring the hard-jawed uniformed cop ready to pounce. "Don't shoot me," Bloom says loud enough for the neighbors to hear. "I'm just getting an envelope from the inside of my truck, okay?" he yells. "So don't go freaking out and shooting me."

HE REACHES INSIDE THE truck and makes a big production of slowly retrieving a manila envelope. Inside are eight-by-eleven photographs taken with a telescopic lens. Jamal Nari is in a black running suit, a baseball cap pulled low. He's getting out of his recently purchased red SUV. The parking lot is dark and I can see the half moon high over the tops of buildings. I remember it was half full at the beginning of the week, just days ago.

The photographs were taken in quick succession, Nari as he walks under tall light standards, his head bent, entering a diner called Jumpin' Joe's in Revere where there are drive-by shootings, gangs and drugs. More images, not many people inside, just a few in line, and Nari stares up at an illuminated menu with pictures of burgers, fried chicken, breakfast sandwiches. He places an order and looks tense. The woman working the counter hands him a white bag big enough to hold several meals. He walks back outside, pauses by his SUV, glancing around, his eyes wide and glassy. He checks the contents of the bag. The last photograph zooms in on his hands, on a small clear plastic envelope of white powder.

"Who've you shown this to besides us?" Marino is incensed. "Not the police I'm pretty sure. Let me guess. You showed it to him, to Jamal Nari to blackmail him."

"I'm not at liberty to discuss."

"You were making sure he drops any possible damages he might get from the school. You may as well answer because I'll find out."

"It's privileged. I don't care what you find out."

"I'm sorry." Mary Sapp directs this at Marino. "I hate to disappoint Joanna, especially at a time like this. I sincerely do," she says and there is nothing sincere about her.

I think about the twelve thousand dollars in deposits that I'm betting will be forfeited. Good luck getting the money back. The legal fees and aggravation won't be worth it, and I wonder what her share is and if Bloom will get a cut.

"As you can understand, the owner can't have something of this nature . . . ," the Realtor explains. "Perhaps you'd be so kind as to make sure she arranges to move out the boxes. They put a number of them in there."

"Nobody's moving a damn thing." Marino's voice is like a gavel slamming down. "This house is now part of a crime scene. In fact your pal here Mister Bloom has made sure it has to be searched very carefully. We're going to need to go through everything in it not only because of Jamal Nari's death but also now that the photos introduce the possibility of illegal drugs. A complicated multijurisdictional investigation like this could take a long time. You know, tests in the labs. They can take months, even a year," he exaggerates. "You might just have a hard time renting it anytime soon. You mind getting a couple of your guys out here to secure this place?" He directs this at the Boston police officer. "I'll be coming back later or someone else from my department will. So we can start processing the house and everything in it, including fuming it."

"Fuming?" Mary Sapp looks genuinely worried.

"Superglue."

"Glue! You can't use glue on . . ."

"For fingerprints," Marino says. "I'm going to need yours for exclusionary purposes."

"Mine?"

"Obviously yours are going to be inside the house. You go through any of their belongings? We going to find your prints on any of their property?"

"What? I don't appreciate the insinuation . . ."

"The glue can make a mess, the dusting powders too." He cuts her off. "You'll want a professional cleanup crew in here after we're done. And we need the alarm code and a key."

"The owner is going to be very upset. This is a very pristine, highly desirable property." Now she looks angry.

Bloom got to her. He made sure Nari and his wife would be in violation of their rental contract. The obvious motive is further harassment, his photographs of Nari disastrous. Had he not died his life would have been in shambles. He may have ended up in prison on drug charges and that certainly would have been the end of his discrimination suit.

"It's a shame they didn't take what we offered when the offer was good," Bloom says to me, and he's clearly talking about whatever settlement Emerson Academy was willing to pay. "You know what they say. A bird in hand."

"Tell you what you're going to do right now with your bird in hand." Marino pokes his big middle finger in Bloom's chest.

"Don't touch me."

Marino pokes him again, hard on his sternum. "You and your bird get in your truck and fly away, and if I find out you're bothering Ms. Cather or anybody else involved in this case, I'll have you arrested for interfering in a police investigation."

"Get your hands off me."

"Not my hands. Just my finger." Marino holds it up, flipping him off.

"I'm reporting you to your commissioner," Bloom yells.

"Knock yourself out," Marino says.

CHAPTER 16

THE SUN IS SHARPLY angled and the outside air blowing through the vents is warmer as Marino takes a different way back to outmaneuver traffic, his efforts hopeless I suspect. President Obama landed at Hanscom Air Force Base twenty minutes ago. His motorcade is on its way to Cambridge.

He's having dinner with key fund-raisers at the Charles Hotel and holding a press conference in Boston in the morning and police and the military are everywhere, closing lanes of traffic, blocking bridges and restricting flight areas, securing the water, land and air. Helicopters thunder over the harbor and up and down the river, Army Black Hawks, Marine Chinooks and Coast Guard Dauphins, low and slow and circling. I hear their thunder and feel their vibration as emergency alerts pop up on the display of my phone.

More than a thousand protestors already have gathered at Copley Square, the Common and along streets near the site of last year's Boston Marathon bombing that killed three and wounded more than two hundred and fifty. Anti-Muslim sentiments are boiling over as we move closer to the trial set for the fall, and members of the Primitive Calvinist Alliance have arrived by the busload to preach their message of hate.

It's the extremists who worry me most, cells of crazies justified by the

Almighty in their twisted minds, jubilant and vile when innocents are shot and blown up at schools, shopping malls, in Afghanistan or last year in Boston. The more people hate, the more they hate. It spreads like a plague, the only cure humaneness and decency, in short supply it seems. Yesterday the president made a statement from the White House urging Americans not to "rush to judgment" about entire groups of human beings.

No words will turn away wrath and I put the CFC on alert the moment I was informed that he was coming to the Boston area. I'm not an alarmist and heads of state visiting here is common but it's stressful when there's so little notice in advance. Despite my close ties with the Armed Forces Medical Examiners and the Department of Defense I knew nothing until two days ago, my ultimate boss General John Briggs calling late Tuesday with a Homeland Security Advisory, high risk he said.

"Think of it as orange," he told me, "but as far as the public goes it's the usual yellow."

"Why?" I asked.

"A confidential report out of Russia," he said. "Their commitment to destroy al-Qaeda after terrorist operations in Volgograd just before the Olympics. Plus what's going on in Crimea and the threat that certain stealth special operatives may go rogue."

"Certain ones?"

"The worry that when Yanukovych fled Ukraine there may have been an exodus of extremely dangerous special ops who were loyal to his presidency."

"May have been?"

"CIA ambiguity about money, drugs and thugs flowing into this country. Then there's the Russian problem in Boston."

He meant the Chechen accused of the marathon bombings. Briggs's warnings weren't necessarily unexpected but they are more alarming than usual and as I say this to Marino I continue to replay what has happened today. I have an uneasy feeling it's somehow related to everything else going on, and if that turns out to be true we have a very big problem, perhaps a global one.

"Except the two cases in New Jersey," he reminds me as we sit in traffic. "How do they fit with Obama being here and whatever's going on in Ukraine?"

"We need to find out if Bloom is connected to some extremist group," I suggest.

"Extremist greedy assholes comes to mind." Marino glowers at cars not going anywhere. "I wish we had Lucy's helicopter right about now."

HIS ROUTE IS A maze as he depends on a phone app to avoid gridlock.

We've been moving very slowly, at times barely a crawl or not at all. In Chinatown, then Boston's North End and we wound around the TD Garden, home of the Celtics and the Bruins. On Nashua Street crowded parking lots spread out on either side of us, then the Charles River Dam, now the Museum of Science, a COLOSSAL FOSSIL exhibit announced on banners draping the building.

Sunlight flickers on the river like a vast school of small silver fish, and in the distance the cables of the Zakim Bridge soar like *Old Ironsides'* rigging. I pay close attention to where we are and what's around us, checking my side mirror and keeping up my scan. I wouldn't be surprised if Rand Bloom is brazen enough to follow us, and I try to imagine exactly what he wants beyond making people uncomfortable. Miserable and extremely unsettled in fact, like Joanna Cather, like Sarah Angiers and in his mind me.

I'll never give him the satisfaction and he should have known that when I was standing on the street looking him in the eye, assuming he didn't already know it before this afternoon. He promised he'd see me around as if that would frighten me, and I smiled and said fine. Maybe he'd like another restraining order or trespassing charge I let him know. Better yet if he shows up at my headquarters uninvited my security will give him a welcome he won't forget.

I didn't mention he doesn't want to tangle with my FBI husband or me on our private property, and that he'd be extremely wise not to come anywhere near my niece Lucy, former FBI and ATF, run off the job because of insubordination and a few bad kills. She is quite skilled with a gun and for better or worse it's in her DNA not to be bothered by much, doesn't care or feel remorse if she decides an action is just.

I didn't need to outright threaten Bloom for him to get the point, and when he drove away from the house on Gallivan it was with an angry squeal that left skid marks on the pavement. A sign of weakness I thought as I watched. But I won't underestimate him. He'd be wise not to underestimate me either.

"He knew me on sight but that's not the most important issue. I got the feeling he expected I'd show up with you," I emphasize to Marino, who seems unmoved by what I'm saying.

"I don't understand why you wouldn't tell me you've got a place in Miami." Suddenly he is stuck on that instead.

"As I've mentioned several times now, I just found out about it yesterday."

"But you've known for a while you were going down there on vacation."

"Yes, for my birthday. I thought we were staying in a hotel," I reply and I've said that several times too.

Marino is digging. For what, I'm not sure. He's acting cavalier but something is gnawing at him as he fixates on Florida where he briefly lived when I had an office there years ago. As is true with most people, he remembers the good parts, and I listen to him while I skim through messages from my office. They land as fast as I can look at them, the most recent one from Luke Zenner.

There was nothing unexpected in Jamal Nari's autopsy except the gastric contents are *interesting*. It's in Luke's preliminary report, which he's just completed and is happy to discuss, and whenever he uses the word *interesting* what he means is peculiar. There was something inside the stomach that he didn't expect, and I wonder what it was. My deputy chief is too savvy to put details in an electronic communication, unlike Liz Wrighton, unlike Bryce Clark.

Left for the day, Liz has let me know. *Thick headed again, can hardly think & keep blowing my nose & coughing my brains out,* she feels compelled to describe, and I wish she would spare me details that a defense attorney would love to use against her. It wouldn't be helpful if a jury hears that she wasn't thinking clearly if at all when she did the ballistics analysis in this case. And then there's Bryce. He truly is impossible, hailing me as he often does with his *Earth 2 Dr. Scarpetta* salutations that make me sound like an eccentric or a space cadet.

R U ever coming to the office 2day? he writes in his increasingly abbreviated text language, and not a minute later another message lands. *OK U've left me no choice. The cat's coming out of the bag. Some of YR very loyal staff R hanging around 2 surprise U. They got cannolis from Mike's.*

Why? I write back.

Hello? YR birthday?

That's very kind but please don't have people wait for me.

I should tell them that?

Of course, I answer.

Do U C that's hurtful?

"No matter what I do," I mutter.

"What?" Marino asks and I tell him and he replies, "I get what he's saying. People want you to care that they would wait. If it makes you happy it makes them feel good."

"What it will make me feel is bad. I'm quite sure most of my staff would like to go home to their friends and family, to enjoy what little bit of the day is left. Do you know what jewelry mix is?" I'm reading something else on my phone.

"Stainless steel shot used in a tumbler," Marino says. "It's different shapes and sizes. Lucy uses it sometimes when she hand-loads ammo. Why?"

"Ernie Koppel." I'm hearing from my most senior trace evidence examiner now.

Usually by late afternoon I've made evidence rounds, stopping in various labs, checking on the status of cases in the works. But I'm trapped in a car because the president of the United States is here, and his presence is like a wildfire that spreads whichever way he goes, shutting down highways, thoroughfares, private air traffic and businesses within a wide radius. But life and death always go on at the CFC and scientists such as Ernie are briefing me. Their narratives aren't detailed but they're enough to give me a hint about developments I should follow up on.

"He got the frag and the mysterious intact bullet from Liz before she left for the day, and he's looked at photographs from the New Jersey cases," I inform Marino. "There's microscopic pitting that he associates with jewelry mix. He says the pitting on everything is consistent."

Ernie doesn't say it's *the same* but that's what he's suggesting, I explain. He's implying the copper bullets that struck Jamal Nari and the ones that killed two other people were polished in a tumbler—possibly the same tumbler with the same medium, jewelry mix that was placed inside the barrel. As it rotated over a period of hours or days, the friction caused by the steel shot removed oxidation and polished the metal. Ernie suspects the final part of the process was the use of a cloth, a manual buffing, and there's also unique machining on the intact bullet that I'll want to see.

"And I remind you that Benton says the pennies may have been polished in a tumbler," I add.

"Bling," Marino says.

CHAPTER 17

BLING?" I ASK.

"A fanatic who treats his hand loads like jewelry. I know guys like that, snipers, competition shooters, Jack Kuster for example. When they eject cartridge cases they never let them hit the ground. As fast as lightning, snapping open the bolt, catching their brass like that." Marino's hand snakes out from the steering wheel as if grabbing a moth from the air. "Considering the type of rifle being used, it's to be expected."

"A perfectionist," I comment as more helicopters thud-thud, three monster Super Stallions, triple turbine engines, seven bladed.

Marino cocks his head, looking up. "Is there an invasion going on that nobody's told us about? I think we already know this person is a perfectionist."

"We probably did but everything else we're finding out is only making matters worse," I comment. "More dangerous," I add. "That's what worries me considerably. Who is it and why? And who is he going to kill next?"

"In cases like this it would be the rule and not the exception that the person is meticulous, even OCD. A precision shooter who might have a smart rifle. This is someone who's got his own shop filled with gunsmithing tools," Marino replies as if he's not surprised and has no doubt. "And I've said it before this homicide. I've said it about the two in Jersey."

"What about the frag from those? Before now was there a suggestion that a tumbler was used?"

"There was so little left."

"Well if anybody could figure it out, Ernie would." He's one of the best microscopists I've ever worked with.

"We were lucky. Especially with the bullet that's mostly intact. Like winning the lottery," Marino says. "Maybe that's your birthday present from the universe. I'm trying to remember how old you are."

"I wouldn't waste any mental energy on it."

"You look good, Doc. Considering."

"That's nice to hear. I'll ignore the *considering* part of it."

"Seriously. When you think about where you work? No sunlight, it's cool. Maybe a constant exposure to formalin fumes. They preserve tissue so it doesn't decompose, right? And that's what aging is." He replays my own joke to me. "You start decomposing, things start dying off, skin, muscle, hair. That's what they say. The minute you're born you start dying. Who would think it? That a morgue might be the Fountain of Youth."

"That's my line you've just stolen. And you've managed to make me depressed," I say distractedly, a visceral uneasiness simmering.

I'm familiar with shooting aficionados who tumble cartridge cases before hand-loading ammunition. Lucy, for example. She has an indoor firing range and hand-loads her own ammo in a shop that has equipment worthy of an armory, including tumblers, all different sizes. But I've never heard of someone tumbling bullets. Brass cartridge cases, yes, but the actual projectiles, no, and then I wonder how the person did it. Were there separate tumblers or did he polish the entire cartridge he'd hand-loaded and -tooled?

We need to talk, I write to Ernie. *How long will you be in the lab?*

A while. FTIR next. On a roll.

He's using Fourier transform infrared spectroscopy, different frequencies of light to analyze a trace amount of a sample. FTIR doesn't digest or destroy evidence the way gas or liquid chromatography do, and I wonder what he suspects. Possibly a chemical, and I think of my niece again and what she's learned from me. Flitz tarnish remover has been around for-ever and is my cure-all for rust, corrosion, calcium deposits and stains. I use it at home on copper, brick, terra-cotta, aluminum and even glass. I've seen cans of Flitz in Lucy's machine shop. That's what she uses when she hand-polishes metal with a cloth.

"Miami? Huh." Marino is obsessing about Florida again. "Don't get some bright idea about moving back down there. You should have told me about the new place."

"I thought we were staying at a resort. Benton made the arrangements. The condo was a surprise. I've seen pictures, that's all, and I don't know why it matters. Your concern at the moment should be that a thug of an insurance investigator seems to be a common denominator in a number of things going on."

"He has nothing to do with New Jersey. With those cases," Marino says.

"Are you certain of that? What about the victims' insurance policies? Any chance their carrier was TBP?"

"Before now I'd never heard of Bloom. I'm not aware of any insurance stuff in connection with the Jersey shootings."

"You'd better ask."

"It's a damn good thing you're my partner or I wouldn't know how to act."

"I'm your partner because you've held me hostage all day."

"Obama has."

"Not earlier."

"We do good working together, truth is."

"We always did," I reply.

"So I'll double-check about the Jersey cases but I think Bloom's a pe-ripheral pain in the ass, a red heron." Marino means a red herring. "Some of the stuff with him is coincidental and we shouldn't be distracted by it."

I DON'T AGREE THAT Rand Bloom's turning up everywhere is coinci-dental. That doesn't mean I'm suggesting he's a serial killer, I explain. But I'm close to insisting he's a common thread somehow.

"It's probably going to take Lucy to figure out exactly what that thread is," I say to Marino as we come to a complete stop again.

"It's my case and I don't want anyone asking her to hack," he answers. "Taking Storrow Drive was a mistake."

"Driving anywhere today was a mistake."

In the past ten minutes we've gone not even half a mile, and I look out at trees along the river, and ahead of us an endless line of cars, heat rising from them, sunlight blanking out glass.

"I would never ask Lucy to hack." I don't add that Marino doesn't hesitate to help himself to anything she offers as long as no one finds out. "In general I avoid asking people to break the law, especially if they're family," I add ironically.

"Would Janet and her go with you?" Marino asks.

"Excuse me?" I look at him and his face is somber. He's not joking.

"It's always a good idea if I know what's going on with you, Doc. If you're thinking of retiring in Miami, I should know."

"Retiring?"

"You could. It's not like you and Benton need the money."

"I didn't become a forensic pathologist with a law degree for the money. That's not my motivation."

"You and him don't have to work another day in your lives if you don't want to. Unlike the rest of us, not including Lucy who's probably on the Forbes List."

"I don't think so but it's not something I check."

"I'd like to be rich even for a week. Just to know what it feels like not to worry about which bill to pay or whether I can afford to trade in my bike for a newer one."

"Fundamental problems are the same for everyone," I reply as we move ahead again, then stop again. "Life, death, sickness, diets, relationships, bills that need to be paid. And if you need something, Marino, you know you can ask."

"I don't need anything. Wanting stuff is another matter. If I had the money for sure I'd have a place in the Keys, get a boat, a trailer for my bike and travel. Take it easy, nothing hanging over my head but an awning on my back porch."

"You'd be bored in five minutes."

"Probably."

"I have no intention of retiring or quitting any time soon if ever," I tell him. "But thank you for implying I'm nonessential and old. That's the best birthday present you could give me."

"What I'm implying is you've been doing this for a while and I wouldn't blame you for being sick of dealing with dead people and dirt-bags. Plus Miami's where you're from so even if you don't want to cash it in," he adds as if I'm dying, "maybe you'd just rather spend your days around palm trees and sunshine."

"I wouldn't."

"Plus you're good pals with the chief in Broward right next door in Lauderdale," he says. "And you teach forensic investigation classes down there three or four times a year. You like South Florida."

"I like a lot of places."

Marino wedges his SUV between two cars, changing lanes as if it will matter. It doesn't. It just pisses people off.

"Why would you bring up something like that?" I ask.

"Because you never know what people are going to do. One day they're your best friend. The next they're a stranger or your enemy. They put you in a situation where there's no right choice if you know what I mean."

"I don't think I do."

"So which is worse?" he asks. "To betray someone or let him get away with something he shouldn't?"

"Both are worse. Are you talking about me? Did I do something I don't know about?"

"That's what I'm saying. You never know about anyone."

I don't tell him he's being irrational, projecting onto me behavior that has to do with someone else. Instead I redirect him. "Bloom usually ends up dealing with Bryce."

"How many times?"

"When I finally returned his call? Not many. There have been several cases." I try to think exactly which ones. "Johnny Angiers most recently."

"How much is the policy for?"

"I have no idea."

"It's enough to push Bloom into overdrive. I'm guessing it's a big chunk of change, a million dollars or something."

"The murder in Nantucket last summer, Patty Marsico." I bring that up. "Her husband sued the real estate company she worked for, and Bloom called once or twice asking me about her autopsy, questions that for the most part I refused to answer. I also was deposed."

"Was he at the deposition?" Marino continues to nudge in and out of lanes, and other drivers blare their horns at him. Some of them mouth obscenities, probably every person on the road around here frustrated and in a foul mood.

"Only lawyers and a court reporter. Before today I had no idea what he looked like." I assumed he was older and wore ill-fitting cheap suits. "He badgered me about something else several years ago." I search my memory. "Liberty Wharf," it comes to me. "The construction worker."

"The one who fell from the top floor of that office building near the Boston Fish Pier. Got impaled on rebar," Marino says as if it's a fond memory. "I had to use a diamond blade saw to cut him loose."

"The focus was on whether his safety harness failed. Bloom tried to make a case for chronic alcohol abuse."

"Blame the victim."

"Whose blood alcohol was negative but he had a fatty liver, CNS lesions, bruising, which I didn't speculate about," I reply. "His death was an accident and the insurance company settled. Again, I don't know how much."

"Maybe you've become an insurance company's nightmare."

"Maybe I am."

"You didn't used to be."

"If you say so."

"What I mean is you used to be more clinical." His scratched Ray-Bans glance at me as we sit on Storrow Drive, going nowhere again. "When we first started working together? You were sort of cold and impersonal."

"I'd take that as a compliment if I possibly could."

"By the book is what I'm saying. You didn't care about the outcome, remember?"

"I didn't want to care about it," I reply.

"Sometimes you didn't even read the paper or watch the news to see what a jury decided after you testified." He glances at me again. "You used to say that the way a trial turned out or what insurance companies did wasn't up to you or even part of your job."

"It isn't."

"Maybe you're making it your job now."

"I might be."

"I'm wondering how come."

"Being the other way doesn't feel right anymore," I reply. "I've had enough of people getting away with things."

"You and me both," Marino says as if something else is on his mind. "People shouldn't get away with shit. I don't care who they are."

"Cold and impersonal," I consider as if I'm amused but I'm not.

"I said *sort of.*"

"You've waited all this time to tell me that?"

"I've said it before including behind your back. You're different now."

"I was that bad back then?"

"Yeah and I was an asshole," he says. "We deserved each other."

CHAPTER 18

HE IMPATIENTLY TAPS HIS thick fingers on the steering wheel as we make progress, inching forward at three miles an hour.

It wasn't what Marino bargained for when he decided to take a creative route back, now on the Longfellow Bridge, locally known as the Salt and Pepper Bridge, its tall granite towers resembling salt and pepper shakers. Rusting train tracks run down the middle dividing four lanes of east- and westbound traffic.

The century-old steel girder bridge spans the Charles River, connecting Boston's Beacon Hill to Cambridge, and traffic is still awful. Right now it has nothing to do with Obama. As if detours and delays caused by his motorcade weren't bad enough, a car is broken down up ahead, the right lane closed. Midway across in the eastbound lanes a twisted wreck is being chained onto a flatbed truck.

A rolling surf of blue and red police lights flash and news helicopters hover like bright dragonflies, three of them rock steady at about a thousand feet. The low sun is glaring and I wonder if that might have contributed to the accident. Maybe the gridlock and road rage caused by a presidential visit did.

"We've talked maybe half a dozen times over the past few years." I'm telling Marino about my conversations with Bloom. "The exchanges are on a par with a number of junkyard lawyers I unfortunately have to deal with. Clearly he's made it his mission to know as much about me as he can possibly find, including what I look like."

"Recognizing you isn't exactly a big surprise," he says. "You're in the news and even in Wikipedia, which you need to correct by the way. It has a bunch of stuff wrong including that you and me had an affair when we were working cases in Virginia. I think they mean Benton."

"Our planned vacation in Florida hasn't been made public." I'm not interested in rumors. "The condo Benton rented isn't. How do you explain that?"

"Lucy might have ideas about it. Some database Bloom got into. Some blog out there you don't know about. I haven't heard jack shit from Machado since I saw him at the scene this morning."

He is sullen for a moment and I let my silence prompt him.

"I thought I knew him," he says and that's what his projection is about.

Marino's anxieties that I might move or abandon him are really about losing his best friend. But a comment he made is digging into me, his question about betrayal and keeping secrets as if a person has done something wrong. That person must be Machado. What did he do and what is Marino hiding?

"I don't know what's gone on but I'm sorry." I'm not going to force the subject. I don't want to come across as cold or impersonal, not even *sort of.* "I know the two of you were very close and that he did a lot to help you get back into policing."

"And I guarantee he wishes he hadn't." Marino is angry because it's easier than being hurt. "You encourage somebody and it's fine until they leave you in the dust. We used to ride Harleys together, hang out at Paddy's, watch the games and get take-out barbecue, ribs and biscuits from Sweet Cheeks. Sox tickets, Bruins tickets, grab Italian, Pomodoro, Assaggio in the North End." For an instant he looks sad and just as quickly his face turns stony. "We had each other's backs."

"You don't anymore?"

"He doesn't have mine and maybe I shouldn't have his."

"It's painful to lose a friend like that."

"Me in pain?" His laugh sounds more like a snort. "Hell no. Not even a twinge. He's a traitor. All the times he said how much he wanted me to become a cop again so we could be partners? Well be careful what you wish for. Now he wishes I was fired or dead."

"Is that what this is about? That you've eclipsed him?" I know how to deal with Marino when he's upset.

But I always thought I did. From the beginning of our relationship I believed in my people management skills. *Cold and impersonal,* and I try to conjure up who I was to him. My psyche wavers like a flame disturbed by a sudden draft.

"Damn right I've eclipsed him. It's the damn truth," Marino says. "There should be some gum in the glove box."

I OPEN IT TO look, nudging the Baggie of polished pennies aside and they quietly clink.

Rand Bloom didn't leave them on my wall. He didn't tweet the poem from Morristown last month. He's too crude and ham-fisted for acts of cryptic symbolism. *Cold and impersonal.* I can't get it out of my mind. When I was hired as the chief medical examiner of Virginia, my first big job, Marino was a jerk. I was reserved. Maybe I wasn't warm but I was fair. I was cordial. I thought I was nice while he went out of his way to make life hard for me.

I dig around and find the gum—Clove, that figures. He loves retro and as I open the slim red pack I'm startled by a powerful rush from the past, images and sounds of my father's grocery in West Flagler, an area of Little Havana that was a safe enclave for immigrants. I hold the pack up to my nose and smell it. Sweetly sharp and spicy, and I remember the hand-painted sign out front, SCARPETTA'S MARKET in big blue letters.

Inside it was always cool, a window air conditioner rattling and dripping condensation on the tile floor, and the first thing I'd see was the candy and gum. Clove, Teaberry, Juicy Fruit, SweeTarts, M&M's, Mallo

Cups filled a wire rack, and on top of the wooden counter were gallon jars of Bazooka bubble gum with comics inside and silvery York peppermint patties coated in dark chocolate.

Marino's phone rings "Hail to the Chief," a ringtone I've heard before but I don't know who it is. I don't pay attention as I envision my father's hands as if they're in front of me, tan with long slender fingers, placing coins inside the nickel-plated cash register, turn of the century and meticulously restored. For months I watched him work on it, a milk crate of pieces and parts on the kitchen table, which my mother made him cover with layers of the *Miami Herald*. He replaced the mechanical keys, added a brass ringer that clanged when the cash drawer opened.

"What's up, Boss?" Marino asks and I'm not listening to him.

I'm listening to what my father used to say as he instructed me, advising me how to live because he knew he couldn't much longer. But I never accepted that until he was gone and maybe not even then. We often spoke Italian in our home and his accent was gentle and lilting, his voice baritone and quiet. *Succedono cose terribili.* He would tell me that terrible things happen and one never knows who's going to come through the door. *Don't turn your back and give a thief an opportunity. Life is short, Kay. It's precious and fragile. There are those who want to take what doesn't belong to them, so many people like that. Very hurtful people.*

Io non volevo vivere la mia vita con la paura del male. I would answer him that I didn't want to live my life fearing evil. I didn't want to fear anything at all, and he said he was teaching me not to be naïve, to be smart. *Non essere ingenua, devi essere furba,* he said one day as he installed a side lock in the cash register that required a key, flat brass, oddly shaped on a fob with a small folding knife he always kept in a pocket.

Later when he could no longer work, I began carrying the key and when he could still talk lucidly he would ask me if it was safe with me. *Sì, Papà, la terrò sempre al sicuro.* It will always be safe, in my jewelry box now, and as I think of it I feel sad. It is an old feeling, vintage and from my past like Marino's chewing gum.

"Okay. I see. You got it from him but he didn't bother sending it to me . . ." I overhear what Marino is saying as I see my father as if he's next to me, thin even before he was sick, sharp featured with blond hair that was wavy and thick.

He'd hold my hand and introduce me to customers when he'd take me to his store, sometimes on Saturdays, and I'd keep him company and do odd chores. Later when he could no longer leave the house I worked the register after school, on weekends and during the summers. At nine or ten I was keeping the books, making the deposits in the bank, meeting delivery trucks and refilling bins with fresh fruits and vegetables. I became facile at cutting and weighing meats and cheeses, an expert in the art of olive oils and crafting homemade pastas and breads. It never occurred to me that I was a child.

My father's leukemia made me old. Maybe it made me impersonal and cold. I stare out the window but don't see the traffic, what I see is the Cuban sandwich shop my father loved, *jamón dulce, ropa vieja,* and Spanish beef stew that I would carry on a tray into the bedroom where he didn't move, lying there with the blinds drawn, the slightest light seeping through. I believed I could make him eat and he would stop losing weight. The headaches wouldn't be so severe and his fatigue would go away if I worked hard and made him happy.

"I'll look," Marino says, not to me but on his phone, and I think about my being impersonal and cold, and I feel anger like a needle stick.

When we first started working together years ago that's what he thought. It seems worse to hear it now. Gratuitous, in fact. He didn't need to say it and I'm not sure it's an accurate description. I was earnest and diligent. Maybe my wry humor was lost on him or it could be possible what he said was true back then. It makes sense that it could have been. I'd learned not to care too much and gradually have unlearned it, which is where I am now. Marino wasn't trying to be cruel. He didn't mean anything.

"I'll look right now." He's unusually cordial to whoever he's talking with. "Because I'm sitting in a damn parking lot. No, I don't mean it literally. Why the sudden urgency?" A pause. "Yeah he got there about an hour before I did. A few uniforms were there. No, not inside with him, they wouldn't have been. Why?" A longer pause. "Like I've said I can't stop him from being the Lone Ranger . . . It's looking like that. Tox will confirm. Right. Bleach." He ends the call and says to me, "That was kind of weird."

I remember the opened pack of Clove gum in my hands. "I think it's pretty stale," I comment, and the anger is gone as if it were never there.

He shrugs. "Hit me twice."

I peel the wrappers off two sticks as hard as cardboard. They crunch when he bites down on them.

"The commissioner," he says as he chews, opening something on his phone, staring long and hard at it. "Help yourself to the gum if you want." His voice is different and distracted. "There's plenty more where that came from. I order it off the Internet."

"The Lone Ranger?" I inquire as he closes whatever he was looking at and drops his phone into his lap.

"I don't really want to talk about it." He goes on to talk about it anyway. "Machado." He tells me the problem started late last year when Cambridge Police Commissioner Gerry Everman mentioned that Marino is one of the best detectives the department has ever had and the word passed down through the ranks.

If that wasn't enough reason for jealousy there were a record number of letters of commendation from victims and witnesses Marino has worked with, and of course he wasn't quiet about it. The more hostile Machado got, the more Marino pushed back. Finally there was a "situation" with a woman that began around last Thanksgiving.

"The straw that broke it," Marino summarizes.

"Someone you were fighting over?"

"This hasn't got anything to do with me and no. I was seeing Beth Eastman until her daughter Julie got killed. The second Jersey victim who was shot when she was about to get on the ferry."

"You dated Beth in high school."

"Went steady and everything."

"She must be devastated."

"Her daughter was a real nice lady." He talks and chews gum at the same time. "The other day I heard a rumor his latest thing is he's trying to get on with the state police, wants to be an investigator assigned to the Middlesex County D.A.'s office." He's talking about Machado again. "If he does, it will be good riddance and my next pain in the ass, which probably is his motivation. He'll try to steamroll Cambridge and interfere with every homicide we get. Sort of what he's already doing on the inside. He was stupid as hell to tell Joanna that her husband was shot."

"I agree it wasn't a good idea to give her an important detail like that." I think about the guitars, their two cases on the bed and other items glowing whitish blue.

"And you know why he's making piss-poor decisions these days?" Marino says. "Because he wants people to side with him, not me. He's obsessed to the point it's crazy. If I turn up dead you know who to look for."

"You've mentioned that twice," I reply. "I hope you don't mean it literally."

CHAPTER 19

We pass the wrecked Smart car in the opposite lanes, crushed, the windshield caved in, the roof flattened. Glass and plastic are all over the road and I wonder if the driver is en route to the CFC.

"May as well be in a tin can." Marino doesn't want to discuss Machado anymore. "I don't understand why anyone would drive something like that."

"It's affordable."

"Yeah a real bargain if you're killed in it. Maybe get something bigger than a bread box. It's cheaper than a funeral."

"Rand Bloom will spare nothing, the end justifying the means." I want to make sure Marino takes the insurance investigator very seriously. "I expect more underhanded tricks and we need to be prepared and pro-active."

"Whenever you say *proactive* it makes me nervous."

"He's been finding out everything he can about us. Let's see what we can find out about him."

"Us? I think it's just you. I don't think he's interested in me," Marino says and I know what I'll do.

"He was in an accident or a fight," I reply.

"Yeah his face looks like someone hit him with a baseball bat. Get in line. Everybody who's ever met him probably wants to beat the shit out of him."

"Let's see what Lucy can dig up about him." An accident or an attack, and there should be a police report, a record of what happened somewhere.

"I think we get the drift," Marino says, and we've reached the end of the bridge and are stopping at a red light now. "Bloom's a shit stirrer, plain and simple. That's why some sleaze insurance company would hire him."

He opens an email and an attachment on his phone, perhaps what the commissioner mentioned to him moments earlier or it could be something new. The head of Marino's department is leaking information to him, and I'm reminded of what was easy for me to forget. Marino is one hell of an investigator. I wouldn't want him after me.

"TBP isn't considered sleazy by the general public," I tell him.

"The Biggest Pricks." He uses two fingers to enlarge whatever he's looking at on his phone's touch screen.

"I don't know what it stands for. The Best Policy comes to mind. If you look them up, it's a great place to work and they've won all kinds of awards."

"Give me a break."

The light turns green. We're moving again.

"It's a formidable insurer and well respected until you actually have a claim," I add. "Then you find out the hard way what they'll do to make sure you don't get what you've paid premiums for."

"Totally disgusting." Marino merges left onto Memorial Drive, and we're back in Cambridge. "What a perfect job for a dirtbag who doesn't give a damn about anybody and has no conscience," he says and he's right.

Jamal Nari's murder this morning didn't deter Bloom from his ongoing harassment of Joanna. In fact he escalated it.

"Obviously he targeted Mary Sapp too," Marino says. "Looks like he may have targeted someone else," he adds mysteriously.

"My question is the same. How does he find out this level of detail about people? How did he know Nari and his wife were dealing with Mary Sapp, that she was the Realtor for a house they wanted to rent?"

"All you got to do is tail someone, keep running into them some-where, to be diligent and focused as hell. Then he passed on info so the rental fell through, getting a dishonest Realtor to do his dirty work. She's happy to keep the deposit and avoid a problem. And who knows how she sweetened the pot."

"Someone in Bloom's position probably gets a lot of pots sweetened."

"Kickbacks, and it's just his good luck that Nari gets murdered."

"His wife loses him now she's going to lose the house," I reply and the Charles River Yacht Club is on our left, the MIT campus on our right, a lot of boats, brick and granite. "She can't stay in their apartment after what happened and suddenly she finds she has no place to go."

Joggers and cyclists crowd the fitness path flanking the river, and lush green trees cast spreading shadows. Rowers and scullers skim over the dark blue water, pumping hard, going fast, ending the day physically and with civility unlike what we're doing.

"A punk. A damn vulture picking on people who've already been vic-timized." Marino goes on to use other descriptive words and phrases that don't bear repeating, but the gist of what he says is true.

Rand Bloom is a thug whose bread and butter is harassment. While we don't know for a fact that he's been spying on me, I suspect he's been doing it since Johnny Angiers died in the woods six weeks ago. It could explain why Bloom was in my neighborhood this morning parked close to my house, and I think of the glint of light Benton saw from the backyard.

Possibly it was Bloom. He or maybe someone associated with him may have been spying or taking photographs of Benton and me during a personal moment to violate my privacy, to gather intelligence, to publicly embarrass. I can only assume the intention is to make sure it's not worth my while to defend what I determined about Angiers's death, and then I think of something else.

"What exactly went out over the radio about Nari's murder this morn-ing?" I ask.

"The address and that Angelina Brown, a resident in the house, saw a man collapsed on the driveway. I've got the transcript if you want to see it. Just sent to me," he adds and I wonder sent by whom. "When we stop I'll forward it to you."

"Did you hear the calls?" I ask.

"I was in the gym and didn't have my radio. Machado reached me by phone. After taking his sweet time. Why?"

"If Bloom was monitoring his scanner he would have heard any calls and recognized the address. He may have been only a couple blocks away. Certainly he was when you and I drove past his truck."

"He wasn't in it," Marino points out. "We don't know where the hell he was."

"If he were near my house he might have seen you pick me up. Did anything go out over the radio about that?"

"When I left my place I radioed that I was ten-eight, responding to Farrar Street."

"Did you in any way indicate you were picking me up and bringing me to the scene?" I ask.

"No. But it was out there that we had a ten-thirty-five."

"A major crime which generally means a homicide. If Bloom heard that, he had an idea what was going on. He may have been watching my house, especially since he somehow knows I'm supposed to be on vacation in Florida. Now it's really interesting for him. He gets to see if I respond to Nari's crime scene or if maybe I'm too busy doing other things."

I envision Benton's arms around me, kissing me. But I don't mention it. I think about Lucy buzzing the house, flying low enough to agitate trees and rattle windows. My mind rapidly sorts through any number of scenes that I wouldn't want photographed and made public.

"Why would he bother?" Marino asks.

"My guess is he's looking for anything at all that might impeach me. It doesn't take much if you plant the right detail and it goes viral on the Internet. I'm no good to anyone if I'm not perceived as credible."

"If what you're saying is true he's more industrious than the damn CIA."

"I'm puzzled by Machado though," I have to say. "If he's so competitive with you then why did he bother to call you while you were in the gym?"

"He knew he'd get there first, have a huge head start working the case. It's like inviting someone to a party late and then ignoring them so they feel like shit. These days he does anything he can to make me look bad and to make himself look better."

"It appears he also was sending you information as he got it, at least for a while," I point out.

"Not him. It wasn't him doing it." Marino doesn't tell me who but I have a feeling I know.

The commissioner is Marino's ally, and that bodes poorly for Machado and tells me something else. Gerry Everman has a problem. I have a feeling he's using Marino to take care of it. My seven-story titanium-skinned building is up ahead, squat with a domed glass roof, and I wonder which members of my staff have waited for me and how I can graciously sidestep socializing and indulging in cannolis. There isn't time.

"I suspect that Bloom assumed when you responded to Dorchester and requested a Boston PD backup that I would show up too," I add. "He had just passed us in his pickup truck. You slowed down to let him go by and I have no doubt he saw us. Then he would have heard you radio the dispatcher to run his plate."

I'm sure I'm right and wish I weren't, and I'm certain the ruthless insurance investigator has an arsenal of dirty tricks I've yet to see. What else has he photographed? What other details of my personal life has he learned, and what will turn up on the Internet? Does he work alone? Who else is he involved with? He tailed Nari and photographed a drug deal, it seems. Maybe Bloom has drug connections.

There's no telling what he's into but he must deal with a lot of claims that have to do with real estate. Injuries and deaths in residences, in office buildings and on construction sites. Has he conspired with Mary Sapp before now and what about the Patty Marsico case, the Realtor murdered last Thanksgiving in Nantucket? It occurs to me that everything we're dealing with right now has happened in the past seven months.

"Why would Bloom go to so much trouble?" Marino turns off Memorial Drive onto a side street that leads to my back parking lot.

"To work on me, to wear me down," I answer. "Clearly I'm a problem for him in ways I don't realize."

"He may be a problem in ways we haven't realized too," Marino says. "I'm going to show you something."

HE NOSES THE SUV in close to the tall black security gate at the back of my bullet-shaped building.

"Obviously he knows about the kid," Marino says as we stop in front of the tall black privacy fence barricading my parking lot, a host of big antennas and satellite dishes on the MIT rooftops surrounding us. "You remember him?"

He moves his phone close so I can see a photograph of a skinny young man with long red hair, black sweatbands and shoes, black tennis shorts and shirt. He's midflight slamming a tennis ball behind his head, birddogging a lob before it bounces twice, a Roger Federer kind of move, probably a photograph from a news story. Leo Gantz. I almost can't believe it.

"The one you threatened this morning?" In fact I'm incredulous.

"Using a leaf blower right there next to Bloom's pickup truck," Marino says.

I think back to the insinuations the insurance investigator made to Mary Sapp. *There's the not so trivial problem of why Joanna really quit her job,* he said and it was obvious he knew about the fifteen-year-old boy's accusations.

"Good God," I mutter. "He knows about Leo because at some point he talked to him."

"You got that right and trouble's brewing. Gerry just sent me this picture and asked if he looked familiar, if I've seen him around Cambridge. Apparently Leo does yard work in Cambridge, Somerville, in your area. Gerry said Machado's going to call me with an update, that the information needs to come from him." When he says that, I know what's happening.

The commissioner has information but is insisting Machado be the one who shares it with Marino. It's a setup, an old bureaucratic ploy. If you want a problem person off the case or out the door make him the messenger of his own bad news. Then the troops don't go after their leader. Whatever has happened, Gerry Everman has no intention of taking the blame. Sil Machado is about to quit or get furloughed, which is the same as being fired except it won't stop him from finding another job somewhere. In fact, the commissioner will probably recommend him.

"You going to open this thing?" Marino asks.

We're sitting before my shut gate of black high tensile steel, its pales terminating in triple-pointed splayed spear tips that are a visual deterrent if nothing else. I open the car door and it's not the first time I've forgotten that Marino doesn't have a remote control. He no longer works for me or has keys or a fingerprint scanned into ergonomic locks, and I enter my code. The black metal gate lurches awake. It begins sliding open on its track. I get back in the SUV.

"I'm still trying to adjust." I open the glove box.

"I didn't leave yesterday. It's been over a year." He loves to think he's missed.

"And you worked for me for more than a decade." I pull out the bag of pennies. "Old habits die hard." That's as much as I'll say about how I'm personally handling his not being my head of investigations anymore.

I've never told him that some early mornings I still find myself pausing by his old office to see if he wants coffee.

"Your spot's empty. You mind?" He drives past employee cars and white vans and crime scene trucks, not waiting for permission.

"These need to go to Ernie." I indicate the pennies Benton packaged as evidence. "Or if you initial them I'm happy to take care of it."

"Shiny like new even though they're nineteen-eighty-one. I think we know why."

"What we need to know is who," I reply.

"You got a Sharpie? The date on them must mean something," he says.

"Or we're supposed to think it does."

He initials the Baggie and hands it back to me. I look at seven pennies too bright to be so old. The person who placed them on my wall knows exactly how to hurt me.

MY PARKING PLACE IS designated by a 1 painted white on blacktop directly to the right of the massive rolling bay door, heavy-duty welded steel, flat gray with no windows. Usually it's retracted when the weather is nice, and next to it is a pedestrian door, also metal with no windows. I scan my left thumb to open the biometric lock.

I detect cigar smoke and Lysol as Marino and I enter a brightly lighted space big enough to hangar a jet, and I'm surprised by the Ferrari, Tour de France blue, the same color as Lucy's helicopter. It's parked in the middle of the epoxy-sealed concrete floor, and I've not seen it before but there can be no question whose it is. The process of elimination is simple when something costs more than most people's houses. I wonder why she hasn't mentioned her latest acquisition to me. My niece has been distant of late. Extremely busy, she says. Mostly we've traded voice mails.

"Maybe she got you a birthday present," Marino says.

"She did. A book." A first edition of Gaetano Savi's *Flora Italiana,* but I don't go into detail.

"A book? That's all?"

"It was plenty."

Lucy gave it to me early, on Mother's Day, because I love gardens, especially Italian ones. I've spent many hours lingering over the beautiful illustrations, remembering places Benton and I have been, the Villa d'Este and the Villa Gregoriana in Tivoli, the Borghese in Rome, the courtyards in Puglia on the Adriatic Sea.

"But not this, not a Ferrari. She wouldn't," I answer Marino literally, and the nonskid floor is damp, the odor of disinfectant stronger as we walk through.

"Afternoon!" Rusty and Harold call out cheerfully from the far end of the bay, putting out their cigars, saving what's left of them for later.

"Happy birthday, Chief! Except you're still here? When you going to Florida?"

"At the moment I have no idea," I raise my voice and it echoes inside the empty concrete space.

They're sitting in a corner to the left of the door that leads inside, the table covered with a red and yellow vinyl French country cloth centered by an arrangement of silk sunflowers, very Van Gogh and washable with a hose. I spot the white pastry box next to the Keurig on top of the hobbled stainless steel surgical cart, a wheel permanently stuck, sweeteners and powdered creamers in a bowl near a big steel sink. Several blue plastic chairs and a pitcher with a water filter have been added to what's come to be called La Morte Café, out of the way of biohazard traffic although it's really not the best idea to consume beverages or food in here. But people do. I'm guilty of it.

We eat, drink and smoke and let the fresh air and sunlight in when we can, when it's not raining or frigid winter. Life struggles to assert itself in a place of death. Downtime in the bay is a way to cope after ugly scenes and autopsies. I miss smoking because it allowed me to check out for a few minutes. I take a coffee or tea now instead. I chat with staff. Sometimes I sit here alone to clear my head.

"You don't need to put out your cigars for my benefit." I say it to Rusty and Harold every time, and it doesn't matter.

They always behave like children caught in the act.

CHAPTER 20

Don't MIND IF I DO." Marino lights a cigarette. "And how are Cheech and Chong today? Miss me yet?"

With his long gray hair and funky clothes Rusty could pass for an old hippie but Harold in his proper suits and ties certainly couldn't, and neither of them looks Hispanic. Right now they're covered up in protective white Tyvek. I notice the stainless steel two-body carrier parked against a wall, the gallons of Lysol disinfectant, Dawn detergent and a nontoxic degreaser on the top tray.

My attention lands on a wooden handle with its large steel head that's missing its mop and a six-gallon yellow bucket with a wringer. The gray melamine storage cabinets are closed and shiny, the red biohazard trash cans emptied and as I get close to the Ferrari I see that there are water spots all over it. Unusually elongated, a four-seater with titanium rims and beefy gray calipers, it has a long sloping nose and a roomy boot. The grille and prancing horse are blacked out. I peer through a tinted window at a lot of carbon fiber and quilted Cuoio leather.

"It sounds like Mach two when she cranks it up." Rusty raises his voice. "A roomy backseat, six-hundred-and-fifty horsepower and all-wheel drive. She can haul passengers in the snow in that thing."

Lucy's idea of a practical car I suppose, and it occurs to me that she must have been planning to pick up Sock in it. That seems a long time ago but it's not been six hours since the ground beneath me opened like a trapdoor. I'm still free-falling with no idea what might happen next except I have a feeling the plans won't include a vacation in Florida, not tonight, not in the morning. I haven't heard from Benton since I called him about Machado, and I wonder what Lucy is doing and if she's made progress on the computers from Farrar Street.

"What was the problem in here?" I ask because I know there was one.

I walk to the table as Rusty and Harold pluck half-smoked cigars out of a Bruins ashtray.

"You sure you don't mind?" they both say at once.

"I never do and don't know why you ask. I'd smoke cigars but I'd inhale."

"You learn to roll the smoke around in your mouth like a fine wine."

"If it's smoke I guzzle. It's not about learning, which is why I stay away. Lucy probably won't thank you for getting water on her car but she shouldn't park that in the bay," I add. "Why did she?"

"Maybe because you weren't here," Rusty says.

"I'm a school principal now?"

"She's lucky if it's only water that got on it," Marino says.

"We told her it was a bad idea just like we always do," Harold replies.

"She never listens," Rusty says. "Probably because the bay seems normal to her. I'm guessing her garage at home is about this size. Well, I hope the inside of her car doesn't stink to high heaven. It was damn awful in here a while ago and some of it was just inches from the tires."

"A leaky body bag," Harold explains, and he and Rusty tend to talk in counterpoint like a Gregorian chant. "The seventy-three-year-old lady who rigged up her car with a hose, killed herself with CO? She lived alone and did it in the garage."

"The case from Brookline," I recall.

"She wasn't found for a while. Nothing makes you want a cigar more than a decomp. It's not true you get used to it."

"Doesn't bother me. I don't even notice." Marino opens the pastry box and picks out a cannoli to prove his point. "Peanut butter? Where the hell's the chocolate chip?"

"The same funeral home we've had trouble with." Rusty sips a coffee in a cheap paper cup, surplus military Bryce buys in bulk. "They use the crappiest bags I've ever seen. They all leak like a faulty bladder sling. A steady drip all the way into the cooler."

"Stunk up the entire bay and the receiving area. Not to mention the cooler."

"Let me guess. Meadows Mortuary." Marino taps an ash and bites into the cannoli, flakes of pastry drifting to the floor.

"I don't know what to do about it," Harold says. "We've even tried supplying them with our pouches but they don't bother using them."

"Probably turn around and sell them on eBay. Same old, same old." Rusty directs this at Marino. "Nothing's changed since you left except I don't mind coming to work now."

"What you do about it"—Marino talks as he chews, licking his fingers, wiping them on his sweatpants—"is transport the damn bodies your lazy ass selves and then you don't have the problem. Instead of sitting here drinking coffee and smoking cigars and eating pastries."

"The cannolis are for the Chief. Nobody made a trip to Mike's with you in mind."

"Very kind of you," I reply.

"To give credit where it's due, it was Bryce's idea and he picked them up."

"And I'm most appreciative. Maybe later?"

"This makes how many cars she's got?" Marino points the cannoli at the Ferrari.

"I've lost count," I reply.

"Can I make you a coffee?" Harold asks me, and by now I know who was waiting here until I got back. "I'm talking to the Chief and not to you," he says to Marino.

"No thanks. Not right now," I reply as I notice there are only four cannolis in the box, five before Marino helped himself.

Harold, Rusty and Bryce were throwing a small party. I'm touched.

"I don't drink your swill." Marino is done with the pastry and back with the cigarette.

"We're not offering."

"Be careful or he'll give you a parking ticket." The joke is always the same. "He'll arrest you for littering or disturbing the peace."

"Can I see your badge, pretty please?"

"Watch out. He has a gun." The Rusty and Harold show continues.

"A damn big one." Marino crushes out the cigarette on the floor as he blows smoke out of the side of his mouth.

He digs cigarette butts from a pocket, drops all of them into the trash.

"We got two cases that just came in from Memorial. MV fatalities not far from here on the Longfellow Bridge," Rusty lets me know.

"I believe we just drove past the accident."

"Anyway, I told Lucy not to park in here." A spurt of flame and Harold relights Rusty's cigar, then his own and I recognize the woody black cherry fragrance of the Bahamian tobacco they like. "Someone scrapes it with a stretcher and imagine what that would cost?"

"BMS is on its way to pick up the drowning from Lincoln," Rusty says, and the acronym is unfortunate.

Bean Mortuary Services. The irreverent comments about the name and its acronym are predictable.

"Kids horsing around a pool at a big house no one's living in," he says. "That and drinking. They're jumping on the pool cover like a trampoline and of course it pulls away from its anchors. Her feet go out from under her and she slams the back of her head on the concrete edge. The little assholes she was with didn't do a damn thing to help. They left her there in the pool, didn't even bother to pull her out, which I can't understand at all. How do you leave someone in the pool? She was on the bottom of it when we got there early this morning after a Realtor found her."

"The kids she was with didn't alert anyone?" I ask.

"Apparently not. Luke says she had a closed skull fracture that was survivable. What killed her is she drowned."

Rusty falls silent for a moment, his mouth set hard as he stares off. He tightens the bandana around his head and won't look at anyone. They went to the scene and transported the body here and it bothers him.

"Fourteen years old and no one noticed she wasn't home all night?" He picks up the cigar and puffs on it. "These days I blame everything on the parents."

"For good reason," I reply.

"When I was coming along if I got in trouble I couldn't leave my room."

"I suspect that happened often."

"You know what I'm saying, Chief."

"I certainly do. Is Luke still here? I didn't notice his car in the lot."

"He and Anne carpooled this morning."

"What they're doing isn't carpooling," Marino says. "And what she's doing is friggin' stupid."

"She knows herself," I reply.

She also knows Luke, an extremely attractive Austrian who is allergic to committed relationships and has a craving for affairs.

"What can we do for you, Chief?" Rusty asks me. "I'm sorry about your plans getting screwed up. If anybody deserves a nice relaxing trip it's you and Benton."

"The Nari case. I want to take a look before we release him. Do we have a funeral home yet?"

"Not that I know of." Rusty and Harold push back their chairs.

"Finish your cigars and coffee first," I tell them, and Marino and I head toward the door that leads inside.

"She bought another Ferrari and didn't say anything to you?" he asks me.

"So it appears."

"She and Janet getting along okay?"

"Why do you ask?"

"Sometimes people spend money when they aren't happy," he says as his cell phone rings.

I don't reply that my niece buying a supercar is like someone else buying a bicycle. She really is that rich from computer technologies she's invented and sold since she was a teenager. Lucy is a genius. She's difficult, quixotic and has been fired from or forced out of every job she's ever had except for the one with me, which she doesn't do for pay. I couldn't love her more, like a daughter, and have since her complicated life began in Miami where she was totally neglected by my sister, who I owe a call. Dorothy left me a message yesterday wishing me a happy birthday. She usually gets the date wrong.

"What? No way." Marino is on his phone. "Yeah I'm with her right this minute." His eyes are locked on me and I can tell by his terse tone that he's talking to Machado. "You don't need to call her yourself. I'm standing ten feet from her. Where is he and where the hell are you?" He listens and gets angrier, then says, "You called them and didn't mention it to me first? You did it on your own?" He's pacing furiously. "You know what? You're out of control. Or maybe you're brain-dead . . . Did you really just say that?"

THE DOOR THAT LEADS inside my building opens.

"Well maybe I will," Marino retorts, his earpiece flashing blue, and as angry as he is it ought to flash red. "Don't you respond there and do one more damn thing until we get this sorted out."

Lucy is here and it's not to say hello. In her black flight suit, she's busy with an iPad, her strong pretty face serious and intense. Before I can ask her what has happened, Benton is behind her dressed for work in a charcoal pin-striped suit, white shirt and gray silk tie. The two of them must have been together, probably in her cyber crime lab. She would have seen me on her closed-circuit video camera displays, and then Bryce walks out the door next.

If anybody deserves a nice relaxing trip it's you and Benton, Rusty just said to me, and neither he nor Harold mentioned that my husband is here. His reason isn't social.

"What is it?" I ask everyone.

"Leo Gantz." Marino is off the phone and looks like he might explode. "This is total bullshit!"

"He just confessed to Jamal Nari's murder," Bryce announces excitedly as if he won the lottery. "It's already trending, *expelled student confesses to murder of controversial music teacher*." He holds up his phone to show me the Yahoo headline. "We've got company. Oh Harold? Rusty? Hello? Is anybody working?" he sings. "We got a pickup. The drowning! Gracie Smithers!"

He pushes a green button on the wall. The sound of an electric motor, and the slatted steel door begins to roll up.

"Leo Gantz called Cambridge PD and us," Benton says to me. "Unfortunately he also tweeted it."

"Just confessed?" I don't understand.

"Not even half an hour ago!" Bryce is energized as if he's about to break into a dance, dressed in his typical uniform of slim fitted jeans, a baggy sweater and red leather high-tops.

About the time the commissioner texted Leo Gantz's photograph to Marino and said for him to expect a call, I realize. That call was from Machado, who has taken the bait, and I look at Benton, trying to read his face. The more impervious he gets, the more certain I am that he has information the rest of us don't. I watch the gears in motion, everything moving right before my eyes, headed to an inevitable conclusion like the game Mouse Trap. Sil Machado is done and not because of whatever he said to Marino on the phone. The call was gratuitous and Marino doesn't know it.

"Already CNN and Fox have left messages plus a producer from *Sixty Minutes*," Bryce gushes. "Look at all the emails piling up?" He holds out his phone again, his boyish face beaming because there's nothing my chief of staff likes more than drama. "This is so huge!"

"Please don't talk to the media right now. Don't answer their emails or calls," I say to him. "So you were already here at the CFC when this happened?" I direct this at Benton. "Why?"

"Cambridge PD requested our assistance," he says as if Marino isn't standing here and I didn't ask what I did. "This was a couple of hours ago, the first time they contacted us about it."

"They asked you twice?" Bryce says. "You big bad Bureau boys playing hard to get these days . . . ?"

"Contacted you about what?" I inquire.

"We won't go into it here," Lucy says and whatever Benton is involved in, it includes her.

"You in on this too?" Marino snaps at her, his face purplish red, his eyes wide and glaring.

He's so angry he's scary, the kind of rage where the brain shuts down like a dog in a fight. I look past him at the widening space in the opening bay door as it occurs to me that there is other cyber evidence besides the computers recovered from the house on Farrar Street. I think of the tweeted poem from Morristown. Then someone tweeted this morning, an allusion to Nari's murder before it happened. Hard drives and security videos have been seized. They're probably inside Lucy's lab and she and Benton have been going through them.

I look at Marino until he looks back. I give him a subtle gesture, the slightest shake of my head. *No*, I'm telling him. *You don't need to react like this. Your war with Machado is over.* He doesn't read my mind. He's not looking at me now.

CHAPTER 21

A VAN DRIVES INSIDE, PATENT leather shiny black.

Bean Mortuary Services is here for the drowning, a fourteen-year-old girl who shouldn't have died. For an instant I wonder about the friends she was with and what the rest of their lives will be like.

I used to get angry over stupid deaths. I was judgmental about drunks, drug addicts, people standing up in the back of a truck or jumping into lakes and pools when they are under the influence and don't know how to swim. The emotions have settled into a deep place with me, not volatile anymore but heavy like gravity. Mostly I feel sad. Mostly I think what a waste. No one starts out in life imagining it will end on one of my steel tables. It's not what people script when they dream about what they'll be and who they'll love.

In the huge square of the retracted door I see the parking lot. It's in shadows, the sky dusky blue, and in the few minutes I've been here more cars have left, employees gone for the day. Few people who work at the CFC exit the building through the bay. It's the autopsy staff who does and I'm always puzzled by forensic scientists who don't want to see a case they're working on. They don't want to be anywhere near dead bodies or even know the details. My entire DNA section wants nothing to do with my building's lower level, what most of them still call the morgue. Some of them call it Hell.

"The confession is extremely problematic any way you look at it," Benton is explaining. "I've been asked to help with that as well."

One of his areas of expertise is confessions, true and false ones.

"Machado!" Marino thunders. "He can't do this! Don't you get it? Godammit, Benton! He can't do this and you need to talk to Gerry!"

"You were asked to help in the investigation earlier or just now?" I pin Benton down because he's being typically evasive.

"Both," he says. "Machado called me directly."

"He had no right to do that," Marino says, and that really is the point.

It would be the equivalent of one of my doctors sending out evidence to the FBI labs without clearing it with me first.

"You've got to call the commissioner," Marino repeats and he's almost yelling.

"What is it you've been told?" I ask Benton.

"Hell yeah. What do you know about my case that I damn don't?" Marino says.

"Leo Gantz claims Nari attacked him this morning, hitting him in the head with a tennis trophy. Leo came back later and shot him. This supposedly occurred inside the apartment on Farrar Street." Benton isn't going to react to Marino's tantrum, and I've given up trying to send signals.

Marino's rage will run its course. Then he'll find out it wasn't merited.

"Of concern is that certain details haven't been publicized yet," Benton says. "I'm not aware it's been released to the media that he was shot."

"It wasn't on the Internet until Leo Gantz tweeted it," Lucy confirms, and I instantly think about Joanna Cather.

She knows we suspect her husband was killed with a gun. She asked me about it, and I wonder if she talked to Leo after Marino and I left her apartment. I have a feeling she did, and I envision the young man with the leaf blower, the quiet anger on his face, the way he didn't back down when

Marino threatened him. Leo Gantz seemed to enjoy the confrontation. He liked the attention even if it was negative, and now he's just gotten a whole lot more, every major news outlet on his trail. By this time tomorrow his name will be a household word.

"He tweeted from his personal account." Lucy's left index finger flicks the iPad's display, scrolling through data as two men open up the back of the black van.

Josh and Diego Bean, in jeans, button-up cotton shirts and sweater vests. Identical twins I can't tell apart, they run their removal service out of their home, are on call twenty-four/seven and consider themselves an ambulance service for the dead. It's a new way of doing business, civilized, minimalist, just gloves and casual attire, and a vehicle that doesn't look like a hearse.

Rusty and Harold have gone inside to get the body of Gracie Smithers. Bryce has left too, propelled by his latest adrenaline rush. I look over at La Morte Café, at the cigars put out and the pastry box. Next I look at Lucy's Ferrari and the mortuary van on its rear bumper. Now and then I'm struck by the absurdity of things.

"The IP is his wireless network at home in Somerville," my niece is saying. "Earlier tweets, and there are a lot of them, indicate an unstable, angry person who mouths off to everyone including the president and the pope. I mean it literally."

I notice her left index finger is missing the large gold signet ring she always wears. It has an eagle on it and has been in her partner's family for more than a hundred years. Lucy never takes it off. She and Janet were flying together this morning when they buzzed the house but Lucy isn't wearing the ring. She must have driven here from the Norwood Airport where she recently built a hangar for her helicopter, which also is new, and I wonder where Janet is and what is going on with them.

"I didn't notice injuries at the scene that might be consistent with his being in an altercation this morning," I say to Marino. "He had no abrasions or contusions on his hands, for example. But I'm going to look carefully."

"Luke didn't point out anything like that," Benton says, and he must have witnessed Jamal Nari's autopsy or asked about it.

"Because there's nothing to point out," Marino retorts. "Leo Gantz sure as hell didn't look hurt when we saw him late this morning, right?"

"He also had a cap on," I reply. "If he had an injury to his head we might not have seen it."

"The kid's lying. You need to look at him too," Marino says to me. "Supposedly Nari whacked him in the head? I'm betting the kid whacked himself in the head, that it's self-inflicted. He probably did it right before he started tweeting his fake story about committing murder."

"I'll examine his injuries if it's helpful," I reply.

"I'm *officially* requesting your assistance," he says snidely.

"The question is where to do that." I ignore his obvious dig at Machado and have given up on signals.

Marino continues punching away at a paper tiger, and it's an inevitable process. It's not up to Benton to disavow him of his assumption that Machado is still working the Nari case or maybe any case. By now I can fill in the blanks about what is going on. Benton is well acquainted with most police chiefs around here, and he certainly knows the one in the city where we live. When Machado took it upon himself to invite the FBI into the Nari investigation, I have no doubt the first thing Benton did was to contact Gerry Everman. The reason was simple. The invitation wasn't Machado's to offer. Added to that is what I said to Benton over the phone about the possibility that someone used bleach.

Machado was inside the apartment on Farrar Street for a while without a warrant. It appears the victim's property was tampered with, the scene staged and a possible attempt was made to eradicate DNA.

"Why don't you wait for her." Marino is talking about me, and it isn't a question. It's a directive. "You can drive her." He continues to boss Benton around.

"I'm happy to but that's not the plan." His reply doesn't invite debate. "A plan is in place that can't be ignored. I'm not the one who instigated it. Your department did."

"Machado's not my friggin' department," Marino fumes.

"I can take her," Lucy says, and I think back to the last time I was with Janet and her.

"Not in that thing." Marino jabs his index finger at the Ferrari. "You're not rolling up to Leo Gantz's house in that."

I also can't pull up in a CFC van or truck. The media and the neighbors will think there's been another violent death. Rumors will fly. I don't want my presence to make matters worse.

"You need to simmer down, Pete," Benton says quietly, and that's as close as he's going to get.

He's not going to let on that Marino doesn't need to worry about Machado anymore.

"You're coming with me," Marino tells Lucy. "All the high-tech electronics kids have today? I don't want even a thumb drive left behind. You're riding with me and we'll see what we find."

"Sure." Her green eyes are hard. She doesn't look happy.

FOUR WEEKS AGO I made kalamata and porcini risotto, and tortas fritas. Italian and Argentine vegan with a very nice Oregon pinot noir, and Lucy and Janet spent a long languid evening with me in front of the fire.

I remember the smell of wood burning. New England was still chilly, but the yard was fragrant and full of color, the Saturday night of Mother's Day weekend, I recall. Benton was out of town. Lucy, Janet and I talked for hours and they seemed fine. My niece had the signet ring on then. I would have noticed if she wasn't wearing it.

She is extremely buff but thinner. Her rose gold hair is tucked behind her ears, longer and a little shaggy. When she's not in a good space she doesn't eat enough or bother with her hair salon. Something is on her mind and she doesn't like Marino ordering her around. She's not going to do what he says.

"Sure, I'll see what's there. That's assuming you have a search warrant." Lucy knows he doesn't.

He couldn't possibly have one this fast if Leo Gantz confessed to the murder within the past hour, and I've been with Marino all afternoon. I haven't overheard him on the phone saying anything about searching Leo's house or even questioning him. It would have come up eventually in the investigation but with all that's gone on there hasn't been time.

"When you get a warrant let me know," she continues. "And I'll be happy to help."

She's saying she's not going anywhere with him. Lucy doesn't want to be used as a weapon in his battle with Machado and I don't blame her. She may also know that it's a battle already over, no winner or loser really. There can't be in something like this.

"It's important that Machado doesn't start interrogating Leo with nobody else there." Benton isn't defensive or overbearing as he again reminds Marino that Machado has formally requested the assistance of the FBI in the Nari homicide investigation.

The official machinery is in motion. Benton rubs it in. Agents have been assigned and deployed, and strategic discussions are under way, he says. It's a process that's hard to stop and Marino doesn't have that kind of authority.

"He's a loose cannon." Marino is very loud.

"Don't give him reason to say you are," Benton warns. "He's asked that we help with the Nari investigation and respond to the Gantz house and that has to be dealt with."

"And I'm unrequesting the FBI." Marino is incensed. "He shouldn't have asked for assistance without clearing it with me."

"I believe the appropriate party to clear it with would have been your commissioner," Benton says.

"So the Feds will take over? They probably already have, right?"

Benton says nothing. He's in his email, on his phone, typing. It's a ruse and Marino falls hard for it.

"What the hell is wrong with him?" he exclaims.

"Let me see what I can do," Benton says, and it's not true. "We need to get this taken care of." He continues to mislead, the situation already taken care of but Marino is none the wiser.

He's too angry to pick up on subtleties and has a decision to make. Marino has to choose where his loyalty lies, and I can see him struggle. I see it in his eyes and in the flexing of his jaw muscles. He wants Machado gone and he hates that he wants it. He has the power to make Machado gone but he's trying to persuade the commissioner and Benton to do it, and they won't, not directly, and it's already done anyway. Marino needs to do the right thing and tell the truth. That's what Benton is waiting for, and I think back to what Marino said about having Machado's back and keeping his secrets.

"I'm not sure there's ever been a time when we were asked and then the requesting department changed its mind," Benton seems to muse. "Paperwork has started. Calls have been made. This is extremely difficult and I don't want to create any exposure. Legally, I mean."

Then the door leading inside my building opens again. Rusty and Harold roll out the pouched body, a small shape in its black cocoon. Wheels make a quiet clatter as the steel carrier is guided down the ramp, the two autopsy techs on either side of it like pallbearers. Past Lucy's car. To the back of the van. Jen Garate appears in the square opening of the bay door. The Bean brothers greet her enthusiastically as if it's nothing to be in a bay with a dead body, as if they just ran into each other in a coffee shop or a grocery store.

"This is how he wants it to go? Fine," Marino says. "I'm texting him right now that he'd better not start without me." He does it as he's saying it. "He damn better just wait until I roll up. He doesn't know shit and he's going to totally ruin this case because he's got something to prove." His thumbs are busy typing.

"I'd suggest that you're careful what you put in writing," Benton says.

"Screw him."

"I'm heading out for the day," I hear Jen Garate say, and she looks at me and waves. "If you need anything you know where to find me," she calls out cheerfully. "Happy Birthday! Her scene photographs have been uploaded if you want to see them."

She means Gracie Smithers's have been.

"But remember you're not supposed to be working!" she adds as she walks outside into the parking lot, heading to her sporty car, a fiery red Scion.

"This isn't helpful, Pete. Be careful and stop texting," Benton says.

"You're just noticing it isn't helpful? You don't know the half of it."

The Bean brothers lift the pouch off the carrier. I can tell by the way they handle it that Gracie Smithers doesn't weigh much and is in full rigor mortis. They're gentle as they place her on a padded quilt in the back of the van and belt her in with Velcro straps attached to the floor. They're talking in low voices that are hard to hear.

"Holy smoke." I make out what Harold says. "Well that's going to make things hit the fan."

I pick up the words *lawsuit* and *congressman,* and Benton is very calm with Marino who says in no uncertain terms he wants Machado pulled off the case. Marino refuses to work with him on any case. Then he throws Machado under the bus.

CHAPTER 22

SIL MACHADO IS SLEEPING with my firearms examiner Liz Wrighton. But that's not the worst of it.

Their professional involvement changed in a manner that is strictly against protocol and is possibly criminal. She moves his cases to the head of the line. She goes out of her way to accommodate, and he returns the favor by giving her information she's not supposed to have, details that could taint her objectivity. Marino claims he knows all this for a fact, and his wrath is dissipated just like that.

"I'm sorry, Doc," he says to me and he looks deflated and overheated. "This wasn't the way I meant for you to hear it."

I don't believe he ever meant for me to hear it, and he should have told me. He should have told me when he first found out. The *problem with a woman,* as he put it earlier today, is this particular one works for me. He's said not a word until now. I'm reminded that his allegiance has shifted away from the CFC and from me. He's a cop again. He walks, talks and thinks like one.

"Is it true?" Benton asks me and I have no doubt he already knows.

"This is the first I've heard of it," I reply with a quietness that belies my anger.

The black van beeps as it backs out of the bay, and Rusty and Harold head our way, guiding the empty carrier. I push the button for the re-tracted door. The motor is loud as the steel panels begin to roll down. I watch the square space get smaller, closing out the dusky sky and the white crime scene vehicles in the parking lot. It's almost six o'clock. Most people are gone. I focus on the metallic blue Ferrari and remember what Marino said about people spending money when they're unhappy. I wonder what else has been kept from me.

Wheels softly rattle as Rusty and Harold walk past us, heads bent, giving us privacy, and knowing them they've heard enough. They push the empty carrier inside, the far wall heavy and solid with stainless steel. I lean against the metal windowless door, holding it open. I ask them to move Jamal Nari's body out of whatever cooler it's in.

"You want him at your station?" They pause by the floor scale and won't look at Marino.

They wouldn't approve of what he just did. They probably think it's hypocritical and unfair. As is true of the general male population here they're enamored of Liz, and Marino has had his share of indiscretions, serious ones that wouldn't have been ignored were he anybody else. He'll continue to be Cambridge's star detective only now he'll be unfettered. I'll probably have to fire Liz.

"Put him in the autopsy room but you can leave him as is on the tray," I tell Rusty and Harold. "I don't need him on the table. I'll be there in a few minutes. When I'm done I'll roll him back inside the cooler if the two of you would like to leave."

"If that's okay. We've got our bowling league tonight. A hair away from winning a trip to Vegas." They don't sound excited. What they just witnessed has made them subdued and in a hurry to get out of here.

"Good luck," I reply.

"Liz Wrighton? You're sure?" Benton asks Marino as I close the door.

I walk past everyone, down the ramp, over to the table with its red and yellow French country cloth. Straightening up and cleaning always calms me.

"Yeah I'm sure." Marino avoids looking anyone in the eye.

"What's your relationship with her? It's important I know." Benton already does.

"Nothing," Marino says. "I know her type and I'm not about to take a chance of fucking up cases or ending up in jail."

I empty the ashtray into the trash. Cigarette butts and what's left of the cigars smell dirty and stale.

"Would Machado say your relationship with her is nothing?" Benton asks.

"I don't give a shit what he says. It wouldn't be his first or last lie about me."

"You would deny it."

"I sure as hell would and he doesn't have a damn thing to prove his bullshit."

I run water in the sink and it makes a hollow drumming sound against stainless steel. Pulling cellophane off a new roll of paper towels, I rip off several sheets.

"Good. That's one problem we can cross off the list," Benton says, and it's not lost on me that Lucy is quiet.

I think of emails, of any indelicate communications. If there were any such exchanged between Marino and Liz, I have a feeling they would have disappeared from our server. Lucy is the system administrator and would protect him. She wouldn't hesitate to scrub his phone. I also have no doubt she would preserve damning emails relating to Machado. Lucy will defend her people at any cost.

"Liz Wrighton has already done the analysis. I suggest we have it done again so she isn't the one who testifies about it." Benton doesn't seem surprised by what has gone on.

He knows her reputation and I also suspect Lucy tipped him off. It's the sort of messiness she would find out. There's nothing she doesn't see if she decides to look. But if she's known for a while she didn't tell me. I'm trying not to be bothered by that. Running water splashes loudly as I rinse the ashtray, scrubbing it hard with my fingertips, the water very cold. I feel Lucy watching me.

Neither she nor Marino told me. For an instant I can't look at either of them. Just as quickly I'm over it. I dry the ashtray with a paper towel and return it to the table. I wipe off the plastic cloth. I pick up the pastry box and walk back up the ramp. I look at Lucy, and her green stare is unwavering. I see nothing in it that might tell me she feels she did anything wrong. I look at Marino and continue looking at him until he gives me his eyes. What's in mine should reassure him that I've already let it go.

Anger helps nothing. What's done is done. Now we move on. I open the door and lean against it. Soft lighting from inside illuminates the ramp, and the security guard behind her glass window smiles at me. Georgia Cruz is new. She was born in Georgia while her career Army father was stationed at Fort Benning, and she's good. I like her. She resumes typing on her computer, rolling her chair back to the 3-D printer inside her bulletproof glass-enclosed workspace, what people call The Fish Tank.

"Maybe you can pass it up the chain about him being compromised and have your *SAC* call Gerry Everman." Marino sounds slightly desperate.

He doesn't like being a snitch and I can imagine what he's thinking. If he couldn't work with Machado before, now he absolutely can't. Marino must have him completely out of the picture but the Cambridge police commissioner doesn't need to hear it from the Boston Division's Special Agent in Charge. A word from Benton would suffice and I'm sure that word was passed along hours ago. As I stand inside the bay with my husband, my niece and Marino, all of us congregated at the top of the concrete ramp near the open door, I watch the mouse get trapped.

Machado is the mouse and it's all played out. It's what Benton does. A simple plan with the end result that the young investigator takes the fall after Marino drops the dime on him. Marino assumes he caused everything to happen but in fact Machado's fate was decided earlier, possibly much earlier. There may have been discussions long before my phone call about the bleach. The rivalry and dirty secrets between Machado and Marino became destructive. One of them had to go.

"It's his fault he didn't recuse himself," Marino says to me, and I don't respond. "The minute you asked her to come in today and examine the bullet frag we recovered he had a chance to do the right thing and recuse himself. He's had chances for months. I kept waiting for him to do what was right."

"He should never have put himself in the situation to begin with." Lucy finally speaks. "And Liz shouldn't have either. But rules don't apply to her. They don't seem to apply to a number of people these days."

It's an ironical comment for my niece to make. She has no respect for rules and no trouble rationalizing anything she does.

"Unfortunately people being who and what they are, relationships happen," Benton replies and he should know.

When ours began we were working a homicide and he was married. We didn't recuse ourselves from anything. We didn't even try. We were smart enough not to get caught. The truth is none of us always does what's right or fair. But when it comes to Lucy, Benton, Marino and me what can always be counted on is that ultimately we will side with each other.

"We need to get things on track and I'll tell you what else isn't helpful." Marino's mood has dramatically shifted as if nothing has happened and he's in charge. "Suits and muscle heads in flak jackets. This is a psychological thing right now, Benton. A fifteen-year-old kid is admitting to something it's not possible he did."

"He's in a lot of trouble," Benton replies. "He's used to lying. Unfortunately for him, he's good at it which isn't unusual when kids have been abused."

"Maybe you can tell me exactly what Machado told you." Marino looks red faced and disheveled in his baggy Harley jacket and sweatpants, while Benton is impeccably dressed, unreadable and cool.

"Exactly this," Benton replies. "At around eight A.M. Leo got into a fight with Nari inside the apartment. Leo returned later and shot him. Afterward he dropped the gun into the sewer but conveniently can't remember which manhole cover he removed to do so."

"And he did that without a lifting tool," Marino says. "What? He pried open a hundred pounds of cast iron with his damn finger? Don't tell me you think there's any truth in this."

"It has to be taken seriously."

"I can tell you what he's tweeting," Lucy says. "He claims that all he did was go there to talk, to give Nari's wife a tennis trophy as a gift and he attacked him. He hit Leo in the head with it. So Leo came back later and shot him. Not one tweet," she says this to me. "Ten of them telling the story."

"A TENNIS TROPHY," I repeat. "It would be helpful if I can see it before I examine him."

"It never happened," Marino says, and I think of the apartment on Farrar Street.

I didn't see a tennis trophy or any sign of a struggle. I think of the guitars and the possible presence of bleach, details I'm betting Leo Gantz doesn't have a clue about. Who was inside that apartment? Who was it really and what was the person doing in there?

I text Anne. I ask if she's still in the building. I want to know what showed up in Nari's CT scans, if she saw anything unusual including gastric contents that Luke Zenner described as interesting.

"You need to keep in mind Leo's tweets were from his house, from its wireless network," Lucy continues to explain. "But not the one this morning that alluded to Jamal Nari's death before it happened. The IP for that is the Sheraton in Cambridge, the business center. The tweet was sent from one of their computers at nine A.M. Then it was retweeted like crazy," she adds as I read Anne's response.

She'll stop by the receiving area where I'm still holding open the door, leaning against it. I listen to Lucy explain that the tweet sent from the Sheraton at nine o'clock this morning was from the Twitter account that uses the name *Copperhead*. Maybe at some level I expected it. Now I have a better idea why Benton is here and what he and Lucy have been doing.

"In both cases a hotel computer in its business center was used," she says. "It made tracing the tweets a dead end because the IP and the machine access code belong to a computer that's used by the public, by guests in the hotel or any person wandering in to print their boarding pass or whatever."

"So you have no idea who *Copperhead* is?" I watch Anne emerge from the corridor, a long white lab coat flapping around her knees and a smile on her plain but pleasant face.

"I know who it's supposed to be," Lucy says.

CHAPTER 23

Georgia SLIDES OPEN HER window in the center of the bright white receiving area.

She says something to Anne as she walks through. Both of them laugh and Anne sasses her back, an inside joke that I don't hear as I listen to what Lucy is saying about the identity of *Copperhead*.

"It's a Twitter account belonging to Michael Orland, who died in February," she says and Marino looks amazed.

"The piano guy?" he exclaims. "I saw him on Leno right before he quit. Maybe it was *Idol*. It wasn't that long ago. I guess it could have been taped."

"That's a shame." Anne walks over to us.

"This Michael Orland was a plumber," Lucy says. "After he died someone hijacked his account."

"How do you know he's dead?" I ask.

"Twitter. His location, bio and contact info make it clear he's the Michael Orland who was a hospital homicide in Florida this past February," she says. "Six patients were given lethal doses of mivacurium chloride. There may have been others. A nurse was arrested and they're still exhuming the bodies of other patients who suddenly stopped breathing. He was from not far from here, New Bedford, was visiting Saint Augustine and had an appendectomy. Soon after, he died. He was single, no kids. It's a fairly typical example of it not occurring to anyone to delete a Twitter account. Some hackers have programs set up that do nothing but search for dormant users. Usually it means the person is dead or for some reason isn't going to notice. Those are good accounts to hijack."

"Whoever did that must have known details about him," Benton says. "There had to be a reason to pick his account."

I wonder if it was always called *Copperhead* and Lucy says yes.

"I suppose plumbers work with copper a lot," she adds. "Who knows why he picked it."

"Wouldn't you need the person's password to start tweeting as if you're them?" Anne asks.

"Knowing the password would be the easiest way," Lucy says. "But certainly not the only way. Scam pages, malware, insecure passwords."

Anne looks perplexed. She also looks happy, a light in her eyes that didn't used to be there. I notice her hair is long and there are blond highlights in it. All must be fine with Luke. She meets my eyes, waiting to hear what I need from her.

"Can you put Jamal Nari's CT scans up on the screen at my station?" I ask. "The essential ones of his injuries and anything else that might be significant."

"There are significant findings all right. Have you talked to Luke?"

"Not about details."

"What findings?" Marino asks.

"Put it this way, if he hadn't been shot he likely would have ended up here anyway," she says. "Do you want me to go into it now?"

"I don't." Not in front of everyone, and I'd rather see what she's alluding to and have a chance to think my own thoughts. "And please find Ernie. I believe he's still here. Perhaps he can meet me in the autopsy room so I can turn this over to him." I still have the Baggie of pennies in hand. "I'm sorry to hold you up. I know you're carpooling these days."

"Luke's gone. A dental appointment." She glances at the digital time display on a stainless steel cooler door. "I'm supposed to pick him up in an hour," she adds as Lucy moves next to me with her iPad.

She shows me the hijacked Twitter account called *Copperhead,* explaining that the avatar was recently changed to a fingerprint, black on white, what looks like an inked print on a ten-print card. The plumber from New Bedford tweeted 311 times until February 10, the day before he died. The tweets resumed some three months later when the account was used to send me the poem on Mother's Day. A month later *Copperhead* tweeted a second time. The Sheraton hotel is very close to here.

"I WOULDN'T BOTHER WITH IAFIS," Lucy says sarcastically, enlarging the avatar with her fingers.

"No pores, bifurcations, ridge endings, cores or anything." I point out there would be no characteristics to enter into the Integrated Automated Fingerprint Identification System or any other database. "There's no minutiae at all. It's not an inked patent print or a livescan."

"It's Photoshopped, fake, like someone's laughing at us," she says. "An image that's actually a logo someone dragged across a browser window onto a desktop."

She executes a search for us, entering the key words *fingerprint* and *logo.* A gallery of fingerprint designs appear on her iPad display. One of them is exactly like the *Copperhead* avatar.

"What's the point?" Marino says. "Assuming you think there is one."

"It's not identifiable," she replies. "It's generic. Someone thinks it's funny."

"A taunt," Benton agrees. "Taunts that are escalating."

"I guess what we're supposed to take from this is the hospital homicide in Florida has nothing to do with the shootings. His identity was stolen plain and simple," Marino decides, and every time he shifts his position, his foot touches the floor scale and a weight flickers on the digital display on the wall. "So we don't need to tie ourselves in knots about a dead plumber."

"For the most part that's right," Benton replies. "There's not going to be an obvious link between the shooter and this Twitter account. The killer isn't someone who died in Florida. But how and why the *Copperhead* account was hijacked is critical to know."

"I checked everyone Orland followed and those who followed him," Lucy says to me. "I did that when the poem was tweeted to you last month. A total of a hundred and six people, almost the same number as when he was alive. Some of them may not know he died and others probably didn't feel good about unfollowing someone who did. And a few of these people are dead too, his stepdad for example. He lived in Worcester and committed suicide a couple of years ago."

"Then he was a CFC case," I point out.

"That's right."

"Whose?" I have a bad feeling I know.

"Yours," she says. "A chemist who killed himself with cyanide."

I remember it. I can almost smell the bitter almond odor of his blood when I opened him up.

"We've also been reviewing the security camera recordings." Benton confirms what he and Lucy have been doing this afternoon. "Now we'll check again to make sure it wasn't Leo Gantz who entered the Sheraton and helped himself to a computer in the business center."

"Or the hotel in Morristown," Lucy adds. "The computer someone used there to tweet the poem last month. We've got that security recording too."

I think of the copper bullet, the frag, the pennies, all of it pitted from being polished in a tumbler. I don't see how there can be any doubt that the person sending the tweets is a killer who has used a sniper rifle to murder at least three people since late December. He probably has been on my property. *Copperhead* might be someone I know.

"So why would a kid confess to something like this?" Marino is asking Benton.

"There could be a number of reasons. Attention would be one. I recommend you get him to your department, into an interrogation room. Kay and I will meet you there when you're ready."

Benton wants to observe Leo Gantz behind one-way glass. He wants to watch while I examine his injuries and Benton doesn't want him to have a clue that anybody is looking.

"It's best you talk to him alone at his house first." Now Benton is coaching Marino. "He's going to be high from all of the attention, his limbic system in overdrive because his name is trending on the Internet. I suspect the phone in their house is ringing nonstop. And he's also going to be scared out of his mind. That's probably starting as we speak. It will be acute when you arrive. Aggression won't work with him. Don't bully."

"Are you telling me nobody's responded to his house yet?" Marino looks shocked. "Not Machado or your guys?"

"They haven't. There's a perimeter in the neighborhood to make sure he doesn't run. But it's invisible. Agents are out of sight and nobody's gone in or approached the residence. And Machado's not an issue. He won't be showing up anywhere."

"OK." Marino nods and suspicion shows in his eyes.

It's coming to him. There was never any real threat that Machado would run the case into the ground. Marino senses he was manipulated but he's not sure how or why or if it matters.

"When you talk to Leo, you need to be his friend," Benton continues to advise. "Can you do that? Don't bully him."

"Who says I bully?" Marino scowls.

"I'm telling you what will be effective. You need to treat him as if he's a victim. He'll respond to that because in his mind he's been mistreated and misunderstood. In his mind he's lost everything."

"The hell he has. He deserves to lose everything."

"Treat him like a victim, Pete. Even if you believe he isn't one," Benton repeats slowly.

CHAPTER 24

WORK AT THE CFC flows in a circle, logical and precisely planned, a thoughtful clinic, I like to think.

The first stop is the digital platform floor scale, high-tech with a low-tech measuring rod near the door where Benton, Lucy and I were talking to Marino before he left moments ago. After a weight and measurement, the newest case is accessioned at the security desk where I'm now standing, the box of cannolis in one hand, the sealed Baggie of pennies in the other.

"Would you like these or know someone who would?" I set the pastry box on the counter of Georgia's open window.

"They went to a lot of trouble to get those for you. What with this gridlock traffic and all."

"Yes and it would be a shame to waste them."

"Well I don't want to know how many points they are, and tomorrow morning I weigh in." She sighs as she opens the lid. "Why are you doing this to me, Doctor Scarpetta? You trying to sabotage Weight Watchers?"

"Never."

"Seven pounds and five to go."

"Congratulations. Do you like peanut butter?"

"Oh no." She groans. "The devil is here."

"Don't forget they need to be refrigerated."

"What are these?" Lucy asks about the pennies and I tell her.

"Why didn't you let me know?" She holds the coins up to the light.

"I just did."

"I'm talking about the minute you found them." She's serious and anger flashes.

"When you were buzzing the house?" I smile at her. "You were a little busy."

"The date's interesting." She returns the Baggie to me.

"I know."

1981. The year Lucy was born and I'm not going to discuss it in front of Georgia or anyone. Neighborhood kids playing a prank or a symbolic gesture for my birthday, and I'm reminded of how light of heart I was when this day started. Everything has turned heavy and savage. As the hours pass and events unfold, the coins burn brighter in my mind and I know the date on them isn't random.

On the ledge of the security desk outside the glass is the handwritten log, heavy and bound in black leather, a permanent record of every case since the medical examiner's system was established in Massachusetts. The large volumes go back to the 1940s and are stored in our records room along with hard copies of files that include DNA cards and in the old days toe tags. Now we use a RFID smart band embedded with a chip that is created on the 3-D printer. All I need is a handheld scanner to tell me who is inside our coolers and freezers.

"Can I help you with anything right now?" Benton is busy with his phone, his electronic tether, looking down at it, a strand of silver hair on his brow that he absently pushes away.

"What would you like to do?" I ask him.

"What I'd like to do? Sit on our balcony in Miami, look at the ocean, have a drink." He lifts his eyes and holds my gaze, and he's elegant in his pinstripes and gray like a CEO or an expensive lawyer.

"Sounds good to me," says Georgia, her golden hair smartly layered and it used to be black with a simple cut, and she has makeup on and then there's her diet.

All of it is since she started working here several months ago, a nice-looking woman, early forties, former Transit Police, and it doesn't escape my notice she's very aware of Lucy who doesn't return the attention. Thank God for that. I don't want one of my most recent hires to be the reason my niece is no longer wearing her partner's ring. It seems to be open season on flirting and fraternizing. Liz with Machado. Georgia with Lucy. Luke and Anne. Jen Garate and her come-hither looks and invasive exchanges with everyone including me. When did my workplace become such a soap opera? What happened to boundaries?

"Until Marino is ready for us I want to continue reviewing what we were looking at upstairs. If you have no objections," Benton says this to Lucy.

"You can pick up where we left off," she answers. "I'm happy to help."

"I need you to stay with me," I say to her.

We're going to talk. That's not negotiable, and I review the log entries, stopping on Gracie Smithers who was just picked up. Marblehead Neck, some twenty miles north of here, a fourteen-year-old white female, a possible drowning. Her body was discovered at eight o'clock this morning in the swimming pool of a house on Ocean Avenue, and I tell Lucy the address.

"Do you mind seeing what you can find on this?" I ask her as Benton places a call, stepping away from us.

"What's on your mind?" She's entering a search field on her iPad.

"It strikes me as strange that the kids she allegedly was with would run off and not report to the police or anybody that she drowned," I reply.

"Doctor Kato signed her out as an accident." Georgia is checking her computer. "It's not pending. Only toxicology is. She's got the manner of death as final and that's what's on the death certificate too."

"The trouble's just begun," I predict.

"According to police the pool cover pulled loose and the kids were drinking." Georgia reads what's on her display, and I remember what Jen said about the water being frigid and her dry suit leaking.

"It's on the market. Being sold furnished, available immediately." Lucy has pulled up the property.

"Sounds like it's unoccupied, at least it was last night," I reply. "I wonder how she and her friends knew it was. You wouldn't help yourself to someone's pool without permission if you thought they were home."

"Friends as in more than one? Do we know how many?" Lucy asks.

"Harold and Rusty seemed to think there were several and probably got this from the police. Maybe Jen did too. But what the information was based on I don't know since it appears whoever she was with left her body in the pool and didn't call for help. And how did these friends get to and from the house? Did someone drive?"

"Maybe they're local." Lucy shows me a slide show of photographs.

THE BIG HOUSE LOOKS turn of the century, gray with white trim, a slate roof, sweeping verandas and tall brick chimneys. It soars dramatically from a rocky rise with wooden steps leading down to a narrow beach, and the black bottom pool is L-shaped with a granite deck.

I remember what the temperature was last night, a low of sixty and on the ocean it would have been quite chilly. It would seem the pool wasn't heated and likely had been winterized and not reopened yet. The chlorine level would be high and unsuitable for swimming. What would possess teenagers to jump on a pool cover in the dark? Not much about this is adding up.

"Do we know if her body was clothed when she came in?" I ask.

"I got the inventory here." Georgia reads her screen and clicks the mouse. "Jeans, a tee, one sneaker."

"That's all?" I watch Benton on his phone.

"Nothing else," Georgia says.

"No problem, thanks, Marty," Benton says to his SAC, the head of the FBI's field office in Boston. "Sorry to pull you out of a meeting."

"Seven thousand square feet, a carriage house garage, a saltwater pool, five acres with a tennis court, listed at six million. Well it was," Lucy adds. "I guess they'll be lowering the price or taking it off the market. It's not good for business if a kid drowns in your pool."

"I overheard a mention of a lawsuit and a congressman," I reply. "Do you have any idea what that might be about?"

"It appears the house is owned by Gordian Knot Estates Corporation which is a personal holding company for Bob Rosado's Massachusetts real estate and who knows what else."

"The congressman from Florida?" I ask. "He has a home here?"

Rosado is the chairman of the Homeland Security subcommittee on Border and Maritime Security. He's in the news often these days because of his controversial push to build a virtual fence on the Arizona-Mexican border. He's also had his share of scandals.

"His wife is from Massachusetts. They have homes here, New York, Washington, Aspen, and the main residence in West Palm Beach," Lucy says and I'm getting worried.

My forensic fellow Shina Kato is bright but inexperienced. She's not board certified yet and would be dismantled as an expert witness in court. Had I been here this morning she wouldn't have been assigned the Gracie Smithers case or at the very least I would have supervised. Luke should have paid attention but he must have been distracted and busy, and I look at the log again. Harold and Rusty transported the body here and I note their initials and also Jen's. I need to review the photographs and get myself up to speed as quickly as I can. There's going to be a stink.

"Gracie Smithers is named in news reports as the victim and it doesn't appear she was with *several friends* when she drowned." Lucy is finding more information on the Internet and Benton is confirming with his office that no agents are to respond to Leo Gantz's house. "Just one so-called friend," Lucy says, "a teenaged male who isn't identified."

"Probably because he's a juvenile."

"They don't say and that suggests to me he's not. I find it unusual the police wouldn't release his name," Lucy adds while Benton goes on to explain that Marino is on his way to the Gantz house and there can be no interference whatsoever.

"My guess is the male who was with Gracie Smithers isn't a juvenile and had a reason to pick that particular house for whatever he really had in mind," Lucy decides. "Sounds like someone powerful keeping things quiet if you ask me, and I wouldn't be surprised if we find out that the person in question is Bob Rosado's son, Troy. He's been in trouble before, cyberbullying a thirteen-year-old girl. She hanged herself in her closet and the Rosados were sued. Apparently they settled. This was Palm Beach County five years ago when Troy was fourteen. Two years later he was stopped for driving erratically. In the backseat was a .416 Rigby with a Swarovski scope, a dangerous thirty-five-thousand-dollar safari game rifle that belonged to his father. When Troy refused to get out of the car the cop tased him."

"It sounds like he's a real personality disorder," I reply.

"It gets worse." Lucy has found something else.

CHAPTER 25

A DUI LAST AUGUST, NO jail time or fine, his driver's license was suspended for a year and he was sentenced to an alcohol-drug program for sixteen weeks," she informs me. "Instead it appears he ended up in boarding school."

"Was this in Florida?" I inquire.

"The DUI yes. But now he's here."

"He's nineteen or twenty and in boarding school?"

"Just north of here, Needham Academy, which is basically a cushy place for rich people to park their messed-up kids," Lucy says. "And it doesn't look like he stays on campus. A month after the DUI and only a week after he started at Needham he was arrested for arson but the charges were dropped."

I watch Benton walking down the corridor, headed to the elevator. I can tell he's listening.

"An apartment building that burned after someone shot a flare through a window. It appeared random, no known motive." Lucy's data mining search engines find information fast and furiously. "There was one fatality, a man in a wheelchair who couldn't get out."

"Smoke inhalation." I remember the case.

"And right after that the Rosados put their place in Marblehead on the market. A suspended driver's license? Right. How is Troy getting around?"

"And why wasn't he charged in the homicide?"

"Apparently they couldn't find the flare gun or link one to him. And by the way, his father is an avid outdoorsman, a big fisherman and hunter. It's not unheard of for a hunter to have a flare gun and he probably has one on his yacht."

"His yacht?"

"An extremely nice one."

"I'm trying to remember where he got so much money."

"Real estate, which is why he could afford to go into politics and have a lot of hobbies. Hunting, fishing, whatever he wants including a beautiful wife."

"He's certainly been in the news a lot but I don't recall anything about the son," I remark.

"They obviously have a crisis management team that knows how to bury things. You have to know how to look if you're going to find what I just did."

What she means is you have to know how to hack. I watch Benton push the elevator button and the polished steel doors quietly open. He's listening to us.

"Here we go." Lucy leans against the counter, focused on her iPad, and Georgia is focused on her. "Uber," Lucy says. "Troy uses the on-demand car service and has the app on his phone."

"And how do we know that?" I ask.

"He may not have been charged in criminal court but there's litigation. Short-lived but enough to create a record if you can find it."

Lucy is accessing Bloomberg Law, LexisNexis, maybe PACER. If she's surfing other sites, ones she shouldn't, I don't want to know.

"The owner of the building that burned and the family of the man who died sued but it was immediately settled," she says. "According to the original complaint, the plaintiffs claim that the night of the fire Troy took Uber to a paintball arena in South Boston. He was dropped off and several hours later was spotted watching the building burn."

"Spotted by whom?" I ask and Benton is holding open the elevator doors, his eyes on us. "And this never made the news either?" It's hard to fathom.

"A firefighter questioned him, asked who he was and what he was doing there." Lucy skims through another file she's mined. "In the firefighter's statement to the police he described Troy as excited by the inferno and indifferent to people being injured or killed. When it was brought to his attention that some of the residents had lost their homes and everything they owned he commented that they didn't have much to begin with anyway."

"Pure garbage," Georgia chimes in with disdain. "They should have drowned him as a puppy."

"You can find the complaint on PACER if you dig through enough subsets of records," Lucy adds.

The Public Access to Court Electronic Records service is a restricted government website that most nonlawyers find difficult to navigate. Even so that wouldn't deter a motivated journalist.

"My question is why other people haven't found the complaint," I point out. "A high-profile federal official and somehow his son has remained below the radar? How is that possible?"

"Crisis management. He must have someone really good," she says and I detect a flash of anger again. "You anticipate what might get legs and kneecap them in advance. Constant online monitoring, constant risk assessment and no holds barred in protecting the brand. Whoever manages this for Rosado is extremely savvy and has leverage. I suspect the person spends a lot of time undercover in proprietary databases, does whatever it takes."

Like you, I think.

"Stealth and manipulation," I say instead. "All you need is enough influence and money."

"A politician's nightmare having a kid like that." Lucy holds her iPad in front of me so I can see a Facebook page.

TROY ROSADO HAS PRETTY-BOY looks, curly black hair and a bright smile but his eyes are dead. *A budding psychopath,* and I glance down at my phone as a text from Benton lands.

If the father or someone on his behalf attempts contact avoid.

The FBI must be investigating Congressman Rosado or maybe it's the son they want.

"That little girl's a real sad one and it sounds like there will be hell to pay. An empty house, a pool and a really deep pocket?" Georgia says, and she continues staring at Lucy.

Sitting straight up in her chair, proud and serious in her navy blue CFC uniform, Georgia likes my niece a little too much.

"The boy is bad to the bone and evil kids are a whole lot worse than adults." Georgia is indignant. "It's some day we got going and I've only been here two hours. TV trucks were filming the front of the building and now you can bet the media will start poking around about Gracie Smithers."

Georgia scans her cockpit of flat-paneled security displays. On them are images of every important perspective including interior scans of the bay, the evidence room and the receiving area where I'm now standing.

"Give me some notice before you head back out," she says, "so I can make sure there are no camera crews lurking around."

"Anything else I should know about?" I return the big black case log to the counter.

"Six cases so far as you can see with two more just arrived," Georgia tells me. "The motor vehicle fatalities. Doctor Zenner says we'll post them in the morning."

"That's fine."

"They came in right before you got here. DOA at Memorial. Newly-weds. It's real sad." She gives in and places a cannoli on a sheet of copying paper. "Also the crane operator from yesterday." She checks her computer. "He's pending and Luke didn't want him released yet."

"Do we know why?" I ask. "Is there a question about toxicology?"

"I think there's just questions period. He was operating that big tower crane where they're building the high-rise apartment building on Somer-ville Avenue. They don't know if he slipped on the ladder while he was climbing up to the cab early yesterday morning or if he had a heart attack and fell." She dabs a finger in creamy ricotta cheese filling and tastes it. "Now I've done it. There's no going back."

"We'll be in the autopsy room," I reply. "In addition to the media there's an insurance investigator named Rand Bloom who I'd like you to be on the lookout for. He drives a big gray pickup, a Ford, and loves to take photographs and trespass."

Georgia is writing it down. "I know exactly who that is." She looks up at me and her eyes are hard and flat. "I've seen that truck around here several times. Just the other day, late afternoon . . . I'm trying to think. I believe it was Monday and he was taking pictures of people pulling in and out. When the gate opened he'd photograph whatever was going on in the parking lot. So I confronted him. I gave him a piece of my mind. A sleaze with a big scar and ugly eyes like maybe he got hit in the face."

"Another thing you can look into for me," I say to Lucy as we follow the curved corridor away from the receiving area, deeper into my dark Emerald City where guests are taken apart and put back together again.

"You're interested in what happened to his face?" she says. "Why does it matter?"

"I want to know who and what he really is and what motivates him besides money. Chances are he hasn't always been an insurance investigator. A lot of people who go into that started out in law enforcement, and he seems to be a common denominator in a number of situations that involve me. Johnny Angiers, for example, the doctor who died in Estabrook Woods. And you heard what we were just saying about Leo Gantz. Bloom has been harassing Joanna Cather and spying on Jamal Nari because of an insurance claim. Then there's Patty Marsico, murdered last Thanksgiving in Nantucket. He's the insurance investigator in that case too because her husband sued her real estate company."

The lights are dimmed inside the evidence room, the door shut and locked, nobody there. Through observation windows I see white paper-covered tables, countertops and drying cabinets with glass doors. A pair of jeans, a T-shirt with some sort of pattern in blue and green, and I see a small sneaker, just one. What happened to her other shoe and her underwear? What about a jacket or socks, and if she had a phone where is it?

"If it turns out this insurance investigator is connected to Gracie Smithers"—Lucy seems to be in my thoughts—"then you'll know something seriously bad is going on."

"I already know it's seriously bad, and you say that as if you're expecting it is, as if you have a reason to." I look at her and don't like what I sense.

A shadow behind her eyes, something dark and impenetrable, and I ask her and she says she's fine. It's not important. I reply that everything is.

"What is it that you think isn't important?" I then ask.

"I don't like to give energy to things like this."

"Like what?"

"Okay," she says. "There are too many weird things going on and people are starting to look at me funny. Not that I haven't dealt with it before but not here."

I pause us in the empty corridor. Just ahead is histology with its microtomes, tissue embedding stations and slide warmers. No one is there at this hour. It's rare for lab workers to stay beyond five. Lucy and I are completely alone.

"What people?"

"When Jen came back from the Nari crime scene she made one of her typical comments to Bryce and of course he couldn't resist telling me instantly. But he's starting to act a little flighty as if I make him nervous."

"Bryce is always flighty."

"She needs to stop saying things about me. She needs to stop Googling."

Lucy has never pretended to like Jen Garate and was against my hiring her. Now this, I think.

"How objective can you be about her when you had your mind made up from day one, Lucy."

"It's a lot of things, Aunt Kay. Things that aren't provable and there's nothing worse."

"Than what?"

"Than when people start acting unsure. Paranoid. And whatever they're thinking they won't say it. They just give you a lot of space."

"Not you too," I reply. "What's wrong with everyone? It's as if my workplace no longer has gravity and my staff's chemistry is altered."

It was better when Marino worked here. Somehow he provided ballast.

"What comments are you talking about? What things are being Googled?" I ask as I think about what Jen said to me earlier today.

Her remark about Lucy flying in prohibited airspace was provocative.

"She wondered where was I this morning when Jamal Nari was shot and mentioned she wouldn't blame me for *offing* him after the way he dissed you at the White House. Bryce said she was joking of course." Lucy acts as if she doesn't care, and I'm reminded of how foolish people can be.

No one with common sense would engage her in a battle, and the more she acts like it doesn't matter, the more I'm sure it does. Lucy has patience. She's stoical. She'll bide her time and then one day the Jen Garates of the world won't have any idea what just happened to them.

"There's no place for behavior like that," I reply. "And I don't understand why she would make a joke about any homicide, much less imply you might have a motive for shooting someone. It certainly isn't funny."

"I've shot people before. That's why the FBI and ATF were happy to send me packing. There are other rumors out there from when I had my own security service."

It's a euphemism for paramilitary government contracts that we don't discuss.

"Does Jen know your history?" I ask.

"There's information on the Internet. More than there used to be. About my past especially."

"Why?"

"Blogs that paint me as dangerous and crazy."

"You must have an idea who's doing it and why," I reply because it's so damn rare she can't find out whatever she wants.

But she says she doesn't. Not really. Not quite. Nothing she can prove, and there's that word again. Something she needs to prove, and I'm not convinced she doesn't have a clue. I worry that she might.

"Let's be honest. If you went down a list I don't look so good," Lucy says and something has tilted her axis.

She seems a strange mixture of energized and slightly spooked. And I also detect excitement.

"If I didn't work for myself no one would hire me except you," she says. "And you shouldn't have and we both know it."

"No one has justification to go down any *list*."

"Behind my back Jen calls me Hack. She says I'm in everybody's email."

"You probably are. And it sounds like competitiveness and jealousy to me," I decide.

We're walking again. The anthropology lab is just ahead.

CHAPTER 26

THE LIGHTS ARE ON and forensic anthropologist Alex Delgado is bent over an examination table covered with a blue cloth. He's looking at a femur, stained brown and damaged, the head of it gone, possibly gnawed off by animals.

Tall and gaunt, Alex is as bald as a lightbulb, his white lab coat buttoned up to his stalk of a neck. Rimless glasses with thick lenses make his eyes owlish and he's a little dingy, almost dusty as if he's begun adapting to his environment like a moth. Moving slowly, deliberately, he begins placing the femur and other bones into a cream-colored cardboard box. As we reach the next observation window I realize he's not alone. Ernie Koppel is with him.

"Good," I say to Lucy as I open the door. "Let's go ahead and take care of this."

A toothless skull on a stand stares with empty eyes as we walk inside and I detect a waxy dead smell, vaguely rancid like suet or tallow. The odor never leaves. I can detect it in bones that are centuries old.

"I was about to call you," I say to Ernie.

"And I was on my way to find you before I head out for the day. Is that your spaceship inside the bay?" he asks Lucy.

"Which spaceship?"

"I bet it's not as fast as my V-four Toyota."

"You must be right," she says, and I find myself searching for the slightest hint of anything unusual from him.

If Ernie is wary of Lucy, I see no sign of it. Alex seems his same self but he's as obtuse as a stone. I find a Sharpie on a cart of pliers, tweezers, rib cutters, brushes, needles, calipers and saws amid tables of skeletons pieced together like puzzles, male, female, old and young, some skulls robust and rugged, others gracile and small. I sign my initials on the bag of pennies and jot what time it is, twenty past six. Ernie takes the evidence from me, the chain unbroken.

In jeans and a blue-striped shirt, he doesn't wear a tie unless he's in court. Already he's working on his tan, a sun worshipper who spends every long weekend and vacation on the Texas Gulf Coast. Born and raised in Galveston he hasn't lost his drawl, and his big stature and rugged looks seem incongruous with what he does. Not a cowboy, he'll tell you, but more like an astronaut exploring the next galaxy of a magnified world where a single-celled diatom is a gem and a dust mite a horror.

"Benton gave me the lowdown on what was on your property this morning and his suspicions about a tumbler," he says to me and I watch carefully to see if he's excluding Lucy.

"Obviously the coins have been polished," I reply. "They're more than thirty years old."

He holds up the transparent bag, tilting it, and the pennies catch the light, and he says, "Nineteen-eighty-one. Does that date mean anything to you?"

"It was a bad year." Lucy looks at her computer again as if she's searching for something. "John Hinckley Junior shot Reagan in March and six weeks later the pope was shot in Saint Peter's Square. In August Mark David Chapman was sentenced to prison for murdering John Lennon, and two months later President Anwar Sadat was assassinated during a parade in Cairo. Four shootings the world won't forget." She recites information I'm quite sure she already knows, and she might just be pulling Ernie's leg.

Sometimes it's impossible to know when she's being funny, and right now I don't find anything about this amusing. Her demeanor is peculiar. It's different. I find her humor angry, maybe hurt, maybe aggressive and spiked with machismo.

"What I remember is Prince Charles and Lady Diana's wedding. My wife was glued to the TV and all misty eyed." Alex opens the glass door of a floor-to-ceiling stainless steel cabinet.

"Some fairy tale that turned out to be," Lucy says.

"You weren't even around yet." He picks up the creamy box and I can hear bones shift inside it.

She doesn't correct him and I don't either.

"We were just talking about the remains from earlier this week." Alex places the box inside the cabinet and shuts the door. "From the well on that old farm in North Andover?"

"The stabbing," I remember.

"A fragment of blade," Ernie says. "The smallest piece of the tip embedded in the left femur in the area of the upper inner thigh."

"Which would be what killed her if it transected her femoral artery," I suggest. "A survival time of minutes at most."

"We may be able to fracture-match the piece of the blade back to the knife," Alex says. "Probably no one to prosecute though as old as these remains are. At least fifty years, possibly more."

They continue discussing sensitive case details in front of Lucy the same way they always have. I don't blame her for being offended by inflammatory blogs and inappropriate quips but she usually has skin so thick it's more like armor.

WE LEAVE ALEX ALONE with his bones behind the shut door. Back in the corridor now, Lucy, Ernie and I move out of view. We find a blank area of wall between a storage closet and the locked solid metal door that leads into the mechanical room.

"You must have been choppering." Ernie indicates Lucy's flight suit. "When are you going to give me a ride?"

"As soon as I finish reading the instruction manual," she says.

Ernie looks at me and gets to what he wants me to know. "A .308 caliber 190 grain LRX bullet shot from a .300 Winchester Magnum isn't something you usually see."

"LRX?" I ask.

"Designed for long range." It's Lucy who answers.

"Solid copper that was polished, and the blue material Luke recovered from brain tissue is a polymer," he says. "I know this isn't exactly my department but Liz and I conferred."

"How many petals?" Lucy asks.

"Four."

"5R rifling?"

"That's what Liz said."

"Are you familiar with Barnes Tipped Triple-Shocks?"

"I'm not a gun nut."

"Premium ammo, match grade, a lot of copper. The gold standard," Lucy says, "and a couple years ago they came out with what some enthusiasts call a long-range BC version of their famous Triple-Shock. Solid copper with a blue polymer ballistic tip that expands on contact into four cutting petals. A clean instant kill and designed for big game hunting at long range."

"As in lions, tigers and bears." Ernie eyes her and I can't tell if he's suspicious or impressed. "Don't tell me you're into hunting."

"Not animals." Her odd dry ice humor again.

"Only the two-legged kind and a lot of them have it coming."

"I don't start it if that's what you're getting at."

"Joking aside," he says. "I didn't realize you know so much."

"I used to be ATF."

"I'm fine with the alcohol and tobacco part of it. But I'm not a fan of firearms. I thought you were a fire investigator anyway."

"I've been a lot of things." Lucy is uncharacteristically generous with facts about her past.

Maybe because of the blogs. Maybe because of the snide comments and gossip. She's asserting herself when that's not her style and I intuit that she's in a competition with someone.

"I have my own firing range, do my own gunsmithing and yes I know a lot," she continues. "This bullet is such a heavy round it usually passes through big game and I'm talking about game a lot bigger than a human being. I'm wondering if the killer has developed a special round with a lighter powder charge load so this one particular bullet would stay in the body and sustain minimal damage."

"The reason?" I ask.

"Because the person didn't want it to exit. The person wanted us to find it."

"Interesting you would say that," Ernie says. "The pitting from using a tumbler, plus FTIR-detected traces of urea monohydrocholoride, an organic acid salt typical in tarnish removers, probably used to hand-polish."

"Same things that's in Flitz," Lucy says. "It's very popular with gun enthusiasts."

"It's on the frag and the intact bullet," Ernie says. "But more important there's something else nobody knows about. Not even Liz. You wouldn't see it with a typical optical scope because there's not enough depth of field."

He examined the frag and bullet with SEM, a scanning electron microscope, and that's classic Ernie. We share the same work ethic. You find answers when you don't know what you're looking for. So you use any means that seems to make a modicum of sense.

"You've heard of ballistics fingerprints?" He slides a folded sheet of paper from his back pocket.

"It's controversial and there's been a lot of talk about it over the years, yes," I reply. "To date I'm not sure it's being done anywhere except in California. A microstamp is etched on a firing pin or some other component of a gun so it will be transferred to a cartridge case. The point is to have a microscopic code that links a spent case with the gun's serial number."

"Do we have a cartridge case? Because if so it's news to me," Lucy says. "I've seen the evidence logged in to the database and what's being analyzed in the labs."

"So far no cartridge case has been discovered here or in the New Jersey homicides. The microstamp is homemade and on the actual bullet." Ernie hands the sheet of paper to me. "Low tech I know but I don't want this in an email."

"How could a microstamp end up on a bullet?" I stare at the photos of the intact bullet recovered from Jamal Nari's chest.

Bright copper, four razor-sharp petals curled back. Then another image, the copper base of the bullet at 150X, so vivid in three dimensions it seems I could hold it in my hand. I know why Ernie is being secretive.

A single digit, the numeral 3, and I can see the microscopic tool marks of the graver that cut into the metal.

"It's certainly not stamped," I observe. "And it wasn't etched by a laser or transferred by a firearm. It was engraved with something very small and precise such as jeweler's tools."

"It was definitely engraved. Then it was eradicated and polished over," Ernie says. "The naked eye and light microscopes can't see it but SEM can. The engraved number three is gone but the deformation beneath the surface of the metal is still there. What the person deliberately did was bear down with the engraving tool, etch the number three on the base of the copper bullet, then grind it away, tumble, polish and hand-load."

"Pretty much the same way people eradicate serial numbers from firearms not realizing they aren't really gone." Lucy stares at the photograph and her mind is racing, her eyes blazing.

Something about her demeanor is unsettling me in an unfathomable place. I don't know what it is. But I feel it like a shadow move. As if something huge and evil is far down deep and looking up at me.

"Similar to indented writing that you can find on sheets of paper that were underneath the one someone wrote on," she is saying.

"I'm of the opinion the killer wanted us to find it," Ernie says. "But he didn't want Liz to."

"How do you figure that?" Lucy seems relieved, as if she just got something she needed as I sense the shadow again as it stirs.

"The engraving wouldn't be seen with the comparison microscopes used in firearms labs, which is why Liz had no idea," Ernie says. "I think it's becoming clear we're dealing with someone who knows a lot about ballistics and how the analysis is done."

"And this person knows you'd resort to SEM?" Lucy asks and I detect aggression more strongly.

"Because of the pitting," he says. "Liz noticed it and asked my opinion. Tumbling cartridge cases is one thing but who tumbles bullets? She saw the snowstorm of pitting under her scope and called me, asking if I could confirm the copper bullets had been polished."

"But you didn't tell her about the eradicated engraving." I fold the piece of paper.

"The only one I've told besides the two of you is Benton."

"We should leave it at that for now," I decide.

"What about Marino?"

"Not today but I'll let him know."

"Okay by me." He doesn't want it leaked, not deliberately or accidentally. "If there's nothing else?"

"Thank you," I reply. "Have a good night, Ernie."

We watch him walk off, the empty corridor curving him around to the elevator in a cloud of soft light.

"He doesn't know who to trust," Lucy says.

"He trusts us."

"What's happening is personal," Lucy says decisively. "A sophisticated highly skilled sniper is jerking you around and wants to make sure you know it. The tweets, the pennies, an engraved bullet that he somehow made sure you'd recover, it's all premeditated and with a goal in mind."

"You keep saying *he*."

"It's easier. And that's what people assume."

"How about you?"

"I'm trying not to assume anything."

"Who and why? Do you have an idea?" I ask and we're walking again, passing locker rooms. Ahead is a hand-sanitizing dispenser on the wall.

I stop and squirt some of it in my palms. The anthropology lab always makes me feel dirty. Maybe other things are making me feel dirty too, this conversation for starters.

"I have a feeling Benton might have an idea," Lucy says.

"But you don't?" The sharp odor of alcohol penetrates my sinuses as I rub my skin until it's dry.

"The way he was acting when we were in my lab this afternoon, his questions and evasiveness," she says and she's the one being evasive. "He wanted to know for example how effective the most advanced facial recognition software would be if someone has surgically altered his features."

He wouldn't mention that unless he thinks it's someone we know.

What I say is, "It seems the government has been dealing with this for years because of terrorism. Not to mention Border Patrol, the FBI, and Benton would know all about it."

Someone hideous from our past, it enters my mind. But why would Benton think that?

"The Feds haven't had much success when it comes to cold hits," Lucy says. "If a biometric portrait changes then you won't get an automated match with a scan in an image database or a mug shot repository. And as far as retinal and iris identification go, your typical security camera isn't going to capture the iris characteristics of someone entering a hotel business center and borrowing a computer. Plus you'd need a scan for comparison."

Someone we believe is gone. There are names I could come up with but I won't. I focus on our conversation because I must. I take a deep quiet breath. I try not to feel the darkness and what's in it. Something is there and Lucy doesn't want to tell me what it is.

"Did Benton seem to be looking for someone in particular when you were going through these videos?" I ask.

"One always has to consider someone who never got caught or has been released from prison," she says. "Something like that."

"Something like that?"

She doesn't answer me.

"Are you bringing this up to see how I'll react?" I ask.

"I'm telling you there's a discussion to be had about familiarity," Lucy says. "A bullet marked with a three intended for a third victim and whoever is responsible wants us to know there's more to come, in other words payback," she says, and I feel myself bristle.

"Seven pennies," I reply. "What? Four murders to go?"

"When Benton asked me to do a low recon over the Academy of Arts and Sciences this morning he suggested I check the trees. Janet and I didn't see anyone suspicious, certainly no one who might have had a gun. What was he thinking based on your own observations when you were with him in your backyard?"

"He saw something flash, possibly light reflecting off a camera lens, probably Rand Bloom looking for dirt, looking to embarrass," I reply.

"I don't think so. Embarrassment can't happen if you don't make photographs public. There's nothing on the Internet."

"Not yet."

"A spotting scope," she says. "It's more likely whoever left the pennies wanted to watch you find them."

We stop outside the large-scale X-ray room and I look for Anne.

CHAPTER 27

SHE ISN'T AT HER console and we step inside. I look through the wall of thick lead-lined glass that connects her office to the scanner room but Anne isn't there either.

The lights are off, the white Somatom CT scanner vaguely illuminated, large bore with a downward tilted table, developed for the military when we went to war with Iraq. Using high-resolution 3-D imaging, we can visualize a body internally before it's autopsied, and I notice what's on one of the desk's displays. Case number CFC979. Gracie Smithers.

"The roof would have been the most likely area if the person was going to get an unobstructed view of your backyard." Lucy continues talking about what she saw when she overflew the Academy of Arts and Sciences. "I had the camera going." She refers to the stabilized camera mounted on her helicopter. "And there was no one but we saw evidence that somebody had been up there."

"Janet was flying with you this morning." I study oblique and axial images of the airway, sinuses and tracheobronchial tree, noting dark spaces indicating gas and froth that are common in drownings. "Are the two of you doing all right?"

"A section of the roof on the second floor and there was a baseball cap and a jacket we could see when I zoomed in," Lucy says. "Obviously someone was up there. We're fine."

"You have a new Ferrari and aren't wearing your ring." Coronal images of the lungs, the distal bronchi are full of fluid, and I click on other images. "You look like you've lost weight and your hair needs cutting."

The maxillary sinuses are also full of fluid and there's a high-density particulate material in the sphenoid sinus. I find more of it around the vocal cords and in the airway and lungs.

Sand.

"Of course a maintenance worker could have left them up there," Lucy says. "But I seriously doubt it."

"I haven't seen you in a month."

"I've been busy."

"Are you avoiding me?"

"Why would I?"

"Because when you do?" I click on images of the head. "It's never a sign of anything happy."

"A surgical hat and jacket," Lucy says.

"What do you mean *surgical*?"

"The patina color of the roof is the bluish green of classic scrubs. The baseball cap and jacket are teal green with a caduceus embroidered on them."

"In other words whoever might have had them on would have blended with the roof."

"Especially if the person also was wearing matching scrub pants and shirt."

"That sounds bizarre."

"Not really," Lucy says. "They blend with the environment and also wouldn't stand out to anybody who spotted this person because a lot of med students and techs walk around in scrubs. That particular section of the cantilevered roof is accessible only by an exterior ladder which is supposed to be restricted to maintenance."

"Supposed to be?" I click on more CT images and what I'm seeing is depressing and cruel. "But anybody could climb up?"

"Yes but just anybody wouldn't."

Sagittal images reveal a linear fracture in the anterior cranial fossae with underlying contusion. Axial images are the problem. They don't show what I would expect if the head injury happened the way it's been described. There's no frontobasal injury with diffuse subarachnoid hemorrhage.

Violence.

"The reason for the new car is we need a backseat and it can drive in the snow," Lucy says.

"Need? As in a Volvo or a Toyota?"

"Okay. Not the right word."

"What else?"

"I'm not wearing the ring because Janet's father wanted it back."

"That's not very nice."

She turns her attention to images I'm clicking through on the display. "What are you seeing?"

"It's what I'm not seeing," I reply.

I explain that Gracie Smithers doesn't have a contrecoup injury and she should if she was jumping on the pool cover and fell, striking the concrete edge.

"There's no bleeding into the inferior frontal and superior temporal lobes." I point out the absence of shadowy areas of hemorrhage on the CT scans. "Blunt force trauma to the back of her head should have caused the front of her brain to hit the front of her skull. There should be injury at the site of the trauma and also opposite it."

"She didn't drown?"

"She did. But not in a swimming pool and this isn't an accident."

We walk out of Anne's office back into the corridor and I ask Lucy if Dr. Shina Kato requested a STAT alcohol on Gracie Smithers. If so there should be a report. Lucy checks the database. The results of the analysis are negative.

"She wasn't drinking," I summarize.

We walk past the tissue recovery room, what looks like a small OR, dark inside, nothing going on, no donated organs, eyes, skin or bones being harvested right now. I push a big steel button that opens the door to the anteroom, a wall of blue lockers for the doctors, shelves of personal protective clothing and other supplies.

"Doctor Kato shouldn't have been the one to do her post," Lucy says. "I guess Luke and the other docs were tied up with what seemed to be bigger more difficult cases. Jamal Nari, the decomp suicide from Brookline. She got Gracie Smithers because at first glance it was an uncomplicated drowning."

"Well it's not." This will be trouble. "See what happens when I'm not here?"

"You should never go on vacation or have a life."

"Tell me more about the Academy of Arts and Sciences roof."

"It's a complex cantilevered system with a series of walkways and ramps so maintenance can reach different levels of piping, ducts, flashing or equipment without stepping on metal and causing damage."

"And you can access these areas from the outside only?" I want to make sure.

"That's correct."

"You went up there." I grab shoe covers and surgical gowns, the same teal green she just described.

"When Benton saw the glint of light the first time this morning it was early, around eight." She sits on a bench to pull the shoe covers over her boots, and it's obvious that he gave her details about what happened.

"And then a second time around eleven," I reply.

"If someone was on the roof to spy on you and your property, this person likely was in position very early and it would have been chilly."

"He might have had on a cap and a jacket," I suggest. "He also may have left and come back."

Jamal Nari was murdered at approximately nine-forty-five. His apartment on Farrar Street is half a mile from our house and the Academy of Arts and Sciences.

"Are you thinking it was the killer on the roof?" I ask.

Lucy gets up from the bench and slips the apron over her head, tying it in back. "On my approach when I was going to buzz your house, he would have heard me and gone down the ladder. It's at the back of the complex where there are woods and a busy street."

"And this person forgot to take the clothing."

"Either that or left it intentionally."

"You retrieved the hat and jacket from the roof and gave them to DNA." I work my hands into a pair of gloves.

"Yes."

"Because you were worried it might have been the shooter up there." I push my point.

"Not with the intention of hurting Benton or you. Not at that time."

"You say this based on what?" I push another hands-free button and the stainless steel door gently swings open.

"Someone with a heavy sniper rifle with a bipod and rear bag rests?" She follows me into the autopsy room. "That couldn't have been disassembled quickly and carried up and down a narrow metal ladder, and the person would have been noticed. You have to envision this logically."

"Help me out."

"A sniper selects a location, a hide. That's the first priority," Lucy says. "After he's completed his mission he's going to break down and stash his gear, possibly in a vehicle or anyplace out of sight where he can come back and retrieve it later. It's more likely he had a spotting scope—not a gun—trained on you early in the morning and then again later. Like I said, he wanted to watch you find the pennies. Maybe he wanted to watch you get a phone call and respond to the Nari crime scene."

"You continue saying *he*."

"For the sake of simplicity. I have no idea who it is."

But the way she says it bothers me strongly.

"Could we be talking about a woman?"

"Sure," Lucy says too flippantly.

The cooler door opens. Billowing fog carries the stench of death and Anne emerges pushing a carrier with a human-shaped black pouch on top.

SHE PARKS THE CARRIER by my table in a vast space of stainless steel wall sinks and workstations.

Natural light fills one-way glass windows, and I flip on switches, and high intensity lamps blaze in the thirty-two-foot-high ceilings. I tie my gown in back, my hands sheathed in purple nitrile gloves, my shoe covers quiet on the recently mopped floor.

"Can you get Gracie Smithers's autopsy records and photos up?" I ask Lucy.

My workstation is the closest one to the cooler, and on a counter next to the sink are a computer screen, keyboard and mouse covered with a waterproof membrane. Lucy logs on to the CFC database. The display divides in quadrants before my eyes and images of Gracie Smithers are there.

"I didn't want to get into anything until I saw you in person," Anne says to me. "In the first place her T-shirt was inside out and I mentioned that to Shina when I was doing the scan."

"Images that you left up on your console so I could see."

"So I could show them to you, yes. I didn't want to put anything in writing about it, to send you an email or anything. Someone inexperienced can easily miss subtlety. You don't want the wrong attorneys to get wind of that."

"I'm not sure how subtle any of this is," I reply.

"Not to you."

"She has significant abrasions on her cheeks bilaterally and also her nose." I click the plastic-covered mouse and more autopsy photographs appear. "Significant lacerations, skin splitting to the back of her scalp, a round area approximately four by four inches. This is inconsistent with her striking the rounded concrete edge of a pool."

"It's more like her head was slammed against a flat surface," Anne agrees.

"That's exactly what it's like," I reply. "More than once," I add. "And she has a thin linear abrasion on the right side of her neck. She came in without jewelry?"

"Nothing. Not even earrings."

Gracie Smithers was pretty but one has to imagine it. One has to somehow get past the way she looked at death, the angry abraded skin bright red, the inside of her lips shredded. Long blond hair, blue eyes, and black polish that is chipped and scraped on her fingernails, and I don't know what Dr. Kato was thinking. Five feet tall, ninety-one pounds, pale and bloodless after the autopsy, and fingertip-shaped bruises are vivid on her shoulders. I can see where someone's thumbs dug into her upper back on either side of her spine. There are more abrasions and bruises on her knees and buttocks.

"Do you want me to get Shina on the phone?" Lucy asks.

"I'll let Gracie Smithers speak for herself," I answer and I feel hard inside.

I don't forgive incompetence and carelessness.

"And what was Doctor Kato's explanation about the T-shirt, the injuries and the sand?" I ask Anne.

"A lot of kids wear their T-shirts inside out because they think it's cool."

"And no underwear?"

"Some kids don't."

"That's what you're saying?"

"It's what Doctor Kato said."

"The first thing I teach our fellows is not to make assumptions," I reply impatiently.

"The abrasions are from scraping the bottom of the pool according to her."

"Nonsense." Now I'm getting really mad.

"And the pool was dirty, the filter, skimmer and everything else turned off or removed for the winter and there was a runoff of dirt from the yard onto the deck. So dirt had gotten into the pool." Anne sums up Dr. Kato's hasty conclusions. "Added to it was what Jen said. The pool had sediment on the bottom explaining the particulate we see in the scan. Some of it was recovered from her lungs. Grit, a brownish sand it seems, and there was some in her hair."

"Did we get a sample of the so-called sediment?"

"Apparently not." It's Lucy who answers. "It's not been logged as evidence turned into the labs. Only the clothing, a shoe and samples for toxicology."

"Then we can't know if the sediment is the same particulate she aspirated."

"Not unless we go back and collect a sample."

"This is bad." I have the autopsy report displayed and I scroll through it.

No obvious injury to the genitalia but there isn't always when healthy young females are sexually assaulted.

"What about the investigator?" I ask. "A Marblehead detective I presume?"

"I doubt the case was assigned to anyone," Anne replies, "since there wasn't a question that she was anything other than an accidental drowning. Even though someone prominent is involved."

"Congressman Rosado," Lucy says. "No foul play and we're talking a civil case. A detective isn't going to care who owns the house or who gets sued."

"See who you can get hold of for me." I log on to Jamal Nari's autopsy records next. "Maybe Bryce can track down someone before more time is lost or more is staged. I'm amending the manner of death to homicide."

I instantly see what Luke Zenner found interesting about Nari's gastric contents. A crowding of vague round shapes in the gastrointestinal track, grape size, dozens of them, and they can be only one thing.

"Condoms turned into capsules. Luke said he counted eighty of them that weighed about five pounds," Anne says and I recall Nari's distended belly. "He said a lot of it was fluid. Tox will confirm but it appears Jamal Nari was smuggling drugs."

"He's driving around like that?" Lucy asks. "Why the hell would he take the risk? All you need is one to leak."

We go through the chronology. Nari left his residence early this morning to shop. He went to Whole Foods, a liquor store and CVS, and time stamps on receipts verify this. Moments after he'd returned home and was carrying bags into his apartment he was murdered.

"In the first place why was he carrying the bags into the house only to move them again this afternoon to the new place in Dorchester?" Lucy points out.

"I suspect his wife alerted him that the lease was falling through," I reply. "Apparently when Joanna Cather showed up at the rental house with more boxes the Realtor told her to cease and desist, to move everything out. Then Joanna placed a call, possibly to her husband. Hopefully it can be determined by phone records but it would make sense that she called immediately."

"And then he drove back to their apartment in Cambridge?" Lucy says. "That would suggest the killer might have missed his opportunity if Nari had gone to the house in Dorchester instead."

"Exactly," I reply. "Suggesting the killer might have had knowledge that the lease was going to fall through. Certainly Rand Bloom knew it was inevitable since he's the one who gave Mary Sapp information that would justify her deciding Nari and his wife were people of questionable character. Have you started going through their laptops?"

"Barely."

"I suggest you check to see if he might have booked a plane ticket," I reply. "That would explain the smuggling. Driving from Cambridge to Boston wouldn't."

"How far along was digestion?" Lucy asks.

"The capsules are still in the stomach. None have passed into the small and large intestines." I show her on the flat screen.

"How long since he'd swallowed them?"

"It depends. The digestive system slows down with stress, especially if he wasn't eating or drinking and was taking certain medications such as ones that treat diarrhea. A side effect of that can be constipation."

I envision the Imodium in the bathroom cabinet, and the unlubricated condoms, boxes of them that luminesced whitish blue when sprayed with a reagent. Nari may have packed them in a Bankers Box. Then they were moved back into the bathroom cabinet, perfectly, obsessively arranged with the labels facing out. Why? But I might know, and something dark stirs inside me again. It's like the guitars returned to their stands, and I think of what Benton continues to say about taunting.

Nari was very busy early this morning, diluting whatever street drug he was photographed picking up at Jumpin' Joes, and cocaine is highly soluble. So is heroin but I've not heard of mules swallowing it in liquid form. He filled the condoms, then cleaned up the apartment, wiping the inside of drawers. Swallowing the grape-size capsules was probably the last thing he did before he got into his car. He had errands to run and a bigger plan.

I move over to the steel carrier bearing his body. I think contemptuously of surveillance and harassment motivated by cheating people out of what they're due. For months he felt he was being spied on and followed. He was terrified the police were going to show up any minute to arrest his wife. Worst of all were photographs that may have caused him to be convinced his arrest on drug charges was imminent.

"It's unlikely he was using drugs again," I explain. "Rarely are drug smugglers also users. It sounds to me this was about money."

I work the plastic zipper down the black pouch and it rustles as I spread it.

CHAPTER 28

A DEADLY COPPER FLOWER THAT gleams like rose gold, the bullet has very little damage. It entered the body and plowed through vertebral bone and soft tissue before its kinetic energy was completely spent. I think about what Lucy said.

A light load.

After Luke removed the projectile at autopsy he took a one-to-one or life-size photograph of it on a blue towel. I notice how substantial it looks displayed on my station's computer screen, and I think about the long-range hunting bullet Lucy called an LRX.

"You can't see the engraving on it with the unaided eye or a light microscope," I'm explaining to Benton, who joined Anne and me moments ago.

Lucy has left, returning upstairs to her cyber lab and I sense that Benton is restless. He wants to head out to Cambridge PD with me but I'm not ready. He doesn't know about the drug smuggling and he doesn't know the oddity of a bullet that should have passed through Jamal Nari's body and fragmented but did neither. Maybe it had a lighter than usual powder load. Maybe it slowed because it was fired from an extraordinary distance. Maybe it's both.

"Not even a shadow of the number three unless you have the depth of field that SEM affords," I add. "We don't know that there wasn't engraving on other bullets. If there had been anything left maybe the same thing would have been found."

"It wasn't on them," Benton says.

"How can you be sure if there was nothing but frag so small some of it was powder?" Anne asks.

"Because it wouldn't have been. Nineteen eighty-one and now a number three engraved on a bullet," Benton says more to himself than to us.

"I'm beginning to think the person's getting unhinged," Anne replies.

"Or wants us to think we are." Benton stares down at Nari's body surrounded by black vinyl on top of the stainless steel carrier. "Ideas of reference are the interpretation of events as highly personal when they're not. A date, a number on a bullet, a certain number of coins left on a wall, and it gets to the point that you don't know if you're assuming all of it is intended with you in mind or if it's completely random. You start thinking you're crazy."

"Do you think what's happening is random?" I ask.

"It isn't. Including the atypical flight path."

"Almost an impossible flight path," I agree. "The bullet entered here." I touch the back of Benton's neck where the cervical spine meets the base of his skull, and I feel his warmth. "And lodged here." I touch the left side of his lower chest at the level of the sixth rib.

As I smell his earthy cologne I'm reminded of our backyard this morning in the sun. Then I smell death. I'm aware of my nitrile-sheathed hands, of his fine attire and perfect grooming, unprotected beyond the blue papery booties he slipped on before he entered the autopsy room. Benton is comfortable in places where it doesn't appear he belongs. He always seems untouched by the ugliness around him.

"The bullet traveled in an acutely downward direction, penetrating the left lung and chest wall and lodging under the skin," I explain to him. "Bilateral fractures of pars interarticularis and complete disruption of the C-two, C-three junction with transection of the spinal cord, and no swelling of surrounding tissue, and no wonder. He didn't live long enough to have a vital response. Death was due to traumatic spondylolisthesis, or hangman's fracture."

"Maybe the bullet was deflected and that's how it ended up where it did?" Benton is trying to envision it and having the same problem I am.

No matter how many different ways I reconstruct the shooter's and Nari's positions in relation to each other, I can't make sense of a bullet entering at the base of his skull and traveling straight down before lodging beneath the skin of his chest.

"Based on what you can see here on CT"—I open a scan on the display—"the wound track doesn't show any sort of deflection. The trajectory is a fairly straightforward path downward and slightly to the left of the midline where the bullet stopped."

"Obviously the shooter was elevated. Typically one might expect on a rooftop." Benton looks at the scan, at the plane of the wound track, which shows the presence of hemorrhage downward through the neck to the left lung apex. "Except there's a problem with that considering the location," he adds.

I open a drawer and find a bullet probe, thirty inches long, black, made of a flexible fiberglass. I tell Anne we need Tyvek coveralls. What I intend to do next is going to be messy.

"I suspect his head was bent as he lifted bags of groceries from the back of his car at the instant the bullet struck him," I say to Benton. "Otherwise it likely would have exited from the front of his neck, in and out, and we probably wouldn't have found it or what was left of it after it struck pavement, a tree, a building. A lighter powder charge or not. Have you heard from Marino?"

"He and Leo Gantz are at the station and almost ready for us. We need to figure out exactly where the shooter was when he killed Nari. There aren't many high-rises in Cambridge and nothing like that near Farrar Street. The tallest apartment building around there is three stories. I doubt that would be high enough."

"I don't know yet."

"It's important we find that out because I believe the flight path isn't a fluke," he says.

"Lucy has suggested this particular bullet may have been hand-loaded with the intention of remaining largely intact and not exiting the body." I pass that along and he has no discernible reaction.

Anne gives me a pair of white coveralls and I lean against the edge of the carrier and pull them on.

Then Benton says, "The shootout in Miami in 1986. The FBI out-numbered the suspects four to one, the two bank robbers shot multiple times with one hundred and ten grain hollowpoints that didn't have suf-ficient stopping power. Two of ours dead and five wounded because we didn't have the firepower, which began the big debate of light and fast ammo versus heavy and deep. The shooter who murdered Nari under-stands the concept and with this one particular round implemented the best of both. That's my theory."

"The recovered bullet is one-ninety grain," I tell him. "Certainly that's heavy."

"But if a lighter powder charge was used the bullet's not going to have the penetration required for exiting the body," he says. "The engraving on it and the lighter powder charge were different from what was used in New Jersey."

"You don't think it's the same rifle in the three cases?"

"I don't think the motive is the same," he says.

"The motive this time is he wanted the bullet recovered," I suppose. "Because he's sending us a message."

"It would seem he's sending you one," Benton says.

"Well unless Leo Gantz is sending messages and has access to a high-power rifle and solid copper bullets super and subsonic, his confession isn't going to hold up." I point out the absurdity of it. "Especially if he claims he came up behind Nari and shot him at close range. I'm guessing he's claiming the weapon was a handgun which he then conveniently dropped into the sewer."

"Unfortunately I've heard of far more ridiculous confessions resulting in convictions," Benton says. "The path of least resistance. Cops love confessions and some of them don't care if they aren't true."

"Marino cares." I spread the pouch open farther.

Bare feet and legs are pale, and I feel the chill of refrigerated dead flesh through the thin layer of my gloves as I check for broken bones and the slightest blush of contusions that might indicate Nari had an earlier struggle with Leo Gantz or anyone. Rigor mortis is complete, the muscles rigid, and I move up past the tattoos covering old scars caused by needles, up to the knees, the thighs and when I reach his genitals I get a surprise.

THE RING-STYLE CURVED BARBELL enters through the urethra and exits through the top of the glans. I wonder if the piercing gave his wife pleasure or pain, and what the healing time was after Jamal Nari got it.

I check Luke's report, and there it is under gross anatomy of the genitalia. "I'm glad he didn't remove it," I say.

"Why's that?" Benton looks on, his demeanor typical. Not particularly surprised or curious.

"It's an awkward item to return with someone's personal effects. Unless it's a precious metal or someone makes a specific request I leave it alone."

"Yet one more example of not being able to judge a book by its cover," Anne observes. "Drug smuggling and body piercing. You don't find out who somebody really is until they end up here."

I move up his torso. I check his arms and his hands, and when I get to his neck I touch my index finger to the wound at the back of it where the bullet entered and separated his brain from the rest of him. A small entrance wound no bigger than a buttonhole was the equivalent of a transformer blowing, and the lights went out instantly. He didn't know what happened. He had no warning and not a moment of fear or pain.

"At least this killer is merciful," I say to Benton.

"That's not why," he replies. "He's not trying to be merciful. What he's doing is practical. It's tidy and efficient and he's also showing off his remarkable skill. This person wants our admiration and he wants our fear."

"Well he's not getting either, not from me." I press my fingers into the area of the chest where the intact bullet was removed.

There's no bogginess, no contusion or tissue response. By the time the bullet penetrated the lung and chest wall, Nari was dead. Picking up a scalpel from a cart I cut through the twine that sutures the Y-incision, opening him up again. The odor is intense and foul and I reach inside with both hands and lift the heavy plastic bag out. It's transparent, filled with sectioned organs and a bloody fluid, and I set it inside the sink. I reposition myself at the back of his head and work my hands under the shoulders, and Anne helps me turn him on his side.

The fiberglass probe slides easily into the entrance wound at the base of his skull and I thread it along the track, making slight adjustments as I feel resistance from ribs, but not from organs because they've been removed. I'm careful not to force, finally stopping. The tip of the probe peeks out of a small incision in the chest that Luke made when he removed the bullet.

I lower the body to the carrier and step away, contemplating the best solution to a significant problem. Rigor is set. Breaking it in muscles of the abdomen, the lower back and pelvis would be like bending iron. It will begin passing in several hours and be mostly gone by morning but I can't wait.

"I could use your help," I say to Benton. Then to Anne, "I need a foot-stool and a camera. But first we need to suture him back up."

CHAPTER 29

A HALF HOUR LATER I'M in an Audi R8, black with carbon fiber blades on the sides. The V10 engine's guttural rumble draws stares from people who admire powerful cars and don't care what they cost or that they guzzle gas like a binge drinker.

Lucy and her supercharged modes of getting around in life seem to be wearing off on Benton. It's not that he didn't have an appreciation of the exotic and expensive but he wasn't conspicuous in his consumption until his FBI boss committed suicide last year. Not sorry or sad, a well-deserved ending to a story rife with the abuse of power and the deliberate destruction of innocents, and that is the truth about how Benton felt. He showed sympathy only to the family Ed Granby left.

In private, my husband didn't care what drove the head of the Boston Division to lock the doors of his house and hang himself. Benton didn't care that he didn't care and then his attitude began penetrating every region of his psyche. He decided he would do what he wants. He would say what he wants, buy what he wants, give away what he wants and be selfish if it was honestly merited. Critical and judgmental people be damned.

A midlife crisis would be another explanation but it wouldn't be an accurate one. Granby was maniacal in his efforts to end Benton's career and eradicate his legacy. He tried to marginalize and emasculate and ended up dead. It was the justice most people secretly wish for but will never express and Benton was liberated in a way I didn't expect. Bad people rarely get what's coming to them and good guys really don't win because the damage exceeds the punishment, assuming there's any punishment at all. Prison and even the death penalty don't undo a sexual homicide or mass murders or bring back a child abused and killed by a pedophile. I heard the bleak remarks and observations so often I stopped listening. Benton used to be cynical. He's not anymore.

In East Cambridge now, armed and dangerous in Italian sunglasses, a shoulder holster under his jacket, he has one hand on the wheel. A black leather and titanium bracelet is loose on his wrist, and he turns his growly car left on Bent Street, downshifting. The engine roars like a dragon.

"The damn smell is caught way up inside my nose." He's complained about it several times since we drove away from the CFC.

"It goes with the turf," I repeat.

"I don't usually get up close and personal with someone who's been autopsied."

"That wasn't typical and you were a good sport." It seems trivial to say but I'm sincere.

"You don't seem bothered. Maybe your sense of smell has gotten desensitized." He's said that before too. He says it often.

"Quite the opposite thankfully. Odors have their own story to tell and the secret is to block them out after they're no longer relevant."

"I can only do that with what I hear and see." He's thinking about his cases, which are the same as mine but our experiences are different.

Vastly and darkly different, the monsters he meets are fond of video-recording the pain and terror they inflict so they can replay it later as they fantasize. I've seen enough to know I prefer the cold forlornness of bodies that can't suffer anymore. I'm left with sensations, not much color, shades of red, a little green, a little yellow, mostly odors and the inanimate noises of metal against metal, wheels rolling, water slapping against tables and floors and drumming against steel.

I focus on newly planted trees with bright green leaves, and glass and granite high-rises in a part of Cambridge called Tech Square.

"I confess I'm not as accustomed to nasty smells." Benton has cracked his window, and the air is rushing in loud and warmly humid. "Phantosmia. I'm not sure it's real."

"It is. Molecules of putrefaction become volatilized like pollution attaching to water molecules in the air and creating smog."

"So I have the smog of death in my sinuses."

"More or less."

"Christ I hope I don't stink."

I lean close to him, and diamond-stitched black leather smells new as I nuzzle the curve of his jaw. "A little cedarwood, a little teak and just enough musk and a hint of cardamom. Bulgari."

He smiles and kisses me, and we're on Sixth Street now. There's still plenty of light but piling gray clouds are advancing like armies. The temperature is on its way to hot. Tomorrow promises to be instant summer, volatile with bursts of rain and wind shifts to the south that could push the mercury up more than twenty degrees. There's too much to do and nature is conspiring against me.

I must get to Marblehead before it storms, and I need to be in New Jersey tomorrow if possible. I intend to see where Gracie Smithers died before rain and wind scrub it away, and a shooting reconstruction is our last hope of understanding the physics of Jamal Nari's homicide. The girl's death is simpler and far crueler. What happened to Nari is sterile and enigmatic with its lack of human contact and explanation.

"It's the equivalent of standing on a tall ladder and shooting straight down at someone who is leaning forward slightly." I'm thinking about our efforts in the autopsy room, what some would view as unseemly and ghoulish.

"A very tall ladder," Benton says and the Cambridge Police Department is just ahead, redbrick with green-tinted glass and art deco lamps.

"Not exactly ninety degrees or perpendicular," I add. "The flight path was closer to seventy-five or eighty."

"Parabolic drop." Benton slows down more, the engine louder.

"What goes up must come down."

"The heavier the round and the lighter the powder charge, the more the bullet's going to lose velocity and gravity's going to pull it down. Like these idiots who fire their guns up in the air and the bullets fall and hit people, the trajectory is vertical or almost."

"That's the important point. Unless an assailant is standing over his victim and firing straight down you don't see a trajectory like this. Certainly not in distant shots. The seventy-five- or eighty-degree angle can't possibly be an accidental phenomenon due to gravity. His spinal cord was severed at the base of his skull exactly as it was in the other cases we know of."

"I agree," Benton says. "What kind of elevation are we talking about?"

"That's what we need to find out. I believe it's key to who's doing this. Someone damn good at shooting and damn good at math."

In first gear now he drives down a concrete ramp that leads into the police department's underground parking. He's careful not to scrape the sloping nose of his car, and abruptly we are in shadows and the air through the vents is cooler.

"Right. Because bullet drop wouldn't explain the flight path unless the shooter did the DOPE and the degree of drop was deliberate." He refers to the military sniper term Data on Previous Engagement or DOPE, which factors in the type of round, the altitude, temperature, wind and barometric pressure.

"Wherever the shooter was, what he did was precisely calculated." I'm sure of that.

"I just hope to hell you never have to show those photos in court. They'll start calling you Doctor Zombie."

I never intend indignity but death has no modesty and the only way to precisely envision the angle that Jamal Nari was shot was to stand him up. So I decided we would. I covered Benton in waterproof Tyvek, and I then hooked my elbows under the dead man's arms while Anne secured him by the ankles. We lowered him to the floor, naked and sutured back up with white twine, and Benton helped hold him straight as I grabbed a camera and climbed a stepladder.

The body was so stiff I could have leaned it against a wall but limber would have been worse, a dead weight as unwieldy as a heavy coil of fire hose, 150 pounds minus the organs. Once rigor passed it would have taken more than the three of us to get Jamal Nari back on his feet, and what Benton said is true. I wouldn't want to show the photos in court, the fiberglass probe protruding from the base of the skull like a black arrow as if he had been shot by Apollo, by a god from above and maybe he was. Only this god is an evil one.

BENTON PARKS IN A reserved spot several spaces away from the police commissioner's unmarked dark blue Ford. Gerry Everman is still here at this hour. Maybe he's observing Leo Gantz through one-way glass. Then I think of Machado and hope we don't run into him.

"I'm trying to figure out the best way to handle this." By *this* Benton means Marino. "Leo Gantz's confession is an interference and a nuisance at best and Marino's going to want to cut him loose, to get whatever information he might have and then get him out of his hair."

"It sounds like you don't feel the same way." I climb out of the car.

"I don't," he says as we walk past a row of white BMW motorcycles tricked out with emblems, lights and sirens.

"Why?"

He pushes open a door that leads inside the first floor of a modern building originally designed by a biotech company that sold out to the city. "The safest thing would be to keep him locked up for a while."

"The safest thing for who?"

"The safest thing for Leo and that might be exactly what he wants." Near the polished granite wall of elevators Benton nods at four uniformed police officers, young and bulky with muscle and ballistic gear, familiar-looking but I don't know them.

They seem strangely congregated by the door and don't nod back at him, riveting their attention on me and I already sense what's coming. I feel uneasiness in my stomach and a cool wariness creeps up my neck. It occurs to me they were expecting us.

"How you doing, Doc?"

"What are you gentlemen up to tonight? It looks like you're keeping the streets more than safe."

"You know who's in town."

"I certainly do," I reply while Benton is ignored.

"Mind if I ask you something?"

"Help yourself."

"I got over a cold last month and am still congested."

"Same thing and I can't shake the cough," another one says.

"Me too," says yet another.

The four of them are talking at once, their attention on me as if Benton isn't here. He's calm and unflappable. He doesn't register surprise at the ruse of a welcome or questions about medical advice from men who sound perfectly healthy. Tension and resentment toward the FBI have been palpable since the marathon bombings and the murder of MIT Officer Collier, a close colleague of Cambridge police, his department within the Cambridge city limits. The FBI is accused of not sharing intelligence and that's nothing new but this time it's as personal as it gets.

They continue bantering with me so they can stick it to my husband. This is for his benefit, passive-aggressive behavior on the way to bullying, and I'm convinced they saw us coming. Benton's car draws attention. All it took was one cop spotting us and tipping off the others so they could lash out, and I can't say that I blame them. Benton presses the elevator button again and I know he's bothered even if he doesn't show it. The doors slide open and we step inside.

"Good to see you, Doc."

"Be safe out there," I reply, and just as I'm certain we've escaped the worst I find out I'm wrong.

"Hey! We're being rude leaving out the FBI." A uniformed arm suddenly juts out and the shutting elevator doors bounce back into their frame.

"Excuse me?" The officer confronts Benton. "Maybe you got something to say?"

"About what?" But he knows.

"Why the FBI thinks it's okay not to share information that might prevent cops from getting shot while they're sitting in their cars."

Benton leans against the open door, his hands in his pockets, his eyes steady on the four of them. And the officer removes his arm.

The officer steps back and says, "Wait until we know something you should be told. And we don't pass it on. See how you feel if something happens to one of your damn agents."

"You wouldn't do that," Benton says.

"Really? Why not?"

"Because you're better than that."

"The FBI should apologize."

"About a lot of things." Fear and intimidation aren't colors on Benton's palette, and the doors slide shut and he meets my eyes. "The Bureau won't. It never does."

"Their hostility might be related to Machado. There's no telling what he's spreading around."

"It's not about him. They said what it's about. They couldn't have been clearer."

"They shouldn't take it out on you."

"They should. I'm safe because I won't go over their heads and complain," he says. "The commissioner is here right now and they know I could head straight to his office. They also know I would never do it."

CHAPTER 30

We ride the elevator up and the confrontation downstairs reverberates. I try to quiet my inner voice but I can't. I'm not a pessimist but I'm not a Pollyanna either.

Resentment of the Feds is at an endless boil, rattling nonstop like scalding water in a pot. It doesn't come and go anymore like it did when I was getting started. Now it's chronic. Absolute power has corrupted and the absence of checks and balances seems complete. There's no place to go but the media, and cops like the ones we just encountered can't do that without permission from the brass, which they'll never get.

"Terrorists score points when they inspire people to act indecently, to misuse what they are sworn to protect." I watch the floors slowly go by. "It started with 9/11 and is building momentum. Our government spies and lies. Those trusted to uphold and enforce the law use it to their advantage instead."

"Not everyone. We don't."

"We probably do. Just not abusively and all of the time."

"Without monitoring what's going on in cyberspace we couldn't begin to anticipate the next catastrophic move," Benton says and I again recall what Briggs intimated about intelligence gathered by the CIA, probably by spies in Russia.

Money, drugs and thugs flowing into this country.

"We work around what gets in the way," Benton adds.

"Like Lucy does."

"We have to dance. We can learn something from Leo Gantz."

"About what? Lying?"

"His is a very calculated dance motivated by a desire to stay safe, to escape a danger that is real but unknown at the moment."

"You say that as if you know it for a fact."

The doors slide open and we step off the elevator.

"It seems to me Leo caused his own danger by tweeting for attention," I then say.

"For attention but not for the usual reason. To inspire hatred and it has," Benton answers. "Especially among certain factions who applaud his allegedly committing murder."

By factions he means people who are anti-Muslim and that continues to be the irony. Jamal Nari was mistaken for a Muslim with terrorist ties when he was neither. A former heroin addict turned drug smuggler, he was a gifted guitarist who didn't play for the right reason anymore. A troubled teacher with penis piercing and old needle scars, he didn't merit hating. His life was a struggle. It was sadly mundane and he was held hostage by his own demons. Had he not died this morning he was headed in that direction.

Lucy has been going through his laptop. He had booked a noon flight today to Canada and it wasn't the first time. He'd been in and out of Toronto on average twice a month since March, probably smuggling drugs, probably liquid cocaine, easy to dilute and reconvert to powdered form, nothing lost except your freedom or your life eventually and inevitably. His routine was to check a suitcase and one of his graphite guitars that he loved so much it merited a tattooed endorsement on his shoulder. He played at live music hot spots, The Horseshoe Tavern, Dominion on Queen and Polyhaus, but what drove him wasn't his rhythm and blues funk or his rock-and-roll riffs.

He wanted money. Judging by the number of condoms inside his stomach when he was murdered he could have been making anywhere from fifty to a hundred thousand dollars cash per month from his trips to Canada alone. Lucy has been following his trail through his emails. What she can't determine is why it appears he turned into a drug mule possibly only three months ago except that was about the time his lawsuit completely stalled. The case continued to cost him with no end in sight. In a way his turning to crime is Rand Bloom's fault, and I'm wondering if it wasn't his influence that caused it.

"I hope this goes away before it's time to eat." Benton is still preoccupied with the odor trapped in his nose.

"I have something that will help as soon as we get where we're going," I reply as we follow a corridor to the end.

HE OPENS THE DOOR to the Investigative Unit, a large open space of grayish blue carpet and cubicles in a grid, the typical police department ice cube tray.

We stop at the front desk where no one is sitting. On one side is a wall of plateglass windows, on the other a line of shut wooden doors, some of the rooms with windows, some without. I hear detectives on phones and the quiet tapping of computer keys. There is no one to greet us and no one pays us any mind as we head in the direction of the interview rooms.

Benton is texting, using one thumb and then he stops, pausing us closer to the soundproof rooms with their shut windowless doors. I can't hear a thing, not even a murmur. Then a door in the middle of the wall opens and Marino steps out holding his phone. He closes the door behind him and walks toward us. His feet make a brushing sound over carpet. He motions for us to follow him to his cubicle in the very back.

A corner office he likes to say, it's nothing more than a workstation with a computer, a coatrack, equipment piled on the floor and photographs crammed on the fabric-covered partition. I notice he's changed his clothes, in khaki cargo pants, a black polo shirt, a black flak jacket. He has on the same black leather high-tops.

"How's it going?" Benton asks.

"He's not budging from his story and the wound on his head isn't pretty." Marino looks keyed up and sure of himself.

"Did he have it treated?" I want to know.

"Nope."

"He continues to say Jamal Nari hit him with a trophy?" I look at a large brown paper evidence bag on Marino's cluttered desk, files, pink message slips and dirty coffee cups, the long cord to the phone ridiculously snarled.

Cop humor. Since Marino has worked here he's replaced his phone cord every month. Overnight it ends up like this. It probably won't happen anymore. I've always suspected Machado.

"The kid's a damn good liar," Marino says. "I've lifted a few prints and swabbed for DNA. There's definitely blood on the trophy."

He reaches for the bag sealed with red evidence tape and snatches two pairs of examination gloves out of a box, handing a pair to me. We put them on. Opening the blade of a folding knife he slits the tape. Heavy paper rattles as he digs inside and pulls out a large silver cup with a rosewood base, what Leo Gantz was presented when he won the state tennis championship last summer. The trophy is spattered and smeared with rusty dried blood. There are smudges of fingerprint powder all over it.

I open my portable kit, this one small and silver aluminum, a modified EMT medical box that includes essential forensic necessities. It's not often I need first-aid supplies but typically when I examine pattern injuries on the living I find their wounds could use a little extra cleaning up and of course I have to replace their dressings. I give Benton an alcohol wipe and he gets the implication.

"Excuse me." He tears it open, turns away from us and wipes the inside of his nose.

"What the hell?" Marino stares and Benton ignores him. "Oh I get it. I guess I know where you've been. Me? I root up there with a wet paper towel before I leave the morgue, as far up as I can reach without causing brain damage. Don't use Vicks. It makes it worse."

I find a tape measure inside the kit and estimate the weight as I hold the trophy by its stem, rosewood embedded with a gold medallion, what looks like a Roman coin. The trophy is heavy, approximately eight pounds, I estimate, and twenty inches high. If enough force were used it could inflict profound damage but obviously it didn't or Leo Gantz wouldn't be sitting inside an interview room. I notice that one of the silver handles is bent and an area of the cup is dented and scuffed.

"Before I take a look can you tell me exactly what he claims happened?" I find my camera and set the trophy on top of the paper bag.

"That Nari took the trophy as if he intended to give it to his wife and then suddenly whacked Leo in the head." Marino watches me take photographs. "He says he didn't see it coming, had his back to him, heading to the door."

"He hit him like this?" I pick up the trophy by the stem and turn it upside down, wielding it like a club. "And struck him with the base of it?"

"That's his story."

I look at the bent handle, at the smudges and smears made by someone with bloody hands.

"I'm going to guess the trophy was already damaged." I point out the handle, which is bent the way it would be if someone smashed it against the floor. "In other words the dent, the bent handle are probably unrelated to the alleged attack."

There's also blood on one edge of the wooden base, crusty and thick and beginning to flake. I turn the trophy this way and that, looking at it carefully.

"How many times does he say he was hit?" I take more photographs.

"Once," Marino says.

"Not possible," I reply. "Assuming he was struck with the base there wouldn't be this much blood on the edge of it unless he was already bleeding. Notice the teardrop-shaped droplets pointing in different directions. The pattern is haphazard and nonsensical. These would appear to be consistent with a medium-velocity impact spatter caused by the base of the trophy striking blood, in other words, striking someone already bleeding. But the problem is it makes no sense that the direction of travel is inconsistent and erratic."

"Because he put the blood drops on there himself," Marino sums it up.

"He could have flicked it." I flick my fingers as if they're bloody, flicking from different angles. "That could account for the droplets and the chaotic pattern. What about castoff?"

"As you know there was no blood inside Nari's apartment, not even any that was cleaned up. Just something like bleach on the guitars, the two cases on the bed, the other stuff. They lit up when we sprayed them but not the same way blood does," Marino says.

"What about at Leo's house?" Benton asks.

"I've got photographs," Marino says. "How about you talk to him alone for a few minutes. Then we'll bring the Doc in and maybe she can get something out of him. I quit."

Benton tucks the used alcohol wipe back into its packet and drops it into the trash.

"My being the good cop didn't work," Marino adds.

Benton doesn't say he's not surprised because he isn't.

"He's the same arrogant prick we saw this morning," Marino says to me. "When I tried to be his friend he went out of his way to piss me off."

"What does he think is happening next?" Benton asks.

"You're looking at him," Marino says to me. "I hope he doesn't recognize you from this morning."

"I never got out of your car."

"So maybe you wander in first," he says to Benton. "Use your touchy-feely magic on him and get him to start telling the truth so he doesn't spend the night in jail."

"He wants to spend the night in jail. He wants to be out of circulation."

"He's probably scared of his father."

"That's not why he wants to stay locked up," Benton says.

"Yeah well maybe if he's lucky they'll give him a vacation at McLean for a while."

The Harvard-affiliated psychiatric hospital is a few miles from here in Belmont, and Benton used to be a consultant there. It would be a good place for Leo, truth be told.

"That's what he wants," Benton says. "He wants exactly what he's getting."

"Then how come he keeps asking when he can leave?"

"Asking you," Benton says pointedly. "He wants to be locked up and he wants nothing to do with you."

"And you're basing this on what?" Marino is getting offended.

"Did you Mirandize him?"

"Now you're thinking I'm stupid." Anger touches Marino's face.

"Obviously he waived his right to an attorney. Obviously he's fully aware and understands the legal process and the repercussions of his confession."

"According to him he's not trying to hide anything so he doesn't need an attorney. Plus I told him three times he could wait for one or his parents."

"This kid is very bright, very logical but his prefrontal cortex isn't fully developed yet," Benton says.

"Give me a fucking break," Marino says.

"He doesn't like the police but he's not afraid of them. He's afraid of something else."

"Like what?"

"The police won't hurt or kill him. Something else might."

"I got no idea what you're talking about," Marino says.

"Leo is impulsive," Benton says. "He's driven by fight or flight, by a need to survive and conquer. He's also driven by the short-term gratification of notoriety, of being a hero and also feelings of guilt. At his young age he's three times more likely to confess to crimes he didn't commit than an adult would be."

"I'm not interested in statistics right now." Marino doesn't try to be diplomatic or anything but annoyed.

"Give me fifteen minutes." Benton walks off.

CHAPTER 31

THE BEDROOM IS SMALL with French wallpaper in a blue floral pattern that is stained brownish in places near the molding. The pumpkin pine floor is badly scuffed. Against one wall are bunk beds. Supposedly Leo's was the top one until he relocated to the basement and began sleeping on a couch.

Marino has given me his desk chair while he leans close clicking the mouse, showing me what he found when he went through the Gantzes' house. What grabs my attention instantly are tennis awards that fill three walls, trophies of all size and description, crystal, silver, bronze, and large medals on bright ribbons. Everything is damaged. Male figures are serving and hitting strokes with rackets that have been removed or broken off. There are blank gluey areas where engraved plates used to be. Platters and bowls are scratched as if someone took a screwdriver to them.

I zoom in on the wooden floor. The scuffing isn't due to normal wear and tear. There are deep scrapes and gouges, and I ask Marino about the bent handle on the tennis trophy inside the brown paper bag on the desk. It appears that someone deliberately vandalized Leo's awards and I wonder if this was discussed when Marino was at the house.

"He says he did it," he replies.

"He ruined his own awards?"

"That's what he said. He'd get angry and couldn't control himself and he'd break something."

"Do you believe him?"

"I don't know."

"What would be the point in vandalizing something that sets him apart in an extraordinary way?"

"To give the impression that they don't mean anything to him. To act like a big guy because he's a wimp, five-six or seven, maybe one-thirty soaking wet."

I ask if Leo's family was home when Marino was there.

"Watching TV in the living room," he says.

"What was their demeanor?"

"Scared but uncooperative."

"And the mother?" I ask.

"Sitting in the kitchen crying. But totally defensive about the father who's a worthless tool, a mean bastard."

"Did you find a firearm or anything firearms related?" I ask.

"The father's got an old .38 special. Unregistered in Massachusetts and I could get him for that too."

"Loaded?"

"No. I didn't find any ammo."

"Is Leo suggesting he might have used his father's .38 to kill Jamal Nari?"

"He's a clever piece of shit. He just says it was a gun he dropped in the sewer. He says he doesn't know what kind it was."

"Where does he say he got it?"

"He bought it on the street."

"He says it was a handgun?"

"Exactly. The possibility of a rifle hasn't come up. I don't think he has any idea that's what was used."

"Did you ask him what type of ammunition was loaded in this handgun?"

"He says he didn't know. That it was loaded when he bought it and the person who sold it to him for sixty bucks said it was *badass* ammo that would explode someone's head like a watermelon. By the way this person is someone Leo doesn't know and can't describe."

"I think we get the picture," I reply. "One lie after another."

Marino clicks the mouse and another photograph opens up on the display. "There was no visible blood so I used Bluestar in the bathrooms, figuring Leo must have cleaned himself up. This bathroom here is the one near the bedroom with the bunk beds." He clicks back several photographs to remind me, then returns to the bathroom.

The chemical reagent causes nonvisible blood to luminesce, and areas of the sink glow a pale sapphire blue, on the handles, around the drain. Splotches and streaks on the tile floor are a ghostly blue like spirit light.

"Someone cleaned up," I agree, "but the question is who and when? And are we to assume he conveniently carried the tennis trophy all the way back. On his bicycle?"

"That's his story." Marino displays another photograph and as he moves I smell cedar and lemon, a cologne called Guilty that Lucy bought for him because she liked the irony of the name. He must have splashed it on when he changed his clothes. "He claims he had the trophy in his backpack," he says.

"Did you find this backpack he mentioned?" I ask.

"Yeah." He shows me photographs before and after he sprayed the inside of it, checking for transferred blood that isn't visible without a special light or chemical.

"Nothing luminesced," I observe. "So it's not likely he put a bloody tennis trophy inside."

"Nope."

More photographs, these of laundry machines in the basement, a front-load washer, then several of Marino's gloved hand holding a white tank top. It's heavily stained with blood that's a dark rusty brown around the edges and a brighter red in the middle. In other photographs he's holding a pair of blue shorts and a large bath towel, also bloody.

"The blood looks damp," I comment.

"It would have dried more slowly from being inside the washing machine with the lid closed. But yeah this didn't happen early this morning like he claims."

"And he also claims he was wearing a tank top and shorts when he allegedly was attacked with a tennis trophy?"

"Remember when we saw him at around quarter of noon?" Marino answers with a question.

"He had on a sweatshirt and long pants."

"Because it wasn't that warm," Marino says.

"And his story is that he was in shorts and a tank top when he showed up at the apartment with the tennis trophy at around eight this morning. No matter how much you emphasized how illogical this is he wouldn't budge."

"It's ridiculous, right?"

"The problem is false confessions more often than not lead to wrongful convictions. Leo Gantz may have a teenaged brain, but he's anything but stupid. Why is he doing this?"

"Maybe I don't care why," Marino says.

"Did you photograph the entire house?"

"Sure."

"Continue to take me through it please."

He shows me the kitchen, the living room, a den, the parents' bedroom, dark upholstered furniture that looks cheap and tired. A lot of clutter, magazines, newspapers, and dishes are piled in the sink. I ask him to return me to the bathroom where the reagent reacted positively, presuming blood.

I click through photographs for a moment. I zoom in and out in an area of brown tile flooring near the walk-in shower. The walls are brown tile too. The toilet and sink are black, and the dark surfaces are fortunate for us. Whoever cleaned up missed some bloodstains and didn't completely eradicate others.

Faint bluish smears and coin-sized stains start at the glass shower door and end at the sink. I click on more photographs, enlarging them over luminescent rings, the outer edges of blood drops that were wiped away while the centers were still wet. Most of them are perfectly round because they fell straight down. It's consistent with someone upright and bleeding. I find the partial shapes of bare feet, and on the wall to the left of the shower stall two handprints glow bluely. The glass shower door is open, the frame is metal with sharp edges and the tile inside is wet.

"He didn't just clean up in here," I say to Marino as I get up from his chair. "This is where it happened."

THROUGH ONE-WAY GLASS I watch Benton talking with Leo Gantz, the two of them sitting at a simple wooden table, their ergonomic chairs angled, not directly facing each other, casual and nonconfrontational.

The interview room is small and bare, and it appears they are alone, that their conversation is private and not adversarial. I can tell by Leo's demeanor that he's not hostile but he's also not opening up or trusting. In a flashy warm-up suit and black tennis shoes, no socks, he leans back in his chair, his fingers tensely gripping the armrests, one leg nervously jumping, then the other, a black cap on his head. I wonder if he has a clue he's being video-recorded by a concealed camera or that someone like me is observing him and listening.

"We're about to wind this up." Benton's voice is amplified through speakers in the corners of the adjoining observation room where Marino and I sit. "But I need to draw your attention to an important fact."

Leo Gantz shrugs, his long red hair loose and unkempt around his shoulders, and I can see a sandy reddish stubble over his lip and scattered over his jaw and chin. The black baseball cap conceals the wound allegedly inflicted by Jamal Nari.

"Despite any consequences for you, and they aren't good ones, Leo, your falsely confessing means the person who really did this gets a free pass. The police will stop looking."

"He doesn't give a shit," Marino says from a corner where he has a chair turned backward, straddling it. "You think he gives a shit about anything besides himself?"

"I'm telling the truth." Leo is looking directly at me, and it's unnerving.

I keep reminding myself I'm far enough back from the one-way glass to prevent him from detecting the faintest shadow or change in light caused by my slightest movement.

"You're not telling the truth," Benton says flatly. "And if you end up wrongly convicted the real killer gets away and might hurt somebody else. Are you protecting the person who murdered Jamal Nari?"

"I'm not protecting anyone."

"You realize you could spend the rest of your life in prison without parole."

"So what." He shrugs.

"You say that now."

"Hell yeah I'm saying it now." His left knee is jumping.

"Do you know who Doctor Kay Scarpetta is?"

Leo shakes his head and shrugs.

"She's an expert in injuries," Benton says and Leo shrugs again. "Her office is here in Cambridge and you may have seen her in the area."

"What area?"

"Around." Benton is vague.

"Maybe I've seen you around too."

"It's possible."

"Are you rich?"

"We're not here to talk about me, Leo."

"The FBI must pay pretty good for you to drive an Audi R-Eight. Or maybe—maybe . . . ! I get it oh yeah! It's an undercover car and you're cruising Cambridge looking for terrorists." His tone is mocking. "Maybe you'll catch them this time before they blow people up. But hey then again probably not. The FBI only catches people who didn't do anything."

"Like you?"

"I've done plenty."

"I want you to tell Doctor Scarpetta exactly what happened to your head," Benton says.

"It's like ten times now I've told the same thing."

"So we'll make it eleven." Benton smiles pleasantly. "Doctor Scarpetta isn't on anybody's side."

"You're funny as hell." Leo laughs derisively, almost hysterically as his leg jumps nervously.

"She's agreed to help out by taking a look at your injury, which is significant." Obviously Benton has seen it. "She may also recommend that you get stitches."

"No way I'm getting stitches."

"Or a few staples."

"Fuck that."

"Let's see what she says. I'm going to step out and bring her in." Benton rolls his chair back from the table.

CHAPTER 32

HE STANDS UP AND absently smoothes his suit jacket while Leo leans back and stares up at the ceiling as if he's desperately bored. Benton walks out of the interview room and shuts the door behind him. Instantly I know that Leo Gantz is clueless about what is going on.

He may be a good liar but he's a novice when it comes to a criminal investigation, and he takes off his cap. He digs into a pocket of his warm-up pants and pulls out a yellow bandana that is spotted with blood. He touches it to the upper left side of his head, the temporal scalp several inches above his ear, and he checks to see if he's still bleeding. Then he presses much too hard to make sure he is, and he winces. He blows out a big long breath, rubs his face, twitchy and anxious. He has no idea he has an audience.

The door to the observation room opens and Benton steps inside.

"Well?" Marino asks. "You get anything I didn't?"

"I'm not sure what you got exactly but he's not changing his story regardless of any incentive offered by my indicating his details are inconsistent with the facts of the case."

"What facts did you give him?" Marino wants to know, and as if on cue Leo yawns loudly and props his feet on top of the table.

"It's not what I gave him it's what I asked him," Benton replies. "Leo wants people to think he committed murder. He wants to feel powerful because he feels the opposite. He feels he has no control and he wants to be locked up. He's also punishing someone."

On the other side of the window Leo tilts the bill of his cap low and crosses his arms across his belly as if he's about to take a nap.

"Why the hell would he want to be locked up? I mean he must know his little game has gone too far," Marino says.

"He needs to feel powerful and he's afraid."

"Afraid of what? To go home? Because his father's a son of a bitch and his brother's an asshole? He's more afraid of them than going to prison? Because he'll be charged with murder as an adult. We've locked up ones younger than him in Cedar Junction. I hope he likes making license plates."

A maximum security state prison where no fifteen-year-old should be, and I hate to think what would happen to him.

"His home is an abusive environment," Benton agrees. "But there's something else. I suspect when he found out Jamal Nari was murdered it frightened him."

"Why wouldn't it?" I reply.

"It's not just one thing. That's what makes situations like this so difficult. We're talking about a series of events that happened fast and now here he is," Benton says.

Suddenly Leo stands up again, looking around, stretching, scratching his jaw. He grabs a Pepsi can off the table, shakes it to see if there's anything in it and crushes it in one hand.

"One reason I say this is because the abusive home isn't new," Benton continues. "His father's had several DUIs and there have been domestic calls on and off over the years. Leo is used to his dysfunctional home life. It's all he knows. Something changed and here he is," Benton repeats.

"Yeah," Marino says. "What's changed is he's confessed to a murder he didn't commit and he's all over the news. And oh yeah, he also lied about Joanna Cather having sex with him, not caring if he ruins her life."

"We don't know what went on between them." Benton watches Leo through the glass.

"Sure we do. Nothing. That's what went on," Marino says. "Another story that didn't add up. He helps her carry the groceries in and they have sex on the couch. It's like the gun being dropped in the sewer. He didn't have details because all of it is bullshit."

"He has strong emotions about Joanna. He's deeply conflicted," Benton says. "He's hurt Joanna, someone who was kind to him, and he may have been coerced to do it because his family needs money. I think Leo feels that he's in danger."

"How the hell can you know what he feels?" Marino doesn't hide his frustration or irritation.

"Because I do," Benton says. "I know what he feels. I just don't know exactly why. And I know he's scared."

"He's scared because he lied about a murdered man's wife. Leo came on to her and she rejected him. That's the real story."

"I suspect the story about them having sex wasn't his idea. And we need to take his fear very seriously." Benton won't back down.

Leo bats the crumpled Pepsi can into a wastepaper basket, his hand flat like a tennis racket, plucking the can out and doing it again, brushing up, top spin.

"He's seen you around our neighborhood," I say to Benton. "There's no telling who else he's seen. Rand Bloom and who else I wonder?"

"You should hold Leo in your lockup for now." Benton directs this to Marino.

"He can stay in jail until he rots. Be my guest."

"I'm talking about a few days at most. Tonight for sure. Best case is at some point tomorrow I can get him into East House at McLean, their inpatient adolescent program where he'll be safely detained while being assessed and treated."

"Don't tell him he's going to a cushy hospital, okay?" Marino says to me. "Don't reassure him about a damn thing."

Benton meets my eyes indicating it's time, and I pick up my silver case.

"Does he know you found blood?" I ask Marino as Benton opens the door.

"I didn't tell him shit."

"Did he observe you spraying a chemical?"

"I made all of them hold in the kitchen while I was checking the bathrooms and the laundry area."

Out that door and Benton opens the one to the interview room. I walk in.

I SET MY MEDICAL kit on top of the table and Leo drops his feet to the floor. We are alone. We can't hear or see anyone but the reverse isn't true.

"I don't believe it." Leo stands up and stares at me, his eyes surprised beneath the bill of his black cap. "You?" he says.

"I'm Doctor Scarpetta." I'm taken aback by how small and nonthreatening he seems.

When I saw him with the leaf blower this morning and even moments ago through the one-way glass he seemed bigger, more formidable. Suddenly he's a wiry boy, unkempt and lost, his defiance a bunker he won't be able to hide behind much longer. Males are his enemy on and off the court. Females are another matter, and Marino couldn't have been a worse choice for being sent to the Gantz house. But Benton knew that. It's why he did it. Now it's my turn.

"I know who you are," Leo says.

"Have we met?" I ask.

"I've seen you working in your yard. You have a lot of roses. I know exactly which house is yours. He's your husband, the FBI agent, the guy in the fancy suit."

"That's right."

"He drives that black R-Eight, a V-ten with titanium wheels. Sweet. I knew I'd seen him before but I couldn't place it until now. I've seen him with you."

"It sounds like you're into cars."

"You name it, I know it. Is the Ferrari yours?" He's fidgety, gesturing a lot.

"I don't own a Ferrari." I smile.

"Well it's somebody's, Jesus Christ." He's animated and talking fast. "I knocked on your door one time to see if you needed someone to cut your grass, rake leaves, wash cars, whatever. And the Ferrari was in your driveway. I couldn't believe it. You don't see cars like that around here."

"I apologize that I don't seem to remember your stopping by."

"It wasn't you who answered the door. Some other lady, young, hot-looking."

"That doesn't sound like my housekeeper." I snap open the clasps of my aluminum case.

"Not unless she drives an awesome five-ninety-nine GTO, twelve cylinder, almost eight hundred horsepower. Gray like a shark with red leather racing seats. She wasn't friendly."

"That wouldn't have been Rosa." I don't say it was Lucy.

"Hell I'd detail it for free. You sure it's not yours?" His face is lively, he's cocky and full of himself as if he's forgotten why we're here.

"It's not."

"Have you ever driven it?"

"Once or twice," I reply and before this moment I never imagined that Lucy's obsession with fast machines could work to my advantage.

At least I'm quite familiar with them. I let Leo think we have something in common.

"What was it like?" he asks.

"A rocket with very grabby brakes." I pull on a pair of gloves.

"F-one shift or did you keep it in automatic?"

"Which do you like?" I find Betadine, a small bottle of distilled water and gauze. I set them on the table.

"Not automatic hell no. I'm going to have a car like that someday," he continues to brag. "As soon as I turn pro and get a lot of big endorsements."

"First we need to keep you out of trouble."

"You're here to keep me out of trouble?"

"I'm going to try." I open the box of gauze.

"It's too late. I'm already in trouble." He seems proud of it and now he's flirting. "What's that? Iodine? What are you going to do to me?"

"I need you to sit down and take off your cap, Leo, so I can take a look at your head."

He sits and carefully lifts off the cap, placing it in his lap, and the lacerated area of his scalp is swollen. It's oozing blood because he made sure of it a few minutes ago. I find a plastic ruler and my camera but I already know at a glance that the tennis trophy I examined didn't inflict parallel lacerations exactly one inch apart and almost three inches long. They begin at his temple and terminate at the curvature of his skull.

"That looks painful." I gently move hair out of the way, noting that the edges of the wounds are clean as if inflicted by a blade but they definitely aren't incisions or particularly deep. "Let me know if I'm hurting you."

"It doesn't bother me." He holds perfectly still, his Adam's apple moving up and down as he swallows, both of his legs jumping now.

"It would be helpful if you could hold your legs still." I douse gauze with sterile water.

"I don't like needles. I don't want stitches." What he does like and want is my attention.

"I don't blame you." I press the wet gauze to his wounds and around them, cleaning up blood as best I can, and his body odor is strong. "There's not much to like about needles. The scalp is very vascular so it's understandable that you bled a lot."

The question is when but I'm sure he didn't get hurt at eight o'clock this morning. There's no way. I also don't think he was injured in the past few hours. The bloody clothing and towel in the washing machine weren't dry and they weren't wet when Marino was at the Gantz house. The bloody items were damp.

"You're very brave but it must have been scary." I use a hand lens to get a better look at the wounds, making sure I don't see any dirt or debris.

"Damn right it's scary when somebody suddenly attacks you."

"The good news is the lacerations didn't penetrate the aponeurosis or the fibrous connective tissue that anchors muscle."

"What does that mean?" His legs are quiet now, his hands on his thighs, fingers splayed stiffly.

"It means the wounds don't gape and you can get by without stitches. But then you probably knew that which is why you didn't go to the ER. Tell me what you did after you got hurt."

"I rode my bike home. It was maybe eight-thirty and I went home and cleaned up."

"Did you let anyone know you were hurt?"

"No. I got the gun and went back to the apartment and shot Mister Nari."

It's impossible. But I don't let on what I think.

"Of bigger concern is any other symptoms you might be experiencing," I reply.

"Yeah like I'm starved. Maybe someone can get me a Double Whopper with extra cheese. I'd settle for a pizza and a large Coke."

"I suspect that can be arranged." I douse several layers of gauze with Betadine, the odor sharply metallic. "This may sting a little."

CHAPTER 33

I CAN HARDLY FEEL IT." Leo doesn't flinch.

"Any dizziness, a headache? What about nausea since you were injured?" I hold the gauze in place using light pressure as I wonder what he fears most.

His father or something else.

"No," he says. "I'm fine."

"Not even a little bit of headache? You have significant swelling. This concerns me. You really should be evaluated. I'm going to recommend an MRI and a thorough exam at McLean Hospital. It's very close to here in Belmont. Possibly you'll need to stay for a while to make sure there's nothing going on with you neurologically."

Marino won't like what I just said but that's too bad. It's not my job to terrorize.

"Well it's kind of throbbing." Leo likes the idea of being detained in a safe place for a while, and I remember how close he was to Rand Bloom's pickup truck.

"It's very important this stays clean so you don't get an infection," I explain. "It probably would be a good idea to get you on an antibiotic. Are you allergic to any medications?"

"Like what?"

"Penicillin or one of its derivatives. Amoxicillin, ampicillin for example."

"You can prescribe anything you want. Maybe Oxys while you're at it?"

"I'm afraid it won't be me doing the prescribing. But I'll have a word with someone before I leave."

"I'm just kidding about the Oxys. Shit, you're serious. Do you ever lighten up?"

"You know what they say about scientists. We're boring."

"I'm good in science." His stare is intense.

He's excited and I feel the transference as it happens. Leo Gantz is bonding with me and my internal conflicts begin to agitate. Do I cross boundaries or not? For the sake of truth and to save him from himself do I let things happen or make them stop?

"Let's talk about how you came to hit your head on the frame of the shower door," I say to him as if it's a given.

"I didn't." He's visibly startled.

"Did you forget it was there and hit your head when you were reaching inside the shower stall to turn on the water?"

"What?" He looks at me with a mixture of amazement and shock.

"I'm trying to reconstruct it based on the pattern of your wounds."

"I don't know what you're talking about."

"I've seen it happen." I position the ruler near the lacerations and with my free hand take a photograph. "A hidden hazard, a design defect. The aluminum doorframe has edges, two parallel ones where the glass door slides in snugly so water doesn't leak out onto the floor."

"He hit me in the head when I wasn't looking. That's how I got hurt."

"You certainly were hit in the head, Leo, but not with the tennis trophy I examined. Last year's state championship. That's impressive."

"I was bleeding in the bathroom," he says. "Because I went in there to clean up after I got home. After he attacked me. And then I went back and shot him."

"You'd been doing yard work. Maybe you wanted to clean up after doing yard work. By this afternoon it was getting quite warm and humid."

"So what!" His demeanor has radically changed from stoical and excited to scared and defensive. "So what if I did clean up after work?"

If his lie is uncovered he might be sent home, and the idea of that overwhelms him with panic.

"Except that based on the amount of dried blood on your scalp and in your hair I don't think you got around to showering." I indicate clumps of his long red hair. "At least not after you were injured. You may not have gotten around to it at all today."

"Y-You're trying to trick me," he stammers.

I use another round of Betadine and gauze, taking my time. "There are no tricks here, Leo. Only the evidence. And what's apparent is that you were in the bathroom, possibly to clean up after doing yard work. You started this morning . . ."

"How would you know what I was doing?"

"I saw you."

"Where?"

"At close to noon you were near my house." There's no point in being coy. He knows where I live. "You were using a gas-powered leaf blower, cleaning dirt and cut grass off a sidewalk next to a gray pickup truck that was parked on the side of the street."

Rand Bloom.

"Shit. You were with that dumbass detective, the one who yelled at me and showed up at my house. It's not even my truck."

I know whose it is.

"I noticed it," I reply. "The driver wasn't in it which is why Detective Marino assumed it was yours. That and it was parked right where you were using the leaf blower."

"I don't have to answer your questions."

"I didn't ask one." I tuck the gauze into a biohazard bag and my used gloves follow.

I roll out a chair in the position I want and sit down close to him, face-to-face.

"I'M WONDERING WHO WAS barefoot." I slide my aluminum medical case off the table and set it upright on the floor next to my chair.

Leo is silent and I detect he's getting more upset. He doesn't want me to leave, and I quickly calculate. How far do I go, and I decide it will be as far as it takes. Marino or Benton can always walk in and stop me. But they won't. Not yet.

"Someone was barefoot in the bathroom where you were bleeding," I say next. "Maybe Detective Marino will show you photographs if you ask. A partial bloody footprint between the shower door and sink, and there are bloody handprints on the wall." I give him information.

Under normal circumstances I wouldn't.

"It appears everything was cleaned up, but with certain chemicals we can still see blood," I continue, hammering a point that usually isn't mine to make. "It's very difficult to get rid of. The police have compelling photographs. Maybe you should see them."

"I don't give a shit about any damn photographs," he says angrily, but he's unnerved.

"At around five-thirty P.M., about three hours ago, you tweeted that you killed Mister Nari." I step over the railing of my boundaries onto the ledge of what I must have. "You tweeted this from your home."

"How do you know where I was?"

"You probably know about IP addresses. You're a very smart young man. You're good in science. Is five-thirty around the time you were injured in the bathroom?"

"I don't remember," he says.

"Your wounds look several hours old. But they might be older. Possibly four or five hours old but definitely not twelve. The question people will ask is which came first. The tweets and your calls to the police or your being hurt. People will ask if you hit your head on the shower doorframe or if someone shoved you or banged your head against it. Perhaps you were caught off guard as you stood there in a white tank top and shorts, perhaps turning on the water with your back to the door. One is bound to wonder if someone got upset when you confessed to a crime as serious as murder."

His abusive father couldn't have been happy with what Leo did. Maybe it would be fine to frame a high school psychologist for a possible payoff. But it couldn't be fine to admit to murder. That's the flip side of encouraging deceit when it suits. You don't get to pick someone's lies, and I can well imagine Leo's father going into a rage when he heard the news. The question is when. I don't know and the wounds aren't going to tell me.

"You're a damn undercover cop pretending to be a doctor." Leo's eyes are angry and suddenly swimming with tears.

"I'm not a cop or undercover but I am a doctor. My specialty is dealing with violence, with injuries and deaths associated with it." I remain seated. I don't dare move. "Let's get back to the gray pickup truck. I saw it again after I noticed you near it this morning. An insurance investigator drives it. Maybe you've met him. He bothers a lot of people."

"What does he look like?" Leo oddly asks and I describe Rand Bloom.

I don't say the name, and Leo stares. I catch the doubt in his eyes. Then fear. Then nothing.

"I got no idea." It's an obvious lie, and I get up from my chair because I know the effect it will have.

"He follows people. He parks in front of their homes," I reply. "That can be very intimidating."

"I killed Mister Nari after he attacked me!" Leo blurts.

"You weren't beaten with the tennis trophy but you or someone smeared it with blood, flicked drops of blood on it to make it look that way." I pick up my medical kit because it's time to leave. "Which was pretty clever and fairly convincing. A lot of people would have been fooled."

"You can't prove it!"

I notice my phone on the table. An alert indicates a secure file has been sent.

Lucy, I think.

"You can't prove it was me!" Leo raises his voice accusingly.

He starts to say something but catches himself. He starts rocking in his chair. I'm about to go and he shows he's scared.

"They'll get me." His eyes are huge and he's begging. "If I walk out of here they'll get me!"

The door opens and Marino is there.

"Nobody's going to get you," he says to Leo. "But I need to know who you're talking about."

Leo shakes his head. He refuses.

"I can't protect you if you don't tell me."

They. It blazes in my thoughts.

"If you don't tell me there's nothing I can do," Marino says.

They. It doesn't sound as if he means his father.

"Okay fine. Have it your way," Marino bluffs. "I'm cutting you loose. You can go home and think about it. When you want to tell the truth for once give me a call."

"You said I'm going to the hospital." Leo stares at me as if I'm the biggest traitor on earth.

I walk out of the small room.

"You said it! You said you wanted to help me!"

When I'm inside the open area with all of its cubicles he screams obscenities, and then I look back at another sound. He's jumped up from the table and he violently kicks his chair. It rolls across the room and slams into the wall at the same instant Marino is on top of him.

"Get off me! Get off me!" Leo is shrieking and struggling, his cap knocked off.

Marino clamps his arms around him from behind and lifts him off the floor as if he weighs nothing.

CHAPTER 34

BIRCH TREES FLASH BRIGHT white in the Audi's headlights. Tall slender trunks with papery bark lean toward the highway from rock piles that dissolve into dark hilly woods. It's almost nine-thirty and traffic moves steadily as we head north to Marblehead Neck, the sky impenetrable with ominous clouds, the wind gusting hard. Distant thunder cracks.

Leo Gantz's story about the attack with a tennis trophy was an afterthought that occurred to him once he had the convenience of a genuine injury. He went so far as to smear blood on the trophy and assume the edges of the square base would account for the pattern of the wounds to the side of his head. He's quick thinking, extremely bright, and I've come up with a theory that I believe is right.

He wasn't shoved into a doorframe because he falsely confessed to murder. It was the other way around. He fabricated a public spectacle after he was assaulted while preparing to take a shower. Leo's tweeting, his calling the police and the FBI was his way of punishing the devil he'd made a deal with and thought he knew.

His father.

"Years of pent-up hurt and anger," I say. "His father probably hurt him earlier today and not for the first time, far from it. Leo's not going to admit it. But he found a way to get him back and at the same time keep himself safe."

"Caught in a cycle he can't break, hating who he loves and loving who he hates." Benton typically weaves in and out of traffic like a slalom skier but for some reason he's holding steady in the far right lane. "Then he's overwhelmed by remorse and the need to punish at the same time he desperately seeks attention."

"And fear," I reply.

"At least he's out of harm's way for now. What happens to him later isn't promising. He's a bigger danger to himself than anyone else might be."

Leo is in the Cambridge Police Department lockup under the watchful eye of an on-call matron, one of their female crime scene techs. In the morning he'll be transferred to McLean.

"It's been going on for a while and escalating, building to combustion," Benton adds. "The murder of Joanna's husband and whatever happened in Leo's house this afternoon lit the match. The fire was set. That's the way it works. One last thing and all hell breaks loose."

Added to this fuel load were severe money pressures with no escape in sight until Bloom entered the scene, we believe. All he had to do was his usual spying to see that Joanna Cather was spending time with Leo and cared about him.

"And their relationship intensified when he started getting in trouble."

"Adjustment disorders, breakdowns aren't uncommon when kids change schools." His eyes move from mirror to mirror. "Leo began high school last fall. He went from a public school to having a full scholarship at a prestigious private academy and quickly began undergoing behavioral changes."

Beyond silvery guardrails houses are tucked back, some of them big and from an era when land wasn't subdivided and highways were cow paths. Benton continues checking his mirrors without turning his head, and it's not traffic he's monitoring.

"Compounded by his dysfunctional home," he says. "A submissive unsupportive mother, a father whose alcohol abuse has reached the point where he's out of work and in serious debt."

Headlights in the lanes opposite and behind us are blindingly bright. I watch Benton watching his mirrors as I look at what Lucy has sent. I continue to ponder it. I continue to think how things get broken with no hope of being fixed. Law enforcement can be one of them, and corruption in the Department of Justice isn't new to us. Rand Bloom used to work for DOJ. That's what he did before he went to work for TBP Insurers.

"Are you worried we're being followed?" I ask as Benton checks his side mirror now, both hands on the wheel, his index fingers on the paddle shifters.

"A pickup truck has been behind us on and off for the past ten miles."

"Don't tell me it's a gray Ford." All I can see in my side mirror is the glare of headlights and I resist turning around and looking.

Benton recites the plate number and it really is outrageous. Bloom is doing it again. But it can't be him.

"White, clean-shaven, a thin face, short light-colored hair peeking out of a cap." Benton is describing someone else, and he's disappointed. "Glasses. Not dark glasses. Regular glasses. Tailgating. I could call him in for reckless driving but that's about it. If it was Bloom we could trump up something to have him pulled over. But I don't know who this is."

"But it's Bloom's truck."

"It doesn't matter. I wish it did."

"We have to do something, Benton."

"I don't make traffic stops. Even if I did I'm driving my personal car."

"But we're being harassed."

"That's not provable," Benton replies and then I think of what Leo said. *They.*

"Get hold of Marino and let him know. If he wants to get the state police involved it's up to him but I seriously doubt he will," Benton says. "There's no probable cause to pull over the truck unless it's been reported stolen. And then it won't be us doing it. Whoever it is knows we've got nothing. He's being a jerk and that's not against the law."

I call Marino's cell phone and when he answers I can tell he's driving. I explain what's going on. He says he just left Bloom's apartment complex and he wasn't there and neither is the truck.

"I'll check with dispatch and get right back to you," Marino adds.

He does in minutes, and the truck is still close behind us.

"I got no idea," Marino announces and I have him on speakerphone, the volume up as high as it will go. "The truck hasn't been reported stolen and Bloom's not answering his phone. Supposedly people he works with haven't heard from him since midafternoon and sometimes he lets people borrow his truck. Maybe he did that to throw us off because I'm sure he figured we'd be bringing him in for questioning. So he's flown the coop and is giving you the absentee finger."

"Does he live with anyone?" I ask.

"By himself in a one-bedroom apartment in Charlestown, which is where I just was. He didn't answer his door."

"What about a warrant for his arrest? Do you have that?" I hope.

"Refresh my memory, Doc. What did he do?" Marino sounds angry and defeated. When he feels that way he's sarcastic. "And you said it's not him in the truck anyway. We got no probable cause at this point. All I can do is question him when he turns up."

"Can the state police check to see who's driving his truck?"

"There's no probable cause," he repeats. "It's not against the law to drive another person's truck unless it's stolen. And his registration is current. He's got no outstanding warrants or violations. Believe me I've checked."

"So someone can have a good time tailing us to a crime scene and there's nothing anyone can do." Now I'm frustrated beyond belief.

"Welcome to my world," Marino says. "You damn sure it's the same truck?"

"Absolutely. It's been following us for the past fifteen minutes or so but we don't recognize the person in it."

"It's probably some dirtbag Bloom works with," Marino decides. "It seems to be TBP's policy to follow people, to do whatever they can to frighten and distract the shit out of them. Unfortunately he's not their only investigator."

I end the call and say to Benton, "I feel as if we're in the middle of some nightmarish nexus."

"Then let's separate what's connected." He's flatline calm, the way he gets when he's on high alert and not to be trifled with. "Let's reduce it to discrete parts. Starting with Leo's relationship with Joanna, who certainly has been in Bloom's sights ever since her husband sued Emerson Academy for twenty million dollars."

"Let's be honest. That's a crazy amount."

"Aim high and get what you get. You know how it goes."

"I certainly do."

"But with Bloom there's no room for negotiation." Benton slows down and the truck is close behind us, relentless now and not subtle about it, as if the driver knows he's gotten a rise out of us. "His M.O. is to further injure and neutralize."

The suit was filed last September and the insurance company offered to settle for ten thousand dollars, an insulting amount that wouldn't have covered Nari's legal fees up to that point. The litigation took the usual course with him opting to take the school to court and to go after TBP for unfair practices, Lucy has let us know that and much more.

"Joanna's friendship with Leo presented Bloom with a perfect opportunity for extortion," Benton adds, and the high cab of the truck on the rear of his low-slung car makes me feel we are about to get run over.

"Imagine what she was going to get thrown at her during the trial," I reply. "She and her husband probably didn't have a clue who they were dealing with." A corrupt former government enforcement official, and the irony is that Rand Bloom's associations and machinations had nothing to do with the assault that disfigured his face.

By all accounts it was random when a homeless person approached his car at a traffic light and beat Bloom with a steel tactical baton, shattering an orbit and cheek and knocking out his front teeth. The incident occurred in Washington, D.C., two years ago, assailant unknown, and I don't believe that part at all. Bloom was uncharacteristically sketchy and passive when questioned about it, Lucy let us know, and I have a feeling that in someone's mind a message was sent and Bloom wasn't going to argue with it.

At the time, he was a lawyer for the Department of Justice's Public Integrity Section and embroiled in a contentious investigation that has me reeling. TBP had been reported for alleged campaign violations in Congressman Bob Rosado's 2008 reelection and a grand jury had been convened. There was no indictment, not even a fine with the Federal Election Commission even though it wasn't the first time TBP had been accused of illegal campaign contributions and bribery. Last summer, Bloom left DOJ and TBP hired him.

Benton watches his mirrors, slowing down more, well below the speed limit now.

"The underside of the rotten log that no one wants to talk about," he says in the same flat tone that belies what he really feels. "Public Integrity, white-collar crime, what we're trained to investigate and prosecute offers the opportunity to abuse power and cozy up to bad guys. Criminal Intelligence analysts become hired guns for murderers, and sleazes like Bloom manipulate the system and make a hell of a lot more money in the private sector. I have no doubt he ensured the outcomes of investigations through promises and backroom deals with influential special interest groups."

"Which I suspect is the insurance company's SOP," I reply. "And maybe Congressman Rosado's too, and here we are on the way to his house and Bloom's damn truck is tailing us."

"And I've had enough," Benton says.

"Just ignore it."

"I'll show you how I ignore things."

He suddenly cuts into the left lane, downshifts, and the speed drops with whiplash abruptness before he swoops in behind the gray Ford's shiny chrome rear bumper, menacingly close, in a low gear, the RPMs high, the engine roaring. Then he floors it, back into the left lane, staying parallel with the truck's driver's door for a second, maybe two.

"Fuck you," Benton says, and we scream ahead.

At 110 the highway opens up as if we are the only ones on it, and he downshifts, suddenly slowing, the engine rumbling and spitting. The truck doesn't try to catch up, and it couldn't possibly. We can't see it anymore and I barely got a glimpse of the driver. Someone small and fair with oversized square-rimmed glasses; the person seemed to be smiling, and an unsettled feeling stirs. I'm not sure of gender. The driver might not be a man.

"I made my point," Benton says.

"But who? We should know who the hell that is." I'm startled by what Benton just did and also by what Joanna Cather said to Marino and me.

Months leading up to his murder, her husband claimed a pickup truck had begun following him after dark, the driver wearing glasses and a cap. Someone had appeared at the bathroom window in their apartment and they began keeping the shades down. Jamal Nari wasn't being paranoid and I no longer believe the person spying was Rand Bloom or at least he wasn't the only one.

They.

"More harassment, giving us the finger, I think Marino's right." Benton is explaining what isn't logical because if that's how he really felt he wouldn't be acting this way.

His sudden flare of threatening behavior on the highway isn't typical of his discipline, which borders on stony, and I look at his sharp profile illuminated by headlights of oncoming traffic, at the hard set of his mouth. I feel his coiled aggression. For a flicker I detect his fury.

WE DRIVE DEEPER INTO the rugged North Shore, winding east to Revere Beach and its former amusement park called Wonderland, now a rapid transit station for the Blue Line.

I think out loud about individual cases, about discrete parts we need to isolate. Patty Marsico, Johnny Angiers, Jamal Nari, Leo Gantz, I spell it out, and now fourteen-year-old Gracie Smithers murdered at Bob Rosado's house. I try to fit the pieces together, looking at every angle, revisiting every detail, and next I think of the two homicides in New Jersey and the tweets we can't trace.

Everything that's happening can't simply be about money. There's got to be more to it than insurance claims, extortion or a wealthy congressman protecting his power and position, and I unlock my phone and log on to the CFC database. I find Patty Marsico's case. I skim through the police report, the scene photographs, refreshing my memory as I think back to her autopsy and what I was deposed about.

Sixty-one years old, a cancer survivor in the midst of a divorce, she was checking on an unfurnished oceanfront home after a nor'easter, and TBP's attorneys argued that the brutal homicide was the work of someone she knew. It was personal and the implication was her estranged husband let himself into the house and beat and drowned her, then took his time drinking beer and cleaning up with bleach. I enlarge a photograph of the nude body suspended by electrical cords tied around the wrists and looped over a ceiling pipe in the flooded basement. I remember standing in the water, feeling its coldness through my rubber boots. I remember sensing evil.

I felt it inside the house and later when I was walking the grounds and the beach with Benton and Lucy. I felt it when we headed back to the airport where Lucy's helicopter waited. Nothing more than intuition, and while I don't rely on gut feelings I also don't ignore them. We have them for a reason, to survive, and a part of my brain was aware of someone being aware of us.

"Patty Marsico had injuries from her head being slammed against a flat surface," I remind Benton. "Fingertip bruises on her upper arms and shoulders from being grabbed and held down as the person drowned her in three inches of water. Her clothing was bloodstained and soaking wet indicating it was removed after she was dead."

"And the killer folded it and placed it inside a kayak that was floating aimlessly when we got there," Benton says. "A gesture that was mocking."

CHAPTER 35

I CAN SEE IT VIVIDLY. Water had poured in from flood-level tides, and when I waded closer to the colorful sea kayak it rocked and drifted away from me like a riderless horse, like a ghost ship.

The killer had placed Patty Marsico's coat, linen pants, blouse and undergarments on top of the cushioned seat, and I remember her pocket-book and keys were upstairs on a table in the foyer, her loafers scattered nearby. She had just entered the house when someone terrified her right out of her shoes.

"Mockery and a total indifference to life," Benton says. "Sexual pleasure from terrorizing and imagining how people will react."

"There was no sign of sexual assault," I remind him.

"The sexual gratification came from the violence." He studied the scene when he was there, taking in every detail silently, oddly, like a peculiar savant. "But that doesn't mean there wasn't a motive," he says. "I've always felt there was, that Patty Marsico was a problem for someone."

"Her husband? He wanted to collect insurance money that he wouldn't be entitled to after the divorce? And he staged her death to look like a sexual homicide? That's what TBP wants everyone to think."

"It's not what happened and there's no evidence her husband was ever inside the house, which is one of many reasons why he's never been arrested," Benton says. "He also has an alibi. He was at work. It was witnessed by at least half a dozen people."

On North Shore Road now we cross Pines River, and the water is dark and empty on both sides of the bridge. To our right, the Broad Sound is as black as outer space. The GPS says we have ten miles to go. At the speed limit it will take us almost twenty minutes.

"Gracie Smithers." I get to what is bothering me most.

"I'm considering the same thing." Relaxed and driving smoothly, he has his left hand on the wheel and I reach for his right one.

I lace my fingers in his and feel his warm smooth skin, the tension in the fine muscles, the tapered hardness of his bones. He glances over at me as we talk.

"She was incapacitated by having her head slammed against a flat surface, then held down in water, her cause of death drowning," I point out. "A murder that was staged and it feels like an ambush unless she was abducted which I seriously doubt."

Gracie's parents didn't know she was gone until they got up early this morning in their Salem home, Investigator Henderson told me some three hours ago after he was assigned to the case. The Smitherses called the police and almost simultaneously their daughter's body was discovered some five miles southeast in Marblehead Neck. A Realtor checking on the Rosado house noticed a vodka bottle near the pool, the cover partially pulled back.

Henderson went on to tell me that at some point late last night when Gracie's parents thought she was asleep she snuck out her bedroom window. He believes she was meeting someone and that this person was Troy Rosado. He's known to party at Salem State College where Gracie's father teaches economics, and several days ago he spotted Troy and Gracie at the college ATM. She was forbidden to see the troubled nineteen-year-old again.

Conveniently the congressman's son is now nowhere to be found, it seems. Henderson contacted Troy's mother who claimed he's supposed to fly to Florida early tomorrow morning for a weekend of scuba diving with the family. She's certain that if the investigator checked he'd find

Troy packing up his room on the boy's residential campus of Needham Academy, getting ready to come home for the summer. For privacy and security reasons she refused to release information about the private jet he's scheduled to be on.

"The important question is whether Gracie Smithers's murder was premeditated or did something get out of hand?" Benton says as we pass through Swampscott on 129 and the darkness around us is almost complete. "Was there expediency in her being killed and I continue to ask the same thing about Patty Marsico."

I envision the murders as if they're happening before my eyes, and what doesn't fit is that Gracie was killed by an impulse-driven teenaged boy.

"He might have gotten sexually aggressive with her," I explain. "Things might have gotten out of hand. But I find it improbable that he murdered her and then had the organization and cool to pull the cover back from the pool and stage an accidental drowning."

"I tend to agree." Benton slowly strokes my hand with his thumb. "And if someone else in fact killed her then this person must have been on the property with them."

"If this isn't about money then what?"

"Whatever is of value. Money is obvious. But equally worth killing for is information."

"Such as being an unwitting observer, being in the wrong place at the wrong time," I suggest.

"Exactly," Benton says. "Patty Marsico and Gracie Smithers might have known something even if they had no idea they did."

In the distance are the scattered lights of Marblehead Neck and beyond are the harbor and the sea. I'm worried about how dark it is, the moon and stars obliterated by building clouds but waiting until morning isn't an option. If word gets out that I believe Gracie Smithers is a homicide then the actual scene of her death may be tampered with. I worry it already has been. I need to see the saltwater pool and I need a sample of the sediment at the bottom of it, and I need to be ahead of heavy rain and winds that are closing in. Moments ago big drops spattered the windshield and then we drove out of it. But advancing thunderstorms will catch up with us soon.

I check my phone with growing concern. Joe Henderson is supposed to meet us and he said to let him know when we were an hour out. I've texted him three times and left voice mails twice and there is no response. I call the police department's investigative unit and the man who answers says that Henderson marked off duty at six P.M.

"Which is about the time I talked to him," I reply. "He agreed to meet me."

"On his own time as a courtesy." It's not a friendly thing to say.

"I wonder if you have a way to reach him. Special Agent Benton Wesley and I are maybe twenty minutes out. This is in reference . . ."

"Yes, ma'am. I know what it's in reference to and you have an FBI agent with you? I'm wondering when the FBI got involved and why no one bothered to mention it?" He's not hostile or rude but he's not warm either.

"He happens to be with me." I don't offer that Special Agent Wesley is my husband.

"Hold on and let me see if Joe's at home. You're aware that we're expecting severe weather?"

"That's why I'm doing this now."

I hear him calling a landline and I catch that his last name is Freedman and he's a detective sergeant. He has a brief exchange with someone and I overhear that Joe Henderson was "meeting the medical examiner at the congressman's house where the girl drowned."

"Sure I know. My thought too and that was about oh-nineteen-hundred hours when you talked last and he planned to come home after he was done? Okay. Sure, makes sense," Sergeant Freedman says to whomever he has on the landline. "He was buying a coffee at that time and since that was more than two hours ago chances are he's been back and forth to Starbucks buying more coffee, addict that he is. How he sleeps at night I'll never know." He laughs. "That and babies, I get it. Thanks again. Sorry to bother you."

Next Freedman is back with me and I'm told that cell reception can be bad on the Neck, possibly explaining why I can't reach Investigator Henderson. He also might be getting coffee somewhere, maybe grabbing a sandwich while he's at it. Something could have come up and then Freedman offers that maybe Henderson forgot.

"Forgot?" I repeat.

"He's got a full plate. Not only on the job but he coaches soccer and he and his wife have three-month-old twins. Let me put it this way. Joe's a great guy, one of our best investigators, but sometimes he's got the attention span of a gnat."

"Just so we're clear," I answer, "if he's not there we'd like to check out the pool area and the grounds but we don't want to alarm the neighbors."

"Not much to worry about. The nearest neighbor's about ten acres away. I was out there this morning when the body was found. It's pretty desolate. Not sure why you're doing this in the pitch-dark. That far out on the Neck and it can be a black hole, and if we get lightning you don't want to be anywhere near it."

"Time is of the essence."

"I'll make sure dispatch is reminded again so no one confuses you with a prowler." He's halfway joking but what registers is the word *again*.

Joe Henderson let his sergeant know about the plans, and information has gone out over the radio. The latter is unfortunate, and I think of Bloom's pickup truck tailing us, I think of the handheld scanner that was inside it earlier today.

"If Investigator Henderson's not there when we arrive I would like another unit as quickly as possible," I inform Freedman and I'm completely professional.

"Hey I'll show up myself."

"Thank you." There's nothing light in my tone.

I end the call and Benton says, "They don't seem to take this very seriously."

"Most people would think that what I have in mind could wait until daylight assuming it's necessary at all."

"Then they don't know you."

"Not every investigator in the world thinks my vigilance is a good thing." I'm no stranger to the gossip.

It gets back to me, usually passed along by Bryce. I'm obsessive. I'm a pit bull who doesn't know when to let go. I overextend police resources and wear out my welcome. I'm Doctor Death. I'm a pain in the ass.

"Not to mention once manner has been established and then I over-rule it, that doesn't always set well either," I reply. "The police in this case were comfortable that Gracie Smithers is an accidental drowning. They don't understand that Doctor Kato is inexperienced. She's not board cer-tified and I won't keep her once her fellowship is complete and I can't say that anyway. I've just made everybody's life a lot harder."

"Doing what's right always does," Benton says.

FOR THE NEXT TEN minutes we wind in and out of narrow roads with different names that lead to large waterfront estates. Lighted windows glow in the dark but don't begin to dispel it, and Benton brings up Julie East-man, the New Jersey woman shot to death at the Edgewater Ferry this past April. He wants to know what Marino has told me about her.

"Only that he used to date her mother in high school," I reply.

"Beth Eastman, the mother, still lives in Bayonne. She and Marino communicate on and off through Twitter." He downshifts and the engine growls loudly in a lower octave.

"I assume this is from Lucy but it matters why exactly?"

"If somebody wanted to know who Marino knows it wouldn't be hard."

"Do Marino and his former high school sweetheart communicate through direct messages or through tweets? Because if it's direct messages, that's not public."

"I worry about hacking," Benton says. "I worry we're dealing with someone who has extreme cyber skills, explaining the tweets we can't trace and possibly explaining your credit card fraud. That's been recent, just the past few months and it's happening repeatedly. Every time you get a new card it happens again, and while I've not wanted to plant un-founded fears in your mind, I've been concerned that there might be a breach in security."

"You blew it off this morning when I brought it up."

"I didn't want to ruin our vacation."

"Well it's ruined so go ahead and ruin it some more."

"Lucy claims it's impossible anyone could be getting past the CFC firewalls but I don't share her confidence," Benton says.

"When did you start thinking this way?"

"It's entered my mind in recent weeks. As the day has worn on my suspicions have intensified."

"Well I do share Lucy's confidence. I'm not sure the NSA could get past her firewalls, Benton." I'm not exaggerating.

By the time Lucy was a teenager she was interning for the FBI and was instrumental in developing their Criminal Artificial Intelligence Network, CAIN. Creating machine language from source code comes as naturally to her as handling powerful machines, and protecting her domain from viruses and malware is automatic and unrelenting. A breach of computer security is something my niece would take extremely personally. It would be a fatal error. She wouldn't let it happen.

"It's easy to get complacent," Benton says.

"You feel Lucy has gotten complacent?"

"She doesn't lack confidence," he repeats. "So much confidence that sometimes she isn't objective. That's the problem with narcissists."

"Now she's a narcissist. A sociopath and a narcissist. How fortunate for her that she has someone close who can profile her."

"Come on, Kay," he says quietly. "She is what she is but that doesn't mean she's bad. It just means that she could be."

"Everybody could be."

"That's absolutely true."

"Are you having misgivings about her that you haven't shared with me?" I think of her aloofness, her paranoia and her reason for why she's no longer wearing Janet's family ring.

"I don't know."

"I think you do." I don't take my eyes off him.

"We've had conversations that concern me about her state of mind," he says. "Her thinking that people like Jen Garate are out to get her et cetera . . ."

"Et cetera?" I won't let him breeze past the remark. "As in more than one person who is out to get her?"

"References and allusions that are disturbing. Suffice it to say I worry that recent events in her personal life have had a destabilizing effect."

"What recent events?"

"Whatever might be going on between Janet and her in addition to evidence that her computer empire is being breached and her adamance that it isn't possible," he says. "Well it is. And the more she protests, the more I have my doubts."

"About what?"

"About who's really doing it."

"Are you suggesting Lucy is contriving all of this? The untraceable tweets to me, the credit card fraud?" I stare at him, stunned. "Are you thinking that Lucy might be shooting people too?"

"*Contriving* is a good word for it," he replies evasively. "Someone is contriving something."

"And the motive of whoever might be contriving what's been happening of late?"

"The tweets like the pennies and possibly somebody using your credit card may be for attention."

"The bullet with a three etched on it?" I add. "The same thing?"

"Yes. A calling card from someone invisible who's in our faces."

"Lucy is in our faces." My eyes are locked on his sharp unsmiling profile as he hints at a hypothesis that for me is out of the question.

"I'm not ready to go that far. I don't ever want to go that far, Kay. But put it this way—somebody is way too interested in us."

"Is this why you were so angry back there that you practically blew the pickup truck off the road?"

"I don't like it." Benton's jaw is set hard again. "I'm not nice when we're messed with no matter who the hell is doing it."

"And the other New Jersey victim? How might that person fit?"

"Jack Segal," Benton replies and the Rosado property is up ahead.

The driveway hooks sharply to the right and is unlighted but I notice there are lights on inside the house.

"He was opening his restaurant, in back of it unlocking the door when he was shot," Benton says.

"Does Marino have some link to him too?"

"No," Benton says. "But you do."

"I do?"

"His son was Dick Segal."

"I have no idea." But the name touches some buried place.

"When you were with the OCME in Manhattan, Jack Segal's son Dick allegedly committed suicide. This was about five years ago. He supposedly jumped off the G.W. Bridge and the family protested the autopsy for religious reasons," Benton says and the case comes back to me. "They had their rabbi pay you a visit, and there was a fair amount of anger in the Jewish community when you did an autopsy anyway."

"Without a CT scanner there was no choice. It was the law, and it's a good thing we abided by it since it turned out Dick Segal had help going off that bridge. I found evidence of ligature marks, and several boys from his school were suspects but were never indicted because there wasn't sufficient evidence."

"Again something that could be known," Benton says. "The case is public information if you know where to look. If we were to chart everything on a whiteboard it starts looking like a web, and you have to be honest enough to consider who might be in the center of it."

"If you know something I don't," I start to say and my heart is constricted by dread.

"I don't know anything for a fact. But whatever the truth, we will have to face it. No matter what it is."

He turns into the paved driveway and I note an unmarked black Tahoe. It's parked near the three-story house that I recognize from photographs. Investigator Joe Henderson is here and it appears he might be inside, which is an unanticipated bonus. I had no expectation that we would be allowed to wander at will through every part of Congressman Rosado's property.

We get out and I'm aware of the wind, the surf, the soft thuds of the car doors shutting and the alarm going off inside my head as I notice several things at once. The back door of the house is slightly ajar, light seeping out onto the brick landing and the steps, and Benton is sliding the pistol out of the holster under his jacket. There is no sign of anyone. Yet the lights are on in certain rooms of the house and the unmarked Tahoe didn't just get here.

Benton touches the hood and confirms it's cold. On the console between the front seats is a take-out cardboard carrier with two large coffees, the lids on, napkins, wooden stirrers and sugar packets tucked between them. The portable radio charger is empty, the driver's door locked. Benton has the Glock pointed down by his side as he walks away from the SUV, scanning, listening, tense because I'm with him but it isn't safe for me to sit alone in his car.

He heads toward the back door of the house, his footsteps light like a cat's, completely silent on old pavers with recently trimmed borders, the grass spreading out on either side lush and well cared for. He makes sure I stay behind him. But if there's a problem there's no good place for me to be. He climbs the steps and at the top nudges the door open a little with his toe. He calls inside for Joe Henderson, shouting several times and no one answers. He pushes the door open wider. I have my phone ready to call the police and Benton holds up a finger, pausing me.

"Dispatch already notified patrol," he says quietly and I get his meaning.

Anybody monitoring the Marblehead frequencies would know we were headed here, and I glance at the time on my phone. My call to the investigative unit was twenty-four minutes ago. Prior to that at about six P.M. I called looking for Henderson to alert him that Gracie Smithers is a homicide, and dispatch raised him on the air and gave him my number. He got hold of me and we talked.

"FBI!" Benton yells, standing to one side of the door, his body shielding me. "Henderson? Anybody in there identify yourself now!"

The wind rushes in from the sea, shaking trees and careening around the house in a low whistle. Silence, no people sounds, no sign of anybody around, and he holds his stance, the butt of the pistol gripped in both hands, pointing out and up, his index finger laid across the trigger guard.

"Call for backup," he says. "Give them the Tahoe's plate number, make sure it's his."

I make the call. Almost instantly I'm startled by the broadcast, a dispatcher requesting a backup, and Benton kicks open the door all the way. Ten feet inside and off to the left a portable radio is on the hardwood floor.

CHAPTER 36

ACRES OF TERRACED ROCKERY span the back of the property, and it's as black as ink, a thick darkness broken by a distant perimeter of throbbing red and blue. Beams of high intensity LED flashlights crisscross the terrain as police search for Joe Henderson.

Marked units and detectives' cars are parked behind the Tahoe, his take-home police SUV, and we have no idea where he is. He doesn't answer his phone and there was no sign he got much farther than the front door when he entered the house, which is furnished but sterile.

A thorough walk-through took no more than thirty minutes and there was nothing in the cupboards or closets, no personal effects, not linens or even soap, only furniture, window treatments, and bottles of water and beer in the bar refrigerator. The house felt unlived in with an air of neglect. Toilets hadn't been flushed in a while, and when I ran water in the sinks it was brown at first.

Yet someone was inside earlier, someone other than Henderson we're sure. This person turned on lights in the mudroom, a hallway, the bar and the kitchen, possibly leaving through the back door without closing it all the way. The detective accompanying us, the sergeant whose last name is Freedman, said Henderson had no plan to enter the house. He had no key or warrant. He must have done the same thing Benton did. He saw the door was ajar.

"Until a couple hours ago this was an accidental drowning." Freedman continues to talk as we follow a stone path toward the water, flashlights in hand, and I detect fear, high-pitched like a dog whistle. "We had no reason to search the house or secure it. The kids were never inside it."

He's talking about Gracie Smithers and Troy Rosado.

"That we know of," Benton reminds him. "I'm going to bet that Troy has a way to get in if he wants."

"When we got here this morning after the body was found the back door was locked," Freedman says.

"And the alarm log?" Benton asks.

"I sure as hell didn't wear the right shoes for this." Freedman is short, heavy with a barrel-shaped chest, and the dress shoes he's wearing with his suit aren't compatible with walking over slippery leaves and rocks. "The Realtor's not very helpful about remembering exactly what time she does her checks of the place, in and out almost every day, nothing routine, just when she's in the area because of worries about vandalism."

"I'm not aware that's much of a problem around here," I reply. "Marblehead is considered safe with very little violence or property crime. But then I don't need to be telling you that."

"I'm passing on what she told me, and the problem with the alarm log is she can't say with certainty if she was in the house at a certain time. For example the log shows the alarm was turned off at ten-fifteen last night and it was never reset."

"And she's saying she doesn't know if she did that?" I don't believe the Realtor whoever she is, and Benton is in front of me, saying little but I know he's listening.

"She says she doesn't think so." Freedman steadies himself, going slowly one step at a time, and he sounds breathless, keyed up and winded, his eyes everywhere. "But she might have forgotten. Suddenly she has amnesia."

"Her loyalty is to the owners." I have no doubt of that, especially considering who they are. "I suspect the last thing she wants to do is cause them trouble and lose her commission."

Maybe lose more than that is the thought that follows, and no matter the Realtor's excuse it strikes me as inconceivable she would check the property daily unless it was being shown that often, which it wasn't. Freedman says it's rare anybody looks at the Rosado estate. It's too expensive for the area and requires a full-time caretaker. Or at least that's what the Realtor told him but she meant it as a boast not a disparagement, and a suspicion begins to take form.

"Troy," Benton says as we follow shallow stone steps, mossy and thick with dead leaves, leading steeply down through hardwood trees. "Is she aware of his ever accessing the property? I know what I suspect but did she say anything about it? He goes to school around here and has been in and out of trouble."

"I don't remember her saying anything about him."

"He apparently has a suspended driver's license"—I pass on what Lucy dug up—"and at one time was using a car service like Uber to get around. All you need is an app on your phone and a credit card on file. You rarely have the same driver twice. The Realtor?" I then ask. "Who is it?"

"A big company that represents a lot of waterfront property here, Gloucester, the Cape, Boston." Freedman tells me the name of the woman he spoke to and it means nothing.

But the real estate company is the same one Mary Sapp works for. I suggest we find out who the owner is behind any shells and LLCs. I remind them that Bob Rosado is a real estate investor who made a fortune from buying devalued properties and flipping them. Then he went into politics and right out of the box won his congressional seat.

"Yeah I know all about Congressman Rosado and his worthless kid." Freedman shines his Maglite down at his feet. "A couple of summers ago I picked up Troy for shoplifting at the liquor store near Seaside Park."

"What happened?" Benton asks.

"His father showed up with the district attorney, that's what happened."

"Nothing in other words," I reply.

"There's a history of that with them. But if Troy's got something to do with what happened to Gracie Smithers? If anything's happened to Henderson? Now we're talking a different ending to the story. I'll put him away if it's the last thing I do. Where the hell is he anyway?"

"I wonder if the Rosados have someone who looks after this place." I suggest what I'm beginning to think. "Someone who's in the area now and perhaps has been since the property went on the market. The Realtor said this property needs a caretaker. The question is did she bring that up because the Rosados have one."

"She didn't mention it specifically and I got the impression she's the one looking after things." Freedman is getting more upset. "I don't understand. Where the hell could he be?" He's talking about Henderson. "What made him drop his damn radio? There's no sign of a struggle. It's like he just vanished in thin air. It doesn't make sense he'd get out of his car and leave his coffee in it for that matter."

ON EITHER SIDE OF the steps is a wall built of the same rough gray stone. The walls get higher the farther down the hillside we go, higher than Benton's head as the earth levels out.

I smell pungent decaying leaves and dead wood, and the wind carries the clean saltiness of the sea rushing against a rocky beach about fifty feet ahead where the trees and vegetation end. Pebbles clatter and twigs snap as we spread out away from the walled-in steps, shining our lights, searching for any sign of Joe Henderson, for any sign of what might have happened to Gracie Smithers before someone dumped her body in the swimming pool.

Ahead and to my right are the ruins of more walls, perhaps an outbuilding in the property's long-ago past, and then I detect another odor. I move downwind and it gets stronger. Charred wood, and the narrow beam of my flashlight licks over cinders and partially burned logs in a small clearing where coarse sand surrounds a fire pit that has been used recently. I note that the sand on one side of the pit is disturbed.

Impressions shaped like hands, shoes, indentations and swaths where people may have been sitting, moving around a lot, and a struggle comes to mind. I step closer and gold metal flickers in the sweep of my light. I sit on my heels and pull a pair of clean gloves out of a pocket of my cargo pants.

"Well that answers at least one question." I brush sand way from a delicate gold chain, a necklace with the name *Gracie,* the curl of the *e* embellished with a tiny crystal.

"So she was definitely here in this spot." Freedman leans close, looking at the necklace in the gloved palm of my hand, shining his light on it.

"Possibly sitting around the fire," I reply, "and the clasp is broken, which is consistent with what I saw in her autopsy photos. She has a very thin linear abrasion on the right side of her neck that could have been caused by someone forcibly removing a necklace."

I open my metal case and tuck the necklace inside an evidence envelope, labeling it.

"You mean doing that while she was alive?" Freedman says and his eyes don't stop moving. "To steal it from her?"

"It could be a souvenir," Benton offers. "But if so why is it still here?"

"It may have gotten caught on something such as clothing if she were undressing or being undressed, for example," I suggest.

"So she might have been by the fire making out with Troy Rosado?" Freedman says angrily, and he's scared.

With each minute that goes by his tension is more palpable. He's trying to focus on Gracie Smithers's murder but he's locked in on Henderson and what awful thing might have happened to him.

"Whatever may have gone on could have been consensual at first," I reply. "What I do know is she didn't die here."

"He could have knocked her unconscious and dragged her down to the water to drown her." Freedman explores the sand and the cinders, his flashlight probing. He's sweating profusely, and I'm aware of Benton.

His attention is on the dark horizon, on blooming black clouds volatile with electricity. He keeps looking up and out to sea.

"There's no evidence she was dragged, no abrasions consistent with that for example." I collect a sample of sand by the fire pit, a coarse granular granite that's a tannish gray.

It will contain microscopic traces of charred wood that I don't expect to be present on the beach, and it's a reflex for me to anticipate the worst. I'm hardly conscious of it. Whatever might diffuse a jury's logical conclusions is certain to be asked, and I already expect the question. How can I state for a fact that the sand Gracie aspirated came from the beach? I'll make sure there can be no confusion, and I envision the delicate fourteen-year-old, a child, and my indignation builds like the thunder cells overhead.

"There's substantial evidence she drowned, inhaling water and what may be beach sand. I suggest we get this tested for DNA immediately." I hand the envelope to Freedman but he's hardly listening to me. "I wouldn't wait. Get it to CFC first thing in the morning if you can."

Benton has stepped closer to the shore, his light moving along the water's edge, waves swelling, heaving onto the brownish rock-strewn sand, fanning out in lacy white foam. The sound of it is loud and pervasive as I creep my light over the beach, illuminating gravel, painting over small rocks that become bigger and then boulders and solid outcrops. Up to a small dry tidal pool where only a storm surge could reach, and what shines this time is tinted glass.

Beer bottles perfectly upright in a shallow crevice, the labels facing exactly the same way, and I'm grateful for my nylon boots with their thick tread as I climb massive granite worn smooth. There are four green St. Pauli Girl bottles, the same beer that was in the bar refrigerator, and a spread-out towel and a faux leather jacket with inlays shaped like flowers. It's zipped up and precisely folded as if it's on display in a shop. I look at the label inside the collar without disturbing the jacket, a size extra small, and I take photographs.

"I can take care of this unless you want to?" I call out to Freedman, who's getting more distracted.

"Go ahead." He hardly looks in my direction.

The wind is gusting, shaking trees and smelling of rain. I pick up the jacket and check the pockets.

"Possibly a house key, a cell phone," I tell him but he's hardly listening anymore, and Benton has moved closer to me. "A lip gloss, breath mints, a five-dollar bill, a quarter, a dime, a nickel." I bag them too. "And four bottle caps." The beer bottle caps are bent on one side from being pried off the bottles, and that's deliberate too.

I doubt Gracie Smithers opened the beers and saved the bottle caps, and there's no bottle opener. It's not here. I refold the jacket and place it inside a bag. Her blood alcohol was negative. She wasn't drinking but someone was, and I suspect this person neatly, obsessively arranged the empty bottles, the towel, the jacket, and I think about the guitars on their stands in the apartment on Farrar Street. I think about the boxes of condoms and Imodium in the cabinet, how perfectly they were arranged. Then my thoughts return to the possibility of a caretaker whose job is to do far more than ensure the safety of Rosado's properties. Troy needs constant monitoring I have no doubt. Someone needs to keep him out of trouble.

"Do you want to get a look?" I raise my voice to Freedman over the heaving surf and wind that's beginning to howl.

"It's about to get bad." He stares in my direction as lightning illuminates dark mountains of clouds and thunder rumbles. "We need to move fast! We don't want to get caught in this!"

I take more photographs and then I pick up a corner of the towel, blue and white with an anchor design. I wonder where it came from. There were no towels inside the house, and I see what's under it and the feeling hollows me out, what I felt when I saw the kayak floating in the flooded basement, what I felt when I found seven pennies on my wall, the same date, heads up, each oriented exactly the same way and as bright as brand-new.

The smear of blood is the size of my hand, dark brown with several long light hairs adhering to it. I take more photographs as Benton climbs up to me. I show him what I've found and he doesn't need to tell me that it's staged. It's not that the blood and hair aren't real. It's not that this isn't the scene where someone slammed Gracie Smithers's head against a hard flat surface, a rounded slab of granite rock. But the rest of it is for the benefit of whoever discovered it, and the message gets only worse.

"Like smoking a cigarette after sex." Benton continues staring off at the sea. "Spreading out a towel over the victim's blood, sitting on it next to her neatly folded jacket, drinking beer, enjoying the afterglow."

"It doesn't sound like something an impulsive nineteen-year-old boy would do."

"No way," he says. "Whatever happened between them likely occurred at the fire pit where her necklace was ripped off. I suspect Troy got sexually aggressive with Gracie, a minor, and it was going to cause a real problem this time."

"Two people are involved in her death?"

"Troy started it and someone far more dangerous, someone in control had to clean up his mess, someone who possibly is paid to clean up Rosado messes and takes pleasure in it. Sexual pleasure," Benton says.

"Are you thinking about Rand Bloom?"

"I'm not. I'm thinking that Congressman Rosado may have his own personal fixer, his own hired psychopath," Benton says as Freedman paces the beach, turning up the volume on his radio.

I get swabs and a small bottle of sterile water out of my case.

"Twenty-seven," Freedman transmits.

"Go to nine," a female voice sounds over the air, and Freedman moves closer to the rock stairs that lead back up to the tiered acres of the property.

I swab blood. I collect the hairs with plastic tweezers.

"Switching now." Freedman sounds very tense. "Twenty-seven with you."

I begin bagging the towel, the beer bottles.

"Affirmative," Freedman says loudly into his radio, and Benton stands up, his attention fixed on the black horizon.

The thunder is louder and closer, shaking the night, and lightning illuminates thunderheads like a face-off between angry gods. We climb down the rocks to the beach and I collect a handful of sand as the rain begins. It is sudden and cold, falling hard with no warning, and Freed-man is busy on his radio as he heads back up the mossy leaf-covered steps, which instantly are wet and as slick as glass.

"We need to find out who that belongs to," Benton says as he stares out to sea.

The sailboat is moored maybe half a mile offshore, its sails furled, a large vessel, at least sixty feet. In the blinking light of a navigation buoy I can barely make out the crane-like davit, the block and tackle, the loops of rope hanging down from the stern dipping up and down in the heavy surf.

"That's a strange place to be moored, the ocean not the harbor." Benton shoves his wet hair off his face, rain drenching us fast. "It looks like it hauls a dinghy but where is it?"

Freedman is halfway up the steps as rain billows in sheets. "The pool!" he yells and he almost falls as he starts to run.

CHAPTER 37

IT WAS THE LAST place the police thought to look, and why would it be foremost on their minds? Benton and I didn't imagine it either, that the scene where Gracie Smithers's body was discovered this morning would be a crime scene a second time.

When we reach the saltwater pool the police have pulled the dark green cover and it's piled on the deck. They stand around the deep end, four uniformed officers and two plainclothes, staring at the body suspended facedown in murky water inches above the sediment-covered bottom. Their collective mood is electrically charged, glimmers of upset flashing, and their aggression rumbles from a deep place, threatening to explode like a bomb going off.

"The cover was all the way on," an officer explains to us above the din of the heavy rain, his voice as tense as a violin string about to snap. "I figured the Realtor did it after the girl was found but I thought we should check."

Freedman is struggling out of his jacket, his shoulder holster, and I grip his arm to stop him from jumping in. I shine my light down in the water and the hands floating up are profoundly wrinkled and chalky white, a phenomenon known as washerwoman's skin, the advanced stages of it. The body has been submerged for a while.

I bend down and dip my fingers in, and the salt water is unheated and chilled, the cover keeping the pool well below the ambient temperature. Hours, I think. Possibly as many as three or four, the dead man clothed in jeans and running shoes, a flash of pale flesh at his ankles, no socks. A loose denim shirt billows up, and I squat at the edge and move my light closer to the surface, and the beam catches an earring, a multifaceted small clear stone in the lobe of the left ear. On the left wrist is a rugged black watch on a black band. His hair is short, dark and curly.

I get up and ask, "Does anybody see a pool skimmer? Anything with a long handle?"

Everyone begins searching at once while Benton stays by my side, and I meet his eyes and don't say a word. I don't have to because he knows me. He knows when something isn't what it seems. I call my investigative unit and Jen Garate answers. I tell her we have another body from the same location in Marblehead Neck. I inform her tentatively who it might be, and Benton is listening. He steps away to use his phone.

"We need Rusty, Harold, a removal service here right away," I talk over Jen's excitement.

"Oh my God. How weird is that? What was he doing there? An insurance person? Oh. I know. The homeowners are afraid of being sued." Her words tumble out. "But who would kill an insurance person? This is creepy. I'm on my way."

"I thought you were off." I remember her leaving for the day.

"Becca had something come up." Jen explains that she took a colleague's midnight shift, and then I inform her I don't need her to come, just a truck to transport the body back to my office.

"You don't need the scene worked?" Her disappointment is shamelessly obvious over the phone.

"I'm working it," I reply as I watch Benton walk off the deck into the sopping wet grass, on his phone, splashing rain drowning him out as he talks to someone.

Next I let Bryce know what's happened. I tell him that whoever does the transport can't be alone at any time, not even for two minutes. There must be a police presence while the body is being removed and he's to see to it because the officers at the scene right now are upset and distracted.

"Call dispatch, a lieutenant if you can find one, to make sure that Rusty or Harold or whoever we get is accompanied by armed officers. It's not negotiable in light of the circumstances," I say and I end the call.

I tuck my phone back in a pocket and Freedman hands me a leaf rake with a blue net and a long aluminum handle.

"What are you doing?" he asks, and he really has no idea, none of them do, but I won't explain until I'm sure.

"I'm going to guide him to the shallow end and pull him out," I reply. "Does anybody have anything we can put him on? I don't have sheets. I'm afraid I didn't come quite prepared for this."

"I've got a weather tarp," an officer volunteers.

"Would you mind? That, towels, anything. And if you could direct your lights in the water for me so I can see what I'm doing?"

I drop in the rake and the silver handle seems to bend in the refracted light, and I touch the body with the frame of the net. I maneuver it flatly against the waist and nudge gently, and the body moves easily. Inching my way along the ledge, I guide the body toward the shallow end and it stops at the steps, the left shoulder barely brushing the rough concrete. From there Rand Bloom is within reach, and I refrain from saying who he is until we are turning him over and pulling him out.

"What?" someone says.

"Who the hell?" says another.

"It's not Joe?"

"Then where is he? That's his car. I don't understand."

"I don't know what Joe Henderson looks like or why his car is here," I answer. "I just know this isn't him."

Benton returns to the pool deck, the rain pounding all around us, the wind tearing at our soaking wet hair and clothing, and I catch the lights peripherally before I turn to look. An orange rigid-hulled Coast Guard boat races through the darkness, blue lights strobing, charging toward the dark sailboat heaving on the angry sea.

WATER POURS FROM UNDER the body as we ease it onto the spread-out orange weather tarp.

Freedman hands me cloths he got from somewhere, microfiber, probably car shammies that are useless. I let the rain rinse the salt water off my hands and clothes. There are no lights in the pool or on the deck, only our flashlights, and in the glare of them Rand Bloom's dead face looks more deformed, more grotesque.

The small vertical slit in the front of the denim shirt lines up with the stab wound I find midchest after undoing several buttons, a single-edged blade that was twisted. His assailant was facing him, and I envision a tactical kill, the knife thrust under the breastplate into soft tissue, angled up into the heart, and I open my medical case. I get out thermometers, a ruler for scale, and the temperature of the body is barely ten degrees warmer than the water.

I take photographs, aware that the Coast Guard boat is alongside the sailboat, blue lights sparking. Then I get Luke Zenner on the phone. I hear music in the background over the splashing rain.

"I realize you're not on call," I say right off, and I can see flashlights in the distance as Guardsmen board the sailboat.

"Not a problem." What Luke means is he's not been drinking and is fit for service, and I explain where I am and why.

"I need you to come in for this, Luke."

"I hope you're headed to the airport and down to Florida . . ."

"We're not."

"But you want me to do the case tonight?"

"Yes and I'm recusing myself."

"Of course. Whatever you need."

"It's best I'm not there at all, not even as a witness," I say and Benton is on his phone again, his back to everyone.

I can see him staring out to sea as he talks.

"That's fine." Luke is moving away from the music. "Do you mind if I ask why?"

"I met Rand Bloom earlier today."

"And you're certain that's who it is?"

"We'll verify his ID but yes. I've had brushes with him in the past, adversarial ones," I reply. "I can't be objective . . ."

"Can you hold, Kay? It's Marino. Probably about this."

I hold as I watch Benton in the dark yard, in the pouring rain, both of us drenched to the skin, and I can't help but think about how this day began and how it's about to end, from bad to worse and what will be next? It's almost midnight and something else occurs to me as I look around at the thick darkness, the rain splashing on the pool and the pulled-back cover and the granite deck. We were inside the house earlier, and I ask Freedman why no one turned on the outside lights.

"We tried." He hugs himself against the billowing rain. "It appears all of the exterior bulbs have been removed."

"Removed?"

"I assumed because no one's living here and the grounds probably aren't shown after dark. Well I'm sure as hell not assuming anything now," he says, and then Luke is back in my earpiece.

"I guess Benton got hold of him," he says of Marino. "You definitely want this done now."

"Since it's the third death today that seems to be connected somehow," I reply. "Yes."

"I ask because Marino wants to come in after he goes through Rand Bloom's apartment. He wants me to give him a couple hours."

"He needs to look for sources of DNA. A toothbrush, for example, and he shouldn't witness the autopsy either," I reply. "He can't be objective. Neither of us can. He almost got into a fight with Bloom this afternoon. I don't want you to wait for him and I don't want him present," I emphasize.

"Is there something personal I should know about? I don't mean to be presumptuous but if there is it will come up, and it's better that I prepare."

"I didn't know Rand Bloom personally." I'm not going to admit that I didn't like him.

In fact I might have hated him, and I watch Benton end his call and look directly at me.

"I have a feeling this is fairly straightforward," I say to Luke. "A stab wound midline to the center chest, posterior to the sternum. The water temp is fifty-one degrees, ambient air seventy-eight now because it's a lot warmer than it was this afternoon. The body temp is seventy-six. He would have cooled quickly in cold covered water and I estimate he's been submerged four or five hours at least. Witnesses will help with when he was last seen alive. Marino and I saw him drive off this afternoon about four. I'm wondering if he left us and came straight here."

"Rigor?" he asks.

"Delayed by the cold water and just beginning to form."

"A wound like that and I suspect he bled out internally," Luke says. "I'll measure how much blood is in his chest cavity and check carefully for any signs of drowning."

"If the blade penetrated his heart or a major vessel, his survival time would have been minutes. If there's any sign of drowning then that likely means he was stabbed very near the pool, possibly on the deck. He would have taken some agonal breaths and that's about it."

"What about blood around the pool?"

"If there was it's gone now," I reply as the rain boils on the deck, and Benton is by my side, the blue lights flashing by the sailboat. "It's a monsoon here." I end the call and meet Benton's eyes. "Please don't tell me there's another one."

"The sailboat," he says.

"Who?" I ask.

"Joe Henderson," he answers. "He's been found alive."

"THE SAME PERSON WE saw in the gray pickup truck," Benton says, and we're trotting back to his car, splashing through puddles in the pitch-dark. "Based on what Henderson says I don't see how there can be any doubt."

At around seven P.M. Joe Henderson pulled up to the Rosado house where a gray pickup truck was parked but he saw no sign of the driver. He got out of his Tahoe and noticed the back door ajar the same way we did, and the instant he pushed it open all the way while calling out if anyone was home he was pepper sprayed. A pillowcase was yanked over his head, his wrists bound in flex-cuffs behind his back, and he felt a gun barrel jabbed into the small of his neck.

"The only thing the person said was *you don't have to die*," Benton continues to relay what the Coast Guard told him.

"Male or female?"

"He told the Coast Guard he doesn't know but assumes male."

"Based on?"

"His impression."

"An easy one since he was overpowered. So he assumes it had to be a man."

"I agree." Benton digs into his pocket, turning it inside out because it's soaking wet.

"How did this person get him down to the beach?" I can't imagine being able to navigate the steep stone steps if I couldn't see.

"It wasn't raining then and it wasn't dark." Benton points the remote and the Audi's locks click free. "The pillowcase didn't have holes for his eyes. But it was left open at the bottom so he could breathe and he was able to look down and see his feet."

"What about the other person's feet?"

"They were behind him. He had no further details except that this person took his phone. The bigger point is whoever it is doesn't hesitate to kill an insurance investigator and a fourteen-year-old girl. He may have picked off three unsuspecting people with a high-power rifle. But he didn't kill a cop."

"Why?" I grab open my door and duck inside. "Does Henderson have any idea?"

"No. He was forced into a dinghy with an outboard motor and taken to the sailboat where he was locked inside the salon. He heard the dinghy leave and managed to get the pillowcase off his head. He estimates he was in the salon several hours when he heard the Guardsmen and started kicking the door and screaming."

"Why go to the risk and the trouble?" I ask. "Why not kill him and leave his body in the pool too or dump it in the ocean?"

"Whoever we're dealing with is sending a message." Benton turns on the heat, both of us chilled despite the dramatic rise in temperature. "This person has his own code about who he kills."

"Do you really believe that?"

"I believe he wants us to believe it."

"*He?*" I have to seriously question it. "The person in the cap and glasses who was tailgating us earlier? I couldn't tell the gender."

"I couldn't either," he admits, and then we say nothing as water drums the undercarriage of the car, the earth cooler than the air which moils with fog.

A woman, and I don't want to think it. Not for a moment do I believe Lucy could have transformed into such a monster but I worry what she knows. I keep my troubled thoughts to myself, back on the highway now, the wipers pumping hard. My phone rings. I glance at caller ID.

Bryce Clark.

"I think you need to hear this from me," he says instantly and with self-importance that's supposed to come across as somber.

"What is it, Bryce?"

"You sound as if you're inside a metal drum being beaten with sticks."

"Go ahead."

"The scrubs."

"What scrubs?"

"That Lucy found on the roof. You know at the Academy of Arts and Sciences?"

"What about them?" I ask.

"Well due to the urgency of the situation, that someone may have been spying on you and maybe it was the same person who shot Jamal Nari? Anyway we had the jacket and cap worked up ASAP and ran the profile through the database . . ."

I interrupt, "What profile?"

"From swabbing inside the cap, there was DNA and we got a single donor profile. I don't know how to tell you this, Doctor Scarpetta."

"For God's sake, Bryce." Of all times for his drama, and I have no patience left.

"Before you jump to conclusions, Lucy knows how to handle evidence without contaminating it."

"Her DNA was on the clothing she found on the roof?" My troubled thoughts begin to throb deep inside my psyche, and my chest feels tight.

"Yes and no."

"Low copy number DNA and she could have breathed on the clothing and that would explain it," I reply in a steady voice I have to force. "What do you mean yes and no?"

"Skin cells on the band inside the cap and Lucy says it's impossible they came from her," Bryce says.

"Then the simple way to resolve this is to get a buccal swab and do the comparison that way instead of using a database match."

"We did and it's not hers," he replies. "That's what I mean by yes and no."

"Now I'm really confused."

"It matches in our computer but not when you do a direct comparison in our lab."

"Are you suggesting that something's wrong in CODIS?"

"We didn't get as far as the FBI's database. I'm talking about ours. Everyone who works here has their DNA in our database for exclusionary purposes," he says. "We do that so . . ."

"I know why we do it," I almost snap at him.

"Lucy's DNA profile in our database is wrong," he says. "Do you understand what I'm getting at?"

"It can't be a corrupted data file because that would assume a false positive, a false match with evidence turned in." I know exactly what he's getting at.

A corrupted file wouldn't have gotten a match with the clothing found on the roof or with anything else for that matter. Corrupted data result in a nonmatch and not a false one, and there's another thought that begins to nag at me. If someone's agenda is to sabotage or frame Lucy then this person isn't trying very hard.

"You're implying our database has been tampered with," I say to Bryce.

"And Lucy swears nobody could do that."

"It sounds like somebody did."

"She says with all of the encryption . . . ? Well I can't explain it the way she does. I mean, hello? Greek? Half the time I've got no idea what she's talking about but she swears the only person who would know how to access those DNA files and alter them the way it was done is her."

"That's probably not a smart thing to say," I reply. "And I'd appreciate it if you wouldn't start a rumor like that."

"Me start rumors?"

"I mean it, Bryce."

"Are you coming in tomorrow?"

"It depends on if we can get out—"

"I checked earlier," he interrupts much too cheerfully. "And the weather's perfect in Florida and nothing has been canceled out of Logan. You can still make it for your birthday on the seven A.M. flight. I mean a tad late but you know what they say? Better late than never."

"Not Miami, not my birthday, I'm talking about getting out on Lucy's helicopter." My God, does he have no EQ at all? "We're meeting with Jack Kuster at the Morris County Sheriff's Department, a firearms expert. We've got to figure out exactly how the killer is doing it."

"If you don't mind my saying it? All the screwy stuff with Lucy? Maybe she shouldn't—"

"I do mind you saying it," I reply.

CHAPTER 38

ROTOR WASH AGITATES THE green canopies of trees, their heavy limbs thrashing beneath our skids. The pale undersides of leaves flash like the palms of upset hands and the wooded hillside abruptly opens, leveling into the airfield.

It's Saturday, June 14. The late afternoon is clear and hot, the storm front having finally moved out around two P.M. We got delayed because of weather and reasons I don't trust and silently obsess about. My mind is caught on the search of Rand Bloom's apartment and what turned up, the sniper rifle with a powerful scope, the solid copper ammunition and a jar full of old pennies including ones dated 1981, the year Lucy was born.

The cartridges weren't hand-loaded. They weren't polished. Neither were the pennies and there was no sign of a tumbler. Bloom's apartment door was open because the lock had been picked by someone skilled who left scarcely a tool mark. Marino believes what he found inside was planted, the scenario a familiar one like the teal green scrubs on the roof, like Lucy's tampered-with DNA profile in the CFC database.

Someone didn't try very hard.

Test fires and analysis will verify the rifle isn't the one we're looking for, Marino is quite sure, and that's not the bigger problem. The manipulations are relentless now and although no one is offering it outright there are darkening suspicions about Lucy. She hasn't been herself of late. Even Benton says it and we're not the only ones aware that she's been acting oddly and in secret, her whereabouts unaccounted for much of the time. Janet has confirmed it.

When I got her on the phone several hours ago she told me that Lucy has been gone often in recent months with no explanation and making large purchases without discussion. The Ferrari and before that she got rid of one helicopter and bought a different one. She said that what Lucy told me about not wearing the ring anymore wasn't quite true. Yes, Janet's father got it back—because Lucy returned it to Janet.

Added to that are other escalating events. Someone figured out a way to send tweets that couldn't be traced, committed fraud with my credit card, hacked into the CFC computer. Now Rand Bloom is dead and items inside his apartment are supposed to make us leap to more conclusions or fill us with more doubt about a former federal agent, my niece. I look over at her. She's the master of her own ship, her fine motor skills impeccable, her focus keen and unflinching.

I don't know what I would do if her seat were empty, if wherever I looked I didn't see her anymore. Should something happen . . . I don't finish the thought.

"I'll tell them we're overnighting. A top-off with Jet-A no prist," I say into my mic and Lucy doesn't answer.

We hover taxi over frantic grass, an orange wind sock twitching wildly as we churn lower and slower toward runways that intersect in an irregular X. There is no wind except ours. The afternoon is hot and dead calm in Morristown, where I've been many times before, never imagining one day it would be for this.

But you should have imagined it. The sotto voce that comes from some deep part of me intrudes upon my consciousness again. *If someone wants to get you badly enough it will happen.* I imagine a weapon trained on us even as I'm thinking this, ready to shoot us out of the sky with no qualms or re-grets as I lightly hold the grip of the cyclic, what most people call the stick.

Black and gracefully curved between my knees, it controls the pitch and roll of the rotor blades, the slightest pressure moving the helicopter up, down, sideways, backward. If I didn't have a gentle touch, I wouldn't be sitting in the copilot's seat. Lucy would have relegated me to the back cabin of cognac leather and carbon fiber trim where our only passenger, Marino, is isolated.

I can't see him. I've made sure I can't hear him and he can't hear us. He's done nothing intentional to piss me off but I no longer pretend when I don't have the emotional fortitude to listen to him anymore. Now of all times I don't. Speculating, hypothesizing nonstop since we took off from Boston. Marino and his bold statements and questions and utter lack of discretion.

He didn't care what Lucy heard. In fact he was picking on her as if it's funny, giving her shit is the way he thinks of it. The killer has got to be someone who knows us, and by the way where was she yesterday? What were she and Janet up to? What kind of arsenal must she have at her indoor firing range? Have I been shooting there recently? His humor is about as tasteful and subtle as his favorite coffee mug, black with a white chalk body outline and the caption MY DAY BEGINS WHEN YOURS ENDS.

I listened to his boisterousness until we got close to New York airspace when I switched the intercom to crew only. He was aware of it when I did it. I doubt he took it personally. He figures it's a busy airspace and knows I'm industrious about monitoring multiple towers and self-announcing our presence to other pilots at every checkpoint along various routes such as the Hudson River. He knows I consider it my inflight job to enter radio frequencies, to talk to air traffic control and tune in the most recent ATIS update about weather, wind, notices to airmen, potential restrictions, and hazards like ground fog or birds.

By aviation standards I can't be trusted with much more than this al-though I'm confident I could land in an emergency. The helicopter might not fare well but I'd get us down safely. The entire flight I've replayed engine failures, bird strikes, every worst-case scenario and how I would respond. It's easier to think about.

So damn much easier.

I press the radio trigger switch without disturbing the cyclic as Lucy skims over grass, holding a speed of sixty knots on a heading that will bisect the mile of grooved asphalt just ahead. The shorter of the airport's two runways, it's oriented north-south some two hundred feet above sea level, as straight and flat as a rolled-out black carpet, heat shimmering on it like a glaze of water.

"NINER LIMA CHARLIE CROSSING thirteen," I announce to the tower, a small white building with a control room on top that looks like the bridge of a ship.

I can vaguely make out the shapes of people inside the glaring glass. The sky is the faded blue of old denim, reminding me of favorite jeans I wore until they literally fell apart, and the past continues sneaking through the back door of my thoughts. I sense the inevitable, a tragedy I can't stop as my life parades behind my eyes when I least expect it. There is something about to happen like an Old Testament judgment. We should have stayed in Massachusetts. There isn't time for this. It's too predictable that we'd come here and I'm seething inside.

You're being manipulated like a goddam pawn.

"Roger niner Lima Charlie," the controller comes back, a woman whose voice I've heard before when I worked in Manhattan and would come to New Jersey on cases that had an ambiguous or shared jurisdiction, usually floaters carried by the current in the Hudson River.

"They already cleared us," Lucy's voice sounds inside my flight helmet.

"Correct," I answer.

"You didn't need to tell them again."

"Roger that."

"Don't want them thinking we forgot," she says from the right seat, her hands gentle on the controls, her tinted visor blacking out the upper half of her face.

All I can see is the tip of her narrow nose, her strong jaw firmly set and her attitude, which is all-business and as hard as metal. The word *rude* comes to mind. It often does with her especially when things are as dangerous as they are right now. But there's more. She's self-absorbed and distant, and something else is there that I can't access.

"Redundancy," I say into the mic against my lips. "Never hurts."

"Does when controllers are busy."

"Then they can disregard." If there's another thing I'm an expert at it's not letting her outwardly rile me, especially when she's right and in this instance she is.

There are no aircraft taking off. There's no traffic in the pattern, nothing moving out here except shimmering heat. The tower granted permission minutes ago for us to enter its class D airspace, cross the active runway and land on the ramp near Signature flight service. In summary my radio call wasn't necessary and Lucy is chiding me. I let it go. I don't trust my mood. I don't want to lose my temper with her or anyone, and it occurs to me that beneath anger is fear. I should get in touch with my fear so I'm not angry.

I'm going to find out this is all my fault.

No it isn't dammit, and when I peel back anger I find more of it. Under more of it is rage. Beneath rage is a black pit I've never climbed inside. It's the hole in my soul that would take me to the place where I might do something I shouldn't.

"Talking to controllers, the less said the better," Lucy is saying as if I haven't flown with her hundreds of times, as if I don't know a damn thing.

"Roger that," I repeat blandly as I stare straight ahead.

I keep my scan going for other aircraft and most of all for him. I think *him* but I don't know who or what, and as of this morning the press has dubbed the killer *Copperhead.* Marino volunteered the name to some reporter, and it will stick as names always do in big cases that seem destined never to be solved. Or if they are it's much too late. *The Boston Strangler. The Monster of Florence. The Zodiac Killer. The Doodler. Bible John.*

I recheck the intercom switch, making sure Marino can't hear a word Lucy and I say to each other. He'd like nothing better than to eavesdrop on us having a personal moment.

You're a bad mother.

It's as if *Copperhead* occupies my subconscious now, hissing ugliness, its fangs filled with poison from buried wounds.

"You got to relax, Aunt Kay." Lucy's twin-engine helicopter is as steady as a rock, directly over the taxiway's yellow centerline that she follows with the precision of a gymnast on a balance beam. "Take care of what's in front of you and don't think too much."

"We don't know what's in front of us. Or behind us. Or next to us."

"There you go again."

"I'm fine."

But I'm not. My vigilance is about to overtorque and while she understands the reason, she can't relate to it, not really. Lucy doesn't perceive danger the way other people do. It doesn't enter her brilliant mind that no matter how accomplished, brazen and rich she is, one day she's going to die. Everyone does. That's my job security as a forensic expert and chief medical examiner, and it's the burden I bear. Long ago I lost the gift of denial. I'm not sure I ever had it.

I know all too well that what separates us from total annihilation is nothing more than a three-pound trigger pull. Struck down by a copper bullet fired from nowhere. Thinking a thought one second. Then gone. We're on the killer's radar. He watches us. He could be in a ghillie suit right now disguised as heavy foliage or sagebrush, and I scan the dense woods beyond the runways and the grassy strips bordering them.

For some reason he has chosen not to squeeze the trigger—at least not yet. I have no factual basis for thinking this but the feeling is as palpable as the turbine engines overhead. I will my mind to stop but it won't, the hissing again, a cold-blooded whisper.

What fun to torture you like this.

And I have a sick feeling, an indescribably dreadful one as we parallel the runway, following taxiway Delta at an altitude of thirty feet and the speed of a brisk walk. The same scenario plays vividly as if I'm watching a video recording of an event that's already occurred. I see myself in the cross hairs of a thermal imaging computerized riflescope that emits no visible light or radio frequency energy. SNAP. Shattering the second cervical vertebra, dislocating the craniocervical junction, transecting the spinal cord.

Lucy gently flares her powerful flying machine as if she's lightly pulling back on the reins of a horse. She couldn't look more composed and sane. She couldn't look more normal.

CHAPTER 39

SHE SETTLES INTO A hover over the ramp's white tarmac where parked private jets and prop planes shine in the sun.

It occurs to me that shooting reconstructions are going to be miserable in this heat. Ballistic gelatin will get slimy and start stinking like rotting meat. Flies, sweat, stench and Jack Kuster, who I've never met, a macho man, a former Marine sniper, 103 kills in Iraq, Marino has continued to brag. I wonder who was counting.

I scan gauges and instrument lights, barely feeling the wheels touch down. I don't bother saying *nice landing*. Lucy's always are. They're close to perfect, rather much the same way she executes everything in life. I'm not feeling charitable.

"Niner Lima Charlie down and secure," I let the tower know as Lucy ground-taxis the helicopter, steering with her toes on the pedals as if she's easing one of her supercars into a parking place.

"Welcome back, Doctor Scarpetta." The familiar controller is slow-speaking and unflappable, and if I met her I could identify her by voice.

"Thanks. Nice to be here," I continue in my typically truncated radio language, and my attention shifts to the passenger's cabin, where I imagine Marino about to open his door while the blades are still turning.

How many times have I told him to wait until we're completely shut down? I envision him in back, headset on, seat belt off as usual, looking out at the woods and hills of New Jersey. I give him five minutes before he starts joking around, talking like the Sopranos, drawing out his vowels and sounding ridiculous. *I fuh-got.* Or *Fuck-dat.* Or *he's a dewsh-bag.* I switch the intercom to *All.*

"Stay put until the blades are stopped," I remind him.

"Naw I'm-gunna get a haircut." His big voice is loud in my helmet.

"You don't have any hair and sound retarded," Lucy says.

"Uh-oh. Not supposed to use that word. You'll lose your allowance."

"What's this Pavlovian thing with you?" Her fingers move rapidly across overhead switches, flipping them off, and the colorful synthetic vision, terrain awareness and navigation screens go black. "The minute you're back in New Jersey your IQ drops?"

"People here are smart as shit."

"I'm not talking about people. I'm talking about you," she says as the engines get quiet, and she begins jotting the flight time and other information in a small notebook.

"I dunno why I ever left."

"You shouldn't have. Then maybe we wouldn't know you." She flips off the avionics master switch before he can insult her back.

Shadows of the turning blades slow overhead in the cockpit's roof windows, and I pull down the rotor brake, take off my flight helmet and hang it by the chinstrap on a hook. Releasing my harness, I arrange it neatly under me on the sheepskin-covered seat so it doesn't dangle out the door and scratch the paint.

In the distance beyond miles of dense woods and on the other side of the Hudson, One World Trade Center rises high above the Manhattan skyline, which I can't see from here. All I can make out is the top of the skyscraper and its spire, a reminder that if you hurt us we'll strike back only harder. We'll rebuild only bigger. As I've watched the construction over the years I'm reminded of the new enemy I face: hate-filled bombers and shooters who know nothing about the people they massacre in a skyscraper, a movie theater, a school building, at a marathon or out by their cars. I think of what John Briggs said to me the other day about the Homeland Security Alert. It's suddenly foremost in my mind again.

Think of it as orange, but as far as the public goes it's yellow.

He wasn't just talking about Obama's visit. He was alluding to intelligence gathered by the CIA, about events in Crimea. He mentioned money, drugs and thugs flowing into this country, and in light of what's happened since he said that to me I wonder what he really meant.

Hot air hits me like a wall as I step down on the tarmac, where Marino is busy opening the baggage compartment, grabbing out black cases, one of them tagged as evidence. He sets down overnight bags, scanning for our ride as a bright yellow Shell fuel truck pulls up and a kid hops out of the cab.

"Where the hell is Kuster?" Marino asks no one in particular. His broad face is red, and sweat is beaded on top of his shiny shaved head, his eyes masked by his Ray-Bans. "I emailed him when we were thirty minutes out and I don't want this shit sitting in the sun."

"Nothing will melt or explode." Lucy grabs rolled-up silver sun shields. "Except you maybe."

"I could fry an egg on the pavement," Marino complains.

"You couldn't." Lucy starts unrolling shields that on a windy day fight her like kites but in this hot calm are completely limp.

"We'll carry everything into the FBO if need be," I suggest.

"Hell no," he says.

He looks sour and irritable even if he's not, his wide brow deeply furrowed, the corners of his mouth pulled down. He parks his sunglasses on top of his head, squinting in the shade under the tail boom to type on his phone's display as Lucy opens the fuel cap. Her rose-gold hair is polished by the sun, and she's nimble and strong in a summer-weight khaki flight suit as she walks around her aircraft, placing the sun shields in the windows. Then she locks the doors as the fuel truck driver who looks all of sixteen clips the ground wire on a skid.

"Afternoon," he says to Lucy. "This yours?"

"I'm just crew." She secures the tires with bright yellow chocks.

"Kuster is pulling up," Marino announces.

"Ready when I'm done." Lucy's not going anywhere until the helicopter has been refueled and she's satisfied it's safe from anyone who might be tempted to tamper with it.

She's obsessive about locking the cabin, cockpit, baggage and battery compartments, the cowling, everything, and her precautions aren't unusual. But I detect her vigilance is in overdrive and I know she's armed, a Colt .45 in a concealment holster under her flight suit. I felt it when I hugged her in Boston. I asked her about it and she shrugged me off.

The security gate slides open on its tracks and Jack Kuster drives through in his dark blue SUV, parking a safe distance from the fuel truck. He rolls down his window.

"Sorry I'm late," he calls out to us. "Been busy in the kitchen."

I HAVE NO DOUBT he's spent the day preoccupied with the onerous task of mixing up ballistic gelatin, creating blocks or molded shapes of a hydrolyzed collagen derived from animal skin, connective tissue and bone.

We have a lot of control test fires to do before it gets dark. We're almost out of time. The day has cheated us. It seems nothing is on our side and I watch Jack Kuster carefully, knowing him only by reputation, specifically the praises Marino sings. Kuster climbs out and grins boldly at Lucy as if they know each other and she doesn't smile back. She holds his stare for an instant, then grabs up several hard cases and bags, whichever are the heaviest.

"The biggest problem was how to mimic bone, specifically the skull," Kuster says as if he's in the middle of a conversation I know nothing about. "I considered putting a motorcycle helmet on the jelly head but it would be too unwieldy. A problem for another day and I gave up after making a mess. That leaves us one to play with." He means one molded gelatin block. "It's not a situation I generally find myself in because usually we're targeting center mass and not taking head shots."

"There's nothing usual about this killer," I reply.

"Well he's definitely aiming for the head, the upper spine unless he's just damn lucky."

"It's not luck," I answer. "Not three times. Possibly more if there are other shooting deaths we don't know about."

"There aren't," Lucy says as if she has information we don't. "Three with more on the way. That's the message we're supposed to get. Number three out of seven."

Because of the seven polished pennies on my wall but I don't bring it up.

"My point is if he's military or former, it's not what he was taught." Kuster rearranges gear in the back of the SUV, making room for what we brought. "We go for center mass."

"Russian special forces don't," Lucy counters. "They're trained for neck and head shots."

"So now we're looking for Russians?" Kuster stares at her.

"There's an exodus of Russian-trained special ops because of what's going on over there," she says as if she's been talking to Briggs. "That and hundreds of billions of dollars out the door, draining the economy. Not to mention drugs."

Benton would know this too. The FBI gets briefed by the CIA. Lucy's information probably came from him.

"It all depends on the weapon." Marino shoves ammo boxes around. "There's a shitload out there now that you didn't have in Iraq." He directs this at Kuster. "And yeah a shitload of stuff they've probably got overseas that's not in circulation here, not public circulation anyway."

"Smart guns, sniper rifles with computerized scopes and we do have them here," Kuster says. "One ballistic gelatin head is what we got and I again apologize for that. I thought about getting a pig carcass. I still could if you've got time tomorrow, if you wanna hang around another day. I also know some pretty good bars."

"No carcasses of pigs or anything else. The gelatin's going to be bad enough in this weather." I open a back door and tuck Lucy's and my overnight bags on the floor because we're running out of room.

"Who? You squeamish?" Kuster says to me.

"I don't do tests on animals alive or dead."

"But you'll do them on people."

"Deceased ones, yes. With signed consent."

"You get signed consent from dead people?" His banter is a blend of flirting and needling that I have no patience for right now. "That sounds like quite a trick. Is that why they call you Doctor Death?"

"Whoever *they* is? You'll have to ask them why they call me that."

"You always this unfriendly?"

"Not always," I reply.

"They've got this synthetic stuff that you don't have to mix and it doesn't stink," Lucy comments as if Kuster was born yesterday.

"That would be too easy. He wants it to be disgusting." Marino's face is slick with sweat.

"We don't have it in our budget to buy premade stuff that's not disgusting." Kuster's attention is fixed on Lucy.

"I'm going inside to pay." She trots across the ramp, her boots light on the blacktop, and somehow she manages to look cool in the sweltering heat.

"You can't afford me," Kuster calls after her.

"Not in the market," she fires back at him.

"Here we go." Marino glowers at both of them.

"How much by the pound?" Kuster yells.

"Out of season." She pushes through the glass door leading inside the FBO.

"No kidding she's out of season all right," Marino says in a loaded way but Kuster isn't listening.

The more he flirts with Lucy, the more she'll flirt back in the way she flirts. I'd be the first to admit that he's a compelling man, in his forties, tall and muscular like a clean-cut Ken doll in cotton twill desert-colored BDU pants and a beige T-shirt, a Smith & Wesson .40 cal in a pancake holster. I have no doubt he's already been told he doesn't have what it takes to wind Lucy's clock. Marino would have repeated his favorite cliché and offered all the details. He might have gone so far as to suggest there are things going on that are suspicious, weird coincidences that are too close to home. Marino and his big mouth.

He opens the SUV's front passenger's door as if he and Kuster are partners and I'm a civilian ride-along. I fasten my shoulder harness. I sit quietly. I can't get out of my mood or begin to fully understand it. I'm angry with Marino. I'm angry with everyone.

"What's new?" Kuster props an arm on the back of the seat, turning to talk to me, his handsome face tan with a blush of a burn on his nose, his eyes grayed-out by sunglasses.

"The FBI's been turning the Rosado estate and the sailboat inside out," Marino answers for me.

I send Benton an email, telling him we're safely on the ground, and at the same time a text message lands from Bryce.

My email password's not working is yours?

Mine is fine, I reply.

Can you ask Lucy?

"Rand Bloom's gray pickup truck was recovered from long-term parking at Logan," Marino is saying. "And remember the white truck you told me about? The one that hit a car at the Edgewater Ferry the day before Julie Eastman was shot? You said it looked like a U-Haul bobtail?"

"You think you found it," Kuster says rather than asks and I'm reminded again of the boxy white construction truck we saw when we were driving to Nari's crime scene.

It also looked like a U-Haul bobtail. Marino blared his horn at it and the driver pulled over to let us pass. The killer may have been right in front of us and we had no idea. It's just like everything else. We're being played, made fools of, following the monster's master plan. How amusing we must be.

"Left at a marina not far from the Rosado house in Marblehead Neck." Marino continues passing along the latest developments, details that I feel certain won't help us. "Plates removed, nothing inside except bleach. You could smell it a block away."

"So the person driving it, probably the killer, ditched it. Then after he killed Rand Bloom he left in his pickup truck and skipped town," Kuster replies as if it's a fact.

And tailed Benton's car, played cat and mouse with us on the highway.

"That sucks but I already knew about it," Kuster says.

If he already knew then the FBI has contacted him, and my anger spikes. They're asking questions, poking around, and I stare at the back of Marino's head. What has he been saying deliberately and thoughtlessly? What CFC business has he divulged without having the common sense to anticipate the harm it might do? The FBI shunned Lucy back in the day and it would shun her now but in a far different way. It would be a different type of judgment, one that could rob her of her freedom and her life.

"A day late a dollar short, that's the Bureau for you. Another waste of taxpayer dollars at work," Marino says as Lucy emerges from the FBO, jogging to the SUV.

"Who's she again?" Kuster asks me, and I don't believe he doesn't know and I don't know how anyone can be playful right now. "Your daughter, your little sister? She really fly that big bird all by herself?"

Lucy slides in back with me.

"Bryce's email," I say to her. "A problem?"

"A security situation. I'll explain later," she says.

I glance at my watch. It's quarter of five. We have at most three hours of usable daylight left.

CHAPTER 40

THE DRIVE TO THE Morris County Sheriff's Department training center and firing range is thirty minutes in the late afternoon traffic.

I feel time. It's tangible like a strong headwind pushing us back into a past that yawns forbidden and immutable. Lucy holds something close to her that she won't share and I sense that eventually I will recognize whatever it is. She's absorbed in her iPad while I stress over tests and reconstructions that I have no faith will catch a killer who has gone viral on the Internet. Since we left Boston *Copperhead* is trending, Lucy has informed us. I can't abide the attention evil people get.

I don't like the reminder that much of my energy is spent building a case instead of stopping the person responsible. It's my job to prepare for future juries, for future attorneys, to make sure I've explored every molecule of an investigation and documented all of it. But that's not enough and I'm beyond being conservative. I'm not sure I'm capable of it anymore.

Alone in my frustrated defiant thoughts I watch the scenery of handsome old homes, of horse farms behind neat fences, and meadows and parks with outcrops of purplish pudding stone. Foliage is lush and shadows dapple the roads, on West Hanover Avenue now, in and out of brightness that hurts my eyes. Lucy is busy on the Internet and I have my back to her as I stare out the window.

You're making this too personal.

I keep telling myself that but it does no good, and for an instant I'm sentimental. Hand-painted signs advertise homegrown produce the Garden State is famous for, and I swallow hard. I feel choked up with emotions I didn't expect. If only life were different. I'd like to pick out sweet corn, tomatoes, herbs and apples. I long to smell their freshness and feel their potential. Instead what's around me is like a noxious fog. Deceit. Lucy has her own agenda and she and Benton have been talking.

She's lying to me and so is he.

Kuster slows the SUV as the sprawling complex comes into sight. The brick and glass crime labs back up to the training academy, a vast tarmac surrounded by shot-up and burned-out buildings, and cars and overturned buses used for simulated scene investigation, for firefighting, K-9 and SWAT.

Beyond are miles of rolling empty grassland with berms and range towers, and momentarily we're bumping over a dirt road not much wider than a path, thick dust clouding up. Recent violent storms hit here first but you'd never know it. The earth has been baked bone dry by the sudden heat, still oppressive at this hour, hovering at almost ninety degrees. Tomorrow will be hotter.

We park behind one of many elevated wooden structures with corrugated green metal roofs, nothing under them but concrete pads, unpainted wooden shooting benches, sandbags, folding chairs. We get out and begin gathering our gear, and Kuster grabs a large black case, a precision guided firearm, a PGF that implements the drone technology of a tracking scope and guided trigger.

"SWAT's latest greatest," he continues to explain as we haul equipment through the hammering heat, setting it on the concrete pad, on the sturdy wooden benches. "I'm not saying the killer is using a PGF but he could be."

"Where does one get them?" I ask.

"The market's mostly wealthy big game hunters, and some law enforcement and the military but not many yet. It's new technology. Twenty, thirty thousand dollars a pop, and you're on a list. It's a relatively small clientele with no good place to hide if you're a proud owner."

"Is anybody looking at these lists?"

"Here come the Feds. Their specialty is pencils and lists." Marino is typically snide.

"I wanted you to see what's possible," Kuster says to me as he continues checking out Lucy and ignoring Marino's bluster. "A bull's-eye at a thousand yards is easy as pie. A novice could hit it. Even Lucy could."

"Where's the soft bullet trap you dreamed up?" Marino snaps open the gun case that is tagged as evidence.

"Right there." He points.

In a weed-infested area of grass below and to the left of where we're setting up is another concrete pad, this one with no roof. At the edge of it and pointing downrange is a section of steel pipe approximately four inches in diameter and six feet long. It's wrapped in a thick foam material typically used for winterizing and "packed with fiberfill real tight," Kuster describes.

"And I got some special loaded subsonic rounds for low velocity," he adds. "Three hundred Win Mags, one-ninety grain LRX, magnum primer, ten grains of Alliant Unique powder. It's not what was used but it will tell us something."

"If you don't think it's what was used then why bother?" Lucy asks.

"For one thing nobody's got to go downrange and try to find it. And for another the bullet remains intact, its open tip doesn't petal and I get to see the rifling picture-perfect and how about you make yourself useful." He's turned up the flame on his flirting. "In the back of the SUV are a headless manikin and an ice chest. Be a good do bee and bring my friend Ichabod and the jelly head here, plus the toolbox."

She doesn't budge. It's as if she didn't hear him and that's one of the ways she flirts back. Lucy likes him. What that might mean I don't know, and for an instant my thoughts return to the missing ring. Janet has left Lucy before and I hope she's not going to do it again.

"In summary"—Kuster has turned his attention to me—"we can fire test bullets with very little damage, collect them on the spot and get a clear look at the twist, the lands and grooves. All this to say that we can use photos from the ballistics labs and do a prelim comparison with the bullet fired into the trap as we stand out here sweating, and maybe spare ourselves losing hours on distant shots with a rifle we probably already know isn't the one killing people."

"The rifle's bullshit." Marino is especially full of himself and seems much too happy. "The question is where the hell did it come from?"

"Somebody bought it factory-prepped and planted it," Lucy says. "There's nothing customized about it. In other words over the counter."

"You should be careful talking like you know so much," Kuster tells her.

Inside the case tagged as evidence is the Remington .308 Marino found inside Rand Bloom's apartment, a stainless steel barrel, a green and black spiderweb finished stock. He picks it up.

"A 5R milspec barrel with a muzzle brake," he says, "and a real nice Leupold Mark 4 scope but there's no fouling. I agree that the damn thing is brand-new. I don't think it's ever been fired."

"Someone knew we'd figure that out in two seconds." Lucy has wandered to the back of the SUV, reaching inside the open tailgate, pulling the manikin out.

Someone. I can't get away from the sensation that she might have an idea who.

"It's not our gun, I can tell you that already," Kuster says. "The barrel's not going to be the same but for court purposes you need more than my word for it. I'll give you a nice chunk of copper that the jury can pass around." His gray-tinted glasses watch Lucy lifting out the ice chest, and suddenly he lobs a pair of hearing protectors and she catches them with one hand.

She clamps them above her ears, and Kuster takes the Remington. He reaches into a foam-lined Pelican case and hands me a video camera.

"I need you to record this," he says. "One thing I know is juries. They like pictures and they like movies. We'll show them the lengths we've gone to, that we didn't just do the DOPE in an air-conditioned lab."

I train the camera on him and begin to record as he steps off the raised pad, down to the one at ground level. He slides open the rifle's bolt, drops in a round, a blue polymer-tipped copper projectile seated in a shiny brass cartridge case. Pushing the bolt home with a sharp click, he lies prone on the grass, resting the butt on a rear sandbag, inserting the opening of the barrel into the end of the pipe closest to him.

"Eyes and ears!" He's flat on his belly, the stock snuggled up against his shoulder and cheek.

A sharp crack and silence, the low velocity bullet is stopped by the tightly packed fiberfill. It doesn't even make it six feet to the end cap.

"Hold." He means to stop recording.

He sits up and takes off his noise-blocking earmuffs. He announces we're going cold and raises a red flag on a pole just in case any new shooters show up. No one is to fire any weapons right now.

"Lucy?" he says. "I'll let you and Marino set up Ichabod downrange and we'll think big, a thousand yards to start with and we can always walk it back if we need to. But I'm thinking this sucker is popping off his prey from a distance. Get the hell on down there while we got God's acres all to ourselves because we usually get a few knuckleheads at dusk getting ready for the next *Zero Dark Thirty*. Then it's bye-bye to going downrange unless you want your head blown off." He says to me, "You didn't record that, right?"

JACK KUSTER UNSCREWS THE end cap from the section of pipe and begins pulling out white filler, what looks like a cloud of cotton. I watch him from a folding chair, the heat pressing down heavily as if I'm under hot water. My khaki field clothes seem glued to my skin, my sleeves rolled up and sweat trickles coolly down my arms, chest and back.

A big wad of filler and the bullet shines like a new penny, a little soot at the rear from the fast-burning powder, and Kuster says, "Well hello. Pretty much what I expected."

I turn my attention to Marino, Lucy and the manikin, a flesh-colored plastic male torso impaled by a shiny rod that at one time was attached to a head and a stand. They grab the ice chest, the large toolbox, hearing protectors parked above their ears. They start moving downrange along the dusty dry path. The sun burns low behind power lines blackly criss-crossing the horizon, no one around, all quiet except the static of traffic we can't see and then Kuster is standing over me with his hand outstretched.

In his palm is a large copper bullet completely intact including the blue tip as if it's never been fired. But lands and grooves are deeply etched.

"Kind of tangles your antennas, right? Like it plays a trick on your eyes?" he says.

"Yes it does."

He slides an iPad out of a backpack, types for a minute and an enlarged photograph appears on the screen, the copper bullet with its four razor-sharp petals recovered under the skin of Jamal Nari's chest. For a long beat Kuster looks at the image on the display, and he uses a 10X loop to study the bullet he recovered from the trap, picking white fibers off it. He gives the bullet to me and it feels warm and weighty.

"Not even close," he says. "This one here that you're holding? It's definitely not a one-ten twist and I already know from the type of barrel, what's known as a Rem-Tough, that it's an eleven point two-five. The upshot, no pun intended, is the firearm we're looking for isn't a Remington 700 unless the barrel was swapped out with something like a Krieger. Not to mention the rounds Marino recovered from Bloom's apartment? They're not Barnes cases. I'll write up my report but unless you or Marino have more questions about this particular rifle, I'm satisfied."

I sit quietly in my folding chair, staring off at the distant figures of Lucy and Marino in the shimmering heat. I feel Kuster contemplating me like a ballistics calculation.

"Try not to show so much enthusiasm," he says.

"I'll try harder not to."

"No discouragement allowed. It's against shooting range rules."

"What I'm trying not to feel is it wasn't a good time to come here and do this. I'm trying not to feel it's a waste to go through the motions of what will be needed in a trial that may never happen," I reply without looking at him.

"We'll get whoever it is."

"We're being toyed with. We're being completely manipulated."

"I had no idea you were such a fatalist."

"I'll also try to stop thinking about who else is going to die while we're out here playing with guns."

"I had no idea you were negative and cynical."

"I don't know what ideas you might have had."

"Is it something I did?"

"Not to me."

"We're not playing." He repacks the Remington in the foam cushioning of the black plastic case tagged as evidence. "But I understand your sentiments."

"I don't think you do." I look at him, at his gray glasses looking at me. "You already knew this rifle isn't the one that shot people. You already knew the answers to your questions before you even asked them."

"And how often do you know what killed somebody before you do the autopsy? How about Rand Bloom? You fished his body out of the pool and saw his stab wound. Did you need to cut him open to figure out that it was an upward thrust and a twist that severed his aorta and took out his heart? Maybe he inhaled a little bit of water with his dying breaths but he wouldn't have survived an arm-pumping upward stroke like that, military style."

"I can see Marino shares a lot with you, and I didn't do Bloom's autopsy. It wouldn't have been considered fair and impartial."

"You were right about what killed him."

"Yes I was."

"But that's not good enough. We have to prove it. And we just did. I'm helping us build a solid case."

"I suppose what you're going to prove next is these victims weren't shot from a ground elevation, not even close."

"You're exactly right. They weren't." Opening another Pelican case, this one large and sturdy, he lifts out the PGF.

It's an intimidating black rifle with a wide-bodied computerized tracking scope, and he sets it up on its bipod.

"And by the time we're done you may rethink your pet theory," he says.

"Which is?"

"That the powder charge was so light he may as well have thrown it. Not quite but I agree the asshole wanted you to find the bullet with the three engraved on it. You've kept that out of the media, right?"

"As far as I know."

"My worry is three out of what? How many is he planning?"

I envision the seven pennies and I think four to go. Marino, Lucy, Benton and me, and then I don't think it. I watch Kuster as he begins pushing cartridges into a magazine.

"Wireless enabled," he says. "Sensors collect all the environmental data, even the Coriolis effect, everything except windage which we have to enter ourselves. It all streams to an iPad which is helpful if you've got someone spotting and I assume our killer doesn't."

"Our? Let's not use the language of relationships."

"The take-home is assholes like this work alone unless it's something that's not important or particularly challenging."

Another open case and he gets out a Swarovski spotting scope. He sets it up on a sturdy Bogen tripod.

"So you can get a good look at what's going on at sixty-X." He stares off at Lucy and Marino far downrange, getting smaller in the low sun, shadows spreading from distant trees. "Although I realize you think we're wasting our time out here playing with guns. Of course if you really thought that, there's no way in hell you'd be here, am I right?"

"I hope you are."

"You're really pissed. I don't blame you."

301

"Maybe I blame myself."

"Yes. What could you have done to better anticipate? What preventive measures should you have thought of that might protect you and yours?" He loads another magazine with five solid copper rounds. "That's why I insisted you come here."

"I wasn't aware you did the insisting."

"Well I did. Two people dead on my turf in Morristown first. Now one in your neighborhood and who might be next? I know what I know and you know what you know. Together we know a lot more than anybody else. So tell me why you're pissed and I'll tell you why you really are."

"Because he's getting away with it."

"Nope," Kuster says. "It's because he's getting the best of you and your usual tools are failing. Lab science is only as good as the evidence turned in, and if evidence is tampered with and planted then what have you got? You've got shit. Like the Remington rifle. No prints on it and DNA will be worthless you'll find out. Same with the ammo Marino found, same with the jar of pennies. A big fat nothing that takes up everybody's time and gives the perp the leisure to plan and get in position."

"I'm afraid you're right."

"I know I am and there will be more of the same with whatever happens next."

"Okay you've got my attention."

"The idea that this killer wanted you to find a bullet? Where's that from? Not you I have a feeling."

"Lucy has suggested it as a possibility."

"She's subjective."

"So you think she's wrong."

"No I think she's right. What I also think is she's wound so tight she's about to pop," he says. "Tactical engagement principle number one is if you don't have a clear and decisive objective the operation becomes disconnected and unfocused."

I don't reply. I'm not going to share my misgivings about her, that she's emotionally involved and not being truthful. She might be disconnected and unfocused, and if not yet that will be next.

"I can help you," Kuster says.

"I'll take any help I can get." I hold his stare and then I say, "Thanks."

"Everybody can stand to learn a few new things in life, even the Big Chief." He opens another box of ammo. "I'm going to teach you to think like a sniper, and you know what a sniper is? A hunter, and I'm going to let you look through this hunter's eyes, through his scope and feel what it's like to pull the trigger and watch someone die before he hits the ground. Why am I going to do that?"

I get up from my chair and look through the spotting scope, light-weight with a large field of view. I adjust the close-range focus on the eye-piece and at a magnification of sixty Lucy seems right in front of me. She pushes her hair out of her face and she's squinting in slanted light. It's that time of day when there's too much glare to be without sunglasses and it's too shadowy to wear them. I take mine off and it's as if Kuster is reading me like a sniper reads his target. He takes his sunglasses off too and I'm surprised by how green his eyes are, almost as green as Lucy's.

"I'm doing it because I know your type that's why," he's saying. "If you see and intuit what this killer does then you'll figure him out. You'll be a lot more clearheaded than Lucy is. I got no doubt about it."

I follow her with the scope as she tears off a strip of silver duct tape that she attaches to the torso's chest, running it over the top of the ballistic gelatin head, translucent like an ice cube and slippery-looking, oval with the vague molded features of a male face. I can tell the tape isn't sticking to it, and she tries another strip, constantly looking around as if someone is looking back. The gelatin is beginning to melt. It won't be long before it's viscous like putrid glue.

"Don't worry." Kuster is reading me again. "This one's mostly for the effect because you're correct. I have a pretty good expectation about what's going to happen. But again I'm thinking about the jury. We'll take out jelly man on video—well actually it will be me who does. I'll set up the camera on a tripod downrange. Two shots at a thousand yards, ten foot-ball fields. One reduced velocity round, one normal. I'm going to get him right here."

He touches the back of his neck at the base of his skull.

"And we'll see what shape the bullets are in and if they exit the gela-tin," he says. "That's about as much abuse as Ichabod's going to be good for. Any other shots we do, and that includes you, we'll simply go after steel targets, see how the PGF calculates the flight paths. Distance isn't my big concern. I'm going to warn you right off that based on this"—he indicates the image of the bullet on the iPad—"what seems to suggest as much as a seventy-degree downward angle? We're talking about a BC that has disturbing implications. That's the problem we've got to solve."

BC or ballistic coefficient is a mathematical measure of drag, of how well a bullet cuts through the air.

"Implications of a flight path," he adds, "that we probably can't simu-late out here unless Lucy is in a mood to let us shoot from her helicopter. We could do that with this thing." He pats the PGF. "We wouldn't even need a gyrostabilizer."

"I wish you wouldn't suggest an idea like that," I reply flatly.

"Why not? Someone's going to."

"What else has Marino said to you?" I look away from the scope, directly at him as he hunches his shoulder, wiping sweat from his neck and jaw.

"That someone might be trying to set her up. That someone might be trying to send her to prison."

"Might be?" I'm blinded by sudden anger.

CHAPTER 41

HE LEANS AGAINST THE edge of the bench, digging his sweaty hands into his pockets, looking down at me.

"I'm not the enemy," Kuster says. "I'm on your side."

"I wasn't aware there were sides." I push down fury I don't want to feel.

"Let's just put it this way. If I thought Lucy was a bad guy she wouldn't be out here on the range with us. But it's not what I think. It's what the Feds think and you know what they say in my line of work. A lot of people get caught because they're obvious and easy. It doesn't mean they did it."

"Your line of work?" The heat of my mood begins to simmer down from scalding to a low rolling boil.

I remember the power of my will. I focus on it. I must stay calm.

"Military. Cops. The school of hard knocks," he says. "I know you're married to the FBI."

"Just to one of them."

"And he's not who you need to worry about I assume."

"Has the FBI been in contact with you?" I want to hear him say it.

"Of course. You'd expect that."

"Benton Wesley? Did you talk to my husband about my niece?"

Kuster slides his hands out of his pockets, sweat dripping off his chin, his eyes like emeralds against his shiny tan skin. "Look, there's a lot of backstory here that you don't necessarily know about. Marino's from Bay-onne and I grew up in Trenton. We've known each other for a while and have been spending a lot of time together the past six or seven months. You're probably aware that he reconnected with his high school sweet-heart, Beth Eastman. They started dating and then her daughter was shot to death as she was getting out of her car at the Edgewater Ferry. Julie was twenty-eight. She'd just gotten a promotion at Barclays and was engaged."

"It's terrible," I reply. "All of these homicides are. Senseless and cold-blooded."

"I've thought for a while that this killer has personal information about all of you and then things quickly began to escalate about a month ago," Kuster continues. "Marino said we need to nip matters in the bud, build a case before someone else does. He trusted me because we're friends and he's known your niece since she was a kid. He knows her history and could see the writing on the wall. The problem is telling whether a former federal agent, a crack investigator like Lucy Farinelli, discovers details be-cause she can or if it's because she's the one who created those details. Like dead-end tweets. Like hacking into your database. Like shooting from an elevation that might suggest a helicopter."

"Why would she?"

"You've heard the story. It's a predictable one. She's confronted stress-ors in her life that have sent her over the edge. I've seen it before and so have you."

"There's no story." Another wave of anger rolls over me. "Someone may be implicating Lucy but not enough for it to stick. None of what you've described stands up to scrutiny."

"And people have been sent away for a lot less. They've been destroyed. We had a case last year you probably heard about. A farmer's plowing a field and digs up skeletal remains that turned out to be those of a twenty-year-old girl who disappeared from Brooklyn in 2010. The more he tried to be helpful, to gather information and assist the Feds, the more suspi-cious they got. Now all he does is talk to his lawyers. He's bankrupt. He's a pariah. His wife's left him. He could end up indicted for something he didn't do all because he was trying to be a good person. See how it works?"

"I know how it works." I realize how upset I am. I'm so incensed it's scary.

"So let me help you catch the bad guy, but you need to sit over here in this chair." Kuster taps the folding chair in front of the bench he leans against, where the PGF is set up but not loaded. "Easy as pie? I want you to find out for yourself."

I stay where I am, standing behind the spotting scope on its tripod.

"Muzzle velocity, wind speed, temperature, barometric pressure and the type of bullet. And the nice thing about this baby"—he indicates the PGF—"is it does the math for you as long as you correctly enter your type of ammo and the wind, which right now is variable and minimal but on its way to stronger. Thursday morning in Cambridge around the time Jamal Nari was shot the wind was ten knots gusting at around fifteen out of the north. Now it's flipped around which is why it's so damn hot."

I move the spotting scope, finding the round red metal targets attached by chains to what are called gong stands at distances ranging from one hundred yards to a mile. The last berm I can see is mirage waves in the heat and the target is nothing more than a red pinpoint. I try to settle down inside. The FBI has come close to ruining Benton more than once and now they'll be happy to ruin Lucy. The anger is huge. It's not going to move.

It's my family. You don't touch my family.

"This shooter clearly knows what he's doing and picked ammunition accordingly." Kuster keeps talking. "Some rounds are slippery in the wind but one-ninety LRX is hateful. It will plow on through the volatile air, through flesh, bone, whatever it hits. Massive expansion and the wound channel looks like jelly."

"What about a subsonic load?"

"I don't think so. That would be a bullet traveling at less than twelve hundred feet per second. But a lighter load, yes," he says. "Add that to a big distance and the velocity drops precipitously. The bullet loses kinetic energy. If you plan it just right it stays intact and gets recovered."

I train the scope back on Marino and Lucy as they secure the ballistic head with more tape, and I can see they've used a rubber mallet to drive the steel rod into the dirt, then placed large rocks around it.

"Play out what you think," I say to Jack Kuster.

"Say one of these leaves the muzzle at 2400 feet per second instead of 2800." He plucks a cartridge out of a box and holds it up. "In other words, a slightly lighter powder charge. Well that's going to drop to less than 1150 feet per second at a thousand yards or an energy of less than 558 foot-pounds."

"And depending on what it hits there could be very little expansion or collateral damage."

"If it hits something soft like a carcass," he agrees. "Or ballistic gelatin as opposed to a hard target like metal or in real life bone. In the round you recovered from Jamal Nari's chest exactly how much bone did it hit?"

"It separated the vertebra and after that tunneled through soft tissue, lodging under the skin."

"That's part of the explanation. The other part is where the hell is the bad guy shooting from?"

"Do you know?"

"I don't." He pulls a small white towel out of his knapsack and hands it to me. "But what I do know is when we're done you're not going to think the same way."

"And what way is that?"

"Like a scientist. Like a doctor. Like a mother or an aunt. I'm going to teach you how to think like a hunter of human beings."

"And that feels like what in your experience?"

"It feels like nothing if they had it coming," he says.

I watch Lucy and Marino swivel the manikin around, turning its back to us. They're talking to each other, now walking in our direction along the narrow dirt road that's barely wide enough for a mule utility cart. Lucy's eyes don't stop moving as she talks and continues her scan. I know her better than anyone. She's worried we're being stalked and she's basing her worry on real information.

"You going to try this thing or what?" Kuster taps the folding chair again.

I walk over to the bench. I sit in the chair.

SWEAT STREAMS DOWN MY face and into my eyes. I can't get comfortable. For someone who has the strong steady hands of a surgeon, I'm shaky as I attempt to center the blue X in the Heads Up Display. The rifle is heavy, at least twenty pounds.

"I don't think I'm even on the right target," I admit.

"You're not. The thousand-yard berm is the big one to the left." Kuster is standing nearby, acting as my spotter, the rifle's scope live streaming video to the iPad.

The jelly man was destroyed in two shots. Kuster nailed the area that would have been the back of the neck at the level of C2, at the base of the skull. At a thousand yards the slightly lighter load didn't exit, there was very little damage and the bullet drop was almost 478 inches, meaning the PGF had to aim more than thirty-nine feet above the target. The heavy load round passed through the jelly head and we didn't find the bullet. Likely it dug deep into the earth.

The intact bullet that killed Jamal Nari must have been loaded with less powder than usual. If so Lucy is right. It was deliberate. I'm not impressed that she would think of it because I'm too concerned about why she did. She's with us and she's not. She's focusing keenly while her attention is all over the place, her eyes moving constantly, and I recognize the almost imperceptible turns and tilts of her head. Her peripheral vision, her hearing are on high alert. The thought moves through a dark part of my mind, a deep off-limits place. Lucy might know who *Copperhead* is. Maybe Benton has his own suspicions too and for some reason they won't tell me.

Now we've switched to metal, and Kuster, Marino and Lucy are seeing exactly what I am. They let me know I'm off target by about a quarter of a mile. I look up, wiping my face and hands on the towel, then I gaze at the spread of parched grazing land, empty except for berms and their back-stops, and far off, clumps of trees. I peer through the scope again. I move the barrel to the left, making very minor adjustments, finding the tiny red targets on the 750-yard berm, and then finally the pale tan berm a thousand yards away, a vague and wavy mirage. It's as if the targets are dancing.

I push away sinister thoughts and a growing sense of hopelessness. What we can't account for is the some seventy-degree downward flight path of the bullet that struck Nari in the back of his neck and lodged under the skin of his chest. Shadows are deepening, creeping in from all angles like nocturnal animals, the sun burning on the horizon and sinking below it in a smoldering rosy orange. I can barely see the red metal targets lined up like lollypops, and I set the white dot on the one farthest to the left and tag it. Then I change my mind.

"Windcall." I realized we've been at this for more than an hour and it won't be long before it's too dark to see. "Maybe the wind has shifted again."

It's picked up and the temperature hasn't dipped below the high eighties.

"I think you should do this," I decide with no one in particular in mind as I reach for my bottle of water, taking a big warm swallow, no one else on the firing line except three men, military I'm sure.

They showed up about fifteen minutes ago, picking a distant steel-roofed concrete pad reserved for close range. The crisp tap-taps of their M4s are a constant bright peppering, and now and then I catch them staring at us, two men, two women with a weapon that may very well change everything we've ever thought about guns.

"If you don't experience it you can't appreciate what's happening." Kuster has said this repeatedly. "You can't appreciate the reality of a weapon system like this."

I press my cheek against the stock, squeezing the rear bag, but the rifle seems heavier the more I try. I'm fatigued and I'm struggling. The more I force things the worse they'll get.

"If he's using one of these, it's not exactly doing all of the work for him," Marino speaks up. "That's the point."

"A point I get all too well," I reply.

"Five miles per hour, right to left," Kuster says.

I press a switch, toggling in the wind speed and direction. The gyroscopes and accelerometer will compensate for barrel movement, and the computerized scope will handle distance, temperature, atmospheric pressure and elevation. I fight with the white dot again, doing a poor job of tagging the target.

"If you don't like it clear it and take another one," Lucy says.

Even my heartbeat bounces the white dot around, and then I get it right and press the button on the side of the trigger guard.

"Nice tag." Kuster stares at the iPad. "Back a little out."

I try again.

"A little more. Move forward on the bench, triangulate with your left arm and try to get comfortable, get really tucked in. Nope, clear that. Try again."

I tag the target yet again, and I'm shaky and my vision is getting blurry. I hold the white dot on the center of the target and push the button.

"Beautiful," Kuster says.

I line up the cross hairs. They go from blue to red as I press the trigger, but the rifle doesn't fire. It's calculating the conditions and any movement a target might make. Then a loud crack and a recoil kicks into my shoulder.

"Center mass about five o'clock. Good enough to get the job done." Kuster shows me on the iPad. "Congratulations, Doc. You just killed someone at a thousand yards."

CHAPTER 42

IT ISN'T TRUE THAT a novice could get hold of a PGF and hit the bull's-eye every time. Jack Kuster demonstrated with excruciating clarity that the killer didn't simply acquire the latest technology and start on a murderous spree that includes hitting nearly impossible targets.

The person we're after is experienced, highly skilled and could be using a smart rifle, a weapon that's a lot smarter than I am I've decided. I learned the hard way that tagging the target isn't *easy as pie*. Typically when I managed to get the white dot just right I moved the rifle and lost the tag, and then there's the problem, the seemingly insurmountable problem of the flight path. After several hours of firing rounds at gong stands and hearing the faint clinks of copper hitting steel Kuster verified what I didn't want to be true.

There are no areas of the range including its towers that are elevated enough to simulate the Jamal Nari shooting. In conditions like the ones Thursday morning Kuster estimates the sniper had to have been as much as three hundred feet above the target. At that distance the most anybody would have heard is a snap of the bullet hitting. He snapped his fingers to show us.

SNAP. I keep hearing it.

He said we'd be "foolish" to rule out a helicopter, and it's just one more thing that the FBI will use against Lucy. A sharpshooter and gun expert, she was flying the Thursday morning Nari was killed, and I feel an undercurrent of urgency as I slide my magnetic card into the lock of my hotel room and open the door. I walk in and drop my bags on the perfectly made bed. I turn on lights and find the desk and a bottle of water, distractedly aware of formal furniture and striped upholstery as I plug in my laptop and sit.

I open a satellite map of Cambridge that was updated eleven minutes ago at eight-fifty P.M. and find the Victorian house on Farrar Street, lit up, tall iron lamps glowing. I recognize the big porch, the bicycles and a scooter chained to pillars, parked cars, the yellow ribbon of crime scene tape still encircling the yard. I zoom out and move due north to the construction site where a tower crane operator allegedly fell to his death early Wednesday morning.

Across the line in Somerville, a tall building, concrete, glass and scaffolding and not much else. I search for information. A twenty-story luxury apartment complex, construction began last summer and the site is exactly point-six miles as the crow flies or approximately a thousand yards from where Nari dropped to the pavement, bags of groceries spilling everywhere.

As is typical of most high-rise construction there's a tower crane for aerial lifting, 250 feet tall, I estimate. The operator cab is tucked in the right angle of the tower and the jib, and the only way up is to climb the fixed ladder, caged inside steel framework that wouldn't prevent someone from falling especially if the person were ambushed. I can't imagine starting my workday climbing up such a thing, wearing a backpack or carrying a rucksack with basic necessities, and I log in to the CFC database and find the case from three days ago, June 11.

Art Ruiz, forty-one years old, with the blunt force trauma and deceleration injuries I expect in a fall from a significant height, and I study photographs of him at the scene and on the autopsy table, noting his lacerated right ear, his open skull fractures, his crushed pelvis and lower legs. Then I get interested in the cuts and ripped nails of his hands. They aren't consistent with someone who suffered a major cardiac event while climbing a ladder, someone unconscious who dropped to his death. I read Jen Garate's report and notice that Sil Machado was the investigator.

Discovered by coworkers at approximately eight o'clock on the morning of June 11th, Ruiz was on his back at the base of the tower crane, his jeans and shirt bloody and disarrayed, one boot and his hard hat off, his backpack on but the straps were down around his elbows and his arms were badly abraded. I notice from the CT scan that both of his shoulders were dislocated, and a close-up photograph of the right side of his face and forehead tell a different story. They show discrete areas of contusion, very faint, a pinkish purple, a parallel pattern that I associate with shoe tread. I call Luke Zenner's cell phone.

"It's hard to know exactly what he hit on his way down. That's one of the reasons I pended his case," he says to me when I ask him about the marks on the crane operator's face. "As you can see he has a lot of non-lethal injuries from hitting the rungs of the steel ladder and its caging as he fell, and he also has narrowing of his vessels, apparently asymptomatic cardiovascular disease. But that doesn't mean he didn't get dizzy or faint. Climbing up two-hundred-something feet of ladder would be strenuous."

"He also could have been kicked." I open another map on my computer, this one of Edgewater, New Jersey. "If someone were already inside the cab, all this person had to do was open the door when Ruiz reached the top. Swift hard kicks to the head and he slams back against metalwork and loses his grip, which might explain his dislocated shoulders. His backpack got snagged possibly repeatedly, and the injuries to his hands indicate he may have attempted to grab hold of rungs and the caging as he fell. What does Machado think?"

"I guess you haven't heard. As of late this afternoon he's no longer with Cambridge. I understand he's taken a job with the state police."

"I'm sorry to hear that." But Marino's better off and that means all of us are.

Another high-rise under construction, another tower crane just blocks from where Julie Eastman was murdered, and I search for government reports, for anything that might have been made public. I ask Luke if there's been any discussion about Ruiz being a homicide.

"Not yet," he says.

"And the construction site? I'm assuming it was immediately shut down."

"Yes. You know what happens when OSHA gets involved."

"Well there was something similar in a New Jersey shooting that's connected to the Nari shooting . . ."

"Hold on. And these shootings are related to the construction death?"

"I'm thinking that," I reply. "A construction site close to the Edge-water Ferry Landing was shut down two days before Julie Eastman was murdered. Apparently there were complaints to OSHA about safety violations and the job was temporarily halted pending an investigation. And six months ago, the shooting homicide in Morristown? Jack Segal was murdered as he was getting out of his car behind his restaurant, which is a third of a mile from another major construction site with a tower crane."

"Was that site also shut down?"

"It would have been," I reply. "Segal was murdered December twenty-ninth and I don't know of any construction site that is active during the holidays. They obviously don't disassemble tower cranes when work is halted and there's nothing to stop someone from climbing up and breaking into the cab."

"To shoot people."

"The ultimate deer stand, hundreds of feet in the air," I reply.

"The question is who the hell would think of something like that?"

"Someone who's been doing very bad things for a while and has no fear," I reply. "A trained killer in other words, the worst rogue imaginable."

AN HOUR LATER IN the bar downstairs, I squeeze lime into a gin and tonic while Lucy drinks beer.

"Are you still convinced *Copperhead* . . . ?" I start to ask.

"It's a stupid name," she interrupts. "A stunt for attention."

"The killer is the one who chose it, not the media."

"Right. Hijacked the Twitter account of a dead plumber, picking a name that would fuck with us."

"How did this person do it?" I follow Lucy's lead. I avoid using pronouns or any reference to gender.

"Easy if you know how to data mine, how to access death records. And we're supposed to start thinking that too. It's all planned and deliberate."

"We are? Us specifically?" I ask and she says nothing. "Why would it enter your mind that this person wanted to ensure we'd find an intact bullet?" I get back to my question as I continue to think about what else Jack Kuster said.

Lucy is subjective. She's wound so tight she's about to pop. She's that way for a reason. Lucy always has one and I'm going to find out what it is.

"An engraved three on a bullet and we're supposed to think about how many other people are going to die and if the next victims are us," she says.

I think *four to go* as I sip my drink and listen to the clatter of the Midtown Express Train. The grand white brick Madison Hotel is close to railroad tracks in a historic area of Morristown that's only a thirty- or forty-minute drive from where Julie Eastman was murdered. The restaurant where Jack Segal was shot is even closer, and a month ago the killer was inside this hotel's business center sending me a tweet.

A poem from *Copperhead* that referenced a silent *hangman* and gold-like *fragments*. A poem that said *tick tock*. A disturbed unsettled flutter starts in my gut as if I'm about to be sick.

"An elevation of several hundred feet." I bring that up to see what Lucy will say. "How is that possible in the area of Cambridge where Nari was shot?"

"You say that as if you already know the answer." She looks at me.

"I might. Maybe I got the idea from you."

"Not from me."

"From my wanting an explanation other than a helicopter, specifically your helicopter," I reply.

"The tallest building anywhere near the house on Farrar Street is maybe four or five stories," she says and then she brings up construction, the high-rise being built on Somerville Avenue where the tower crane operator died.

"So you thought of it too," I reply and I tell her he might have been murdered.

"That would make sense," she says.

"Why would it?" I ask.

"It was smart of you to figure it out and I agree. It makes sense," she repeats.

The bar is pleasantly dark with wainscoted walls and bare wooden floors, and there's a piano at the far end, nobody playing right now. It's almost eleven and we've showered and changed, both of us in jeans and polo shirts, finishing salads, going easy with our drinks after hours in the heat. I feel the unpleasant flutter again as I confront her about helicopters because someone else will and may have already.

"You were flying Thursday morning around the time Nari was murdered." I sip my drink and focus on my stomach to see if the tonic water might settle it.

"*After* he was murdered," she corrects me. "I took off from Norwood at eleven-oh-eight and that's on an ATC recording. It's an indisputable fact."

"I'm not interrogating you, Lucy. But it has to be cleared up. I think the shootings are being done from tower cranes but we have to talk about helicopters."

"Go right ahead, interrogate. You won't be the only one. In fact you aren't."

"What time did you begin monitoring the Boston-area frequencies Thursday morning?" The tonic water isn't helping and I don't know what's wrong. "You routinely do that prior to a flight. You check weather. You check area traffic and notices." The waitress is heading our way, a young woman with short spikey hair, in tight black pants and a white cotton dress shirt. "Could there have been another helicopter up that might have . . ."

"Might have what?" Lucy interrupts. "The killer put it on autopilot and fired a heavy weapon system out the window? Or maybe had an accomplice who was doing the flying with a door off? No way. You were smart to think of the cranes. I guarantee you're right. It makes sense."

"Need another?" The waitress smiles at me and glances warily at Lucy as my feeling gets worse.

"A shot of gin on the side and extra tonic water please." It's a bad idea and I probably should go upstairs to bed but I can't possibly.

"Do you have Saint Pauli Girl?" Lucy asks boldly and I'm stunned.

"Yes." The waitress sounds nervous.

"Now we're talking." Lucy is intimidating her and she hurries off.

"What just happened?" I take a deep slow breath, waiting for the nausea to pass. "How did you know about the beer?"

"You mean the empty bottles lined up on the rocks where Gracie Smithers had her head smashed? You took photographs at the scene and uploaded them into the database. You also took plenty of photographs at the Patty Marsico scene in Nantucket. Do you remember what was on the windowsill inside the flooded basement? Four empty Saint Pauli girl bottles, wiped clean of prints, the DNA destroyed by bleach, the labels facing out. You know who owns the real estate company, the one that Patty Marsico's estranged husband tried to sue? Gordian Knot Estates, the corporation formed three years ago by Bob Rosado."

"You just scared the hell out of our server." I finish my drink and don't feel any worse or better.

"I don't want her hanging around."

"I don't think she has any interest in hanging around. Are you ready to start telling me the truth? Do you think I don't know when you're not?" I touch my forehead and it's hot.

"You know everything," she says.

"We'll sit here until I do."

"Why's your face so flushed?"

"No more lies," I reply.

"It's not lying. It's about timing, about my feeling it's safe to share information. So far it hasn't been safe and I wasn't sure of it."

"Why?"

"Maybe you won't approve. Maybe you won't believe me the same way certain other people don't."

"What other people?"

"Marino. I know what he thinks."

"What did you tell him that you haven't told me?"

I hold her stare, trying to read what's going through her mind, secrets she doesn't want to trust me with, and she's not afraid. She's not angry. She's something else I can't quite define and then I catch the scent of it. I feel its motionless presence, its stare like a majestic animal perfectly camouflaged. And I know what it is.

Lust.

"The signet ring that's been in Janet's family." Sexual lust, bloodlust, I sense both raging inside her. "You stopped wearing it and then Janet's father got it back. Not the other way around."

"She shouldn't be talking to you." A glint of hurt darkens Lucy's eyes to the color of moss.

"Some months ago you suddenly got a different helicopter . . ."

"I like the Agusta better. It's twenty knots faster."

"And recently you bought a new Ferrari."

"We need a backseat and I'll bet Janet didn't bother telling you why."

"She didn't."

"She should tell you. Well it's not important anymore. At least a backseat is helpful when I pick up Sock."

"What isn't important anymore?"

"You need to ask Janet."

"I'm asking you."

"Her sister has stage-four pancreatic cancer."

"I'm so sorry. Christ. I'm so sorry. What can I do to help?" I've met Natalie and what races through my mind is the rest of the story.

She's a single mother with a seven-year-old son.

"Janet promised to take Desi," Lucy says and I'm not surprised.

Of course Janet would and even if it weren't the right thing to do I also know she wants children. She's not coy about it. Former FBI, an environmental lawyer now, she's gentle, settled down and would be an excellent mother. Lucy worries she'd be a bad one. She's always said she couldn't deal with kids.

"Of course I'll help. I'll do anything you need," I repeat.

"I can't do it," she says.

"Desi adores you."

"He's great but no."

"You would let him end up in social services?" I can't believe she would be so selfish and cold. "Well that's never going to happen. I'll take him before that happens, and you of all people know . . ."

I don't finish. I'm not going to say that if it hadn't been for me stepping in and being a surrogate mother to her there's no telling what would have happened.

"Natalie was diagnosed a few months ago," Lucy says, her eyes bright with tears for an instant.

At least she feels bad about it. At least she feels something.

"It had already spread to the lymph nodes, her liver." She looks around the bar and she doesn't look at me. "It's stage four and all of us have prepared for the worst. I got the car. I've done everything I can and it was fine until last month when I decided no. I told Janet no I can't. She should do what she needs to do but I can't."

"Of course you can."

"No. It's not possible."

"Last month." It occurs to me. "Why did you decide this last month?"

Lucy takes the last swallow of her beer. "I've told her she shouldn't be with me. Especially if there's a kid, neither of them should be with me. But she won't listen and I can't tell her the reason."

"That's why you stopped wearing her ring. You want to break up. Are you seeing someone?"

"Yes I want to break up."

"Yet you and Janet were flying Thursday morning and buzzed my house. You're clearly very hurt. I know you love her. You never stopped loving her all the years you were apart. You found each other again and now you do this?"

"The past is the problem. It's anything but past and that's a problem as big as one could ever get," she says and I feel it again, the huge beast I can't see and then the sensation, the flutter in my gut.

"It doesn't sound to me that you really want to break up." I hear my own voice and it isn't convincing or strong as I try to push down nausea.

"She needs to move out. She should have already. I told her I'll give her whatever she wants but she needs to get as far away from all of us as she possibly can." Lucy's face is stony and beneath her hard cool surface is a desire too hot to touch, molten and flowing like the core of the earth.

"You just said *all of us.*"

"I was with Janet when it began. First Quantico and then we were living together in D.C." Lucy says what seems to be a non sequitur. "But Janet wasn't on the radar and now she is."

"On whose radar?"

"Janet would be on it now and it's incredibly dangerous, it couldn't be more dangerous with only one way it can end. Anything I care about she wants me to lose."

"Janet doesn't want to take anything from you."

"I'm not talking about her."

"Then who?" I'm suddenly chilled and sick.

I put my jacket on. I press my hands against my face and they're so cold my fingernails are blue. I think about rushing to the ladies' room. I sit still and breathe slowly. I wait without speaking until the attack passes, and I see it again. I see it move.

CHAPTER 43

"THE BEER. THE SAINT Pauli Girl," Lucy says and the great beast is as big as the Rockies.

I feel its unblinking stare and its smell is strongly sour.

"You don't find it everywhere and this bar doesn't have many people who ask for it."

"You know someone who drinks it," I reply, and she nods, and the air shifts and the smell changes.

A gamey wet odor that I know is an olfactory hallucination as a primitive part of my brain somehow knows what's coming. It's threatening enough that I can't give it form. I can't capture it as a conscious thought.

"On the night of May eleventh, Sunday, Mother's Day, at eleven-thirty-nine P.M. to be exact, this particular server"—Lucy looks across the room at her—"waited on a woman who sat at that table over there near the bar." She indicates a corner table that is occupied by a heavyset man in a suit, drinking whiskey. "This woman ordered Saint Pauli Girl, four of them over a period of two hours, and when she ordered the third one at exactly eleven-twenty-two P.M. she got up to use the ladies' room. But that's not the only place she went."

"She stopped by the business center." I can see where this is headed and I feel myself resisting as the flutter comes back powerfully and moves up my throat.

"Yes," Lucy says and our waitress returns with a St. Pauli Girl, my extra shot and a large carafe of tonic water, cold with tiny gas bubbles suspended in it.

She sets them down and doesn't linger.

"She thinks I'm going to cause her trouble, but I'm not." Lucy picks up her beer.

"Why would she be in trouble?" I pour the gin into my melted ice and fill the glass from the carafe.

"Because the beers were comped. Maybe one would have been okay but not all four of them. She says she did it because the woman scared her. She was quote *weird* with creepy eyes, and after she was finished drinking each beer she placed the empty bottle in her tote bag. She didn't use a glass and she wiped off the table and her chair."

"Why?"

"Why do you think?"

"She didn't want anyone to have access to her DNA or fingerprints. Did the waitress tell you this?" The gin and tonic helps wash down the bile sneaking up. "And when did you have this conversation?"

After we checked into the hotel I was busy on my computer. I made phone calls to Luke and then to Benton, who's not answering, and I showered and changed, meeting Lucy here at ten-fifteen. She got to the bar before I did and gathered the information she needed, and it's no wonder the waitress is avoiding her.

"She's seen what's all over the news about the shootings here and in Cambridge," Lucy says. "I made it clear she would be wise not to hold anything back from me and if she keeps her mouth shut so will I. Four free beers and Carrie, who came on to her, gave her a hundred-dollar bill for a tip, tucked it in the front of her pants."

"Carrie?" The beast steps out of the brush and it's unbelievably noisy and I smell how old it is. "Carrie?" I repeat, and Lucy smiles thinly, coldly.

"This time she loses for good." Hatred and that's not all. "I won't allow collateral damage. Not Janet, not a kid, not anyone."

I lean forward in my chair and everything that's happened crashes through my mind, charging right at me. The shootings, the tweets, the pennies, Patty Marsico, Gracie Smithers and the sailboat, the corrupted DNA profile and apparent planted evidence and now the beer.

"Carrie Grethen." Lucy's matter-of-factness is more terrifying than the name itself.

The beer. The beer. The beer, my inner voice isn't quiet anymore. In this very bar. Lucy picked the Madison Hotel, not me, and she doesn't see what's happening. A buried plague like an ancient virus waking up in thawing permafrost, and she's as bloodthirsty as she's lustful. She'll be infected and probably is and always was.

> *Hey DOC,*
> *Tick Tock . . .*
> *LUCY LUCY LUCY and we!*

Another poem sent to me, this one from Wards Island, New York, the women's ward of Kirby Forensic Psychiatric Center where Carrie Grethen was committed because she was too dangerous to be contained in any other facility. Criminally insane, too mentally unfit to stand trial, but it wasn't true. It couldn't have been more false. She was never crazy, was anything but crazy, and I remember what Benton said after she escaped from maximum security:

Carrie Grethen hasn't finished ruining people's lives.

"She's dead." I say it quietly, carefully, my hands cradling my drink as I hold Lucy's stare. "We saw her helicopter blow up midair and crash into the ocean after you fired an A-R-fifteen at it through your open door."

It was a white Schweizer that was no match for Lucy's Jet Ranger or her skills. But we were low on fuel when its pilot, Carrie's killing partner Newton Joyce, opened fire with a submachine gun, hitting our skids, our fuselage. Lucy didn't want to crash over a crowded beach, over occupied

324

buildings and busy streets. So she banked and headed out over the Atlantic Ocean where we could die without taking innocent people with us. That was thirteen years ago.

"She isn't," Lucy says. "Carrie's not dead. You won't prove it through fingerprints or DNA. Those files are never purged from IAFIS or CODIS and she knows all about it, is too smart to be caught that way, and not with trace evidence or ballistics either. Someone who helped me engineer and program the FBI computer system and you think for one minute any traditional means will stop her?"

Nothing was too violent, too monstrous for her. She picked a killing partner, a sexual sadist who had been disfigured, horribly scarred. He abducted objects of his obsession, people who were beautiful to him. He cut off their faces. He had a freezer full of them.

"To Carrie forensics is nothing more than Tinkertoys. Rudimentary and childish," Lucy goes on and she could be describing herself.

I envision the tiny piston helicopter exploding into a ball of fire, breaking apart and raining down into the sea. There would have been no survivors. But I never actually saw Carrie Grethen. I saw the pilot, a glimpse of his scarred face. I assumed Carrie was in the other seat. Everyone assumed it. Her remains were never found, only part of Newton Joyce's charred left leg.

"QUANTICO," SHE SAYS. "The Board Room, the Globe and Laurel, our hangouts when we were developing CAIN. That's what we drank together, our favorite German beer. She knows I'd think of it. *Tick Tock . . . Watch the clock BIG DOC.*"

Copperhead is Carrie Grethen.

"And the poem sent to you on Mother's Day has the same language," Lucy says. "*Watch the clock Doc. Tick Tock.* It was always you she hated. She was jealous of our relationship and couldn't stand that you weren't afraid of her."

During one of our earliest encounters we almost came to blows, I disliked her instantly and that much. I remember lying in wait at a spy shop in a Northern Virginia shopping mall. Had there not been other customers present when Carrie walked in with coffee I'm sure she would have thrown it in my face. I see it. I hear it. As if it just happened, the way I led her to an empty bench by a fountain and spoke to her in a way she wouldn't forget.

There's no point in wasting your charm on me because I have you figured out.

Lucy was a teenager when she began her internship with the FBI, working out of Quantico's classified Engineering Research Facility, the ERF. Carrie was her mentor and I can see her clearly from back then, her eyes a dark blue that would turn violet on their way to steely hard, and she had a rare beauty, fine featured, a brunette, and I envision the person driving Rand Bloom's gray pickup truck.

Short hair possibly dyed light blond, big glasses and a cap pulled low, and it could have been Carrie and then I'm sure it was. When I first met her at the ERF I couldn't tell her age but she's older than Lucy, well into her forties now. Carrie is vain. She would have taken impeccable care of herself. She'd look younger than her years and be extremely fit, the two of them, Lucy and Carrie. They're each other's good and evil other half.

"Okay I'm listening. I'm open-minded and reasonable. I'm listening carefully." My voice doesn't begin to convey what I feel. "She didn't die."

"I've always wondered about it." Lucy's attention is all around us as if Carrie Grethen might be here. "I must have known at some level that she wasn't inside the helicopter."

"Then who was?" I ask and the nausea has completely passed.

"The glare on the windscreen and Newton Joyce started shooting at us," Lucy says. "It could be that no one else was in it. I don't know. But Carrie wasn't and she's not dead."

"That was a long time ago. Where's she been and why now?" I want to argue it away but I know better, and my focus couldn't be keener.

"She used to tell me how much she hated America. God knows she hated the FBI and only went to work for them so she could steal technology." Lucy has lost interest in her beer and her eyes are everywhere. "She used to talk about moving to Russia and working with military intelligence. She was an admirer of the old Soviet Union the same way Putin is and felt that the demise of the USSR was a tragedy."

"And you didn't think it was unusual for an American who worked at Quantico to talk like that?" I'm careful not to sound like I'm blaming her. I notice our waitress gathering her belongings from behind the bar. I motion for her to bring the check.

"I was in college," Lucy says. "She was very persuasive and manipulative and I admit it. I thought she was really cool. Maybe I just didn't think period. And I was a rebel. I hated rules."

Some things never change. What I say is, "Let's focus on what happened after we assumed she died in a helicopter crash."

Then silence as the waitress leaves the check in front of me and walks off swiftly.

"Carrie may not have gone to Russia immediately." Lucy resumes talking quietly, intensely. "But she was there for at least the past decade and probably longer, part of a Russian intelligence service notorious for its expert marksmen who wear hoods and have no identifying insignias on their camouflage. Until early last fall Carrie was in Kiev."

"How can you possibly . . . ?"

"When you began having the problem with credit card fraud I became suspicious that our server was compromised," Lucy says. "The breach happened through your bank. Specifically a hacker exploited the Heartbleed Bug in OpenSSL encryption software that's widely used to secure websites and Internet transactions."

"Such as making purchases online."

"Bryce," she says. "It began after he used your personal bank card to purchase a new laptop in March and Carrie captured his password. Only at first I didn't know who it was. But I knew it was someone sophisticated."

"And the ongoing fraudulent charges on my card?" They weren't for large amounts, not as much as they could have been, and I found it odd.

"Bait," she says. "Carrie wanted to see if I'd change Bryce's password and as long as I didn't she assumed I wasn't aware that the CFC security had been breached. I continued to suggest openly that you were using your physical card and someone was getting the information that way to commit fraud. I said it to Bryce in emails. I said it to Benton."

"Because you wanted her to see them. Because you know how she thinks."

"It works both ways."

"Someone who once was your teacher," I say.

"I had to be very careful she didn't realize I was on to her, that every time she was in our server, I was tracking her."

"And you let it continue. You didn't change Bryce's password until today."

"I couldn't. Not if I was going to figure out who was doing it."

"But you knew it before now, Lucy."

"I had to track her and pretty soon I was in Carrie's email, in everything," she says and I don't believe her.

She's obsessed. She's addicted to a game that only Carrie knows how to play with her.

"And she was in everything of ours." I point out what Lucy doesn't seem to see. "She was able to access extremely confidential documents that might include Social Security numbers, social media accounts, personal effects and addresses that would make it simple for her to show up after a death and steal something the person won't need anymore, such as a license plate or a Twitter account."

Pieces fit together just like that. The tweets I've gotten from the hijacked account of someone who died, the stolen tag of another deceased person on a truck that was spotted at the Edgewater Ferry Landing the day before Julie Eastman was murdered and now possibly recovered at a marina in Marblehead Neck. Things stolen from dead people with Massachusetts ties.

"How could you allow her into our server? Why would you even chance her corrupting information?" It would be an incomprehensible disaster, enough to shut me down.

"Bryce doesn't have the level of user privileges that allows him to alter anything on our server," she says. "He can view certain data but he can't change or delete them and I've kept our server backed up. I've made sure we're safe."

"Your DNA profile was changed. That required more than view-only privileges."

"Carrie's locked out now and I've restored the database to what it was."

"So she found a way in that could have been massively destructive. It sounds like you got so caught up in your cyber war that you underestimated her."

Lucy meets my eyes. She doesn't answer because she can't.

"And where was she when all this started?" I ask. "The mutual spying. The game of tag in cloud computing that let her into our back door."

"She was in Kiev until last fall."

"What prompted her after all these years?" I repeat.

"She knew it was time to leave, that Yanukovych would flee Kiev and Ukraine and she wouldn't want to be around when he did. That's what Carrie does. She plays whatever side of the net suits her at the moment. She allies herself with powerful males. Powerful patriarchs, powerful predators, powerful politicians."

"Like Congressman Rosado?" I ask.

"Money laundering, drugs," she says. "Hundreds of millions out of Russia that he launders mainly through real estate. Carrie didn't connect with him in the U.S. She connected with him over there three years ago. Rosado's got quite the crisis manager in her. Someone with a tremendous ability to manipulate the Internet and take care of problems, to do whatever's required but she has her same flaw. She's not independent. She's a parasite. She always has been. She's weak and eventually breaks her own rules."

No matter Lucy's disparagements it sounds like she's bragging. It sounds like she's impressed all over again.

"I assume she's changed her name." I study Lucy's face for visible signs of what I suspect.

"No one's looking for her anymore and hasn't been. But she has plenty of aliases and I've given all of them to Benton."

"Then he's aware."

"Now he is."

"I wouldn't know. It's the first I've heard about any of this and that shouldn't be the case."

"Before she murdered Jamal Nari and Gracie Smithers it never entered my mind she was the shooter who took out Julie Eastman and Jack Segal," Lucy explains. "Then you got the tweet on Mother's Day and I traced it to this hotel."

TICK TOCK DOC. The same language in the poem Carrie Grethen mailed to me from Kirby thirteen years ago.

"Troy Rosado took Gracie Smithers to his family house in Marblehead Neck after she sneaked out a window." Lucy goes on to give me details she didn't get honestly. "He picked her up using a car service he charged to his credit card. It's in emails Carrie deleted but as you know nothing's ever really gone."

"And she knows that too, doesn't she. Carrie knows all of the same things you do."

"Gracie had no idea what a little shit Troy really is until things got out of hand when she was alone with him on the deserted estate, and then Carrie stepped in as she always does." Lucy is much too animated and much too sure of details she can't know for a fact.

"She killed Gracie. And then she killed Rand Bloom and abducted Joe Henderson." Carrie's the monster she's always been, only I'm deciding that now she's much worse, and Lucy is more vulnerable to her than ever.

"As you probably know the sailboat was stolen," she says.

"I didn't know," I reply as something else occurs to me.

"Carrie can't be traced through it and Gracie won't be talking," Lucy says and the question looms large.

"Why are we here? Why really?" I ask. "Were you hoping you would find her here?"

"Why would she be here?"

"Because we are. Because you are. You want to see her."

Lucy takes the bill, covers it with cash and I push back my chair.

"Don't you see what you're doing . . . ?" I start to ask but she's staring at the TV over the bar, transfixed by it.

"Jesus Christ," she says. "Are you believing this?"

I can't hear what the news correspondent is saying but I see the aerial footage of a sleek white super yacht before a backdrop of what I recognize as the South Florida shoreline. Then quick clips of Bob Rosado in the Oval Office, the Rose Garden, at his congressional desk in D.C. and the soaring iron gates of his estate in West Palm Beach. He's a smarmy man, balding and heavyset in handmade suits that are too shiny and a gold watch that's gaudy.

Congressman Bob Rosado has died, the crawl slowly goes by at the bottom of the screen. *He was scuba diving with family in Fort Lauderdale late afternoon. Officials haven't released cause of death but a source has suggested possible equipment failure.*

CHAPTER 44

INSIDE MY ROOM I sit on the bed and call Benton again. He doesn't answer our home phone and his cell phone goes straight to voice mail. I write an email and decide against it.

Lucy claims Carrie has been locked out of the CFC server but I can't help it. I don't trust anything right now. I send an email that simply says *call me please,* and then I worry that the IP will come back to this hotel. But Carrie could already know we're here. Emails were exchanged about it. Next I text Benton and there's no reply. Marino obviously is in a loud bar when I finally try him, and I suspect he's with Jack Kuster.

"Have you seen the news?" I ask.

"I was going to call you. It happened at around six and we're just now hearing about it at midnight? Weird right?"

"Considering who it is, no it's not weird. But his death is too coincidental."

"He might have had a heart attack." Marino isn't in great shape. "It's the leading cause of scuba deaths."

It's not true but I'm not going to argue.

"Sure hit me with another one," he says to someone else. "Sorry." He's back to me. "You should be here with us. They got this karaoke thing going and the prize is up to five hundred dollars."

"I hope you're not going to sing."

"You never heard me in the shower." He's drunk. "Another theory? His tank. It may have been accidentally filled with too high a blend of oxygen, which is combustible."

"Baseless theories are worthless. I'm tired of theories. I'm damn tired of them, Marino."

"I'm just saying."

"I can't get hold of Benton."

"I haven't talked to him."

I start to say *why would you.* Marino can't stand Benton and I feel alone.

"You sound upset. You want me to come back to the hotel now?" he says above the din.

"You don't think this is too coincidental?" I repeat.

"What?" He's very loud and I turn down the volume on my phone.

"Rosado dying now? In light of everything else? He was probably well on his way to getting arrested as is his son."

"I don't know . . ."

"Well I do."

"Someone like him? Politicians like him are bulletproof and freaky timing happens, maybe it's poetic justice," he says and I can tell he's walking outside where it's quieter. "You don't sound so good."

"I'm fine."

"Like you're pissed. What a fucking long day sweating our brains out."

I ask if Lucy has told him about Carrie.

"Shit." A pause and he says brusquely, impatiently, "Yeah I talked to her earlier before you two went down to the bar. She said she was going to talk to a waitress or something and it went on from there, and I hate to say it but it's not a hundred percent new. I've heard rumblings before that's made me think Carrie was back inside her head. You know what I mean by that?"

"I'm afraid I do."

"I remember like it was yesterday. I don't have the right word for it. Some hypnotic thing like Sengali."

Svengali but I don't correct him.

"Yeah this addictive thing. These people who get so deep under your skin you can't pull them out. Like Doris."

"I'm sorry about Beth Eastman." I haven't really said that to him yet.

"The first girl I went steady with. It's kind of unbelievable to look at each other now. I kind of wish I hadn't and the truth is there's no going back. I remember when she was on the homecoming court, you know, the prom and all that shit," Marino slurs. "Lucy's stuff about Carrie is just ridiculous any way you look at it, Doc, and I think she should see a shrink and she'd better get a damn good lawyer."

When I don't reply he's silent for a moment.

Then he says, "You're not telling me you believe her, that you think we should be chasing a fucking ghost?"

"There's no physical evidence that Carrie Grethen is dead," I reply. "Only circumstances and a long silence that could very well be explained if she was living in another country for the last decade or longer."

"What Lucy needs is a shrink and a lawyer, Doc. The best she can find. I know the friggin' FBI's sniffing around her. Some suit called me asking questions but I didn't give him shit."

I hear the spurt of a lighter.

"There's a lot going on at home and maybe she's not thinking right," says Marino the de facto big brother, the de facto uncle who taught Lucy how to shoot, how to drive his truck and ride a motorcycle while she taught him how to be tolerant. "You know, the stuff with Janet's nephew. They've already fixed up a room for him and Lucy doesn't want a kid. Let's be honest. She'd probably suck at it."

Tears sting my eyes. He knew before I did, and I hear him smoking. I tell him to be safe and not stay up all night. I sit on the edge of the bed staring down at my phone until my vision is swimming and what I see is the dark road dividing FBI field offices from firing ranges and then a clearing, barbecues and picnic tables beneath the dense shapes of trees. The wind is humid and smells like summer. As the wind moves through leaves it sounds like rain, and their voices drift toward me. I hear the spurt of a match being struck.

I can't hear what they're saying as I get closer in the dark and a lit cigarette glows as it's passed back and forth. The FBI Academy when Lucy was barely more than a child, and her voice was wounded and filled with longing. Carrie's was soothing and in command as they shared a cigarette and it was then I knew.

Why did it have to be you? Why did it have to be you!

I remember what I sensed and what happened when I said it.

I saw you in the picnic area the other night. I brought it up in normal conversation as if it was nothing.

So now you're spying on me. Lucy said it as if she hated me. *Don't waste your sermons.*

I'm not judging. Help me understand.

The child I had helped raise was gone. I didn't know this Lucy and I agonized over what I'd done wrong. What had I done to make this happen, to make her choose something so damaging and dangerous?

You can't possibly make me anything, she said, and it wasn't what I meant.

What I meant is the same thing I would mean if I were saying those words to her now. Her first taste of solid food shouldn't have been poison, and all these years and what I've felt, and I would eradicate Carrie Grethen from the face of the earth easily. It dismays me how little I'd care if I could make her dead, really dead and forgotten. Maybe I should be ashamed that I loathe anyone that much but it's true of human nature. People are more alike than they're not.

"I'M SORRY TO BOTHER YOU. This is Doctor Scarpetta." I have Benton's field office on the line.

"How can I help you, ma'am?"

"I'm looking for my husband."

"Who's your husband, ma'am?" Some young agent working the desk on midnight shift, the usual wooden demeanor that makes me want to touch him with a cattle prod.

"I'm Doctor Scarpetta. Benton Wesley's wife."

"What can I do for you?" he says and my anger burns colder, harder like frostbite.

"I'm trying to reach him. It's important and please stop saying ma'am."

"I'm not allowed to give out information . . ."

"I'm the chief medical examiner. I'm his wife and it's urgent I get hold of him."

"Have you tried leaving a message?"

"No. I'm too stupid to think of that."

"No offense intended, ma'am. I'll pass along the message. I believe he's tied up right now."

"You believe?" It's all I can do not to yell at him.

"When he checks in next I'll make sure he knows you called."

"Checks in from where?"

"I'm sorry but . . ."

I hang up on him and throw my phone on the bed and it bounces. I go to the minibar and open the door. I find another gin but put it back. I grab a bottle of water and turn off the lights. I wait for it all to go away like an awful dream but it can't.

CHAPTER 45

I SNAP ON A LAMP and imagine distant gunfire. Not an explosive noise or a sharp crack but more like the dull snap of a raw carrot, a celery stalk, a green pepper I break in my bare hands. I envision my kitchen and remember I'm not home.

I turn off the alarm on my phone after a poor night's sleep. It seems I was awake every hour, speculating, working out problems, worrying about Lucy as Carrie Grethen ranged back and forth through my mind like a rabid animal. I saw her eyes and the way she used to pierce me with her stare. I know she wanted to hurt me. I know she wanted me dead. I sit up in bed.

Soft light illuminates antique furniture, cut glass fixtures with ivory shades, the wallpaper creamy damask. I remember where I am. The Madison Hotel. On the fourth floor, a corner room facing the courtyard and my attention finds a space between the floral drawn drapes, complete darkness showing through. I feel a tug of impatience and my awareness kicks up a notch.

Despite my efforts the drapes didn't stay completely closed even after I propped a chair in front of them, shoving the heavy fabric panels together, pinning them against the glass. At some point they crept open and as I stare at the black vacuum in the gap I'm reminded of what Nietzsche said:

When you look into the abyss, it also looks into you. I lower my feet to the floor and rearrange the chair.

I'm not afraid of the dark but have no intention of making it easy for someone to spy on me as I read or work on my laptop with lights off or worse as I sleep. All it would take is a high-resolution night vision scope and then Carrie is there. I feel her inescapable presence. I turn to see her and she steps around me. Whichever way I look she's behind me like a long shadow when the sun is in my face.

Predators watch their quarry. It starts with the eyes.

Benton penned those words in sepia ink on a sheet of watermarked stationery, his initials *BW* engraved in an understated script, no address, phone number or personal information. I still have the letter, the first one he wrote to me more than twenty years ago when he was married to someone else. I feel empty from missing him but at least he's safe, texting me at three A.M. to say he'd call. He hasn't yet. I point the remote at the TV to catch the news.

The usual economic woes, local crimes and disasters. A small plane crash, four killed. A fire, two hospitalized with smoke inhalation. I remove my bags from the closet and set them on the bed as the anchorwoman begins an update on Bob Rosado.

" . . . His body was transported to the Broward County Medical Examiner's Office last night but still no details about what might have caused the congressman's death while he was scuba diving off his yacht late yesterday," she reports. "Let's go to Sue Lander and see what she has for us. Sue? Good morning."

The dark back parking lot of the medical examiner's office materializes. White scene vehicles and palm trees are barely visible in the glow of sodium vapor lights, and the correspondent named Sue grips a microphone, a blank look on her face, then recognition that she's on the air.

She says, "Good morning."

"Sue? What's happening at this early hour in South Florida? Have there been any updates?"

"There was quite a media presence here most of the night but now you can see how quiet it is. What we do know is Doctor Raine drove out of this parking lot about two hours ago and hasn't come back."

More footage, this time the silhouette of the flat-roofed one-story stucco complex, the bay door loudly cranking open and the sound of a rumbling engine as a white SUV drives out, headlights blazing on hibiscus bushes. A pack of correspondents and a constellation of shoulder-mounted lighted cameras surge forward, and through the driver's window Abe Raine's face is resolute. He won't look at anyone and that's not like him. Young, energetic, a former quarterback for Notre Dame, he's not the sort to duck a confrontation with journalists or anyone else.

"Doctor Raine?"

"Doctor Raine!"

"Can you tell us what's going on with . . ."

"Do you know what killed Congressman Rosado?"

"Any suggestion of foul play?"

Their answer is ruby red taillights as the chief medical examiner drives slowly through the parking lot, past the void of an artificial lake, then gone, and we're back to the Morristown news desk.

"So he was there all night, Sue? That's a little unusual?"

"He was inside the building until just two hours ago as I've mentioned," her voice says off camera. "And the most recent statement released by his office confirms that the autopsy will be finished today."

Finished? I think. That's a strange way to put it. I take off the loose cotton scrubs I slept in and find clothes I brought for my idea of yoga, which is mostly stretching, staying limber. My personal time as I call it. I do it alone in my room. Spandex shorts, a sleeveless top with a built-in bra.

"Then it's definitely not been done yet. Maybe they're waiting for special tests?" the anchorwoman suggests and that can't be the reason.

Knowing Raine as well as I do, I don't accept that he wouldn't do the autopsy immediately in such a high-profile fatality, and certainly the delay has nothing to do with any types of tests he might order. The longer he waits the more he'll be swarmed by the media, and the rumors will get legs—which is what's already happening.

Assuming the jurisdiction is his and probably isn't anymore.

I revisit the same suspicion I began to entertain late last night when the news first broke, only now I feel a certainty, an inevitability. I envision Raine sequestered in his office on the phone making arrangements, discussing strategies, taking directions and orders. I'm betting he's handed off the case like a hot potato, and there's at least one good reason for him to do that.

Florida's Sunshine Law makes state government records accessible to the public, including photographs, reports and any other documented information related to a medicolegal investigation. If Raine wanted absolute discretion there's a way to ensure it. All he had to do is request assistance from the Armed Forces Medical Examiner (AFME) and the FBI. He can legitimately claim that Rosado was a federal government official and therefore not Florida's problem.

He could have called me but the proper protocol was to go straight to my boss, John Briggs, and I suspect that both of them have an inkling about other disturbing factors. Rosado died suddenly when it was only a matter of time, perhaps only hours or days away before he would be publically sullied by serious crimes. Gracie Smithers's murder and his son Troy's part in it, a murdered insurance investigator linked to Rosado's real estate and of course the possibility of money laundering and a crisis manager, a psychopath named Carrie Grethen who isn't dead.

Gordian knot, a knot impossible to unravel, and Alexander the Great solved the problem by cutting through it with his sword, in other words by cheating. A provocative name for a corporation and I wonder who came up with it and then she's in my mind again. It's the sort of cryptic name she would conceive, one that hints of using violence whenever it suits or in her case whenever she pleases.

She doesn't work alone.

Her *Clydes* as Lucy used to call them. Carrie has always had a killing partner. Temple Gault. Newton Joyce. There probably have been others and her newest might be Troy Rosado, and that bends my thoughts back around to my niece. She was a teenager, about the same age as Troy when she and Carrie worked together at Quantico and began a relationship that hasn't ended, I don't care what Lucy claims.

Sitting on the edge of the bed with my laptop I log on to the Internet to see what else I can find about Rosado's death, and the most complete coverage is in the *New York Times.* There's little that's not already on the news, a few additional details from police and first responders who wouldn't allow their names to be used.

The fifty-two-year-old congressman died at approximately six P.M. while diving the *Mercedes,* a German freighter sunk in the 1980s, now an artificial reef in ninety feet of water barely a mile offshore. He chose to dive the shipwreck late in the day because he didn't want other divers or their boats around, not only for privacy reasons but also for his safety.

As chairman of the Homeland Security subcommittee on border and maritime security he was a potential target for drug cartels and organized crime, and if what Lucy says is true he was a bigger thief than anyone who might be out to get him. For his first dive of the day, I continue to read, he was witnessed stepping off the dive platform, taking his giant stride into the ocean. He was floating on the surface with his buoyancy control device, his BCD vest inflated, when it appeared his tank malfunctioned. A sudden release of pressurized gas made "several loud popping sounds" and spun him into the air.

Why several?

I ponder this as the anchorwoman starts in on the local weather, warning that the high today in New Jersey will be record setting.

Popping sounds, as in more than one?

I flick off the TV and skim for an explanation, finding nothing further, only theories and wild speculations. His neck was broken. An O-ring was loose or failed. Someone tampered with the first stage of his regulator. A bomb was attached to the anchor line. A shark got him. His gear was sabotaged by the Mafia. Maybe his wife wanted him gone. I decide against my floor exercises. I sit on the bed and think. I wait for my phone to ring because I'm sure it will.

General Briggs is an early riser. He's usually up by four. Unless he's somewhere else, Florida for example, he should be in his office at Dover Air Force Base port mortuary where several years ago I spent long months of radiologic training. I wait a few more minutes, pacing the room, and there's no answer at his office. I try his cell with no better luck. Maybe he's still at home and I enter that number.

The phone rings three times, then, "Hello?"

"Ruthie?"

"Yes?" His wife sounds barely awake and startled. "Oh my God. Kay? Is he all right?"

"Is there a reason he might not be?"

"Then you're not with him." She sounds congested and upset from crying.

"No. I'm sorry to call so early. I woke you up. I was hoping to speak to him about the Rosado case in Florida."

"I assumed you might be with him." Her voice is shaky and depressed.

"No, I'm in New Jersey," I reply.

"I see. John's down there and whatever's happened exactly? I don't know but I can tell you he was very stressed. He flew out the door last night like a bat out of hell right after he got the phone call."

"About the congressman?"

"A few minutes before seven last night."

I was on the range then and Benton wasn't answering his phone.

"As much as he hates the CIA as you well know since it seems to be their favorite pastime to harass him? Spying, showing up with their latest accusation about him leaking information," she says and I didn't know she was so paranoid.

In fact she sounds almost hysterical.

"And you know what I say? I say John? How are you any different? A life of secrets, lies and threats of being locked up in Leavenworth. There. If anybody's tapping our phone I don't care. I turn fifty next week and . . . Life is short and I don't need to tell you that. Will you talk to him?"

"About what exactly?"

"His blood pressure and cholesterol are through the roof. He has Raynaud's syndrome and had to have his beta-blocker changed because his heartbeat is so slow he was almost blacking out. He's not supposed to dive! He was specifically told not to!"

"He's planning on diving?"

"He took his gear so what do you think? And it's strictly against his doctor's orders but you know how he is. Everything he sees, everything that kills people and he believes it will never happen to him!" She starts to sob. "We got in a big fight about it before he left. Please don't let him. I don't want to lose my husband."

CHAPTER 46

MOVING THE CHAIR AWAY from the sliding doors, I step out onto the balcony, the concrete warm and dry beneath my bare feet.

I know how stubborn Briggs can be, and scuba diving is out of the question right now especially if strenuous underwater searching is involved. Hard-boiled Army he's fearless. He thinks he's invincible. He's ungracious about aging and fiercely proud. He'll kill himself if he's not careful. I will have to outmaneuver him.

Stagnant air settles over me as I check the weather app on my phone. It's already eighty-six degrees at five A.M., hotter than South Florida, which is a balmy seventy-three with afternoon thunderstorms expected. The sound of traffic is a constant rush like a heavy surf or the wind. A power line hums. If diving is required then something needs to be recovered and I wonder what it is.

I look down at the illuminated swimming pool as blue as turquoise in the hot darkness four floors below. I can barely make out red umbrellas furled like rock candy swizzle sticks and white lounge chairs lined up like piano keys. I return to the coolness of the living room and check flights into Fort Lauderdale. There's a nonstop Virgin America flight out of Newark in two and a half hours.

I'll be on it but I'm not going to tell Lucy yet. She'll try to come with me and she can't. She'll insist she send for a private plane and I'm not going to let her. Whatever is happening can't involve her because it already does. Carrie Grethen. Lucy still has feelings, old powerful ones. Love, hate, lust, a murderous loathing, whatever it is it's deadly not just to herself but also to everyone. I place a pod in the espresso machine. I listen to the pumping of hot water forced through injector holes as I replay our conversation from last night, recalling the look in her eyes and what I perceived. I smell the bold Brazilian blend flowing through the nozzle into a glass cup as I make the plane reservation.

I'll let Lucy know what I'm doing after I've already taken off. She and Marino need to go home. They need to stay out of it. I leave my spandex shorts and top on and pull cargo pants and a polo shirt over them. I skip a shower. I don't bother with makeup. I know what I'm going to do, and I pick up the espresso, black with a tan froth on top.

I'm about to try Benton again when he calls me first. I'm right about where he is and why. Rosado was murdered. He was shot. Briggs got in around midnight and did the autopsy. The reason it *isn't finished yet* is biological evidence has yet to be recovered from the dive site, from the bottom of the sea.

"We have the rifle," Benton continues to explain. "It was on the yacht. A PGF 300 Win Mag with a muzzle brake and rounds with solid copper bullets, Barnes one-ninety grain polished like jewelry."

"Are any of them engraved?"

"No."

"Did you find the tumbler? Did you find where the gunsmithing and hand loading were done?"

"Not yet but the rifle belongs to Elaine Rosado. There were no prints on it. After it was swabbed for DNA it was sprayed with a chemical reagent and a residue lit up like Saint Elmo's fire."

"Bleach. Someone wiped it down and made sure any DNA was destroyed."

"Apparently Mrs. Rosado bought it for her husband," Benton says. "Several times a year he did big game hunting in places like Tanzania,

Montenegro, Cambodia, and apparently no one noticed the rifle was missing from a locked gun closet in their West Palm home."

"What has Lucy said to you about Carrie?" I sit on the arm of the couch.

"After she left you last night we were on the phone. It sounds like Carrie is in league with Troy and that's classic. It's what she does so well. The male thinks he's dominant and he couldn't be more mistaken," Benton says.

"Marino doesn't believe it."

"He doesn't want to believe it," Benton says. "Let me back up. I suspect the rifle was transported to West Palm Beach yesterday morning when Troy flew home on his father's G-Five. At some point prior to the shooting it ended up on the yacht, which is where the police found it when they searched it last night."

"What about spent cartridge cases? Did the police find those?"

"No. The magazine is missing and I'm guessing it went overboard, that Carrie tossed it. The Rosados know her as Sasha Sarin, the name on a passport and other documents stolen in Ukraine last year. When Troy flew down here yesterday there was a second passenger on the plane by that name."

"Did Congressman Rosado know the real identity of the crisis manager he hired?"

"I'm sure not," Benton says. "No one in his right mind would hire Carrie Grethen."

"SARIN," I REPEAT, AND she must have found it enormously amusing when the opportunity presented itself, a person with the same name as a deadly nerve gas.

"The pilots described her as attractive, in her forties, thin with light blond hair and large framed glasses," Benton says. "When she got on the jet with Troy yesterday morning she was carrying a guitar case. The same type of guitar Jamal Nari had and as you recall there was a case missing from his condo. Three guitars but only two cases."

"A guitar case?" I'm baffled.

"I strongly suspect that's what Carrie had the rifle in. If it was broken down it would fit just fine, a RainSong guitar case that she carried on board herself. One of the pilots noticed it because he's a musician, and he said she buckled it into an empty seat and carried it off after they landed. She wouldn't let them touch it."

"She was in Nari's house, unpacked his guitars and placed them back on their stands? Then stole one of the cases?"

"Yes."

"When? Not after he was shot. There wouldn't have been time," I decide. "If he packed his guitars before he went out to run errands then Carrie must have gone inside their apartment while he and his wife were out."

"Locks and alarm codes have never been a problem for her. She would have reveled in walking around the apartment, thrilled by the fantasy of what she was about to do. She stole something her next victim cared about, taking a souvenir, a symbol of him in advance. When he returned home and was carrying groceries inside he would have noticed his guitars were back on their stands and wondered how the hell that happened. It probably was one of the last things he ever thought."

Benton recites all this as if it's indisputable. He sounds dispassionate and sure of his facts as if he's talking about a chronic illness that went into remission for years and now is back. He can predict its progression and every symptom, and I'm desperate to get to Florida. My anxieties are in overdrive as I envision what he describes, and I wonder if Carrie intended to kill Rand Bloom. What was he doing at the Rosado house? Was he meeting her and did they know each other?

In his former career with the Department of Justice Bloom made sure charges against the congressman were dropped. Rosado had a faithful ally and protector in Bloom. But he may have become a liability, a problem.

He must have known about the drugs, the money laundering, assuming all of that is true. Maybe Bloom knew too much. Maybe Carrie didn't want anything to do with him anymore. Or more likely she was just in the mood when she thrust a knife into his heart, and that's what Benton thinks too.

"She felt like killing him whether she planned it or not," he says. "And then she didn't feel like killing Detective Henderson when he showed up. It was more fun to abduct and terrorize him and she's reminding us she can be decent because in her mind she is. What motivates someone like this has little to do with expediency. Some of it is scripted. Some of it isn't. But she has an end game, a goal. It's Lucy. Carrie's come back for Lucy."

"To do what?" The thought of it is so enraging it's all I can do to talk. "What exactly does the damn bitch want?"

"In her blighted fantasies she may think they'll get together again."

"Lucy's in extreme danger."

"All of us are. Maybe more than she is, frankly. Carrie wants to get to her and we're in the way. In fact we're weapons she can use to hurt her."

"Was Carrie on the yacht when Rosado was killed?"

"She must have been."

I walk into the bathroom to pack up my cosmetic bag as Benton goes on to describe the aftermath of the shooting. There was so much panic and chaos it wasn't discovered right away that Troy was gone and most likely Carrie was with him.

"The yacht has a rigid inflatable tender, a twenty-foot RIB which also was gone," Benton says as I zip up an overnight bag. "It's presumed he took off in it. The crew was in the wheelhouse and the main galley at the time of the shooting and they couldn't have seen anyone on the uppermost deck unless they were specifically monitoring that part of the yacht, which they weren't. Positioning on the helipad would have placed the shooter thirty-six feet above the water and some sixty yards from where Rosado was killed."

"It must be a very big yacht."

"A hundred and seventy feet."

"Why the helipad? What makes anybody think the shots were fired from up there?"

"That's where the rifle was found. In a deck hatch where aviation equipment is kept, life vests, extra headsets, things like that. I just sent you CT images from the morgue and the video clip his wife took. She was filming her husband's dive. It's only about two minutes. When she realized something bad had happened she turned the camera off."

I look while we talk, the empty ocean a ruffled dark blue, a red dive flag on a yellow float moving with the chop, and I overhear voices in the background talking about cutting up another cantaloupe. A woman— Elaine Rosado I assume—tells a member of the crew that the cantaloupe isn't cold enough and she wants another martini. She points the camera at her husband, the recording herky-jerky at first and then steadier.

I see his image in high resolution, his scant dark hair plastered to his balding head, his heavy jowls and chin tan and stubbly. The amber lenses of his dive mask are looking directly at the camera as he holds up the BCD's power inflator until he's comfortable with his buoyancy. It's a stiff chop and the regulator is in his mouth.

"You all right, hon?" his wife calls out. "It looks rough. Maybe you should just come back in and have a drink!" She laughs.

He forms a circle over his head with both gloved hands, giving the universal dive signal that he's okay. Everything is fine, and he floats on the surface, waiting to descend the mooring line. I press pause.

"Who was he diving with?" I ask.

"The dive master had gone down first to make sure everything was clear around the wreck, making sure there were no other divers, specifically spear fishermen. As you know it's legal to use scuba gear while spearfishing in Florida and there have been some accidents, both serious injuries and fatalities. There was someone shot in that area just the other day."

"Ninety feet is a long way to go to do a recon," I reply. "Rosado would have to wait on the surface for at least ten minutes and that's a long time too, especially when he's already got the regulator in his mouth. He's going to suck in a lot of air in ten minutes."

It occurs to me that the dive master may not have wanted to be anywhere near him. Maybe he was involved in the homicide. I suggest this to Benton.

"There's no evidence of it and I don't think so," he says. "Apparently it was S-O-P for him to check out a site first to make sure no one else was diving it and that everything seemed safe, the visibility adequate etcetera. An Australian guy who works on the yacht full-time, he'd filled the tanks the day before, checked all the gear."

"How much air was in Rosado's tank?"

"He started out with thirty-three hundred PSI."

"And when he died?"

"We don't know and in a few minutes you'll see why."

I resume the video, and Rosado is floating alone. He looks at the dive computer on his wrist. His head jerks slightly forward and to the right, and next he's facedown in the water. He's just been shot. I back up, watching that part of it again and again as I remember what Jack Kuster said about starting out test fires at a thousand yards. If it was too far we could always "walk it in." Sniper terminology.

When a shooter is attempting to hit a target he might fire multiple times, recalculating the DOPE, each shot landing closer and I look for water splashing. I scrutinize the rolling swells around Rosado, the dark blue water rising and falling, lifting and settling smoothly as he bobs with his mask on, his regulator in his mouth, waiting, leaning his head back, looking around.

There. A tiny splash, like a small fish breaking the surface. I back up and play it again, a splash, as if someone threw a rock. About ten feet from Rosado and I see another splash, this one closer and he seems to sense it. He turns to the left and instantly he's facedown. Three seconds later there are two loud pops.

He's lifted completely out of the water and spun through the air like a limp frog, and I study this for a while, zooming in, detecting the spray of blood in the bright blueness as his body is propelled by pressurized gas blasting. The regulator is out of his mouth, its hoses whipping around as he pirouettes before his mask and BCD rip off. He sinks into the water, his head caved in, one side of it gone.

"Bob? Oh my God! Bob! What's happening!" his wife screams and then there are no images, no sounds, and I open another file, this one a CT scan from the Broward County Medical Examiner's Office.

The entrance wound is in the back of the skull, just to the right of the lambdoidal suture, a small tangential hole. The solid copper open tip bullet expanded on impact, its four petals causing devastating damage as they buzz-sawed through the occipital, temporal and frontal lobes. The bullet exited through the left side of the mandible, which is missing as are most of the teeth and part of the skull.

"The flight path is downward from right to left," I say to Benton. "It required at least four shots. If you replay the video clip and look closely you can see the shooter walking the bullets in closer until Rosado is hit. Then two more rapid shots struck the tank. That doesn't sound like the other cases. Granted Rosado was a moving target, bobbing in a heavy surf but it doesn't seem the same. I don't believe it is."

"Troy," Benton says. "Someone who's not experienced or skilled with a PGF or firearms in general."

"A shooting gallery," I decide. "Almost an entire magazine at only sixty feet."

"I suspect taking out the scuba tank was deliberate, intended to horrify those watching and to mock and degrade the victim. Carrie would have found it entertaining watching him lifted up and twirling in the air. She probably told Troy to do it."

"Well I don't think it was her who fired those shots. At that distance and with a tracking scope it was someone who didn't know what he was doing, someone who was even worse than I was yesterday. Why kill him?"

"Why kill any of them?"

"Are you going to dive?" I then ask.

"We'll be looking for a number of things. His mask, his BCD and tank, the magazine missing from the rifle and any cartridge cases. The marine unit's Moose Boat is going to pick us up as soon as it's light."

351

"On your way out did you grab everything?" I envision our bags of dive gear, our luggage by the front door where we left them early Thursday morning.

"I thought we'd leave it down here in the condo. So I grabbed yours too. Why?"

"Take mine on the boat with you."

"No, Kay."

"You can't let John dive. At his most recent physical he wasn't given a clean bill of health, Benton. Far from it. We don't want anything happening to him and we don't want further complications with this case if he has an unfortunate episode while he's helping collect evidence."

"Good luck stopping him."

"I'm going to call him but you need to tell him too. I'm fine to handle what needs to be done."

"You don't need to come down here. I don't want you to."

"Teeth and bone are somewhere down there."

"I can look," Benton says. "You don't need to."

"Biological evidence is my jurisdiction."

"Are you giving me orders now?"

"Yes."

"You really think you're going to find anything? Christ almost a hundred feet down . . ."

"I'm going to try," I reply. "I'm heading to the airport. I'll see you early afternoon."

CHAPTER 47

HIS SILVER HAIR IS pushed off his forehead, dry and messy. He's slightly sunburned and the impression in his skin made by his dive mask has faded.

He's been out of the water for hours when I step inside the cabin of the Moose Boat, drop my bags and kiss Benton hello. His lips are salty from the sea. Behind him is the electronics display, including a GPS plotter that shows where we are off the coast of Fort Lauderdale, almost a mile out. He's sitting in a pilot's seat, the twin engines turned off and the boat rocks gently. I hear water softly lapping.

"I feel like I've really inconvenienced everyone." I open my bag on the fiberglass floor. "But I had no idea you'd be done this fast."

"It's not a good thing that we are."

"I know."

"But we have the boat. You're always worth waiting for. We'll give it one more try." Benton stares off and I can tell he's bothered.

His black dive skin is pulled down to his waist. The sleeves are tied around him, what he always does during surface intervals and this has been a long one. Outside on the bow two police divers are drinking water and eating fruit. I already know they've found nothing so far, not one damn thing and I also know this is unexpected if not inexplicable.

"How does a forty-pound tank disappear?" I sit on a bench and pull out a wet suit, dive socks and fins.

"You're talking about tons of rusting iron at the bottom." He watches me take off my cargo pants, my shirt.

Underneath are the spandex yoga clothes. I came here straight from the airport. I dig around some more and find my mask.

"We obviously can't get near it with a metal detector. The vis is maybe thirty feet. But I agree with you. Three of us spent the morning doing a circular search, doing sweeps out from the wreck, shifting the center point and starting again until we were well beyond where I would expect anything to be."

"There's a lot of silt and sand that could have covered things." I reach behind me to grab the long tab, zipping up my wet suit, and then I pull on the socks. "What about sonar?"

"We found all sorts of crap with the side scan but nothing we're looking for." He works his arms back into the sleeves of his dive skin. "We got here around eight this morning and gave up by noon. It's crossed my mind that someone might have gotten here first, either earlier or even last night."

"Searching after dark?" I say dubiously as the police divers get ready to go back in.

"With the right equipment, sure. In a perfect world a dive team would have been deployed right away but there was so much pandemonium and confusion. It wouldn't have occurred to anyone until after Briggs and I showed up. So here we are. Or at least I am." Benton's eyes smile at me. "Whatever you said scared him back to Delaware."

"He wasn't scared. But I reminded him that the Pentagon wouldn't be pleased if he conducted an underwater search and recovery on a high-profile case when he doesn't meet the physical fitness standards. In fact he admitted his Army doc ordered him not to even think about diving unless he gets a pacemaker."

I follow Benton out of the cabin as the two police divers take their giant strides off the dive platform, one of them holding a lift bag in case he gets lucky and finds Rosado's missing BDU and the perforated tank, which would have filled with water. It would be quite heavy and less likely to have been relocated by the current, and I squirt defog in my mask. I check the inspection stickers on a filled tank clamped into the side of the boat, and I remove the valve cap and release a quick hiss of air.

"Well it's sounding pretty hopeless but I have to say I tried." I loop my BCD strap around the tank and clamp it tight. "As usual we have to worry about the trial and some dream team focusing on the missing pieces of skull, the mandible and teeth and how finding them would have changed the interpretation of things."

"It's such bullshit." Benton swishes his mask in a drum of clean water.

"Unfortunately it's not. If I were a defense attorney it's exactly what I'd ask." I line up the top of my vest with the upper rim of the scuba tank and then I sit down on the bench. "The question will be distance. By the time they're done the jury will doubt the shot could have been fired from the yacht, that instead it was a sniper a great distance away on another boat, possibly from the top of a high-rise onshore. They'll compare it to the other cases and say it couldn't have been Troy."

"Or they'll blame it on the person who's supposed to be dead. Carrie."

I scan the sparkling blueness all around us and the closest boat I can make out is maybe a mile south of us. I notice it's moving very slowly in our direction.

"A shark could have eaten the bones I guess." Benton fastens his BCD and pulls the straps tight.

"I doubt it." I lean over to slip my feet into the fins.

"There's nothing down there anymore and I think for good reason," he says. "A lot of old tires. I saw plenty of those this morning."

"Why bother? Assuming you're thinking what I suspect you are."

"We know for a fact she was on Rosado's jet yesterday morning," Benton says.

"Well Sasha Sarin was."

"If she's still protecting Troy and the family then it would have been a shrewd move to make sure any evidence on the ocean floor was gone by the time we started looking."

"Like wiping down beer bottles and the gun and using bleach to destroy DNA." I pick up my regulator, the mouthpiece in my right hand, the computer in my left and I mate the valves, tightening the connectors on top of the tank.

"That's right, Christ when you know who it is. That's probably exactly what she did," he says. "It fits the pattern and there's nothing left down there to find so why the hell are we still bothering? And we have your birthday condo all ready. If ever I was tempted to scrap a mission it would be this one."

"That would be ungracious." I attach the low-pressure hose to the nozzle of the inflator. "Our police friends are down there waiting for us."

I place my regulator in my mouth and inhale, and the membrane resists, moving forward, exactly what it's supposed to do and I turn on my air. My attention continues to be drawn out into the blueness everywhere, to the small boat I noticed earlier. It isn't moving now but I can hear the outboard motor running and see someone sitting in the back. The dive flag is moving through the water, someone drift-diving the artificial reef.

Benton follows where I'm looking and says, "Don't worry. If any other divers get close Rick and Sam will shoo them off."

"They'll flash their badges under water?"

"Something like that."

"I'll make one sweep around the wreck, in and out of the immediate area and then we'll quit."

"All so you can say you did."

"That's ninety percent of it these days." I dig into my bag for my dive computer watch, for my knife, blunt tipped and short bladed. "Come on. We haven't been dive buddies in a while."

Rinsing my mask with its mounted minirecorder, I work my arms into my vest. I try my regulator and octopus again, making sure I'm getting air. Then I purge them. I put my mask on and recheck my computers, and I lean forward to dislodge the tank from its holder and I stand up. I pull on my gloves and walk carefully in my fins to the platform. My regulator is in my mouth and I place one hand over it, the other over my mask. I take my big step in.

THE WATER IS WARM and I add air to my BCD and float, waiting for Benton, giving him plenty of room as I ease my way to a mooring line attached to the dive buoy. He's in with a splash and we meet each other's eyes and nod. I bleed all of the air out of my vest and we begin our descent, the water full of light near the surface. It gets darker and cooler as we go down.

My breathing blasts loudly in my head and I pinch my nose, clearing my ears as we go deeper, and I feel the water weighing heavily and cooler as the pressure increases and the light dims. I look for the two police divers, Rick and Sam, for their bubbles or their movements and don't see them. I check my computers repeatedly and then I see the sunken freighter, a broken hulk of a silhouette on the murky bottom. I can make out the bow facing north, the angles of twisted metal. I don't see anyone around.

At ninety feet a large shape is a sea turtle on the rusty hull and a toadfish deflates its bladder, flattening on the brown silt bottom. An orange-striped triggerfish makes kissing movements with its mouth as it glides past, and I see a conch that looks exactly like a rock until it moves along like an old Winnebago.

A sea fan waves and I see a large gray grouper with spots, a sea bass, a broad-snouted shark that aren't the least bit interested in the two of us. A crowd of yellow angelfish swim close to my mask as if I'm part of the artificial reef, their round eyes cartoonish. A sea horse hovers. A venomous lionfish has fins that look like feathers, and I adjust my buoyancy with my breathing.

I sink down to dark holes in the ship's side, and I drop lower into an opening that had a hatch cover in an earlier life. I shine my light and it's a reflex when I flutter my fins to back off from the other diver and what

I notice doesn't register at first. A barracuda zigzagging out from under him, and there are no bubbles as he's floating inside the hull. I paint my light over his arms and hands, and his masked face is down. I move closer.

I touch his neoprene-covered back and he moves a little, and I see the hoses hanging down and the straight line of a spear embedded in his chest. There's someone else below him inside the bulkhead. The second one, both police divers dead inside the hull, and I bolt up with powerful kicks.

I find Benton inches from the bottom, moving along, searching with his light and I tap my knife against my tank to get his attention. A faint sharp clank, clank and he looks up at me. I urgently point toward the barge, and its gaping holes in the dark greenish blue water where particles are suspended in my light. Then I hear the sound. A faint rapid vibration like a distant power saw. I turn in its direction as I catch something move darkly around the hull, what I think at first is a large fish but it can't be, and the vibration gets louder.

The shape moves rapidly toward me and I shine my light into a face with eyes wide and wild, framed in a sinister black mask and she has a black torpedo shape on her tank, like a turbine engine, whining on and off as she stops and starts, moving unnaturally fast. I don't see the spear gun until she swivels and points. I hear a spit and feel the hit like a jolting punch.

EPILOGUE

THE DOUBLE LOUNGER IS made of a tropical wood I can't identify, possibly teak but the driftwood finish confuses me, sort of pickled, sort of plastic. The cushion is ivory and the bright throw pillows are in an abstract cubism design that reminds me of Picasso, also sort of.

Day in, day out I sit on the wraparound terrace of my birthday condo, looking at the ocean change color, at the shapes of clouds that shadow the rolling surface, waves rising and crashing softly, sometimes louder and violently when they hurl themselves on the beach as if they're angry. I gaze at them with sunglasses on and I listen. I don't miss anything, not a helicopter that goes by, not a low-flying banner plane, not people on the boardwalk ten floors below. I don't say much as I watch what goes on.

Everyone around me has the best of intentions, first Lucy and Benton, then Marino got here, and day before yesterday Janet and Desi showed up. Their efforts are relentless, and they don't listen when I say it's enough. It's as if I died and am in a different dimension. I see them rearranging towels as if they're shrouds. They place pillows behind my lower back and under my knees. They worry about my neck, my hair, do I need a different hat and what about a manicure as if I'm about to be put on display at a wake. My only noninvasive friend, all seven years and four feet tall of him, is Desi, who sadly and soon enough will be adopted. At least it will be by Janet, his mother Natalie's only sister.

He has huge blue eyes and pale brown hair that grows in different directions, cowlicks everywhere. Very small for his age, he was born three months prematurely, carried by a surrogate but it was Natalie's egg. She's dying of pancreatic cancer. In hospice in Virginia, it's a matter of weeks and she doesn't want Desi to see her like this.

Janet and Lucy don't push back about it and they should. He should see his mother. He should be with her when it happens and already I can imagine how things will go. Lucy and Janet will need my help until I give it. Then they'll say I interfere. It will be true. I'll interfere on a regular basis and they'll have to get used to it.

"Quiz time," I say from my lounger, and as usual Desi is perched on the edge of it.

He doesn't take up much room, and the sun is giving him freckles all over the place.

"Where's your Avenger special cream? Remember we talked about it?" I nudge up one of his sleeves to remind him as I reach for the lotion for babies, SPF 50 on the small square pickled-looking table. "What happens if you get sunburned?"

"Cancer like Mommy has." His back feels narrow and bony pressed up against me.

"She has a different type of cancer. But too much sun exposure isn't good, you're right about that. I can't remember who you are this minute. Is it Hawkeye or Iron Man?"

"That's silly." But he loves it.

"It's not silly. We have to help people, don't we?"

"We can't save the world, you know." He's very wise all of a sudden.

"I know but we have to try, don't we?"

"You tried and got shot."

"I'm afraid it's the thanks I got."

"It must have hurt." He says the same thing on and off all the time and my answer isn't enough. "What did it feel like? Nobody ever really says what it feels like and it's not the same as a movie."

"No it isn't."

"Maybe it's like getting stuck with an arrow."

"That would seem right but it didn't."

We continue to have this conversation because it's important to him. It's not really about me.

"What then?" He presses against me like Sock.

I try to think of a different description and come up with one. "It felt like I was punched by an iron fist." I rub his back and it's very warm because of the sun, because he's a little boy with so much life in him.

"Were you scared of dying, Aunt Kay?"

He already calls me that and of course he can, and he uses the scared word a lot and it's not a new question. Both of us look at the ocean, at a squadron of pelicans flying past our terrace, so close I can see their eyes as they spy for fish.

"What do you think dying is?" I ask him what I have before and no discussion will take away the sadness.

"Going away," he says.

"That's a good way to think of it."

"I don't want my mommy to."

"Going away like on a trip but that doesn't mean she's not around anymore. It just means she's not where everybody else is right now," I reply.

"But I don't want her to."

"None of us do." I rub lotion on an arm he holds straight out like a stick.

"It would be lonely."

"Maybe it isn't for the person who left." I start on the other arm. "Wouldn't that be a good thought? It's lonely for us but not for them."

"I would have been scared if someone shot me under the water," he says, and there's little I remember but what I don't doubt is that I knew exactly what was happening at the time.

I heard the spit and the spear as it hit my scuba tank, glancing off, and I couldn't get away as she placed the butt of the gun against her hip, jamming another shaft into the barrel. Then I was slammed in my right thigh and she was rushing on top of me and the vibration was loud, the propulsion vehicle like a lightweight jetpack mounted on her tank, battery charged, controlled by a handheld switch. What I remember most vividly is Benton's face, the water pressing his cheeks flat. He was unnaturally pale, as pale as death.

I don't remember struggling. I have no recall of stirring up the bottom, deliberately creating a brownout. I don't remember slashing at her with my knife, cutting open her face from her temple to her chin, through her left cheek. Then she was gone as if she'd never been there, and I don't remember the blood clouding out in her wake.

I don't remember anything. I wasn't aware of Benton getting me to the surface, holding my regulator in my mouth. My mask-mounted camera ran the entire time. It captured at least some of what happened. I don't know how much. The FBI has my mask, my tank, my knife, everything. I've not been shown the list of what they've seized. I've not been allowed to review the recording yet for reasons not even Benton will tell me. What I'm left with for now is a black hole as if Carrie Grethen is dead again but I'm told she's not.

It's like a weather report I get on the hour. The latest prediction of the heat and humidity, the latest storm moving in or out and what to expect next and should we go somewhere else. I look for her as I convalesce, taking an inventory of how I feel and what I've been through, details I won't share with Desi until he's much older, maybe as old as Lucy was when I began talking openly about life's ugliness.

In truth it's been awful. A punctured quadriceps above the knee and a debridement surgery not to mention decompression sickness as gases came out of solution, migrating to areas of my body where bubbles don't belong. Severe joint pain as if I didn't hurt enough, and hyperbaric oxygen therapy in a recompression chamber which I have no idea about. Except I have vague impressions, ephemeral like gauze, and that's probably the origin of my comic book theme with Desi.

I think I believed I was in a space warp or on a Galactus ship. Since he got here he rarely leaves my side. He reminds me of Lucy at his age, a hovercraft constantly staring at me and asking the same questions repeatedly that are hard to answer honestly.

"How about you roll the Ferrari over here?" I say to him.

"It's not really a Ferrari and pretty soon you won't need it." He trots to get it.

"When my leg is better you're in big trouble."

"Why?"

"Because I can catch you," I reply.

He rolls it over to the lounger and the walker isn't bad for such a thing, racing red with black swivel wheels and handbrakes.

"It's like an old person," he teases yet again and he's enormously amused by himself.

"It's not."

"Like a cripple person."

"What would be a nicer word, Desi?"

"An old cripple person!" He shrieks somewhere in the range of two octaves above high C.

"You owe me another quarter."

"When we had a dog he got hit by a car and couldn't walk anymore. He had to be put to sleep." He follows me through the open slider.

I push the walker along, moving my wrapped-up right leg without bending it much.

"That bad lady should be put to sleep," he says. "What if she comes here?"

The living room with its earth-tone furniture is empty and quiet. Benton, Marino, Lucy and Janet went to the Taco Beach Shack to pick up dinner and after that they picked up my mother, and I'm annoyed. Take-out food every night and it depresses me. I look for Sock. He's probably snoozing on the bed again. When everyone gets back Benton needs to take him out.

"You may not know this about me yet but I'm a very good cook." I roll the walker to the kitchen and open the refrigerator door, then I maneuver myself to the pantry. "What would you think of spaghetti with tomato and basil, a little red wine, olive oil and some garlic with a dash of crushed red pepper?"

"No thanks."

"I'll write your name on the plate with a noodle."

"I don't want it."

"So it's tacos again. And that root beer you like so much. When I was your age they had birch beer. Have you ever heard of it?" I get a root beer out of the refrigerator and twist off the cap. "In a glass?"

"No thanks."

"I didn't think so but it's nice to ask." I hand it to him. "They had a place down here called Royal Castle. There might still be one on Dixie Highway near Shorty's Barbecue. I'm going to have to find you a birch beer somewhere. We have birch trees in New England. Lucy has a lot of them on her property. They have peeling bark like white paint peeling off."

"Am I going back to Virginia?"

"Do you want to?"

"I don't know," he says. "Mommy's sleeping I think."

"It would be fun if all of us lived closer, wouldn't it?"

"Were you ever seven, Aunt Kay?" He lifts the bottle and takes a sip as I hear a key in the front door.

"My mother tells me I was. You know her. The notorious Grans."

"What's notorious?"

"You'll find out soon enough."

"Then what happened?"

"When I was your age?"

"Yes."

"I grew up to be disappointed that you don't want my spaghetti."

"Oh don't worry I'll eat it!" That laugh again as he runs to the door.

I smell Mexican food as everybody walks in, and I take off my tactical gun pouch. I tuck it in a cabinet out of reach for a little boy.

BENTON AND I ARE alone, both of us in the lounger for two. The low sun smolders over the ocean in hot pinks and oranges, diffusing over deepening shades of blue that heave languidly. Soon it will be as dark as velvet.

"The latest isn't much better and may be as good as it's going to get." Benton holds my hand and drinks red wine as he explains the update as of half an hour ago. "If she received medical treatment we can't find any hospital or private practice that might have treated her. She's vain enough to want a plastic surgeon, but we can't find it out. We probably won't. She could be anywhere now. At least we know the RIB we recovered is the boat you saw. That we're sure of."

"The drift divers were the two of them. Right there. Right under our noses as usual." I reach for the bottle and he beats me to it. "Troy was in the RIB and we know where she was."

"Well we know she was the one diving and that it was a ruse so she could take us out. Leaving Lucy by herself. That would have made Carrie very happy." Benton fills my glass.

"I should have asked about the damn RIB when I saw it out there. Why didn't I? What's wrong with me?"

"Anybody seeing the dive float moving would assume it was normal," Benton says. "Just people drift-diving the reef and that the person in the boat would eventually follow and pick up whoever it is."

"She did that because she knew we'd be looking. And obviously she abandoned the float and line attached to it so we'd have no idea how close she was to us." The wine is nice and I'm getting sleepy. "She knew we'd see the RIB and the float some distance away and think exactly what we did."

"It was meticulously planned—as I would expect from her," he agrees. "And the RIB's registration was painted over, which is why it wasn't noticed by police, the Coast Guard or us. After the incident it appears she ditched it in a marina in Pompano Beach. That's where it was found this afternoon."

"No sign of Troy."

"No," he says. "I'm sure he's with her somewhere. Her new partner."

"And more people will be hurt or killed. It's my fault. I saw the damn RIB. I should have asked about it."

"You shouldn't be hard on yourself about any of this, Kay. You need to stop."

"I wonder how long it had been there in the marina. One more thing under everybody's nose."

"I don't know. It was docked right there in the open but again the number had been spray painted over and a new one applied with a stencil. An expensive boat, a Scorpion. If it wasn't for that we'd still be looking. I suspect she ditched it there soon after the incident."

"Maybe we can come up with something besides *the incident*. I feel as if my life has been reduced to a police report. What are we supposed to do now exactly?" I went easy on the tacos and can really feel the wine. "She managed for thirteen years and no one was the wiser. If she wants to disappear she certainly knows how. She's smarter than we are."

"She's not."

"It feels like it."

"She'll need money again. Whatever she's got won't tide her over forever. Not the way she lives and moves around." Benton leans back in his side of the lounger and when the warm moist air moves I smell his cologne. "The fact is we'll always have to be vigilant."

"If it's not her it's someone."

"Always the optimist." He turns his head and kisses me and I taste wine on his tongue.

"Marino needs to take my mother home. We should say good night." I lower my bandaged leg to the tile but I don't put any weight on it.

Benton wraps an arm around me and I limp a little as he helps me inside. The damn walker is parked just inside the open slider where Sock is snoozing on the cool marble floor. I place my hands on the grips and roll it in the direction of Desi shrieking again, his small feet galloping, and he screams around a corner just as Lucy snatches him up and lifts him over her head, his arms and legs pumping.

"She hates children," I say to Marino.

He's in baggy shorts, a Hawaiian shirt and flip-flops. He hasn't shaved in days.

"Being a designated driver sucks." He's holding the car key, nothing subtle about it.

Then another noise, a toilet flushing down the hall, a long pause and the door slowly opens. My mother's white hair is a halo in the light spilling out but there's nothing angelic about her as she rolls her walker toward me.

"This is what you get for being disrespectful," she starts in again as she rolls closer. "When you were Desi's age and you laughed at the older people who came into your father's market with their canes? And this is what you get."

"I never did such a thing," I reply and it does no good. "Desi, don't listen to her."

He isn't, and now Lucy is a helicopter flying him around the room while Janet looks on from the sofa, in a cotton shirt and loose pants, pretty and at ease as usual. She meets my eyes and smiles because we both know what we're dealing with, and then my mother has to pointedly look me up and down and make another comment, her eyes faded and magnified behind her glasses. She's spilled salsa on her dress, another floral pattern with a hem that looks uneven because of the way she stoops and seems to cock herself like a gun about to shoot.

"Katie?" When she calls me that I know it's coming. "Dorothy is happy to keep Desi and I think it's a better idea than him being around all these women. It's nice to have a man. A boy needs the influence of a man."

Dorothy, Lucy's mother, my only sister, isn't here of course. I'm not sure she even understands exactly what has happened. She knows I was hurt. She did ask if I'd be able to wear shorts again.

"Great idea, Grans," Lucy says as she lowers Desi to the floor, and his cheeks are an excited rosy red. "She did such an amazing job with me and there were so many men I can't remember them."

"That's not nice, Lucy." My mother rolls closer to her, and if it's one thing I've learned from witnessing all this night after night is I'll never use a walker as a weapon. "You should be ashamed of yourself wearing no more clothes than that. Those skintight shorts are indecent. Are you wearing a bra?"

Lucy pretends she's going to lift her shirt to check and Marino guffaws.

"Are you ready to go home, Mother? Marino is happy to take you."

"Well all right then. That's only the third time everyone has asked. I know when I'm not wanted. I don't know why you even bother having me over." She slides her feet, rolling her walker to the door where Marino can't wait to open it for her.

"Come on, Grans. I'm your chauffeur. I hope you don't expect me to wear one of those fucking prissy caps."

"I'll wash your mouth out . . . !"

"I've heard you do your share of cussing." He holds the door for her, and then they're in the entranceway and he pushes the elevator button.

Sock has gotten up and is cowering. My walker scares him.

"I don't even know such filthy words as that," my mother says.

"Then how'd you know what it was? See? That's why I'm such a good detective."

I wait until they're gone before I shut the door, and Lucy and Janet tell Desi it's time for him to brush his teeth. He bolts over and hugs me. He stares up at Benton rather dubiously.

"Good night, Mister Bentley," he says. "I'm going to be an FBI agent someday."

They head down the hall.

"I think we should take the rest of the wine to bed, Mister Bentley." I push the walker and envision my mother pushing hers.

I start laughing. I laugh so hard I can't go anywhere quite yet. Then Benton helps me down the hall to the master suite, where the slider is open all the way, the warm breeze blowing in. A huge moon is low and reflected in the swells of the waves. Boats are out. Some of them like small cities on the water. Lights wink red and white on distant planes flying in and out of Miami. I listen to the rhythm of the surf. It sighs loudly and sounds like breathing. Sock cowers again when I park the walker out of the way. He flattens himself on the floor.

"Oh I'm not going to hurt you for crummy sake. Don't be so dramatic," I say to him. "I'm sorry I didn't handle it better," I say to Benton as I lower myself to the bed and Sock jumps up.

Benton unbuttons his shirt, arranging pillows behind me as if I'm back where I started, in the double lounger again.

"I'm ashamed I didn't," I say to him. "No matter what you say the fact is she was right there and I let her get the best of me."

"You didn't. You sliced open her face and probably saved both of us." He says the same thing as he sits next to me in his boxer shorts. "You're the most perfect person I've ever known. And you don't panic. You didn't and that's the difference between you and almost everybody else. Don't ever forget it."

"I didn't fix it. Nothing's fixed, Benton."

"We never fixed it. No one did. It's not just you. Maybe we never fix anything. I don't know what's gotten into Sock tonight. He's sticking to me like shrink wrap."

"Probably because Lucy was horsing around like she's ten years old again. Sock isn't used to so much commotion. He's used to being around two stick-in-the-muds. I won't mention names."

"I love you, Kay."

I reach for the lamp. I switch it off and I hear it.

SNAP